W9-BCZ-304

ELVIS *and* NIXON

ELVIS *and* NIXON

a novel

jonathan lowy

CROWN PUBLISHERS • NEW YORK

Grateful acknowlegment is made to the following for permission to reprint previously published material:

Fantasy, Inc.: Lyrics from "I Feel Like I'm Fixin' to Die Rag," © 1965/renewed 1993 Alkatraz Corner Music Co. BMI. Words and music by Joe McDonald. Used by permission of Fantasy, Inc.

Jondora Music: Excerpts from the lyrics to "Fortunate Son" by John Fogerty. © 1969 Jondora Music (BMI). Copyright renewed. Courtesy of Fantasy, Inc. All rights reserved. Used by permission.

Special Rider Music: Lyrics from "A Hard Rain's A-Gonna Fall" by Bob Dylan. Copyright © 1963 by Warner Bros., Inc. Copyright renewed 1991 by Special Rider Music; lyrics from "Gates of Eden" by Bob Dylan. Copyright © 1965 by Warner Bros., Inc. Copyright renewed 1993 by Special Rider Music. All rights reserved. International copyright secured. Reprinted by permission.

Warner Bros. Publications U.S. Inc.: Lyrics from "I Put a Spell on You" by Jay Hawkins. © 1956 (renewed) EMI Unart Catalog Inc. All rights reserved. Used by permission. Warner Bros. Publications U.S. Inc., Miami, FL 33014

Published by Crown Publishers, New York, New York.
Member of the Crown Publishing Group.

Random House, Inc. New York, Toronto, London, Sydney, Auckland
www.randomhouse.com

CROWN is a trademark and the Crown colophon is a registered trademark of Random House, Inc.

Printed in the United States of America

Design by Lenny Henderson

Library of Congress Cataloging-in-Publication Data

Lowy, Jonathan.
Elvis and Nixon: a novel / by Jonathan Lowy. — 1st ed.
1. Presley, Elvis, 1935–1977 — Fiction.   2. Nixon, Richard M. (Richard Milhous), 1913 — Fiction.   3. Presidents — Fiction.   4. Musicians — Fiction.   I. Title.
PS3562.094E48   2001
813'.6 — dc21   00-043178

ISBN 0-609-60818-5
10 9 8 7 6 5 4 3 2 1
First Edition

To my parents, Judy and Art,
for teaching me how to spot the bad guys,

and to Dawn, for everything.

ACKNOWLEDGMENTS

I would like to thank my agent, Deborah Grosvenor, for her unrivaled perseverance and assistance; those who read early versions of this book and provided editorial assistance and encouragement: Dawn Nunziato, Judith Lowy, Chris Knott, George Garrett, Dave Scheurmann, and Doug Barry; and my editor, Rachel Kahan, and everyone else at Crown Publishers.

I just want to ask you one favor.
If I'm assassinated, I want you to have them play
"Dante's Inferno." And have Lawrence Welk produce it.

— Richard Nixon

We have all had our My Lais
in one way or another.

— Billy Graham

ELVIS *and* NIXON

ONCE UPON A TIME, in a nation called America, in a town known as Tupelo, there lived a girl and boy, who wanted for much—money, for starters—and to them were born two babies, twin boys. But as the first baby (whom the couple had named Jesse Garon) attempted that treacherous journey through the doors of this life, Death did snatch him before he could exit the womb. And so the girl, Gladys, told her sole remaining child, "The Lord has chosen you to carry on with the spirit of two souls, Elvis Aron" (which is what they named him). "You have a special purpose," the point of which she was not certain . . . even after the day, some eighteen years later, when Elvis (then a truck driver) would rent some studio time to record a song to give as a present to his beloved mother. . . .

And once upon another time (twenty-two years and a day before the birth and death of Gladys's babies), in a town known as Yorba Linda (same nation), a woman named Hannah and a man named Frank also wanted for much, and to them was born a child whom they named Richard. And Hannah did instruct her child that "Your relationship with your Creator is the most important thing in your life," and "the Creator loves nothing more than honesty and faith." And Frank did teach Richard a thing as well, using the cold angry strap of his belt, and one day when he caught his son swimming in the town irrigation ditch he grabbed him by the scruff of his neck and hurled him into the watery depths. Richard was terrified as he dropped to the bottom, and as he clawed back to the air he could hear his father hollering, as he had so many times before: "To win, Richard, isn't the most important thing; it is the only thing. . . ."

And when young Elvis was still a baby (and his father, Vernon, had been locked away, leaving Gladys alone to raise him), young Richard traveled east where he immersed himself in the texts of politics and law, earning high honors at Duke University Law School, and from there he traveled on to the city of Manhattan, intending to join the great law firms on Wall Street, where (he was certain) John Foster Dulles and other learned veterans of high government service would bestow upon him the vast monies, wisdom, and repute which his hard work had earned him. But the great firms denied him entrance, and that too taught Richard a thing about the world.

"Fuck the bastards," said young Richard, as he crawled home to California to take all that was offered him (a humble law practice in his small hometown). "Fuck 'em all."

And time did pass. And young Richard did become President of all the nation. And young Elvis became known as the King. And life, for Richard and Elvis, did take a turn or two.

PART ONE

Saturday Morning

MEMPHIS TO WASHINGTON

1

ELVIS

THEY WERE AFTER HIM. They were after him and there was nothing he could do.

"Lord, Elvis, what do you think you're doin'?!" Vernon was waving a stack of receipts at him, eyes all accusation and certainty. "Just look at these! You go to Kerr's and you buy yourself eight—count 'em!"—the papers smacked Elvis in the nose—".357 Magnums. Now why in hell you need all them? That's over three thousand dollars right there. Then there's three—four is it?—Colt .45s, one for one thousand twenty-five and fifty-six cents. What's that made of, gold? Let's see what else. There's a Luger, seven more .45s, rifles, shotguns, ammo—"

"But Daddy—"

"And—wait one minute there, son"—Vernon paused: *worked up the strength and fiber to take you on, boy, my own flesh and blood*—"I ain't even started yet. That's thirty-five thousand in guns alone!"

Elvis shook his head, put his hand to his face. Felt his lip trembling. The upper lip, the right side of it, twitching totally out of his control.

Hell: Daddy should know well as anyone why he needed the guns. This was 1970 and things had gotten godawful crazy. *They* were everywhere, and just crazy enough to take a shot at him, all to prove whothehell knew what. The phone calls in the night were just the first step, sure as sunrise.

"Then there's the cars"—still thumbing the invoices—"eighty-five thousand in cars in a day? Cadillacs, Mercedes. We got fifteen of those already."

"Daddy, it's Christmas."

It *was*, just a few days away, and if Bo got a Benz then Tubby would want one too, and Joe and the rest of the guys, and if he didn't keep all the girls happy there'd be paternity suits for New Year's: oh, that was all Priscilla needed—

"But Elvis, that's over a hundred thou in two days' shopping! And you've already given a car to everyone you know in Memphis, and L.A. too, more 'n' likely. And then there's—"

And, and, and, and.

He tried to block it all out, the petty-ass bitching. Either it leaked out like some huge faucet the size of the swimming pool out back, drip-drip-drip just beyond the reach of his ear at night, or it rushed at him like a flood, torrents of dickering over dollars. And this from the servants—yes, ever since Daddy went on salary it was true—the folks who fed off him. Rats, all of them: Elvis put his hand out to offer the poor bastards a few crumbs and next thing they were nibbling his skin, then gnawing on the bones, gathering at the wrist, working their way up the arm. . . . He had created them, constructed each one out of his will and his graciousness and his talent and his power—yes, his Power—and his dollar bills, scraped and clawed for. But they had run amuck. Grand things were going on around the life of one Elvis Aron Presley—involution, evolution, a new faith—and the talk here was dollars (he had said it all before, if not to Vernon then to Tubby or Bo), but they no longer had faith and so his power was impotent, within these walls. . . . Things they did not understand . . . and so, things out of control.

They were in the living room at Graceland; not the one with the billiards and games, but the business room, where Vernon and the Colonel kept the books, invoices, profit and loss statements (*as if there were ever losses when Elvis Presley was on a marquee!*), though, like all the rooms in the mansion, the walls were lined with plaques, mementos, golden records, platinum records, and photos of Elvis, on tour, in movies, at home with Priscilla, Lisa Marie, or shaking hands with Governor Wallace, Vice President Agnew, Sheriff Morris. Looking over Vernon's shoulder now, an old photo caught his eye: he was on stage in '55, a guitar swung over his shoulder, propelled outward by his undulating hips, eyes raised up to the sky, like he was in church back when Momma was alive—damn did he look good back then. It was the picture that had been projected in his skull for what seemed like hours now, ever since Vernon had first launched into him when he walked in the door, home.

"Now I know how you feel about Christmas, Elvis, I mean ever since you was little—"

Good Lord, Daddy: Like you would know.

"—it was something mighty special for you. Your mother, God rest her soul, used to think the same—Lord, what Gladys'd do to make Christmas special. Spend half a year's food bill on a day; that's probably where you got your indulgences from—"

"Daddy, it's only money." He thought he said it out loud. "More where that came from."

"—I know, I know, but Elvis"—Vernon shook his head, wiped some drool off the corner of his mouth—"all I'm saying—and Priscilla's behind me completely on this—is that there are limits—"

"'Cill—?!" Elvis stopped himself after just letting out a yelp, an indecipherable syllable.

Damn: there went the lip again.

"—even with you playing Vegas now, there gotta be limits, Elvis. Priscilla, you tell him."

And there she was, suddenly appearing beside Vernon, her hair hanging down almost hippielike, the way someone other than he must have a passion for; her face sullen, eyes smoldering. They just stood there, she and Vernon, glaring, but the sense Elvis got was that the two of them were marching in lockstep toward him, closer and closer.

The picture—of him young, onstage—was over 'Cilla's shoulder now, and he locked on to it. He could see the arms of the young girls reaching up, grabbing at him from the front rows. Even now he could hear their screams, see them fainting. . . .

And here he was now, onstage again, he felt like, but before an audience angry and disillusioned: *You blew it, King,* they were saying. *Had it, then lost it.*

"Elvis," Priscilla started, "Vernon's right. Some of these folks you're buying for, they aren't even friends of yours, really. I mean—we can just go down the list—"

Now she wanted to talk with him, all the sudden.

"You know it, Elvis," Priscilla still, "now I don't usually—"

Vernon looked at Priscilla and she at him: *Gonna be more difficult than we thought. Better bring in the heavy artillery.*

"And Elvis," Vernon now shrunk back a step, more his sheepish self, "the Colonel's got it all worked out, a budget you see, and—"

"And Elvis," Priscilla said, "it's not like the old days. I mean, I know we've got money, but it's not like you're the Beatles either. . . ."

Oh, Priscilla knew where the open wounds were. Elvis closed his eyes and could imagine those girls in the old black-and-white chasing John Lennon now, grabbing at his long hair all crazy.

"I mean, you're still the best, honey, but . . . you've seen the charts—"

He hadn't, in fact, looked at the pop charts recently, not in *Billboard* or *Variety*, but that was just because he knew that faggot Lennon would be up there, riding atop, all over him. Probably riding Priscilla too, soon as Elvis left town.

"And we know you've been working hard, and it's not like we don't understand—"

Elvis felt his entire body quivering now, like some girl had sucked on his big toe, then rammed it into a socket and the voltage was wending its way up from his tapping feet to his vibrating legs, all the way to his neck, which was now rocking back and forth from Vernon to Priscilla like one of those Rock 'm Sock 'm Robots after taking an uppercut, head teetering on a thin springy wire, back and forth, back and forth. He tried to straighten himself out—he figured if his body could stop moving then so would his racing, blood-boiling mind—but he just couldn't. The greens were in his pocket but if he pulled them out Vern and 'Cilla would get into him for that too. The best he could manage was to quiet his voice down to a low, sultry decibel.

"You can't understand," he said.

The urge he had was to pull out the .357 Magnum he had holstered to his hip, hold it out in front of him with both hands like Clint Eastwood himself, aim it right at that traitorous pair of leeches staring at him now like he was a madman, and shoot over their shoulders—Daddy's left; Priscilla's right—whistle it past their ears, and watch it smash glass in the heart of that damned black-and-white that had ingrained itself in his head since he couldn't remember when, as if that would kill that youthful, beautiful image.

2

SHARPE

STANDING OUTSIDE ON THE lawn in the Rose Garden, near the roped-off area where, just minutes from now, the press would fire away with their cameras, Max Sharpe was stuffing the fingers of his left hand deep into his mouth. The tips of the two middle fingers were firmly between his teeth, and now he clamped down hard. He had already gnawed off the tips of the fingernails while the advance staff set up the chairs for the crowd. It would still be another five minutes before President Nixon would even emerge from inside the White House to begin the ceremony, to make the short speech honoring the veterans now standing on the podium. And that would be the easy part; the speechwriters would get the blame if the President honored the boys as heroes in the war "in Cambodia," rather than "in Vietnam" (Ray Price, who had written most of the speech, was careful to avoid all reference to that taboo *incursion,* but Cambodia was so much on the President's mind these days that such a slip would have surprised no one), or if Nixon veered off the script entirely to lambast *those bums,* or *the Negroes,* implying that they were responsible for removing the body parts which each of the honorees had lost in Vietnam. All that would be somebody else's problem.

Not that a simple Rose Garden awards ceremony was any big deal in the grand political scheme of things: just a simple fifteen-minute slot penciled in by Dwight Chapin, the President's appointments secretary, on the presidential calendar. (When Sharpe had snuck into Chapin's office early this morning to make sure the event had survived on the day's schedule, he had noted that the event was marked only *in pencil,* a dictatorial slight by Herr Chapin, denoting that the ceremony was subject to EBCs—Events Beyond Control.) But Max Sharpe knew that in the Nixon White House you had to make the most of opportunities, especially if you aspired to take that long, high vault from the second tier of White House aides (Sharpe being Staff Assistant to the Assistant to the President for Domestic Affairs; his boss and mentor, John Ehrlichman, being *the President's* Assistant for Domestic Affairs) to a front-row leadership post in the upcoming '72 campaign, or even an inner circle spot in the Cabinet or White House staff, a position with independent power and authority. (Only thirty-one, but Max Sharpe was not satisfied, not a bit.) In the sort of football analogy the President would appreciate, Sharpe now was in the defensive secondary of the administration, remembered only for the plays not made, touchdown passes thrown past him; chances to blitz and sack the quarterback few, the uncommon interception expected. To get to the inner circle was difficult, the field before him crowded thick and fierce. Ambition was not enough.

Ehrlichman had given Sharpe the task to select the list of victims (honorees, Sharpe knew Ehrlichman had meant to say: heroes), and Sharpe had done so carefully to provide the President with a healthy mix of amputations: one arm severed off at the shoulder; one leg lost at the knee; a quadriplegic in a wheelchair (broken spine); one pair of functionless limbs (arm and leg, both on the right side), presented in a wheelchair (the redundancy of the two chairs disturbed Sharpe initially, but he remedied the situation—a brilliant stroke—by placing each on opposite ends of the line, giving symmetry to the tableau). He had covered every base. And then there was the *pièce de résistance*: a man with both legs completely removed below the hip, displayed on a round, wooden platter with small three-inch wheels which he shimmied from place to place with his hands. Needless to say, the Platter Man was front and center, so that, in photographs of the event, he would be just over the President's right shoulder. (Sharpe had cordoned off the photographers on a small riser and to Nixon's left, making the angle unavoidable.)

Sharpe had even taken the step of including some racial diversity among the vets. It was a bold move—uncalled for, some would say, since only whites were going to vote Republican (worse, said Pat Buchanan: *A sign of weakness; shows we're scared of them*), but Sharpe argued that it would, if nothing else, baffle the usual critics, throw them a curve. (He also thought the President would appreciate an occasional sound application of risk; the Mad Dog theory: creative, confident.) Sharpe stuck to his guns, and his boss and mentor had supported his decision. So there, standing on the podium (he *was* standing, having lost only his right arm), was a Negro.

His name was Benjamin Rollins.

A local boy, Rollins had grown up just blocks from the White House, where, in high school, he had been an All-City quarterback and pitcher. Besides that he was a good student; and Rollins had never been arrested which, in Rollins's part of town, Sharpe felt, meant that he had taken a brave stand against the drug culture itself.

Not that any of that made Sharpe any less nervous. He hadn't had time for as thorough a check of Rollins's contacts and current friends as he would have liked. And failure, in the Nixon White House, was many things, but never an orphan.

He tried to imagine the ceremony going smoothly, no glitches in the President's speech; then Nixon would say the words "a just and victorious peace in Vietnam," which meant that he had finished, and would then drape medals around the necks of the boys. A personal touch: Sharpe's idea.

Yes, Sharpe thought, Ehrlichman would be impressed. Maybe even the President himself would note the brilliance of the event, its many layers of meaning (at bottom, read the symbolic message, this was a war like any other in America's history: ordinary salt-of-the-earth heroes risking life and, in these cases, limbs, for the eternal fight of good against evil), and afterward Nixon would glance at Sharpe's High on Life memos, then reward him with a plum job in the '72 campaign that would propel him upward, like a rocket, into the clouds of the Republican Party firmament. His good works would be rewarded. If everything went according to plan.

Sharpe looked at his watch: eleven fifty-five. If the President was late, even by five minutes, it would be enough to knock live coverage off the noon news, and any more delay would jeopardize coverage in the afternoon papers. . . .

Max Sharpe stuffed his fingers even deeper into his mouth, chomped down hard, so even if he wanted to scream during the ceremony, he wouldn't be able.

3

SITORSKI

"It's Christmas," the President said.

Nixon was standing at the far end of the Oval Office, gazing out the window. In fact it was December 19, the Saturday before the holiday, but Colonel Alex Sitorski had learned long ago not to correct a president. The key was to develop a somber studied look of meditative reflection when the President spoke. *Yes of course, Mr. President. I never thought about it that way. Brilliant, if I may say so.*

"It's Christmas so goddamned early."

The President turned around. He was not looking his best. His best was not great—on camera Richard Nixon was not a handsome man, and he was less so in person—and still, he was not looking his best. For one thing, he was tired, so red semicircles rimmed beneath his eyes, his face was a pale white, and the combination made him resemble a raccoon. Thick whiskers darkened his beard and his hair was greased to his scalp, adding a cartoonish quality, as if his skin was shaded with Magic Marker. Richard Nixon had not been sleeping well and, tired as he was, his shoulders hunched more than ever. Uncomfortable as always with human contact, he lapsed even deeper into the comfort of his awkward mannerisms: puttering about the office, shaking his jowls, hands clasped behind his back.

"You." Nixon turned and nodded his chin toward the center of the room where his two top aides, Bob Haldeman and John Ehrlichman, were seated in chairs. (Rarely did the President use names; either he didn't remember them, or he chose to avoid the soft fuzziness that such reference suggested.) "Next year you keep me out of this Christmas business, all these . . . fuck it." He rotated his hand in circles.

"Events," Haldeman said.

"Right," Nixon said. "There's the fucking midterm returns, this Cambodia business going on, the Haiphong harbor plan we discussed, My Lai, and I'm lighting Christmas trees, watching carolers and such. It's no good."

"Certainly, Mr. President," Haldeman said.

"The tree lighting though," Ehrlichman said, "I think we should keep. It's traditional. People expect that of a president. Not that I'm certain about the history of it—"

"Well, of course the tree," Nixon said. "Richard Nixon is not going down in history as the first president to refuse to light the national tree. No, that wouldn't do. Not for the historical angle."

Nixon continued to nod his head now, holding his chin with his left hand, his neck hunched down toward his chest, puckering his lips out, almost baboonlike, so they neared his nose: the classic pose of Nixonian contemplation.

They were in the Oval Office. In between Haldeman and Ehrlichman, Vice President Agnew was slumped on the couch. Behind them, in the back of the room, Dwight Chapin sat, quiet and out of the way, and on another couch sat a higher-up from Defense. On this Saturday morning Melvin Laird was not in attendance; his understudy was an undersecretary: Walter Popkins. Popkins didn't offer an excuse for his boss, just announced that he, Popkins, was standing in for him this meeting. Not a good tack, thought Alex Sitorski, *you cover for your superiors, take the blame yourself.* The sort of mistake Sitorski might have made, say, two presidents ago.

The meeting had already meandered through a number of issues that Haldeman had noted beforehand on his Agenda Memo (a more detailed supplementation of Chapin's bare-bones daily schedule): Vietnam; Cambodia; Laos; the schedule of upcoming antiwar protests; how bad were the midterm election results, really; James Reston's latest brutal assault on the very institution of the Presidency (launched from his secure perch on the op-ed pages) . . . and the President's inevitable digressions.

Before he had ventured off on this latest diversion, President Nixon had been receiving body counts. Colonel Alex Sitorski was giving him the news, standing before his easel, displaying charts. At this moment Sitorski was still pointing to a bar graph showing the number of casualties suffered in Vietnam in the last quarter—September, October, and November 1970—as well as the first two weeks of December. He had just explained the Vietnamese side of the ledger (the

North and Communist-sympathizing side): the dead were red rectangular bars; serious casualties (suspected loss of at least one appendage or major organ) were white; nominal injuries in blue; all against a black background. Red stripes dominated the posterboard Sitorski had just exhibited, with white bands underneath almost as long, and only a splash of blue. It had been a good few months.

Sitorski looked at the President, tried to gauge his response to the presentation. During the decades Sitorski had spent slowly moving up the ranks in the Pentagon public relations department, he had immersed himself in the numbers of the dead and wounded, but recently—the past year, and the past week especially—he had become obsessed with the effect that data had on the living. What message did the dead send in their last act? How did one deal with the news? Every president Sitorski had briefed had his own style, his own response to the roll call of the dead: Kennedy was cool; Ike sought historical parallels (the bodies so few in those days, death could be rationalized with relative ease); while Johnson—with the dead piling up around him—showed emotion of a higher, more intense pitch; there was agony, there was angst. (Though Sitorski often wondered, as the war took over the country and the Presidency, whether the angst was for the dead or for himself. Or whether Johnson realized that it was for himself, and that only gouged the wound all the more.)

As for Nixon, Sitorski recalled when he had first presented the particulars of My Lai 4 to him in March 1969, over a year and a half ago. Sitorski had noted that the . . . incident ("Only the Reds and the *New York Times* call it a massacre," Agnew would say) had occurred a year earlier—information had been suppressed from moving up the chain of command—but now it was clear that an army company, led by Lieutenant William Calley, had rampaged through a small village in the south, though they never faced enemy fire. During Sitorski's exposition of the details Haldeman and Laird had peppered him with questions: "How many are certain kills?" "There was a strategic advantage to be gained by the incident, wasn't there?" "You'd agree, Colonel, it was justifiable on one level, at least?" while Nixon had remained silent, pacing. Then he turned to look at the paper on Sitorski's easel—an aerial shot, poster-sized, of the village of My Lai, showing the bodies lining the paths between the burned-out remnants of huts. "There was a ditch," Sitorski had just said, "where Calley and the others tossed the bodies," when Nixon looked up from the photo on the easel, then turned to Alex Sitorski.

"Bastards," Nixon said, and it was impossible to know to whom he had been referring: Calley, the Red Viet Cong, the South Vietnamese, or whether the term—on principle—was generally applicable. The President caressed his chin in reflection, then said: "Can they prove it?"

And now, a year and a half later, there was no question that Calley and his boys had done the killing, and that it had been unprovoked, and as the army's court-martial trial against Calley had begun weeks before, My Lai was back in the news. . . .

Nixon was standing, pacing behind his desk in front of the large French doors at the back of the office, picking up memos, reading a paragraph, skimming quickly to the end ("Hmm, that so, that so"), grabbing a *Post* ("Fuck the bastards, Ben Bradlee and all his damned—whatcha say, Colonel?"), gliding through the briefing like a ghost through walls: in-and-out, in-and-out.

Sitorski looked at his chart, but the President was now ignoring him.

"Fucking Manson's a hero to the kids," Nixon said, and the others—Haldeman, Ehrlichman, Popkins—nodded, mumbled in agreement.

"They're not kids," Agnew said. "They're bums."

"Bums," the President said. "Right," and Nixon nodded vaguely, moving quickly to suppress any notion that he, the President, might not be as tough as his Vice; the phrase had slipped his mind, but Nixon, of course, never imagined that the students who protested the war each day, across the street in Lafayette Park and everywhere, the entire long-haired counterculture ("*Anti*-culture's more like it," Agnew would say, "no culture I can make out"), could be anything other than bums. The President continued. "But Calley, to them—the bums I mean—Calley's a murderer. What they mean is Richard Nixon's to blame. Nixon's a criminal. And then if we pull out Richard Nixon's the first president to lose a war." He lifted his head up, looked at the couch, at Haldeman and Ehrlichman. "Can you win with those fuckers?"

Agnew shook his head, firmly and decisively: No. With bums you could never win.

Now the President, for the first time today, turned to Sitorski.

"Colonel, speaking of Calley, what sort of . . . collateral damage"—Nixon smiled as he threw in this bit of Pentagon-speak, cool as an unscripted "Do svidaniya" dropped to Brezhnev, catching him unawares—"did we end up with down there? Percentage, I mean."

Alex Sitorski wasn't ready for the question: when the meeting wandered from the issue of body counts, he had assumed that his role was over, and he had allowed his mind to drift. Out of character for him, but today Alex Sitorski was not himself. He was thinking about tonight. About seeing his son. He would see Al Junior tonight, in just a few hours. And he still wasn't sure what to say to him.

He had not seen his son in almost three years, not since he'd left for Vietnam. Though Junior had returned to the States almost a year ago, he had been traveling ever since, who knew where, and had only communicated through his mother—hell, she had a name: Elena—and Elena would just say that he was doing fine, working things out. Which meant, to Alex Sitorski: moving away from me. Distancing himself; learning to blame, under his mother's expert tutelage.

All this was on his mind, but the President's question was so simple Sitorski could handle it without even having to recall the mnemonic devices he used to store such data (brick walls, usually: each body a brick, each battle a row, each war a wall), for a rudimentary ML-4 breakdown was easy as hitting an arcing softball out on the Mall on Saturday afternoon with Junior at a father-son, long ago. And though the My Lai death count was uncertain, the collateral percentage— the ratio of Vietnamese civilian deaths to American deaths—was definite, and ingrained in his head.

"Mr. President sir, one hundred percent was collateral," Sitorski said, standing rigid, nose pointing up to the crystal chandelier. "Vietnamese total dead was minimum three hundred and forty-seven, but now estimated upwards of five hundred. American dead: zero. Vietnamese by gender and age, we have a breakdown only in rough categories: women, babies, children—that is approximately four to fourteen—"

"Kids?" Agnew said. "When they're old enough to blow away our boys?"

Sitorski didn't answer; he knew the Vice President wasn't interested in answers.

"We can do without the breakdown, Colonel," Nixon said.

Then Nixon paused, and all in the room were silent, waiting for the impending presidential pronouncement. Sitorski, still rigid, now cut a sideways glance to get a look at the President, saw his brows had begun to furrow up and down. Nixon then dropped into a crouch, disappeared behind the easel, and emerged on the other side, hands behind his back. He then appeared behind his desk, where he rested his hands palms-down on the desktop, and leaned forward.

"Now this My Lai business, Colonel," Nixon said.

"Yes Mr. President sir." Sitorski snapped his eyes up to the ceiling, ironed his back straight.

Nixon cut Haldeman a quick glance and a surreptitious shake of his head, then Haldeman did the same to Ehrlichman.

"You've got a kid over there," Ehrlichman said, suddenly, "haven't you, Colonel?"

Sitorski looked blankly at him, his eyes, he felt, giving away a hint of shock. He tried to keep his two worlds separate as possible, but today he couldn't help it; he felt that Ehrlichman could read his thoughts. If the President's men wanted to, they could find out anything, but why would they bother with him, Alex Sitorski? Maybe he was just paranoid.

"In Vietnam, I mean," Ehrlichman added.

The others—Haldeman, Nixon, Popkins, Agnew—studied him. It struck Sitorski that to these men—who controlled the destiny of all half a million American soldiers, and several times that number of Vietnamese, Cambodians, and Laotians—his son, a boy none of them knew, whom Sitorski himself had not seen in years, was the closest link they had to an actual fighting man. They were curious.

"Yes," Sitorski managed to say. Junior was probably in the air now, flying across the country to see him. Sitorski tried to picture him, but the boy's face was hidden. Which was fitting. The obfuscating clouds were Vietnam. Images meant something. "I mean, no. He was there, yes, but he's home—back—now."

"OK, is he?" Haldeman asked.

Sitorski rubbed his eye with his index finger. No: he wasn't crying. That was good.

"Yes sir. Fine sir."

Haldeman turned to the President, and the two smiled at each other, Haldeman having proved a point, apparently. It wasn't all body bags and mayhem. Our boys have a job to do and they did it. Some came home heroes.

"What does *he* think about Calley?" Ehrlichman asked. "About this My Lai business?"

"I don't know that we've ever discussed it," Sitorski said.

"Come on, Colonel," Popkins said, "at ease, boy. You must have an idea."

"No," Sitorski said. "I'm sorry, sir, but I can't say that I know what his view of that whole . . . situation . . . is."

Nixon looked up at Sitorski, stared at him a good fifteen seconds. Richard

Nixon believed that every situation could be summarized by a sports coaching adage, and for this one, My Lai—like almost all others—one could aptly say: Every challenge is an opportunity. Or something like that. Though that is not what the President said to Colonel Alex Sitorski on this particular Saturday morning in December 1970.

What the President said was this:

"Colonel," the President said, "I have one question. How will it play in Peoria?"

4

THE WRONG ANSWER

NIXON WAS STARING AT SITORSKI from behind his desk, and Ehrlichman's eyes were on him too, and Haldeman, and Popkins and Agnew, all staring and waiting, as if his very face emanated the breakdown of collateral damage at ML-4, and with it the entire political situation that it presented to the White House, the administration, a month after the midterm elections.

Which is what Alex Sitorski assumed Nixon was asking about.

"Mr. President sir," Sitorski said, still standing at attention, "I'd rather not speculate."

"Jeeze." Haldeman shook his head, laughed. "You have nothing to say? About Peoria?"

"I don't think it would be appropriate for me," Sitorski continued. "The political implications of—it's not my position to—"

"Mr. President," Dwight Chapin said, standing up and raising his hand in the back row, "I hate to interrupt, but I don't think there's time for any more. We have that Rose Garden ceremony. The veterans' awards? We're a little behind. . . ."

Nixon looked quizzically at Chapin, then at Ehrlichman.

"It'll just take fifteen minutes or so," Ehrlichman said. "We discussed it the other day? You'll give a brief speech—Price drafted something—then give medals to a few local veterans." He glanced at his watch. "I think we've screwed with Dan Rather's lunch plans enough."

"What kind of vets we talking about here?" Nixon said.

"Amputees," Ehrlichman said.

"That's good," Nixon said. "Let them try to attack us for that, giving an amputee his due. Who's the friend of the fighting man then? Just let them try to attack us."

"Oh, just wait," Agnew said. "They will."

"Mr. President," Dwight Chapin said, tapping the face of his watch.

"You heard that, Colonel," Ehrlichman said, turning back to Sitorski. "The President's busy. Is that how you choose to leave your answer?"

Alex Sitorski glanced at Ehrlichman, then at Nixon.

"Yes sir," Sitorski said. Then he turned his chin up, but saw, out of the corner of his eye, President Nixon looking back at him, then at Ehrlichman and Haldeman, frowning at each of them. Then the President nodded his head and waved his hand toward the door, communicating by silent gestures, then turned his back to them all, looked out through the French doors behind his desk, out toward the lawn. The room was silent for a moment, and all Sitorski heard was the faint beating of a drum from across the street, in Lafayette Park.

"Colonel," Haldeman said, turning to Sitorski. "You're excused. Thank you very much."

5

ESCAPE

BACK AT GRACELAND . . . Elvis didn't follow his urge to shoot his image; his hands shook so violently he knew he couldn't aim the gun steady enough. What he did was turn around, run up the grand, winding stairs, then down the hall and into his master bedroom.

Against one wall was the walk-in closet that held his stage suits; he opened the door, flicked the light on and stepped in. Inside there were shelves littered with police badges, sunglasses, jeweled rings, belts with huge metal buckles, rods sagging under the weight of gold medallions, and clothes he leafed through: jumpsuits made of velvet, polyester, and silk, embroidered elaborately with glittering designs of eagles in flight, the Mayan sun god, rising and (more fitting, today) setting, Kung Fu karate fighters . . . in bright shiny gold, rich navy blue, red, silver, and pink . . . matching capes. Elvis scanned his collection and picked out one of his favorites—a stage suit that Priscilla had given to him (*"Given" him; right. With whose money?*)—but hell, he loved it. He slipped off his pants and jacket, kept the same shirt on, a white high-collared job, gold chains dangling around the neck, leaned over to slip into the suit, then snapped the cape on behind. Peeked up at the mirror and there he was, the flab of his gut drooping down, his cheeks bloated. Behind him was reflected the black leather suit he'd worn two years before, on his television special (Lord, had he sweated and starved to strap himself into that thing; the closest he'd come to looking like he did in the old days), and for an instant he tried to recall the feeling of what it was like back when he was young, meditate so the sensation would take him over and carry him back: the body thin, the legs sexy and lithe, the soul pure; the future vast, uncertain, and awesome in potential, limits not something on his mind back then. No end to that road. Checking himself again in the mirror, the leather suit displayed like a trophy, he thought: *What happens to calfskin when it hangs unused? Atrophy, or stiffen like a corpse?* . . . He reached in the pocket of the pants he'd just taken off—white polyester loungewear—pulled out a couple of pills—quaaludes: something to calm him down—and popped them in his mouth, thinking for a second that they could bring back the old feeling, make Vernon and Priscilla disappear, leave him without the worries, the money, the phone calls in the night ("Presley's a dead man," Bo told him the most recent one had said, a week or so ago; Sheriff Morris said not to worry, probably just some crank), the touring, the Vegas dates, the obligations, the rigidity of it all—limits—just one way to sing, to look, to be: the end of things. Closed his eyes, thought that when he opened them everyone would do what he wanted, they all would, and they would believe in him again and he would lead them and everything would be all right . . . but the feeling didn't come.

On to the gun closet, he pulled a few holsters off the hooks on the walls and strapped one over his left shoulder, another over his right, bent down and hooked another around his left calf; ducked underneath the rifles and shotguns hanging on the rack against the far wall and opened the safe, from which he pulled out a few prize guns: a gold-plated World War II commemorative Colt .45; a German Luger; a .38 Savage; a couple of knives, with their own holsters. Then he grabbed a handful of ammo from each of the boxes on the shelf, stuffed it all in his pockets and stepped out of the closet. That should do.

On the floor by his bed lay the belt the boys at the Vegas Hilton had given him—the buckle was a huge slab of gold topped with jewels scooped like an ice cream sundae; big enough to disguise his paunch and guns—and he slipped it on. From his bookshelf he quickly grabbed a handful of some favorites—*The Secret Doctrine, The Tibetan Book of the Dead, The Impersonal Life,* and of course, Madame Blavatsky's *The Voice of Silence*—stuffed them into a soft leather valise. Rushed back in the closet and tossed his badges, the whole collection—they might come in handy—in as well. Next: in his bedside table was the stash of pills Dr. Nick had given him yesterday, bottles upon plastic medicine bottles: high-charging, blood-thumping reds, Dexamyl, Dexedrine, and more; and a variety of downers, Placidyl, quaaludes, greens and yellows mostly (it was the downers—still more of them—that he needed now, his heart thumping like a kettledrum, hands shaking like a snare); he pulled out the shelf and dropped all of them into his valise, then emptied a few in his pockets. Then he charged back down the stairs, slamming the door ("ELVIS!" Priscilla screamed, with a "Now look what you've done!" glare at Vern, "where you going?!"), charged into the Benz parked farthest away from the house, along the turnaround, and drove out the front gate.

6

THE LEAK

"ABOUT CALLEY," THE PRESIDENT SAID. Nixon was staring straight ahead as he said it, walking down a hallway in the White House with Ehrlichman on one side, Haldeman on the other, Popkins right behind. Dwight Chapin and a few Secret Service men were in front, leading them to the Rose Garden. Ehrlichman had been quickly briefing the President on his speech for the veterans' awards ceremony, but Nixon wasn't interested. "That, that general," Nixon said, "the one who just left . . ."

"The colonel?" Ehrlichman said. "Sitorski?"

"Yes," Nixon continued. "He's the one, you know. I can sense it. You noticed that too, John?"

"Mr. President?" Ehrlichman said. "I'm sorry, but—?"

"The Calley business," Nixon said, impatient and gruff. "Peoria. Someone's leaked the idea, and that fucking general's the man. It was obvious, so fucking obvious. There's always some bastard with one hand on the telephone to the press."

"I haven't read anything that would implicate," Ehrlichman said, "I mean, that would show us as having a hand in the idea. The *Times* had some references to the 'mood in the Pentagon' on Calley, that sort of thing, but nothing that would harm us."

"No," the President said, shaking his head, "of course there haven't been any *overt* leaks yet—nothing obvious—but I *know* that there's been . . . talk. I can smell a rat. I've been smelling rats for thirty years. That colonel—"

"Sitorski," Haldeman said.

"Yes," Nixon said. "That colonel's our rat."

"Well of course," Ehrlichman said, "we do have to be careful with something like this. Can't be too vigilant."

"And he seemed a little odd today," Popkins said.

"I want an eye on him," Nixon said, leaning to mutter in Ehrlichman's ear. "The works. On the colonel, I mean."

"Right away," Ehrlichman whispered.

"It won't do any good to have a man like that in his position," Nixon said.

"Of course, Mr. President. Absolutely."

They turned the corner. Just ahead of them, at the other end of the hallway, were the French doors that opened outside, leading to the terrace walkway to the Rose Garden. Through the glass they could see, faintly, the crowd outside, seated in lawn chairs. As soon as the door opened the band would begin playing "Hail to the Chief," and the RNC staffers would wave the little American flags that had been distributed to them. The President stopped for a moment, as if anticipating the applause, preparing his face for a spontaneous flashy grin, a high wave of the hand over his head.

"And the bulbs," Nixon said. "I want them red, white, and blue."

"Mr. President?" Ehrlichman said.

"The Christmas tree. When we light it I want red, white, and blue bulbs. So when Madalyn Murray O'Hair and the ACLU and the Jews go to court to stop the thing, it'll look like they're trying to stop the flag. And when Walter Cronkite sneers at us on the nightly news, I want the American flag over his goddamned shoulder."

7

THE ROAD

DRIVING, DRIVING, FAST AND forward on the highway, Elvis wasn't thinking where he was going, just staring ahead of him, waiting to see where his hands would take him. *You aren't really in control, so why act like you are?* A voice was speaking to him, the Voice of Silence that had whispered to Madame Blavatsky herself. *You have been chosen for a reason, and you will be guided. Go with it.* If he were back at Graceland, Tubby and the rest of the guys would be snickering as he tried to enlighten them, acting like they were listening but joking all the while that it wasn't no voice, but only Elvis's karate teacher, Mr. Rhee, who'd said it. *Oriental crap, like chop suey two hours later. . . .* Truth was, it was his friend Larry Geller who had turned him on to the spiritual stuff a good five years back, but *turning on* was all—showing him the books—then Mr. Rhee had carried him up another step, but most of the journey Elvis had taken himself, immersing himself in the books in hotel rooms on tour, or at home in Graceland, or L.A., alone or with the guys, when Elvis convened them to read them the tracts. . . . Dumbass good old boys was all they were: good for girls and protection, but what did all them put together know about the Inner Quest? About involution and evolution? Or Avichi? Had a one of them even heard of the Buddha, and more to the point, of Siddhartha's transformation into the Buddha *at the age of thirty-five?!* Elvis would turn thirty-six in just *three weeks!* Didn't they understand the implications?! No, no, and no. At least Bo understood that Big Things were circulating about the life of one Elvis Presley: why else was he picked out of the crowd of poor white trash dreamers in his housing project back in Memphis to rise to such heights? But even Bo only understood enough to get his paycheck every week. Enough to hear, maybe, but not to listen.

Which was all another reason to get out of that trap, Graceland.

He let another hand take the wheel, tried to unpack his mind. . . . He had just come back from a hellish concert tour, more hellish than he wanted to admit to the guys. Ten years in Hollywood had taken their toll on his endurance level, that and old Father Time; and now, performing live again, two shows and a hundred miles a day wore him down . . . then home to the vultures, Vern and Priscilla, clawing his bones for money . . . Christmas was less than a week away, but what the hell did that mean now? There wasn't time for it, for one. And presents meant nothing: everyone had everything. And the jig was up with old man Jesus: Elvis had pulled the curtain on that magic show. Once you discover that you, yourself, are a Master, what's the deal about the birthday of another?

Check it out: driving now, he spotted a cloud in the sky, a dark ominous sucker, and he locked his vision onto it like radar. Elvis could make out forms in the sky like nobody—a special connection there; he understood the images—and the shape of this cumulus was obvious: it was Elvis, his own face, when he was young, in the picture that had transfixed him back at Graceland. Now he willed it to move: *When I drive straight ahead I command you to move on out of the way, so I don't see you no more, not ever. And I mean double time.*

The signs he saw directed him to the Shelby County airport, and that is where his car drove, turning right off the highway here, banking to the left there, then following the signs to American Airlines . . . and parked his black Mercedes sedan in the lot nearest the American entrance. Though he was trying not to think, his mind was racing: the reds he'd taken when he was shopping had got it going, and the green downers he'd popped at Graceland had slowed it sudden-like, a failed engine, so now his head was mush, crashed in a slushy swamp thick as molasses, though an occasional idea, a flurry of thought, would take off over the ooze, then plummet just as fast back into the mire.

He walked across the parking lot, twirling a walking stick in his hand (he'd found the cane in the car) like some gentleman, Maurice in one of those French dandy movie roles, and the thought that came to him was: Quest. *I'm not escaping; that's not it. I'm searching. But what for? What in God's name am I looking for?* Then the notion vanished, though intermittently throughout the next forty-eight hours the idea would fly through his consciousness again and again, even in sleep (especially in sleep), so that the notion of a quest ingrained itself in his head like a thought implanted by aliens, a false memory.

Confucius on pills.

He walked quickly through the lot, turned to shield himself from the occasional passersby who gave him a double take as they got in or out of their cars. But once Elvis reached the sidewalk beside the airport's main artery, just across the road from the terminal, a Volkswagen Beetle slammed on its brakes, and before it even came to a full stop a couple of longhairs got out.

"Hey look, man! Look who's here!"

"Cool!"

One of the kids, a boy with hair longer than Priscilla's, all greasy and stringy and down to his butt, stood just in front of him.

"Dig it," the kid said, almost poking a finger into Elvis's eye.

Elvis tried to smile at him. The car was coated with those stick-on psychedelic flowers, all fluorescent pink and yellow, and bumper stickers: "MAKE LOVE, NOT WAR," "DROP ACID, NOT BOMBS." Beatles followers, he bet. John Lennon's boys.

What they probably didn't know, Elvis thought, was that he understood them better than the Beatles did, versed deep in the recurring cycles of life and rebirth as he was. The Masters, The Quest. Avichi: theosophic hell. Had that bastard Lennon ever witnessed even a single embalming of a real human being? While Elvis, he could make a ready-for-the-next-life mummy if he wanted, explain the autopsy scars and perform the Tibetan rites while you wait. And he could read your thoughts, too. See if ole John Lennon could pull off that trick.

"Kids," Elvis said, "you're lost. I can tell."

Maybe he hadn't said it out loud; no one responded.

"Hey!" Now it was a girl who emerged from the car, a flower child in patched elephant-bell jeans, petite, with a beaded headband over her straight blond hair. Not a bad looker, actually, he could see as her young face looked up at him. "Didn't you used to be Elvis Presley?"

Then came the mad rush. He heard the screams behind him ("ELVIS! OH, ELVIS!" "I'VE LOVED YOU SINCE . . ."), and he turned around to see an army of old ladies, round balls of fat wrapped in flowered dresses and eyeglasses, handbags swinging like wrecking balls, running toward him.

He waved at them, and waited a moment, waited for Bo to pull him into a waiting limo, seemingly against his will, while Tubby, Charlie, and Joe moved in front to form a wall, protecting him from the oncoming mass. Waited, but nothing happened, only the screams got louder and the ladies got closer—though still a good thirty yards away—and now in the other direction, behind the flower children, another crowd was approaching. It came to him that he had lived his life in a cocoon, encased in Plexiglas from where he could hear the cheers, screams, and cries from his fans, and they could see him, but that was where it ended: a smile, a wave, maybe a few words after a show. Besides that, he was up onstage, the little people down below, and between them there was the wall.

"ELVIS!"

"LET ME KISS YOU, YOU SWEET LOVELY MAN!"

"I PRAYED TO YOU LAST NIGHT, ELVIS! YOU HEARD ME, DIDN'T YOU?"

The ladies were now just a few yards away, and there were a few scattered onlookers on the other side even closer. A few of them held papers and pens out toward him, and one woman held out a baby who, it seemed, was being offered to him.

There was no wall.

He ran across the road toward the terminal, grabbed a baggage cart half filled with luggage, tossed the walking stick on top and rolled it toward the approaching army.

But just before he stepped inside the terminal he stopped, turned around and looked up at the sky, just to check. As he had commanded it, the cloud, that dark ominous bastard of a storm cloud, was nowhere to be seen.

8

HIGH ON LIFE

IT WAS 12:05 AND THE Secret Service had only their advance men stationed in the Rose Garden: still no sign of the bodyguards, the entourage, and certainly not the President. The press was in position, cameras at the ready, growing restless. Coverage of the ceremony on the noon news was virtually impossible now, and play in the afternoon papers was in jeopardy.

Sharpe had to take some action, that he knew, but his options were limited. He couldn't just knock on the door of the Oval Office: a staff assistant didn't merit that degree of access to the President. He couldn't buzz his boss and mentor, not because of a mere scheduling glitch. The truth was, he didn't know what he could do, but he was sure he could get more done inside the White House than outside. It wasn't just this awards ceremony that depended on the President's timely arrival, no; the future of the Get High on Life campaign—and its creator, Max Sharpe—hung in the balance.

Sharpe had devised "Get High on Life" (he called it HOLE; Nixon would appreciate the acronym), to show Ehrlichman—and Nixon himself—that Max Sharpe possessed within his skull the most brilliant, incisive political mind to which the Republican Party had been privy since . . . well . . . since young Richard Nixon himself, and that at the same time he understood how the young mind worked nowadays. Max Sharpe knew about those rock and roll musicians; *dug* Bill Haley, and even owned a Simon and Garfunkel album (which actually wasn't half bad). And Sharpe knew history; had studied how Nixon had leaned all his weight on Alger Hiss to vault into the Vice Presidency, how Wallace clinched the South in '68 armed only with a quixotic vision of a segregated future. And, of course, he was conservative . . . the perfect mix of talents, a mix that was being wasted on John Ehrlichman's petty errands (not that he didn't appreciate the opportunity his former law firm boss had given him; Sharpe was a team player, too), but would blossom when given license to paint on the vast canvas of a national political campaign. . . . Max Sharpe had great confidence in ultimate justice; that he, his boss and mentor, and Richard Nixon would one day be rewarded with the wondrous fates they deserved.

Sharpe allowed himself to imagine that his latest memo (Re: "Get High on Life"/Get Out Young Vote; To: John Ehrlichman, H. R. Haldeman; cc: Pat Buchanan, Ray Price) had piqued some interest, though he had yet to hear any actual responses. Perhaps John Mitchell, the now–Attorney General expected to lead the reelection campaign, had floated a copy up to the President himself, who noted in the margin, *"Effective manufacturing of grassroots impetus propelling citizens into movement without realizing it. In the end, who knows which came first? It's a chicken-egg thing. . . ."*

"Max, I've got to talk to you."

It was his boss and mentor. Sharpe had just stepped through the side door of the White House and walked a few steps inside the hall. The Secret Service men were in front of him, leading the way outside. Sharpe craned his neck to look inside the pack, saw Haldeman, Undersecretary of Defense Popkins, and the ubiquitous Dwight Chapin, but could not see the President.

Ehrlichman put his arm around Sharpe's shoulders and led him against the far wall as the entourage walked past them.

"John," Sharpe stuttered, "the ceremony. I've got to go see—"

"You will," Ehrlichman said, "in a minute."

Sharpe could hear the crowd of White House and RNC staffers erupt into cheers outside. The President must have walked through the door, then stepped to the podium, perhaps patted the Platter Man on the head. A nice gesture, if the President thought to do it.

"It's the My Lai business, Max," Ehrlichman whispered. "We think we've found the leak."

"What leak?"

"There's a . . . well, RN's convinced that that colonel's talked to the media. Sitorski."

"Alex?" Sharpe said. Maybe the applause outside had caused him to mishear. "Alex Sitorski?"

"That's right," Ehrlichman said. "You know him?"

"For years. Alex wouldn't—"

"Well, Max, RN thinks he would," Ehrlichman said. "He thinks he's leaked Peoria."

"Peoria?"

"Oh that's right, you don't— Well, you don't need to know the details, Max. It's a leak situation, and RN smells vermin. See what your friend's take is on Calley, this My Lai business. If your friend believes in Peoria, if he's for or against us, and if his belief is, well, waning. Look into it, then deal with it . . . appropriately. RN wants a job on him to make sure—a tail, taps. The works."

Looking at his boss and mentor, Sharpe now knew he had heard correctly.

Ehrlichman looked out through the glass-paned doors. Haldeman was standing on the far end of the podium, motioning for him to come outside.

"Max," Ehrlichman said, "we can rely on you." And though Max Sharpe wasn't certain whether he could actually do what his boss and mentor requested, he nodded his head, over and over.

9

SHARON

SHARON TEELE, THE ATTENDANT working the American Airlines ticket counter at the Shelby County airport that Saturday afternoon, did not believe in miracles. Though she had been raised to: a good Catholic girl, Memphis from birth, in church she had mouthed belief in the Second Coming, the Immaculate Conception, the miracles of Jesus . . . but her life had yet to offer her evidence that such wonders could be true. When her husband, Hank, went off to Vietnam she stopped going to church entirely. And though, since the army had delivered the news about Hank one month ago, she had tried to accept the words of her friend, Wendy Root, that miracles did indeed occur, that hero stories—the Bible, the Buddha, and the Bhagavad Gita—all played themselves out each day in Memphis, still, she just couldn't. Faith, it seemed, had up and died on her.

So, when Sharon looked up and saw the blinding sunlight stream in from the windows of the terminal, then an image appear before her—black hair thick as the mane of a fine thoroughbred, sideburns big and bushy all around—her first thought was, *Wendy was right: the gods do walk among us. They taketh away— bless you, Hank—but Lord do they giveth, too.*

She had a new coif, a half-a-foot-above-the-forehead-combed-back do, like the First Lady's but with a single curl looping down just above her eyes (after all, she was nearer Julie's age), which she had given herself as a reward, a special treat. Things had been . . . tough . . . for her recently, to put it mild. Real mild.

And now there he was, right in front of her. He had been dead to her for years, since she was a girl, but now he had risen to save her. . . . Elvis was there.

"Next flight, ma'am?" is what he said. (Truth be known, his words weren't all that clear: even screening out the overlay of slurred, garbled sounds—which

33

took some doing: a wrinkled, puzzled look from Sharon, a reiteration or two from Elvis—it sounded more like: "Neggsfla, mmmm." But seeing as she was working behind an airport ticket counter and was wearing a red polyester American Airlines pantsuit when he said it, Sharon knew he probably meant *flight.*)

She wanted to say . . . she wasn't sure what she wanted to say (the sight of Elvis had melted her mind into a soup of recollections and wishes, opportunities lost, dreams dashed). She was lonely, her husband gone forever, though she wasn't sure how she felt about Hank's death, thought maybe she was happy, angry only at the time she had wasted married to him, or maybe that was an excuse, something to soften the pain for her . . . whichever . . . Elvis could sort things out for her and explain . . . make it right. . . . But all that emerged out of the jumbled, stormy soup was an image, clear as day: her mother running her out of the living room, years ago, having caught her watching him "swivel that godawful pelvic region" (Mom's words) on Ed Sullivan (was it really almost fifteen years ago?), and Sharon had run up to her bedroom, locked the door and cried. Then, with raw revenge pulsing in her temples, salty beads leaking into the corners of her mouth, and lust, lust, lust (and images of forbidden Negro love, and the bursting temples such an interlude would create on her daddy's forehead; but Elvis, young vibrant Elvis, was wrapped in that fantasy too, in ways she was not even completely certain), she had ripped down her panties and masturbated with a fury.

"Mr. Presley—Elvis—I—wonder if you have—do you?—a particular—"

Cool it, girl.

The words didn't come. So she grasped at convention: her role as a representative of American Airlines, Inc.

"Mr. Presley," Sharon said, "where would you like to go now?"

Which, thought Elvis, smiling at Sharon from the other side of the counter, was one hell of a question. A question that required some thought to answer.

Elvis's mind, too, was an anarchic jumble; no longer molasses but now a speedway in which Elvis was only a bystander, snapping his head back and forth as thought-cars raced through at warp speed, trying to make out something more than the choking exhaust they left in his face before they drove out his far ear. Racing through the jumble (and would be, throughout his travels during the next two days) was this:

Thought: Christmas coming, six days or so—in three weeks Jaycees make me one of the Ten Outstanding Young Men in America; need a speech—just like the Vice President told me the other week, there's a damned near revolution out there, hell-bent on breaking out any instant, those damned Beatles leading the charge—America needs a superhero, part James Bond, part J. Edgar Hoover and George Wallace combined; a powerful man versed in espionage, undercover work.

Thought: *Washington needs me.* Washington, D.C. Just received marching orders from Above, the Colonel in the Sky. The center of Power—and the FBI— was in Washington and, now that he thought of it, hadn't his friend John O'Grady told John Finlator, head of the FBI's Bureau of Dangerous Drugs, that Elvis would like a meeting? (Bo, or one other of the boys back home, would know for certain. *Hell, if Elvis Presley was supposed to remember every god- damned appointment he was supposed to keep . . .*)

Anyway.

Washington—and Finlator—it was.

The girl behind the counter was staring at him; a fixed, vapid gape. A fan's look: a follower.

"Washington," he said.

"Washington, Mr. Presley?" she repeated. "Washington, D.C.?"

Yes, Elvis nodded. But then he shook his head. No.

"Name's not Presley. It's Burrows. Colonel Jon."

"Burrows?"

Elvis had suddenly fixed on the idea, as if he had planned it all along: he would travel to Washington incognito, under the name of Colonel Jon Burrows (the name had bubbled up into his head—one of the aliases Colonel Parker used for security).

"That's right."

"And you'll be paying for this by—?"

"Paying?" *Where was Bo, Tubby?* "I'll—"

"We could send the bill to you at Graceland, if you—"

"That'll be—yeah. Thank you."

He glanced at the door. The ladies. The old wrecking ball ladies had just stepped inside the terminal, and now were looking the other way, then—

Elvis ducked his head, then stepped over the baggage scale to Sharon's side of the ticket counter.

"Tell me when they're gone," he whispered, as he crouched down behind her.

"The-the-they?" He was so close—almost touching her—she was shaking.

"The biddies," Elvis hissed. "The old ladies."

Sharon forced herself to stop staring at Elvis—his bent knee *had* touched hers—and looked across the counter, saw the ladies running away (actually, most were Elvis's age), toward the other side of the terminal.

"Yes," she whispered. "Gone."

And Elvis got up, walked back over to the passenger side of the counter.

So close. So close.

She held her hand out to him, and Elvis saw that now she wanted to give him something, though he wasn't sure what.

"Your tickets?" she said. "Mr. Pres— Burrows. Colonel."

Elvis took the packet of tickets, tried to stuff them into the inside pocket of his cape. But he missed: the mush of greens and reds had screwed with his coordination, made his hand jittery. So he tried to slide the tickets inside his belt, but there he ran into an obstruction: hard metal. He knew what that was. He had forgotten until then, but now he knew.

The girl was pointing off toward the heart of the terminal.

"Gate Three, Mr. . . . Burrows," she said, somber now, and he followed the direction of her finger to a flashing arch lined with security guards, uniformed types.

The gate. A metal detector.

Shit.

Thought: the leather holster, the gold-plated .45 within. The Luger in his boot. Somewhere he had his faithful .38 caliber Savage, too. Triple shit.

There he was: tickets to Washington in one hand; a priceless Colt .45, et cetera, strapped to his body; metal detectors and guards in between. As if God, for a joke, had dropped him here.

Thought: Need credentials, some serious gun permits. A federal badge would probably do the trick. Wouldn't hurt my collection, either.

Finlator would solve problems like these, for the future anyway. (Finlator, hell! Once Elvis'd walk into that office in Washington, Hoover hisself would want to see him, and Nixon would join in.) But all that would come later. Here, now, Colonel Burrows couldn't get away with this trip.

"Ma'am?" He turned back around to the American Airlines girl. Still ogling at him, like she'd been frozen with her jaw jut down since she'd first laid eyes on him. "I ain't Colonel Burrows," he said. "I'm Elvis Presley."

"Yes," she said. Sharon had begun to have doubts, saw herself an unworthy, rejected disciple, but now the faith returned. "I know."

"An', the crowds 'n' the like, y'understan', I mean—"

Sharon began to step around from the counter; he needed her on the other side.

"The gates, the security," he went on, "I jes can't—"

"Of course, of course."

Oh, she had been chosen: part Moses, she thought—a tidal wave of old Bible study suddenly splashed on the shore of her skull—part Mary Magdalene, and a bit of Ann-Margret in Sharon's favorite Elvis movie, *Viva Las Vegas* (not as busty, of course, but more pert and sincere). Things made sense, suddenly: the years wasted with Hank were for a reason; the war, the waiting, the mourning, it was all a prelude to today. A beginning. She would take Elvis by the arm, escort him to the VIP lounge, and on the way, gradually, slowly, they would get to know each other, nothing forced you understand, just easy and—

Then another hand—not Elvis's—grabbed her by the back of the shoulder as she neared the baggage scale, just about to cross over to the customer side of the counter.

"Miss-us Teele." It was Mrs. Honeycutt, "Sour Honey," the matron in charge of the girls behind the ticket counter. It could as well have been Momma grabbing her on her way out the door to the graduation night party, or God knows how many other nights. She knew what was coming.

"Miss-us Teele, I believe you're needed behind the counter."

She was smiling, Sour Honey was; that is, the corners of her lips were pointed up, setting off ripples of old dry skin and pancake makeup that reverberated in circles round her cheeks . . . and still with that nasty glare, a look that'd uncoil like a scorpion's tail at half a chance.

"Mr. Presley"—now Sour Honey stepped out from behind the counter, brushing past Sharon like a stuffed, over-regulation-sized suitcase, or the godawful Queen of England and Elvis was newly knighted—"I'm Gladys Honeycutt."

"Pleestammeyamm."

Sour Honey looked to Sharon for help, a translation, and Sharon, too nice for her own good (her curse: mistakes that would hound her till the end), announced, hushed but official (though tears were beginning to well up in her eyes already), "Mr. Presley is traveling under the name of Colonel Jon Burrows, Mrs. Honeycutt. For privacy and security, you understand. But he'd like to be escorted through security, private-like, away from the crowds and such—"

"Well of course he would," Sour Honey said, grabbing an elbow of Elvis. "Why wouldn't he now!"

And the two strolled away, Sour Honey's fat arms wrapped around Elvis like a Roman guard's, leading him up Calvary to be strung up and entombed, while Sharon Teele just stood there, watching.

It was like Wendy had told her: *Devils walk among us, too.*

This was her whole life, over and over.

1 0

THE MEDAL

STANDING ON A PODIUM IN the Rose Garden, Ben Rollins was waiting for the President to finish his speech and give him his medal so he could get out and go home.

Ben had grown up just five blocks from the White House, on 14th Street near Thomas Circle, and had walked past the building hundreds of times, but he had never been inside the grounds before. Now inside, he felt that the place had an unreal quality, what he imagined a Hollywood set might feel like. Photographers and cameramen were snapping shots, and though they focused mostly on the man to Ben's right, a legless stump resting on a wooden platter with small round wheels underneath, Ben couldn't help but feel that he, too, was a model, an actor playing a part, which added to the surreal, unnerving atmosphere.

Ben and the other honorees had arrived early and met each other, and it hadn't taken long for them to figure out what they had in common: they had all left body parts in Vietnam. After realizing their bond, all the veterans on the podium were silent, except for the stump, the laughing, rollicking torso whose legs had been removed from just below the hip. To the man on the platter, everything was a joke.

"Where'd you lose yours?" he said to Ben, offering a hand to shake. "I'm still limbs ahead of you and every bastard here!" Soon others were joking, but Ben, who saw he was the only black on the podium—and in the Rose Garden—was still uncomfortable.

Most of the other men had family in the crowd, but Ben did not. The truth was he was ashamed to be here. Hadn't even mentioned it to his sister,

Angelina. You earn your medals in fair competition, on the football field; that is where he had earned trophies in high school, and that is how he wanted Angie to think of him. And since he'd returned from the war a month ago, even the sight of her depressed him. In the time they were apart she had lost even more than he had.

While Ben had told his friend Lester that he was going to the White House, he was sorry he had. Lester had teased him, joked that if you were going to be on a podium with the President, why wouldn't you attack him: *one life can save so many.* And at some level Ben agreed: what a waste of an opportunity. At such close range.

When Max Sharpe finally made it back outside, the President was still speaking.

"You hear them night after night on television," Nixon said, "the people shouting obscenities about America and what we stand for. You hear those who shout against the speakers and shout them down, who will not listen. And then you hear those who engage in violence. You hear those, you see them, who, without reason, kill policemen and injure them, and the rest. And you wonder: Is that the voice of America?"

It was an old speech, one the President trotted out often on the campaign trail. Then Nixon improvised, riffing on it like a jazz musician.

"This," the President said, waving his hand toward the veterans on the podium behind him, "these are the voice of America."

Nixon stepped from the dais and moved to the one-legged man, a couple over from Ben, to give out the first medal. It made things easier for Ben to look away from Nixon, try to transport himself back to Lester and his friends in the park. Tried to convince himself that Lester was only joking that violence was the answer. If Martin Luther King had not been shot dead in Memphis a year and a half ago things would be different: racism, this war. . . . Even Richard Nixon could not help but listen and learn from a pure soul, a good heart.

Sharpe looked around for Ehrlichman, but couldn't find him. When he turned back to face the podium, Nixon was giving the right-legged amputee a final shake of the hands, but the man wasn't ready for it, had already grabbed hold of his crutches so when he let go to shake with the President he wavered, unsteady, looking like he might fall for a second, but then grabbed Nixon's hand—the Secret Service men behind him jerked a step forward; Sharpe bit his teeth down hard on the middle knuckles; felt he drew blood—and the man caught his balance, and righted himself.

Sharpe hadn't heard anything about peace in Vietnam, but surely the President knew best about that. Time constraints must have forced Nixon to leave out a few paragraphs of his speech. Yes: that had to be for the best. Moved things along, closer to the climax, the *pièce de résistance*. Maybe he should have dispensed with these preliminaries altogether.

Lord, Max Sharpe prayed, just get Nixon to the Platter Man.

Now the President stepped over in front of Ben Rollins.

"Congratulations," Nixon said, pausing as he read the name tag on the chest of his uniform, "Private Rollins."

Nixon smiled, his whiskers darkening his jowls even now, just past noon.

Ben Rollins saluted the President.

Nixon extended his right hand to shake, then looked up at Rollins's shoulder, saw that the right sleeve was dangling from it, empty and limp.

"I'm sorr—" Nixon began. "Brave boy."

Then the President reached out his left arm, and when Ben did the same Nixon grabbed his hand but then wriggled his fingers upward, as if trying to grab Rollins's thumb. Rollins swiveled his hand to match Nixon's movements, so the two rotated their hands against each other's, pivoting at the point where their palms touched. The gestures looked like some new, funky dance craze. Finally, the President grabbed Rollins's wrist with his right hand, pulled it down and cuffed his fingers over Rollins's, so their thumbs interlocked. The President had, finally and only after dogged perseverance, succeeded in performing the hip young people's black power shake.

The President lifted their interlocked hands up in the air to show the spectators in the crowd, who now were clapping and laughing.

"Right on, brother!" the President said, grinning.

Then he turned around and was handed the medallion, shook out the nylon ribbon to prepare the loop for Rollins's neck. Ben Rollins bent his neck down, just as the others before him had done, but then he straightened up before Nixon could get the medal around him. Rollins extended his hand out and the

President, after looking around and receiving an affirmative nod from Ehrlichman, placed the medal in Rollins's hand.

Ben Rollins looked down at the medal for a moment. Then he looked up at Richard Nixon. Ben could hear, from across the street in Lafayette Park, the beat of a drum, slow-paced and steady, and he knew that it was Lester, keeping his peace vigil. Ben pictured the scene, the world of protesters in the park: long-haired guys and girls, barefoot with patched elephant-bell blue jeans; shirts made of American flags, single-starred Vietnamese flags, hammers and sickles, funky tie-dyed designs, peace sign pendants dangling around their necks, peace sign earrings, bumper stickers coating guitar cases and the guitars themselves . . . one band of hippies, fifteen of them maybe, following each other in rotating circles, dancing like an Indian rain dance, singing: "All we are saying/Is give peace a chance," over and over, and "War is over/If you want it . . ."; other groups dancing similarly, chanting "Make love, not war, make love . . . ," their long stringy hair bouncing up and down, covering their faces, though a few had towering, moplike Afros, and there were even a few brothers in the crowd; placards, hand-made, posted in the ground: "DROP ACID, NOT BOMBS," "BUILD HOMES, DON'T BURN THEM," "FIGHT HUNGER, NOT COMMUNISTS," "WANTED FOR MURDER: NIXON, WESTMORELAND, CALLEY," "WE HAVE FOUND THE ENEMY, AND IT IS U.S."; pictures of Lieutenant William Calley, with notations on and around the photo: "SCAPEGOAT," "ONE MURDERER CAUGHT, THOUSANDS AT LARGE," "MANSON-CALLEY, NIXON-AGNEW: ANY DIFFERENCE?" and meditators sprinkled throughout, seated in the lotus position, eyes closed, palms pointed upward, some silent, some humming, mumbling, speaking aloud to themselves or to the sky ("Lord let them learn, let them see, let them stop"), in circles holding hands; and incense everywhere, thin burning rods or small cones in hollow metal sculptures of doves, deer, frogs, unicorns, or, of course, the peace symbol, with holes to let the smoke rise out . . . so much incense that a thick, pungent aroma filled the area, and a cloud of smoke hovered over the one square block of grass of Lafayette Park (though still, the unmistakable marijuana odor couldn't be disguised); music, too: guitars, tambourines, recorders, and flutes; folk songs ("Where have all the flowers gone? Long time passing") ("We shall live in peace, one day"); rock music blasting from portable radios, Hendrix, Joplin, the Doors, and the Beatles, everywhere the Beatles; and a constant pounding, more military and melodic, a steady, slow thump (pause: one, two, three), thump (pause: one,

two, three), thump, booming like cannon fire, lingering between beats so long
that, like villagers under enemy fire, you had to think maybe they'd stopped,
gone home for the day, and then—*thump*—the sound came again.

Ben looked back up, and there, still in front of him, was Richard Nixon. Then
back down at the medal. *Sometimes you just act. Do what you feel, what is right.
Consequences, the long view, can mess all that up.*

He looked down at the medal for what seemed like a very long time (to Max
Sharpe, sitting in the back of the Rose Garden, then standing, gesturing madly
to no one in particular, then sitting again, it seemed that time had stopped) and
then Ben Rollins spat on the medal, cocked his arm back, and threw it, so it
sailed hard and high into the air and the sun's light caught the medal at its zenith
and from there formed a blurred beam that tracked the entire distance of its
measureless decline, a vast ray that curved over the entire crowd, the bowed
necks of the television cameramen on the raised platform to the left, the length
of the Rose Garden and the White House and the lawn out front, the White
House fence, the tourists lined up on the sidewalk outside and the guards in
their kiosks beside them. . . .

In his mind Ben Rollins could see the medal sail over all this, a high rounded
arc, until it settled, magically, peacefully, deep in the bowels of the protesters in
Lafayette Park, at the base of the African conga drum which a young black man
was pounding, in slow, measured beats.

GRACELAND

BACK AT GRACELAND, all hell was breaking loose.

Colonel Parker (his voice bellowing from the telephone) was saying he wanted Bo's head.

Bo (hand over the mouth of the phone, shout-whispering asides) was saying he wanted Vernon's and Priscilla's heads.

Priscilla (sipping a drink, glaring down at the others from the far end of the room) was saying she wanted Vernon's head.

Vernon (sheepishly lurking, eyes buried in the bear skin rug on the floor) wanted Priscilla's head, but didn't say a word.

And Tubby didn't care if it was Bo's head, or Vernon's or Priscilla's, long as it wasn't his own.

But the truth of it was, they all really wanted Elvis's head, but they also knew that, without Elvis, they weren't worth more than, as Tubby would put it, "nigger shit." The point being that, with Elvis slipping out of their grasp, they were all in one hell of a conundrum, though that wasn't a word that any of them would use. "Nigger shit" was more like it.

The Colonel wanted to get to the bottom of it.

"Bo, good God, he's a grown man, six plus if he's an inch, going on three hundred if he's a pound, and he's only the most famous godawful face on the planet, thanks to Colonel Tom, none to you. HOW THE HELL COULD YOU LOSE HIM?!!"

The Colonel was barking so loud that Bo (anchored to the telephone stand like a ball and chain) actually pulled the phone a good foot away from his ear, just to save the drums.

"Now Colonel, that's just the point—I mean, after all, he is a grown man, and he can, I mean, you know—the man's got a right to walk out of his own house—"

"Rights, you say? Well, Martin Luther Christ, he's got the right to drive a diesel per mile, which he'd be doin' right now if it wasn't for yours truly. Holy Christ. Rights."

"He may have just gone out for a drive. Maybe down to Tupelo."

"And maybe he could crash 'maybe down to Tupelo.' Maybe he could keel over and die 'maybe down to Tupelo.' Maybe you'll be in the poorhouse 'fore you know it." Bo waved at Tubby, Priscilla, and Vernon to come closer while the Colonel continued to rant. "Remind me why it is you get a paycheck, Bo. A three-hundred-pound man he loses. Just walks out the godawful bigger-than-life door."

"Now Colonel, it's just been a couple of hours—"

"'Now Colonel, a million dollars walked out the safe. Now Colonel, the Hope Diamond strolled out the door, and just drove on down the driveway.' 'Maybe down to Tupelo.' 'Now Colonel . . .'"

Bo let the Colonel go on with his tirade, cupped the mouthpiece with his hand.

"Tubby," Bo whispered, "you dim-witted ass, what the hell did you do now?"

"Hell, Vern done it," Tubby said, and for once he was right. "'Cilla, too."

Bo grabbed Vernon, who was pacing the floor in front of him.

"Vern!" Bo said, in a loud whisper. "What happened? And quick."

"He jes walked on us, Bo. You know how his temper's been flyin' these days. He jes snapped. And like you said, he's a grown man 'n' all, jes like you and me."

Priscilla cut her eyes at Vernon, shook her head.

"Vern, you holdin' out on me? That what you sayin', Priscilla?"

"Bo," Priscilla said, "Vern and I were after him a little, but only for his own good—"

"That's right, Bo," Vern said. "It was—"

In the background the Colonel was still screaming about a million dollars walking out of his safe, after the security guard handed it the key.

"—he got a little hot," Priscilla went on. Bo thought she should have been more upset, what with her husband getting up and leaving to parts unknown. But then again, Bo had his own inklings about Priscilla Presley. "So he went up and changed. Then he stormed out."

"Why were you after him?" Bo said. "You know what he's like, Priscilla, with the phone calls we been getting, and then this last tour. I mean, for godsakes."

"He was spending like a drunken sailor, Bo. I mean, we were just pointing out—"

"Look at these!" Vernon shoved a handful of papers into Bo's face. "Look at them yourself! Then tell me who's what and why."

Vernon dropped the papers on the telephone stand (a mahogany bar stool from the Hilton in Vegas; a gift to Elvis for a week of sell-outs), then paced to the far end of the room.

"My own son," Vernon said. "My own flesh 'n' blood. Can I give him a talkin' to now 'n' ag'in? S'pose not."

"Bo!" The Colonel again. "You vanished on me, boy?"

"No, Colonel. I'm here." Bo leafed through the papers on the stand. Invoices, receipts from the past week. A pearl-handled Colt .45 for $3,500 from Kern's. A Derringer. Another Colt. A Mercedes sedan for $12,000. Ten more Mercedes. He tried to add up the totals quickly: over $100,000 in a three-day stretch. Merry Christmas, boys, from the King.

"Bo, you get back to me when you hear word one about my boy. Comprehendo?"

"Yes, Colonel."

"And Bo?"

"Yes, Colonel?"

"In case you see two fat cheeks walk out the door, you better stop them."

"Yes, Colonel."

"Hate to see you lose your brains."

And the Colonel hung up.

1 2

THE CAPTAIN

THE STEWARDESSES—THE whole crew of them—had escorted Elvis to the front row of the plane, and tired, worn out already, he sat down. He had popped some greens on the tarmac, and though he had fought their draining effect to survive the security crisis and get on the plane, now they kicked in. Sleep was in order. He took off his cape, then his jacket, placed them on the aisle seat. When he looked up at the stewardesses he saw that their eyes were looking down at his midsection, bugged practically out of their heads. And it wasn't, as he first thought it might be, at the outline of Little Elvis, now limp and inert (but ready to spring into action at any time): no. Their eyes were agog at the gold-plated Colt .45 holstered to his shoulder, and at the .38 nestled above his right hip.

Elvis homed in on the girls, tossed them each a wink. Like sweat-soaked scarfs to sweethearts in the front row: magic to make the problems go away.

And it seemed to work, at first. They each (one blond, one brunette) returned synchronized winks back. But that was all. Before they could do more a uniformed intruder elbowed his way in front of them.

"Now Mr. Presley," it was the copilot, "those guns"—pointing down—"they're just—not permit—you know—Washington calls the shots—wish I could—not my baili—"

And then a barrage of "Mr. Presley, you don't understand," "federal regulations—weaponry—prohibited" sprayed at him, all rapid-fire bureaucratese. If they asked Elvis (no one did), and even if it had made sense at all (land of liberty, my ass!), what they were talking was petty laws for the everyday Joe. Not Elvis.

"Let me explain it to you," Elvis said once there was a lull in the firing. "The threats, they've been comin' heavy. 'Presley's a dead man,' that sort of thing, middle of the night, then click. First by telephone, but next thing they'll be over the fence, Bo's called the Feds and they're onto it, but what can they do? There's a war out there, I see it on the news same as you. Those boys are serious."

In Memphis all this didn't need to be explained—Panthers, hippies, us/them—or if it did, Bo or the Colonel did the explaining. But not with this crowd.

So he reached in the pocket of his cape, then pulled out a badge, an honorary one the sheriff had given him out in Vegas, and handed it over.

"This should cover it," Elvis said. "See? I'm deputized." Then he dug out a handful more badges, quickly examining each before handing them over to the copilot. "That one's from Memphis," a palm-sized silver crest, "and this," a circular gold one, "this one is too."

Which was the beauty of these badges, why he brought them along. *Symbols brought power, right?*

But they didn't, the problems, go away.

"They're awful pretty," the copilot said, badges pointing at the guns. "We'll take care that they go to—" and the man had the Mother-of-God balls to reach down and grab the gold handle of Elvis's prize Colt.

The magic had faded.

"TO HELL YOU WILL!" Elvis yelled as he smacked the little man's hand off the gun. Then he stood up. More like he unrolled himself out of his seat, unsteady and staggering, hands grasping the armrests, propelling his hips out, caught himself before he fell forward, then steadied himself, like a rubber pole bouncing itself out, settling down.

"Elvis Presley don't have to take this crap. Can't trus' me with ma guns"—he gathered up his cape and jacket, whipped them onto his shoulders—"then ah'll find someone tha' does."

He walked the few steps to the door—the stews had been readying to close it when they'd spotted the guns—and stepped off the plane, then down the stairs outside.

Elvis now stood on the tarmac just a few feet beyond the steps, having stopped in the midst of each slow pace to give the appearance of walking while not really moving. No need to rush back: he wanted to give the crew ample time to reconsider.

Turned out again. He tried to imagine what Madame Blavatsky would say on the subject of the unrecognized Master: *They who show the door to Him, who do not understand . . . they do not know. They know not who is in control. . . .*

Control. That was at the core of things right there, the hot center of it all. After all, it wasn't just clouds Elvis Aron Presley could guide; it was people. Didn't understand it when it was happening to him first time 'round—'55, '56—but since then he'd had time to consider . . . the meaning of things.

He stood still, his back to the plane. Closed his eyes. *Turn around, boys.* He said it to himself, he prayed it. *Change thouest small-ass minds and invite old Elvis back. Girls, disposeth thy brassieres, and boys, lay out the red carpet with velvet casings for the guns.* (Suddenly the image of a sweat-soaked scarf flashed into his head—didn't know why or where; wasn't trying to summon it—but instead of Charlie draping one 'round his neck onstage, damn it if it wasn't loose around some bathroom pipes, slipping off.)

It would be a slow ride back to Graceland; an escaped prisoner returning himself. *Boy can't make it on the outside.* Vern and 'Cilla'd slap the cuffs on him, then march him down to Colonel Parker for his licks. *Had it comin'. . . .*

Control, he thought again. *Get me back on that jet. If I am a Master, if there was a reason for all this, then give me wings. Invite me back on the plane. Back at Graceland, Lord, I'm dying.*

Then he heard a bang, then another, and Elvis turned around toward the plane. It was the captain, running down the movable stairs, to the tarmac.

"MR. PRESLEY!" he screamed.

"You all don't want my business," Elvis said, patting his holster, "I'll take it elsewhere. I been cut off at the hips before. They turned me out of Florida, too. See who needs who."

"Elvis," the captain said, now reaching his arm around Elvis's waist to escort him back, "won't you forgive us?"

1 3

IN THE GARDEN

THE AWARDS CEREMONY HAD just ended, and though the platform was empty, Max Sharpe could still see Ben Rollins snatch his White House Medal of Honor out of President Nixon's gracious, giving hands, then toss it toward that cauldron of rapacious counterculture types in Lafayette Park, who then devoured it as if it was the staff of political dominance everlasting. All this in front of the *New York Times*, the *Washington Post*, the *Los Angeles Times*, CBS, ABC, NBC, AP, UPI . . . Nixon could blackball Sulzberger and Cronkite out of interviews to punish them for editorializing the event, but it was too late to suppress the straight news coverage of the Rose Garden ceremony . . . Rollins's black face would be splashed across the front pages and the nightly newscasts with a top-of-the-hour flourish; Cronkite would laugh (off camera, of course) as the screen filled with the ashen face of the stunned President, the Negro cocking his arm back as if to deck him (Nixon flinched—ever so slightly, but enough for his enemies to sense weakness, and—Jewish liberal sharks—they would *home in*); but then he tossed the medal: a forceful act, though technically nonviolent. *Lieutenant William Calley is being prosecuted for the murder of over one hundred civilians in Vietnam*, the *Post* would pronounce tomorrow (Sharpe knew exactly how the editorial would be written: trenchant, hyperbolic analysis; he had drafted enough Letters to the Editor to know—always from "Mrs. Abigail Jones" or "Bobbie Rae Todd," and postmarked from Muscatine, Iowa, or Selma, Alabama): *American boys are dying each day for a war that every rational man recognized long ago cannot be won*—Bradlee snickering as he wrote that one, implying that RN was neither rational nor man—*and, more pointedly, a small group of veterans invited to the White House yesterday have already lost a vast variety of limbs. And what does this White House offer them? Imminent peace? Heartfelt apologies? Increased benefits, with medical care worthy of their valor? This administration offers only cheap medals . . . the only honest response to the situation was offered by the true hero in the Rose Garden Saturday: one Benjamin Rollins. . . .*

Sharpe imagined the scene that followed: full of pomp and ritual, but with the cold brutality of a Mafia hit. The first thing the President would say to Ehrlichman would be: *Who got the Negro?* And when Sharpe's name was mentioned, the President would just give Ehrlichman a wink—*You know what to do, John*—and he would know . . . though Sharpe, still a trifle naive to the ways of the Nixon White House, was not certain what would happen to him, which made the impending punishment, and the agonizing wait for it, all the more painful. . . .

"Max, I've been looking all over for you."

It was his boss and mentor, walking up the aisle between the seats, toward him.

Sharpe shook his head, as if that would prompt his blood to immediately course, a nonchalant air to permeate his body.

"I thought you'd be back at your office by now, Max. Nobody knew where you were." Ehrlichman sat down beside him. "We need to know. In case of emergencies or whatever."

Did that mean that this was or wasn't an emergency?

"Sorry," Sharpe said, "I was just trying to think things out. The HOLE campaign, the ceremony—"

"Just talked to Bob and RN about that," Ehrlichman said. He was smiling, which in Sharpe's state of mind made things seem only more sinister.

"Really?" Sharpe's voice cracked in between syllables. "About the memo I drafted? The High on Life campaign—?"

"No—"

"—because I was wondering what they—"

"Look, Max, we were talking about this . . . business . . . today. This embarrassment."

Sharpe didn't say anything.

"The Negro," Ehrlichman said, "what's his name?"

"Rollins." Sharpe's throat could barely expel the vile name. "Ben Rollins."

"Rollins, right. You know what the press will do."

"Of course," Sharpe said. It was the media's fault; RN would understand that it was just the usual cabal of Jews. "The damned press. Love the Negroes like a brother, as long as they don't move next door."

"Right," Ehrlichman said. "Another rotten egg thrown at the motorcade from Lafayette Park. Of course, it's worse that he got inside the White House gates. But if I know Ben Bradlee, the *Post* will put a man on this kid Monday morning, take an in-depth look at him, so by Tuesday, Wednesday at the latest they'll have a full-blown spread on him. That's our real problem. *Your* real problem." Ehrlichman paused, looked out at the White House in front of them. "You see, Max, RN's a visionary. He can *see* political events as they may occur in the future, then, with a little legwork, change them. Alter the course of things."

Sharpe wasn't sure where this was going. Which frightened him.

"If Bradlee has his way, Ben Rollins will become a hero, a guest of honor at every protest rally from here to Berkeley. That's one reality, as RN sees it. That's the history you wrote by putting Rollins up on that stage. It's not a pretty story. It's not a true story, either. But Ben Bradlee is going to write that Ben Rollins is every Negro and every vet and every average American invited to the White House. That's a lie."

Ehrlichman turned toward Sharpe and looked him in the eye.

"I *know* what the truth is. Max, *you* know what the truth is."

Ehrlichman turned to face the podium, which a work crew was now disassembling. Sharpe looked with him. He could see the kid's eyes when he cocked his arm back to toss the medal, two hundred years of resentment forged into hot, pent-up rage. Rollins could have gripped the medal in his hand and, using it as a makeshift set of brass knuckles, decked the President with a mighty left hook, then stomped on him before the Secret Service could get to him. . . . Wasn't that what was in his heart?

"Remember," Ehrlichman said, "history is what is written about the past; nothing else. It isn't what happened. If you don't understand that, you don't understand RN, his obsession with history. What I meant when I told you that he sees the future, that he can alter history."

Alone in the garden, listening to the words of his boss and mentor as he gazed at the pristine image of the White House before them, Sharpe sensed that the scene was almost biblical: Ehrlichman being a prophet or disciple. But who was Max Sharpe?

"Yes. I get it."

"You altered history, Max. You need to undo that. Make it true."

Sharpe nodded his head.

"What do you want me to do?" he said.

Ehrlichman stood up, looked at the podium again, then turned to face Sharpe.

"Well, what if the facts are so counter to the story Ben Bradlee wants, that with whatever little conscience he may have, he cannot go through with it?"

"OK," Sharpe said. "But how do we make that happen?"

Ehrlichman paused.

"Max, listen. When I recruited you, I knew you had some potential in this business. Not every lawyer is suited for politics, but some have all the skills and more. RN, for one. I thought you had it, Max. I still think you might. Maybe RN will see it too. In time."

Looking at him in the eye, Ehrlichman had an honest face. Sharpe could tell.

"Use Finlator for this," Ehrlichman said. "He's a good man. And he can solve that Pentagon leak too. The Sitorski problem. Peoria. You do a good job on both of them, and then maybe I can catch RN's ear on—what's that you're always rambling about?"

"'Get High on Life.' It's a campaign, you see, where—"

"Right." Ehrlichman took a step away. On the other side of the lawn workmen were stringing lights on the White House Christmas tree. "You want to give RN something special for Christmas?" he said. "Wrap both of these jobs up by Monday."

1 4

ON THE AMERICAN AIRLINE

ELVIS HAD OVERCOME the problem of the guns; the captain had escorted him back on the plane, and the stewardesses had set up a special section for him, near the cockpit. From here on in his voyage—fully armed—he would be Colonel Jon Burrows.

No one would know his mission.

The truth was, at the moment, he wasn't sure what it was himself.

Since leaving Graceland, he had ridden the pills all the way up and back down again. *Why had he left? Where was he going?*

Destiny, karma had led him to American Airlines. Now on his way to the capital of these United States, in the VIP section up front . . . he had fast nursed a Jack Daniel's on the rocks . . . then another . . . to Washington . . . to sleep . . . then to the men's room, where now he stood, eyes closed, Little Elvis dangling between his fingers.

Things had come to a head back at Graceland. Many forces at play there; the surface (the words Vern and Priscilla had screamed; money), that was just the half of it. Though what the other half was Elvis couldn't say. It was just something he felt, that was all, bubbling under the surface but percolating up, a blowup in the works, a long time coming.

Elvis, Vern had pleaded with him, *the Colonel, he got it all planned. . . .*

Planned: damned straight. Graceland was a prison, all the sudden; Bo and Tubby, guards. All of Memphis, in fact, ensnared him; the way Sheriff Morris and his boys knew him, and everyone else, you couldn't get away. *Elvis, sign this! Elvis, I love you! Here's my phone number, Elvis; my husband's on the road this week. Elvis, Elvis, Elvis!* They had him handcuffed and bound, but on a treadmill, whipping him to run faster. Chasing those damned Beatles, that was what they wanted, for him to run up and grab John Lennon by the ponytail and pull him down to the dirt, then see who the girls flock to.

Elvis reached into his pocket, pulled out a medicine bottle, checked his supply of reds. What with his crazy-assed schedule (*Want to catch a movie? Better rent out a whole theater at two in the morning*), the touring (say good night to Lisa Marie, fly out to Vegas for a week of night shows that'll keep you revved up till sunrise; and the Colonel had another gig, another make-Elvis-a-laughingstock-everybody-laughing-behind-his-back-for-a-few-million-for-the-flick-a-few-more-for-the-album movie; then back to Memphis, Priscilla bitching about his being away when he's just earning her keep, when he's the money tree is all; Vern, Bo, Tubby climbing up and shaking him down. . . . Elvis needed his medication.

He popped a pill and closed his eyes, felt the meds splash down in his bloodstream, course like a riverboat. . . . On the road in '55 was what came to him. Twenty years old, two years out of truck driving, one year after "That's All Right, Mama" played on the radio in Memphis and the phone lines had lit up like tits on his Barbarella pinball machine; driving 'round the country with Scott, D.J., and the boys, young and hungry, five hundred dollars in one fat pile, handed to him backstage by Hank Snow, scared to come onstage after Elvis was done ("And get the hell out of town, boy!"); beginning to catch on big but not there yet . . . you could still find a nook of privacy, and just because a girl caught his eye and he caught hers that didn't mean that the quivering upper lip of Elvis Presley alone gave him free license to slip a hand under her shirt; no, there was still charming to be done; and back home there was Momma . . . the workaday past just down the road a piece, the all-the-dollars-and-girls-in-the-world future so close; pedal to the floor, driving down that road, top down and singing to the wind; grinning with enough aw shucks confidence to halfway hide the fact that he was scared all to hell—rising so fast up the charts who knew where that road ended?—and the crazy-ass girls, screaming, crying in the front rows like they'd seen the Lord himself, only sexy and hung like a farmhand nigger—maybe those girls in a frenzy would devour his heart in their luscious, virgin mouths, knowing not what overtook them. . . . He had never been richer and, if you didn't count dollars, never would be so rich again.

Then what? Drove off the cliff. Constructed people like robots—Vernon and Priscilla and Bo and Tubby—then lost all control of 'em.

Elvis opened his eyes. He was still standing, alone in the cramped bathroom. Looked to his right. Out the airplane window clouds were racing by, he told them to stop but they wouldn't. Somewhere down below was Graceland. He smiled: left all that. For damn sure.

Then someone banged on the bathroom door.

"We'll be arriving in Washington in fifteen minutes, Mr. Presley." A stewardess outside in the aisle.

So this is where you fell, off the edge of the cliff.

What would he do there? Was he to mingle with the people—his people? Was he to discover/uncover what had happened to America in the fifteen long years since he'd taken over the joint? The young minds of America were no longer so sharp, so fresh, so filled with compassion and, yes, love . . . Communist mentality seeping into the American brainscape, poisoning the wells. . . . Oh, he knew their brainwashing ways. He'd studied the Commies, talked to FBI agents, cops . . . and other, less official paramilitary types . . . back in Memphis, Vegas, and L.A. It was the drugs, rock 'n' roll, eating away like a cancer.

Was he, Elvis Aron Presley, the undercover agent of President Nixon's dreams, of Director Hoover's fantasies? Yes and yes.

Would he subvert from within?

Yes!

Shit. He had pissed on himself. He had forgotten that he was in an airplane and, in particular, in the bathroom, fly open, Little Elvis in hand . . . and a drop or two had landed on the leg of his pants, on the inside of his thigh.

In his other hand he still held a green plastic bottle, almost full: a fresh supply from Dr. Nick. Yes, oh yes; the riverboat was cruising now. He would be Jon Burrows, an FBI special agent, burrowed—get it?—in the rock 'n' roll drug culture ("President Nixon? Burrows—hey hey hey—yes it's me, sir . . ."), and if all else failed, at least he'd get a nice badge, something to give him credentials to flash at poor bastards he'd pull over on the highway, back home with Bo and the guys. Hell yes. Power there, in symbols.

He forgot about the spots on his pants, buttoned up, and walked out of the bathroom, down the aisle. He was floating—the reds rolling, as the Fogerty boys sang, on the river—and float he did, smiling, waving, blowing kisses to the ladies in the aisle seats . . . until he was back, ensconced in his seat, not sure even if he was awake, or back in Graceland, or in Hollywood on a shoot, or in Vegas between sets, or fifteen years ago, on the road. . . .

"Another drink, Mr. Presley?"

It was a stewardess, a long-legged red-haired youngster. Priscilla ten years ago, though who could judge tits in that polyester smock? If he was Elvis Presley, if this Natalie—reading her name tag—were in Graceland, if Bo, Tubby, and the boys had rounded her up for a party and he was peeping in at her through the wall, watching her sip G&T's with the rest of the night's recruits, he might have chosen her, her and another girl, and they would have been presented to him in his Master Chamber, the personal guests of Elvis Presley, the King of Rock and Roll, of Pop, of Hollywood, of Las Vegas, of the South, of the Silent Majority, of Mothers Everywhere, of Daughters—yes, of Daughters—Everywhere. Of Everyone Everywhere. Guests of Elvis. And Little Elvis.

But this was not Graceland. And he was not Elvis.

He had work to do.

"Must be a mistake, ma'am," he said, looking serious as he could manage, straight ahead.

The girl was shocked.

"Burrows is the name. Colonel Jon Burrows."

1 5

FINLATOR

JOHN FINLATOR TOOK THE long view. Saturday afternoon, as was his custom, he was in his study at home in Georgetown, sitting back in the regal, wooden armchair he had commissioned from the finest North Carolinian backcountry craftsman with whom he, during his long years of fieldwork for the Bureau, had ever dealt. The chair was cushioned with goose down, packed tightly into smooth sheaves of calves' leather to create an unearthly lightness. The feeling he had, sitting now, was that he was adrift on a cloud, and the billows of smoke that surrounded him, created by the pipe he was puffing, accentuated the feeling. Reviewing FBI surveillance files, he imagined this is what heaven was like.

Over the years some of the work in which Finlator had been forced to engage was . . . distasteful—there was no other way of putting it—but, in the long run, it had all been worth it. Take his work in the South, for example, when he had come in contact with the craftsman. Finlator would obtain information from the Bureau's Negro agents working undercover in the civil rights movement: reports of upcoming marches, sit-ins, boycotts, and most important, the activities and interests of the leaders, Martin King in particular (Finlator refused to sully Luther's name by association with the Negro subversive), with a premium on rumors of sexual trysts, adulterous flings, proclivities for drugs, boys, white women, or, of course, dalliances with Communism. As he would meet these double agents in rat-infested, snake-laden shacks in the deepest backwoods, Finlator could never be sure if the snap of a branch or a slither in a swamp was another agent of the Bureau, an enforcer from the Klan, a hunter, an alligator, rattlesnake, or prancing doe (those treacherous bayous were microcosms of the nation itself); and not infrequently the Negro agent—unhinged by the same uncertain fears—would race out of the shack and meet his end at the barrel of a rifleman, or chained to the trunk of a tree. . . . Bastards on all sides in that scene, the worst of them being the double agents he would have to coddle and pamper. But still, there was a war which the Bureau was fighting, in which J. Edgar Hoover was captain, Richard Nixon now the general, John Finlator a soldier, and everyone had his role. . . . And now, years later, the woods were thick with saplings off the Communist tree. The war was raging still.

But John Finlator believed in ultimate justice. After all, in December 1970 Martin King was dead, those Kennedy boys (after thumbing their Harvard noses at the Director and caving in to Castro) were dead too, and Richard Nixon was alive and well. Now, as head of the FBI's Bureau of Dangerous Drugs, Finlator was at the point where all threats converged, the main nerve of the Revolution. The long view had paid off.

His pipe was out—the last drag he inhaled was just ash and hot air—so he pinched some tobacco from the tin on his desk, tamped it down in the bowl of his yellowed calabash, lit it, and breathed deeply so the inside glowed. Then he walked over to his bookcase, picked up a few volumes: Freud, a Black Panther newsletter, and a couple of internal FBI manuals, one on the threat to American civilization posed by the inner cities, another on effective use of the *agent provocateur*. A few inspirational texts that might interface at some fundamental plane with the tasks at hand. Director Hoover had taught him never to be satisfied with a simple law enforcement effort unless they were converted into events of maximum effect. A simple street bust of a few ounces of heroin that might lock up some inner city thug for ten years Hoover saw with the long view in mind: use the boy as a fulcrum to tear the lid off the decaying social jar, so one could remove the debris with tweezers, then place a magnifying glass over it and, *voila!*, a laser beam is created that zaps the life out of the Movement, the so-called Revolution. A genius, Finlator knew Hoover was a genius, and his creative use of law enforcement was augmented by the inclinations of the current President, whose mind ran, he knew, along similar wavelengths, creating a synergistic effect.

Finlator puffed his pipe again, cracked open each book and pamphlet and laid them out on his desk, scanning his eye along the pages.

The phone rang. Finlator picked up and, per his custom, said nothing, waited for the caller to speak.

"Mr. Finlator?"

The voice sounded ill at ease, a lost boy wandering in dark rooms. He knew the voice.

"Max Sharpe," Finlator said.

He had known Maximillian Sharpe for a couple of years now: a kid, really, a thirty-some-year-old hot shot who John Ehrlichman had brought in to run Nixon's anti-drug program, and had since been bumped upstairs to the White House.

"Nixon Crime Summit, 1969," Finlator went on, "and not so much as a card from you since. Any more luck on that High on Life business?"

"HOLE?"

"I doubt it, but an interesting concept, still. But that's not why you called. A favor, surely. What is it?"

There was silence for a minute as Finlator puffed his pipe and Max Sharpe, on the other end of the line, wondered if Finlator had a bug on him.

"Actually," Sharpe said, "it's two favors. Orders, I mean. Jobs."

"Ord—?" Finlator reined in his tongue. Then he listened and, as Sharpe explained the tasks at hand, he jotted notes on his pad: *Ben Rollins*; *White House guest*; *Viet vet*; *Negro*; *no right paw*; *local DC boy*; *Bradlee/Post story coming*; *need to change that*. As Sharpe babbled on about Ben Bradlee getting history wrong, Finlator scrawled next to the name of Ben Rollins: *agent provocateur or setup job*.

"Enough, Max," Finlator interrupted. "What's the other job?"

"Well," Sharpe said, "the President thinks there's been a leak."

Finlator listened and wrote more notes as Sharpe went on. *Col. Alex Sitorski: suspected leaker, Calley/My Lai, "Peoria"?*

"We need these wrapped up quickly," Sharpe said when he was finished. "By Monday. The President wants to nip all this in the bud, before the media runs with it."

"Don't you worry your little head about that," Finlator said. "Just let Uncle John work out the details." And he hung up. Finlator never allowed anyone, save the Director himself, to leave him hanging on the line, alone with a dial tone.

Then Finlator thought for a moment, and jotted down a note next to the name of Colonel Alex Sitorski. *Tail. Bugs. Deal appropriately.*

Distasteful jobs, picking up the refuse low-level White House flunkies left behind, *by Monday at the latest!* . . . Finlator resented any White House infringement on Hoover's law enforcement turf, and these petty tasks . . . it wasn't going after *the problem;* a waste of resources . . . but the Director himself had ordered his boys to be particularly receptive to White House demands, a change of pace from Hoover's inclination in administrations past to treat the Bureau as a separate power base, in some ways more powerful than the President's. . . . *Who, after all, had the goods on whom?* . . . The rumor was that Nixon was getting pressure to squeeze Hoover out of office before his impending retirement, thus inspiring the Director's calls for Bureau-wide graciousness . . . which was a way to see even this detritus as part of the long view.

Finlator leafed through his Rolodex of agents. The Sitorski job required some delicacy: a sophisticated quarry. The job demanded one of Finlator's best men. Ronnie Bonnard had just finished an undercover stint with some Mobilization to End the War offshoot: set up a ringleader with an acid sale, then offered him a deal if he turned counteragent. With Ronnie Bonnard, quarries always did. Next to Colonel Alex Sitorski's name, Finlator wrote: Ronnie Bonnard.

The Rollins job was another matter. The quarry petty and powerless, but the inner city setting brought some risk. He focused on the lowest rung of agents: rookies, trainees, veterans on the way out or returning from probation. Ideally he would use a Negro, but they were few at the FBI, and he realized as he fingered through the scant number of brown cards, they were all occupied as counteragents, mostly as Black Panthers. Finlator's fingers continued to leaf through the Rolodex, and now he reached the last card. It was orange—that is, the card was yellow, signifying the lowest rung, and it was encased in pink plastic, which meant he had just returned from a suspension that was not his first. The card read: *Palmer Wilson. Probation ended: December 14, 1970. Previous probations: three. Drinks.* That much was typed, part of the form Finlator's secretary used to complete each card, but underneath Finlator had written in his own hand: *father—Wallingford Wilson.* Wallingford Wilson was one of the great old men of the Bureau; he had helped develop an internal security and intelligence system before there ever was an FBI. Though the elder Wilson was in his eighties now, Hoover himself was said to call on him for advice on occasion. Which explained Finlator's note at the bottom of the card. It meant: *This man cannot be fired, regardless of circumstance.* Finlator understood that clearly.

Each time Finlator placed Palmer on probation he had slipped back into the bottle soon after. An *agent provocateur* job could prove the answer for Palmer, where his recklessness and irresponsibility could work to his advantage, encouraging those qualities in his quarry. And if not . . . well, even Hercules had stables to clean.

16

PALMER

PALMER WILSON EMERGED OUT of a thick cloud of cigarette and incense smoke, dense and foglike, making him visible at the exact moment that Elvis, still flying overhead toward Washington, closed his eyes.

"Freshen it up, Ray, will ya?" Palmer said. He was leaning over the bar at Ray's Saloon on O Street, just off 14th, ten blocks or so north of the White House, banging his glass on the counter. "For our fearless boys in the field!" Palmer raised his glass and laughed. "For the gunmen on the grassy knoll! For black bag jobs from Marilyn Monroe to Martin Luther King, Lord love 'em."

One P.M., so no one was on stage entertaining (economic necessity having forced Ray O'Reilly, the owner, to sully the place with nightly burlesque shows and strippers), and Palmer had been sucking Jack Daniel's out of a glass like it was the hump of a camel and he was stranded between sand dunes.

The glass was empty.

Palmer looked down, and instead of seeing a bottle of Jack Daniel's, saw only Ray O'Reilly's outstretched palm.

"You know I'm good for it, Ray," he said, but Ray shook his head. So Palmer fished his hand into his pants pocket, dropped the contents on the bar: a fake Maryland driver's license under the name of Omar Al-Khamal (the Bureau had supplied him with the alias and a beard when the picture was taken back in '64, during his early days as an agent), two foil-wrapped condoms of uncertain vintage, six pennies, three dime-shaped slugs. Then he pulled out from under his belt a silver flask, the metal dented, but polished bright. He patted it fondly, then unsnapped and removed the leather holster that covered the bottom, from which a single dollar bill fell out. The dollar he gave to Ray. The flask Palmer carefully returned to his pants.

"Now Ray," Palmer said, as Ray poured him another, "did I ever tell you the one about Oswald, how Ruby was able to get such a clear shot at Lee Harvey?"

Ray set the bottle down behind the bar, began polishing a thick-bottomed whiskey tumbler, and nodded. Yes, he had heard the story about how the FBI had played a hand in the lax security, how Palmer's father, the legendary Wallingford Wilson (famous, though Ray had never heard the name other than from his ever-present patron), had tipped Ruby off to tie the last loose end of the Dallas job.

"What about Memphis, Martin Luther King? Nineteen sixty-eight and all hell is breaking loose, the Negroes are taking over the joint like a speeding bullet"—Palmer stood up from his bar stool and, pinching the tips of his thumb and forefinger together to form a point, mimicked a slow traveling bullet—"and up jumps Wallingford Wilson, pater fam—il—i—ass! And with a few loyal compadres, history, just before it's derailed in the hands of the radicals, gets back on the right road. That is," Palmer said quietly, sitting down, "*his* road."

Yes, Ray nodded his head again. He had heard that one before, too.

"What about RFK?"

Uh huh.

"I ask you, Ray," Palmer said, "when your dad's done it all, what's a guy to do for a second act?"

Ray O'Reilly said nothing. He was not warming up to Palmer. Far from it. Oh, early on in the day, they made a fine pair, as they did every morning, what with Palmer knocking on the bar instead of even saying, "'Nother Jack Daniel's, Ray, straight up if you please," the pair's powers of communication being that closely attuned. But around ten Palmer's antics began to wear on Ray (again, the day's usual pattern), who long ago had heard Palmer describe J. Edgar Hoover's choice of hose (it depended: with a formal black dress, he tended toward a shocking fishnet pattern; in summer he wore white), that the Director had gotten the goods on that rascal Jack Kennedy and forked them over to that other rascal Lyndon Baines, thus getting LBJ the Vice Presidency and ultimately (wink, wink: *Ray, you gotta see the FBI files on the witnesses at the grassy knoll; and I ask you, bottom line: who had the most to gain in Dallas?*). Ray knew all this and more, and even if he believed some of it (though never the stories about Hoover cavorting in drag with his FBI buddy; that was too much) he just didn't care.

"You should hear what old Nixon's got cooked up for the '72 campaign," Palmer rambled, "talk about your black-bag jobs! If I was in that Democratic National Committee, I'd watch my mouth, let me tell ya. . . ."

On and on and on and on. If Ray O'Reilly died at that moment, he feared, he would hear only the voice of this old drunken bastard, making up stories as if he really were some FBI man, on into eternity. And that was the bright side: if Palmer was telling the truth, his one repeat customer was a bright white FBI agent of the Nixon administration, the embodiment of the Southern Strategy, the Klan, the murder of Martin Luther King, Medgar Evers, Cheney, Goodman . . . all wrapped in one drunken, overprivileged package (he could hear the talk: call a drunken brother a bum, call a drunken honky a bureaucrat).

The phone rang, and Ray picked up the line.
"Hello."
Silence.
"Who is this?"
No response.
"Wendy?" Ray said.
Nothing.
Which got Ray thinking. A shiver ran down his spine, like long nails on foil.
"Elvis?" he whispered.
Still nothing.
Finally, Ray heard an electronic sound, then an odd, distorted voice that seemed to undulate in volume and pitch between a soft feminine whisper and a loud booming baritone, with an overlay of scratchy white noise.
"Palmer?" the voice said. "Palmer Wilson?"
Ray placed the phone on the bar, pointed to Palmer.
Palmer's first reaction was to look behind him, unable to believe that there was anyone out there who would drop a dime to make contact with him. But besides Palmer and Ray, the bar was empty.
Palmer straightened out his shirt, picked up the phone, and spoke as soberly as he could.
"Palmer Wilson. May I help you?"
"You're at a bar, am I right?"
"Uh huh." Palmer held the phone out in front of him and examined it. "How did you know?"

"And you're sitting on a stool, in front of the bartender?"

Palmer nodded. The voice was beginning to scare him.

"Look, I don't know who you are, but you should know that I'm a registered agent of the FEDERAL BUREAU—"

"Be quiet, Palmer!"

"—OF INVESTIGATION! And my father, Wallingford Wilson, you may have heard of him—"

"SHUT UP!" the voice thundered. "Hang up the phone and get out! That's an order!"

17

WASHINGTON

THE PLANE LANDED, SLICED down through the clouds and into National Airport
. . . and the stewardesses wanted to know if they should phone ahead for him.
Did he have a concert planned in D.C.? Did he want to see the cockpit? (draw-
ing out that last word: cock—pause, slowly lick red lips—pit). But no, though
she was sweet (the stalking redhead), he was just Jon Burrows, out to see the
Nation's Capital, and the redhead's eyes turned to stone (she would become a
bitter woman). . . . As he walked off the plane there were the obvious stares, calls
for an autograph or two, a request to sing a bar of "Love Me Tender" or
"Heartbreak Hotel" (a longhair even mock-hummed "Jailhouse Rock," muttered
a few satiric verses, then was pushed away back to the cheap seats). He did let
the girls walk him down the movable stairs to the tarmac, then deposit him in
the lobby of the airport terminal, and there wasn't a damn thing he could do
about them stuffing scraps of paper in his pants pockets, front and rear—phone
numbers, love notes: he knew without looking—but then he shooed them away,
as if there was some reason he had to be seen alone. . . .

In the lobby the girls left him, and the captain walked past and saluted, and
the fellow passengers (the longhair flashed a closed fist toward him) . . . and
then, in the terminal, he heard a choir of boys and girls singing, "O come all ye
faithful, joyful and triumphant," and the herds of passengers rushed toward
him . . . "O come let us adore him, o come let us adore him," anticipating him
apparently. . . . There Elvis stood, in the center of it all, waiting for them to
gather 'round and listen . . . "O come ye, o come ye" . . . but the people rushed
past, not interested, or too busy . . . the waves of humanity washed over him,
around him, then peeled away in ripples . . . he stood . . . like a statue, a rock in

the water . . . no press, no entourage . . . no Bo, no Tubby, shuttling him back and forth, from city to city, shepherding the girls in and out . . . and Elvis, standing there in the lobby of National Airport, began to feel invisible. Began to forget he was Elvis Presley.

He walked straight ahead, toward the TAXI/LIMO sign, shaking his head no to the "Are you really . . . ?" stares, the gaping autograph seekers. "No," he muttered, "the name's Burrows."

Outside there was a line of yellow cabs, and a uniformed Negro—*another captain?*—herding people behind a set of parallel ropes, a serpentine path leading circuitously from the exit doors to the sidewalk. The captain spotted Elvis, ran up to him and—to the "What the hell about us?!" of the others waiting on line—grabbed him by the elbow.

"Where to, my good man?" The captain was smiling.

Elvis drew a blank.

"Where you headin' this fine day, Mr. Elvis? Or should I say King?"

Elvis had no earthly idea where he was going.

He looked straight ahead; a street sign with an arrow, next to which was printed: Washington.

"Washington," Elvis said.

The man looked puzzled.

"Uptown? Georgetown? Downtown?"

Elvis nodded slightly.

"Where're your bags?"

Elvis held up his valise.

"Travelin' light? Travelin' light but travelin' right!"

The man led Elvis along the sidewalk, past the yellow cabs, snapped his fingers and a long black limousine appeared. He opened the door and, pushing Elvis gently in the back, guided him into the back seat.

"The King here's going into the city," the man told the driver, who remained seated in the front. The driver nodded. "Pleasure serving you," the captain then said, and held out his hand.

Elvis didn't say anything. He was leaning back in his seat now, waiting for someone else to say something for him, to do what was necessary. Offer him a drink, fill him in on the schedule for the day. But there was no one, so there was silence, and the silence wasn't being filled.

The man's hand was still extended. Empty, and extended. The man stared at it. Which made Elvis stare at it.

"What's your name?" Elvis said, finally.

"Jones. Clarence Jones."

"Clarence, this here's the land of opportunity," Elvis said. "I'm living proof of that."

Clarence slammed the door hard, actually bit down on the sides of his mouth to keep from cussing.

"It's a great country," Elvis said, as the limo drove off. "Hang in there."

18

BO

Bo Price was in Elvis's bedroom, upstairs at Graceland.

He tried to imagine scenarios of where Elvis could have gone, play the alternate possibilities out in his mind, look for leads. What were Elvis's plans? Or what if there weren't any plans?

First, he separated what was possible from what was not. Bo could not imagine Elvis far from Graceland, certainly no farther than Tupelo. And he would be driving: Elvis had never taken any other form of transportation alone, and given the recent threats on his life, the fear those calls had struck in Elvis's heart, he certainly was not going to start now. And he was so used to being around the guys, traveling in the center of an entourage, Elvis would get lonely in a hurry. . . . Elvis would not be gone long. He'd come on home. Or, more likely, call to be picked up. By Bo. The best tack, if Bo had his way, was to wait a few hours, let Elvis work out of his system whatever it was that had gotten into it.

But the Colonel wasn't buying that. And though Bo could pull rank on the rest of the guys at Graceland—Lord, did it rile Tubby!—in the kingdom of Elvis it was the Colonel, not Bo, who called the shots.

In all the years Bo had served Elvis, Colonel Parker lived on the fringes of Elvis's day-to-day life, intervening only when Elvis had an outburst, just enough to smooth things over with the front desk of the Hilton, say, if Elvis and the boys had gunned down Tom Jones, Robert Goulet, John Lennon, or Ralph Abernathy on a series of televisions, and other guests had complained. Or if he happened to be backstage at a concert when Elvis lapsed into one of those long monologues, first the story of his life, smoothed over and sanctified into comic book/Horatio Alger/superhero stuff, then veering off into mumbled, half-stated jokes, keeping the punchline to himself, biting self-parodies, or rambling, paranoid fantasies . . . all this in mid-song, for so long that the guitarists would give up on their background riffs, then the snare drums would stop, leaving Elvis alone to speak his piece . . . and the Colonel, were he around, would signal for the band to rise again, loud enough to drown Elvis out and end with a crescendo with the lights going bright, then out . . . though Elvis still had points to make, messages to transmit . . . or if a paternity suit got filed, some farm girl with an autographed concert ticket stub attached to her complaint as Exhibit A, as if that were proof that Elvis had deigned to keep company with her . . . Colonel Tom Parker only dirtied his hands at the extremes. The Colonel's realm was mostly the business end of the operation: setting P.R. strategy, cutting deals for movies, products — Elvis statuettes, teddy bears, scarves, fan magazines, publicity photos — contracts with TV, with record companies, the Hilton . . . then let his boy do the rest. Other than that, to Bo it seemed that counting the money was the Colonel's main duty. That and bending your ear with a story, from his carnival days most likely: "So after I've sold 'em the tickets, you see, and I got them all in the tent, tied up the entrance so they're stuck watching the bearded lady, the muscled midget, whoever, and while they're all occupied I go around the back exit and make sure the horses, donkeys, and such go about their business, so when the act lets out the first customer sees smack in front of him a turd big as Texas, and there's one of my boys at the ready, offering a donkey ride escort over the wasteland, all for an extra couple of bits!"

The Colonel's point? "Son, I was making money when all I had to sell was donkey shit, and that I mean quite lit-er-al-ly." Now that he had himself a bona fide product it was Bo's responsibility to take care of it. Keep Elvis standing up with a voice box: let the Colonel do the rest.

But now the guys had lost the Colonel's product. Didn't even know where he was, for chrissakes. And Bo was in charge of bringing him back. The Colonel had made that godawful clear. There was no bounty waiting for success; after all, this was Bo's job. But failure? Well, what was Bo Price worth, exactly, without Elvis Presley? That was something the Colonel wanted to know.

Bo had wanted to get help from the police, but the Colonel insisted that Priority Number One was to make sure that the press not get wind that Elvis was on the loose. This — as Elvis playacting like James Bond would say — was an inside job. A hush-hush deal.

So tracking Elvis was Bo's job alone.

OK, then.

Bo had told Tubby to check out the hospitals, look into the worst-case scenarios, while Bo would stay at home base to call friends, stay around the phone. Vernon would take to the streets, drive to Elvis's haunts and see if he'd been spotted by any car dealers, gun shops, or at the movies. As a rule Elvis wouldn't dare visit any such places during the day (to avoid the public he'd have them open the place for him at three in the morning), but he wouldn't dare do what he just did, either. Anything was possible.

So Bo was sitting on Elvis's bed. Looking for clues.

He pulled open the upper drawer of Elvis's bedside table, dumped out the contents, and began sorting through the scraps. On top were a few photographs, old black-and-whites of Elvis onstage in the '50s: arms raised, guitar hanging from his neck, his hips in mid-swivel; Elvis leaning over, just beyond the grasps of the clutching arms of the girls in the front row, kids screaming, crying as they reached up at him. Then a photo of Elvis in '68, sitting on a stool during the taping of his television special, thin again. Bo had watched the image develop; had seen Elvis become *Elvis*. Back in Humes High when Elvis'd strut around in that oddball D.A. haircut ("Only an asshole'd wear a duck's ass," kids would say, then take a swing at him) and funky clothes from Beale Street that only a Negro would wear, he was meek and shy, but with a surly air to him, a sense down deep that he was something special—Bo sensed it too—and all he'd get for it was his ass kicked, until Bo came to save him (yes, Bo was bailing Elvis out back then, too) . . . but Elvis hung on to that look, that attitude . . . let it grow. Alone among the guys, Bo believed Elvis when he said that God had chosen him special to rise out from the poor, dark underbelly of Memphis life . . . and that was only the half of it. Call him a star and you missed the point.

Bo looked down and saw a book that had fallen out of the bedside drawer, and inside were portions of more photos that had been ripped apart. Putting them together, roughly, he could see that they were publicity shots for Elvis's recent Vegas shows, ones Elvis and the Colonel had rejected; couldn't hide his blubbery jowls, the bulging paunch. Among the fragments was an old black-and-white that was intact, one Bo had never seen before: it was Elvis standing with his arms around a couple of Negroes, singers he figured, in a studio, in '57 if Bo had to guess. Everyone was smiling, joking around. Not the sort of picture the Colonel wanted to flaunt, which probably explained why Bo had never seen it. And the Colonel certainly would not have wanted Elvis's public to see the photo the way it was now—especially his fans today (those middle-aged white ladies who'd mortgage their daughters for a sweaty scarf Elvis ripped off his neck during a show): in the picture Elvis's face was colored in with a black Magic Marker, just leaving some white around the eyes, so he was blacker than his friends in the studio, and across the page was scrawled, "AM I? AM I?"

Bo laid the photo on top of the bedside table, picked up the book that had been in the same drawer: *Theosophical Writings.* The spine was cracked open to a page where Bo figured Elvis had stuck the photos, and Bo turned to it, saw a passage circled at the bottom and an exclamation point scrawled in the margin.

Avichi, the circled passage began, *meaning Hell. A long drawn-out dream of bitter memories, a vivid consciousness of failure without volition, or the power of initiation. A dream of lost opportunities and futile regrets, of ambitions thwarted and hopes denied, of neglected duties, abused powers and impotent hate. A dream ending ultimately in the oblivion of utter annihilation.*

Bo didn't think Elvis had ever read that passage aloud to him, though he might have; try as he did, Bo could only absorb so much from Elvis's sermons on the Masters, theosophy, Buddhism, whatever. Bo never pretended his mind was a match for Elvis Presley's.

1 9

CHANNA

THE EYES STUDYING HIM in the rearview mirror had an Oriental look about them, Elvis thought. *Wisdom there. Hidden mysteries.*

"Elvis Presley," the driver said, and Elvis thought maybe the man had expected him all along. "My God."

"No suh," Elvis muttered. He was tired and now he closed his eyes. "The name's Burrows. Confused me with, with this . . . Presley character."

"The King. 'Knock me down, step on my—'"

"It's a common mistake, really. People make it all the time. Colonel Burrows—"

"'—face. Doncha step on my blue suede shoes!'" The driver had pulled the limo out of National Airport onto the George Washington Parkway. "Your momma raised a charmed man, Channa Stalls."

"Channa?"

The meaning of the name flashed in Elvis's mind: the driver who took Siddhartha outside his castle gates for the first time, leading to his ultimate enlightenment. *Everything for a reason.* And then the thought vanished, just as quick.

"Where we off to today, King?" Channa said. "To see the world? How we live and die down here?"

Elvis had popped another pill—maybe two, or was it three?—since his foray into the airplane bathroom, and it was as if each pill had pumped helium in his head, causing it to float, higher and higher, his neck holding it to his body like a tether. Then the gas coagulated, thick and heavy, so his neck could not hold it up . . . then it floated up again. At sea, rocking, floating, in the back of the limo.

Thought: somebody, tell the driver where Elvis is going. *Know where the hell
I am, tell me, then tell me where I'm going.*

"A hotel in the city?" Channa asked.

Elvis had been looking at the water—a river, it seemed—to his right. His first
thought was: the Mississippi. Must be heading into Arkansas, West Memphis . . .
and then: this wasn't Memphis. That wasn't the Mississippi.

"Going to Washington, am I right? A hotel, I suppose?"

"Washington . . . ? Right, Washington. Hotel?"

"Washington Hotel it is then. Good Lord, you must be goin' to the White
House! Goin' to see the President!"

The President, the White House. Yes, it was coming back to him now.

"Elvis Presley meets Richard Nixon." The driver laughed, glancing back at
the rearview mirror. "That'd be a sight! Tricky Dick hisself."

"President Nixon's doin' his best," was all Elvis could say. His head was floating again, tugging at his elastic neck. "It's a great country, and they're trying to
ruin it. They're doing their damnedest, I'll tell you what."

The driver switched off his smile.

"Who 'they,' Colonel?" he said, as he pulled the limo off the parkway, onto
an exit ramp, then to a bridge crossing the river.

"They?"

A rough, gritty blues was playing on the radio. When Elvis didn't answer, he
could see that the driver began to sing along: "'I put a spell on you, 'cause you're
mine. Better stop the things you do, I ain't lyin'!'"

Who was singing? Screamin' Jay Hawkins? Oh, Elvis knew what the driver's
point was, blasting his ears with the stuff: *Gotta live tough to get that edge to your
voice; you earn that edge. If you were colored, you wouldn't be no King. You'd be
nothin'. Just warmed-over, pasteurized white blues; that's all you ever was. In your
prime, even with the full range.* And Elvis thought, in answer: Bullshit. Hell,
Elvis had lived those blues, then bottled and stuffed 'em in his arsenal to pull up
at his will. He was no musical thief, no sir, that missed the goddamned point of
everything. Listen: Junior Parker moaning "Mystery Train" never got the girl,
just whimpered watching that train chug away with his lady in tow. Listen to
Smiley Lewis, one repentant guilt-ridden hombre after that "One Night of Sin."
Listen to Hank Williams, or the good old Carter family, bowin' and scrapin' for
one brooding-ass God, heavy into damnation, working stiffs, and doom, doom,
doom. So what did Elvis do? Oh, only jumped that train, searched out that Night

of Sin and reveled in it, laughing . . . God was never gonna wreak vengeance on Elvis Aron Presley; wasn't no petty-ass prude keepin' score of transgressions; his world was a joyride. . . . That was the message, the new gospel, and in each song the hero was Elvis, sniveling before Nobody. Oh, Elvis had fucked with the cosmology of song; a guitar wrapped 'round his shoulder, maybe a wad of toilet paper down his pants, a wiggle and a smirk, he'd grappled with that old doomsaying Lord, showed him Fun was not Evil, Sex was not Bad, not in this land of fast cars and bobby sox, not with so little time, so many girls; a foot on James Dean's shoulders, the other on Brando's, he'd overthrown the God of Junior Parker, Smiley Lewis, Hank Williams, Hank Snow, and the Carters, and lived. . . .

The city lay before him. Memorials he had seen in grade school books: marble domes, great pillars, statues. There was Abe Lincoln, out the window, big as a drive-in movie star.

"'Ain't gonna take none of your—foolin' around,'" the driver sang along with the radio. "'Ain't gonna take none of your—hand-me-downs.'"

"My momma never had much use for that Lincoln." Elvis thought he said it out loud, meant to anyway. *Provoke 'em a little. Jab 'em in the ribs.* "Down in Tupelo, we don't have much use for ole Abe Lincoln."

"I *know* a lot of folks down south don't have much use for Mr. Lincoln," the driver said, then turned around to stare Elvis down in the back seat. "But who 'they,' Colonel?"

Screamin' Jay, or whatever colored bastard had been singing, was finished; on the radio now the news was on. Nixon . . . plans for Christmas at the White House . . . Vietnam . . . pending prosecution of Lieutenant William Calley for his part in leading the massacre at My Lai . . . protests . . . Vietnam, Vietnam, Vietnam. A goddamned shame is what it was.

The gas in his head had thickened again, frozen solid. His neck could barely hold it up.

"The President's doin' his damnedest." Elvis was mopping sweat as he spoke. "Vietnam? Hell, he'll beat those Commies back to the Stone Age."

Elvis heard a rhythmic beating outside, tribal drums; looked out the window and saw a colored kid, his Afro in the trees, tie-dyed shirt, blue, yellow, and pink circles, what was left of a pair of army fatigues, beating his hands on a conga drum, over and over. And there, right across the street, was the White House.

"That is," Elvis continued, "if the Beatles give 'im half a chance. Send 'em back. If they don't like it, send 'em back. Pack 'em up, cut their hair, send 'em back! You understand what I'm saying?"

"I'm hearing it, Colonel. I'm *hearing* what you're saying. But who 'they'?"

" 'They'? They're beatin' the drums. And they can't sing the blues either, anyway. Never hear those Beatles sing the blues, didja? Or gospel? No sir."

Channa didn't say anything.

And Elvis thought, suddenly: *Got this quest figured out.*

"Now give me a pen." Elvis thrust his hand toward the driver's seat as he pulled some American Airlines stationery out of his pocket. "I got it all in my head; just give me a damned pen."

The driver cranked the volume of the radio up: "Mystery Train," the original blues version by Junior Parker, was now on. Channa must have slipped in an eight-track, having saved it for this moment. Then, in his own sweet time, the driver held out a Bic and Elvis took it from him.

Elvis spread the stationery out on his leg.

His head was floating again.

The driver stopped the car, leaned over the seat and unlatched a table that fell just above Elvis's lap.

"Thank ya," he mumbled.

Channa was shaking his head, muttering, "I *know* who 'they' is, Colonel. I know."

But Elvis wasn't listening.

Dear Mr. President, he wrote.

I have the greatest respect for you.

COMING HOME

BEN ROLLINS WAS A FEW blocks away, walking home from the White House. As soon as he had thrown his medal away the Secret Service had pounced on him, wrestled him to the ground, handcuffed him, then dragged him into the basement for an interrogation.

What was that about?

Nothing.

Who are you?

You've got my wallet.

Benjamin Rollins, 1375 O Street, N.W. How long you lived there?

Since I got back.

He's been planning it. Staying close.

Bullshit. I grew up there.

Thomas Circle?

Rollins, Rollins. Not the Ben Rollins from Eastern High? The quarterback? Man, Charlie, this boy could throw like you wouldn't—

Losing that arm's gotta hurt. Blamed the Commander-in-Chief ever since—

Don't like what the President's doing in Cambodia, you and your friends—

What the Hell did you think you were doing?

Friends helped you?

Just tell us who and you'll get out of here quick.

It was just something I did, Ben said.

He didn't say much else.

Since he hadn't attacked anyone, and it was his medal to do with as he pleased, there was nothing to charge him with. So they let him go, eventually.

. . .

Now he walked across 14th Street, his body cutting through the clouds of steam rising up from a manhole cover. The white billowy steam brought back memories he couldn't get away from. It was napalm. Vietnam.

On the other side of the steam, on the sidewalk across the street, he now saw Angelina sashaying away from him. How long ago was it when she was his bright-eyed kid sister, tagging behind him after a football game like he was a conquering hero? Only slivers of eyes now, hollow and empty. Angie was always a little slow, easy prey, but Ben and his friends could protect her . . . when he was around . . . then, when he went away the streets sucked her in like a monsoon sewer, she drifted away from him, grabbing the drugs she could get a hold of, doing whatever she could to pay for them. . . . Who was she now?

In Vietnam, at first, he thought of girls he met as Angie. The girls were a place to get away, whisper sweet bullshits until they laughed their way into your arms, ran you onto the cramped cot in the room they shared with five other girls . . . and after the Saigon giggles, after the sex, Ben would lie on his back, close his eyes and the girls would hand him the "poppy smoke," and listen to the fan whip around over his head, feel it stir the heat up in tiny cyclones, let the scene take him back: high school, king of Thomas Circle. Big things were going to happen to Ben: college ball, and then who knew . . . who could stop him? Simple, good times back then. Where the hell was Vietnam?

And then Ben's number came up . . . and now, since he'd come back, he reversed his perception: now he saw, walking down the street, a Saigon whore sashaying down 14th Street the way he saw them at the end of his tour, their true selves, hollow, burned-out, and tough (frisk you with sloppy kisses all the way down, while a girlfriend picks your pockets clean), which is how you grow up, in Saigon and Thomas Circle, how you get by. *Isn't that what Angie had told him ever since he'd come back, eyes droopy, body spent?* He had left and she had gone down and he had come back and she went down some more. *You lose your dreams and then—what's the point?—you lose everything.*

"Yo! Yo, Bennie!"

"The man himself!"

He whirled around and there, strutting up the street behind him, was his old crew, but nothing like he remembered them. Before he'd left they were skinny laughing kids, but now there was T-Squared, a cube of tough muscle topped with a 'fro so outrageously high it said *I can get away with this bullshit, motherfucker;*

and Horse, chomping down on his anger like a bridle; and Dex leading the way, all flashy in his bright-patterned dashiki.

Ben nodded, tried to smile.

"What's up, Ben?" Dex said as he slapped Ben on the back. "Where you been hidin' out, man? We've been looking for you."

"White House hero too big for us?" T-Squared said, Horse play-punching him in the shoulder.

Ben could see Dex nod to Horse, who nodded back, then quickly walked away. It was a silent language Ben no longer understood.

"Just settling back," Ben said. Yards away, Horse had stopped Angie on the sidewalk, and now he held out an empty palm, yelling something at her.

"That's just some business," Dex said, grabbing Ben by the shoulders, turning him away so he couldn't see his sister without cranking his neck around. "Like what I wanted to talk to you about. My man could use a little spending money, now that you're back home, couldn't you?"

"Danny's lined me up something, Dex," Ben said, "and I figured—"

"Danny? You want to clean floors like your momma?" Dex cut his laugh short soon as Ben fired him a glare. "Hell, Ben, it's too late for after-school jobs. We're not kids anymore. I'm talkin' real money."

"I know what you're talking about." Turning around Ben could see Horse pocketing something, while Angie snapped up her purse.

"I'm just trying to help you out, brother. Get you in with the program." Horse came back over and slipped something into Dex's hand. "Unless you still think you can make it in the pros." Dex glanced at Ben's empty sleeve. "But Tricky Dick and his boys fucked that dream for you, didn't they?"

Dex licked his thumb and counted the money Horse had handed him, then tucked it away in his back pocket, exposing the butt of a gun wedged under his waistband.

"You got to understand how it is, Ben," Dex went on, turning back to Ben. "I'm the man, now. You want to do business in this here community, you go through the Dex. I could make life a little easy for our conquering hero. For old times."

Old times: Ben would snap his fingers and Dex and T would come running, shoo the dealers away from Angie.

Angie was starting to walk away from him and Ben felt a twinge of pain in his arm, the arm that wasn't there. He thought he could recall an instant in the jungle when he looked at his arm, blinked his eyes, and the next moment it had vanished, just white light that first blinded his eyes and then enshrouded him, transporting him to some dream state where silent racing doctors and nurses bent over him, and there was blood and screams and bodies, and then he was home. Maybe that was some pivotal moment when time shifted, separating then from now, when Dex became a king, and the drugs took over Angie, and Ben . . . where did that leave him?

"What the fuck happened to you, Dex?" Ben said, all of a sudden. "What's it been? A year and a half since high school? You weren't into all this shit. And Angie, man. I figured at least you'd stay away from her. Protect her while I was gone."

Dex had been buttoning his coat over the gun and the money, but then he stopped and stared hard at Ben.

"Ben, you've forgot a lot, man." For once Dex's smile was switched off. "This is Thomas Circle, remember? You do what you can. Angie—she needed some help, so I gave her a little. A chance to make a little bread, and something to make it all go down smooth, besides. She's got no head for business, you know that."

The two watched Angie walk down the street away from them, staggering a little, floating down the sidewalk from side to side. Ben thought he'd take a swing at Dex, grab that money out of his pocket and run Angie down, take her away. But she was so weak, so light, and Dex and his boys so solid, Time and Fate tucked securely away in their wallets, there was nothing Ben could do.

"Ben," Dex said as he began to walk on, Horse and T on either side of him, "you been away a long time."

2 1

DOUGHNUTS

"I'M HUNGRY," ELVIS SAID, all of a sudden.

After writing the first line of his letter to the President, Elvis stopped *(what else was there to say, really, to Richard Nixon?)* and realized that what he needed to continue his rhythm, to finish the letter, was food.

The idea of his quest had vanished.

"Well, I'll have to double back, Colonel," Channa said, stopping the limo at a light. "This ain't exactly your kind of neighborhood."

Which was an exquisite example of understatement.

Elvis looked out the window, his sunglasses almost pressed against the glass, and saw the sidewalks cluttered with more Negroes than Beale Street at midnight: hoboes and hustlers flamboyantly covered shoulder to toe with thick fur coats, ponderous rings, and jewel-studded pendants. Hovering over the limo, above the Afros, Elvis could see an arching peacock's feather poking out of a broad-brimmed cowboy hat, under which flashed a shining gold tooth. Women paraded back and forth along the sidewalk, swishing their wares like models on a runway, though some looked like hogs at the county fair, legs painted with bright pink, yellow, or blue tights under miniskirts that were little more than bands of cloth, leaning over carefully from their spike heels so their breasts wouldn't slip out of their costumes, chattering to the drivers slowing on the curbside, "Party today?" "See something you like, lover?" then stepping back toward the storefronts as a police car rolled by.

One girl on the street caught his eye: a young, slim colored girl with a sweet, soft face, eyelids drooped to half-closed slivers, her walk unsteady, more the aimless drift of a balloon at the mercy of a gusting wind than a drunk's mindless stagger. Away from Memphis, the guys, the Colonel, the press, Elvis thought he could talk to her. Things now he could do.

"This is fine," Elvis said. "Back in Memphis, I'd be the only white boy on Beale Street." Which was true. Twenty years ago.

The girl walked past an unlit neon sign that said DANNY'S, suspended above a huge plastic doughnut. Before Channa could pull over to the curb lane Elvis got out, smack in the middle of the road, and stepped onto the center line. A car stopped short inches in front of him, tires screeched, horns beeped. The sidewalk traffic stopped too, followed him when they saw what it was that got out; few believed it could really be Elvis Presley who had walked out of a limo in the middle of 14th Street, but still, the spectacle of him drew their attention: fingers studded with jewels—real ones—big as golf balls, more jewels encrusted on the huge belt buckle, the purple cape that caught air as Elvis now trotted across the road.

By the time he reached the sidewalk, the crowd was gawking and pointing at him. Elvis lifted a hand to welcome them, to quiet the applause that wasn't there, then looked down the street. The girl had vanished, disappeared on the other side of the sign, but as he looked closer for her the plastic doughnut caught his eye; four feet in diameter, it must have been, emanating the sweet smell of chocolate melting on oozing, sugary glaze.

He trotted under the DANNY'S sign, into the shop.

The place—a narrow aisle cramped against a glass counter showcasing what was left of the day's goods—was empty, save for a rotund Negro in a white apron, chef's hat, and name tag that said DANNY. Empty, but not under the glass counter. There was still a smattering of doughnuts: glazed, chocolate-covered, lemon custard, and cream filled; and maybe six cinnamon buns, another five pecan twirls. Elvis looked at the display for a long time. When he looked back up he saw twenty-five sets of eyes that had followed him from the sidewalk, now lodged against the window of the place, looking in.

Maybe it was the emptiness in his stomach that only now, gazing at the sweet feast before him, he fully appreciated, or the pills he had downed, or the exhaustion that was just hitting him, or the fight with Vern and Priscilla, the charge to the airport, the flight . . . the eyes watching him . . . whatever . . . he began to feel woozy; his head again transformed into a balloon that floated upward, to the clouds.

"May I help you?"

It seemed to Elvis that the eyes looking at him from the outside—especially those on the tall skinny guy with the gold tooth leaning against the window— were dead set on his rings.

"You want doughnuts? Coffee?" Danny said, gruffly. "I haven't got all day—"

"Yeah, sure," Elvis said. "One chocolate."

Danny bent down and picked out a miniature version of the oversized plastic doughnut that had compelled Elvis to come inside.

"Another one."

Danny bent back down.

"Make it three."

Danny looked up as muffled laughs rippled through the crowd outside.

"And a lemon custard."

Another glance from Danny, who was now bobbing like a rooster behind the counter. Each glance at Elvis was a little longer, more angry than the last.

"And two creams. And a cinnamon. Make it four. Five."

Danny stood up and looked hard at Elvis.

"Now look, boy. I don't care who you are, but make up your mind."

"I'm hungry."

In Elvis's head were flashing nightmares: he would walk out of the shop, and in an instant they would converge on him, the eyes on the street wild boars, rutting and tearing him to pieces. Rage was seething within each of them, he knew; rage at any white man, any whiff of money; what was denied them was the fault of whoever had the ill fortune to wind up in Danny's Doughnuts on a certain Saturday afternoon; every time was the wrong time, every place a bad luck scene, every white man rich and ready for sacrifice. Add that he was Elvis and you had an all-out war on your hands. He had read about such scenes, though Tubby and Bo had kept him away from experiencing them for real. Why in hell had he left Graceland, anyway?

"Better make it all of 'em."

"All?"

"Uh huh."

The idea that had come to him, all of the sudden, was this: he would buy out the store; then, if the crowd chased him, he'd toss it all up in the air—doughnuts, pecan twirls, coffee—well, maybe he'd keep a chocolate for himself—and make a run for it. That should distract them enough so he could get back in the car. Thinking of which: where the hell was that damned limo? He couldn't see it through the crowd outside.

"Everything? You're sure?"

"I said it, didn't I?"

And Danny went about picking out what was left of the day's supply, dropping it in bags.

"That's seventy-five doughnuts—you want the pecan twirls too?"

"Everything." The eyes seemed to have multiplied, the faces and bodies squeezed out for lack of space so only eyes lined the glass outside, from sidewalk to ceiling, peering in.

Then the door opened.

"Quick," Elvis said. "I need—"

"I'm not finished—"

"—whatever you got, then. Gotta get out of here."

Danny set five bags on the counter, began to ring up prices on the register.

Elvis recognized who had just walked in; it was Gold Tooth, the tall, wiry one with the peacock's plume. He stepped beside Elvis at the counter, nudged him and smiled.

"How much, how much?" Elvis said. Behind Gold Tooth, Channa, the limo driver, was coming in.

"Slow down," Danny said, still working the register.

Elvis turned his back to Channa and Gold Tooth, leaned over and pulled out his wallet, close to his chest like a poker player. Damned if it was empty. And why not: where in Memphis did he ever need cash?

"Just give me the bill," Elvis said. "Let me sign for it."

"Sign?"

"Yes sir. Send it to Graceland. Hell, double it if you like. Treat yourself." Elvis cut a smile across the counter, but it wasn't returned. "I'm Elvis Presley, man!"

"Out here you need cash, King," Channa said.

Gold Tooth had made his way to the door, and now held it open. Flashed a maniacal grin.

Ben Rollins saw the crowd gathered around the door of Danny's. Must be a fight broke out, or some druggie run amuck inside. A holdup on Saturday afternoon seemed, to Ben, unlikely, but you never knew.

He elbowed his way through, saw T-Squared, Dex, and Horse; and nearest the glass were the old-timers, the craps game apparently having recessed to check out the commotion, allowing LeRoy, Ernie, and the rest time to suck down Colt malts as they waited to roll the dice again.

"Crazy bastard thinks he's Elvis," Dex said, laughing.

"I tell you, that bastard *is* Elvis Presley," LeRoy said. "Saw him in '56 in La Crosse, *Wis*-con-sin. Remember him like it was yesterday."

The two shook, a gentleman's bet never to be cashed. And LeRoy held the door open. Ben patted him on the back as he walked inside.

The shop was relatively empty: only Roland, his old basketball buddy, by the door, Danny behind the counter, some chauffeur in the back, and . . . him. Standing across the counter from Danny, over six feet easy (though the platform shoes had to help); the flair and outrageousness of a 14th Street pimp or dealer played out to unimaginable extremes, part circus show trapeze artist, part comic book superhero. But the face was something else: ashen white, haggard and scared; veined eyes darting back and forth, bloodshot as any strung-out druggie on the street (Angie in her lowest throes), and a sadness behind the fear, a lost look. The contrast, between the in-your-face glamour of his costume and the meek terror in the man's face, brought a lump to Ben's throat. He wasn't sure if the man was Elvis, though there was a sense of the extraordinary, how everyone around him reacted. He figured that was what faith does. It didn't mean things were real.

"Get the hell out of my shop!" Danny yelled.

"Make it triple. Take a hundred." Elvis's upper lip was trembling. "Money's not a problem."

"Maybe not for you it ain't, maybe not in 'Graceland.' Crazy son of a bitch."

And Gold Tooth—Roland—grabbed Elvis by an elbow. Elvis flinched.

"Ben," Danny said, "seems the King here wants a gift from his subjects." Elvis saw he was talking to the kid in the army uniform who had just walked in. "What do you say? Do we look like wise men?"

And there were the eyes again, all around him, circling him from the sidewalk as Elvis faced the door. Only now the eyes were attached to bodies, long, broad, hard-muscled bodies, all black, all with a latent, awesome power, now ready to erupt, and they were walking through the door, coming toward him. There was the money thing—you got it, we don't—and there was the old slavery thing, the Civil War thing, the southern thing, all that black and white angry crap. But there was something else, Elvis felt, at the core of the rage, a special anger for Elvis. It was this: *You stole our music, you white bastard. You ain't no genius. You ain't shit, truth be known. You a fraud, boy.*

Gold Tooth pulled Elvis's arm toward the door, and as Elvis looked around him now it seemed as if they had all moved closer, everyone was muttering, they were laughing, talking, maybe they were trying to talk to him. Junior Parker, they were saying. Big Boy Crudup, Sleepy John Estes. Sang the same songs and they *really* couldn't afford a doughnut. *You a thief, boy.*

Envy, envy is what it was. Envy and greed. You can't work for it—not can't, but won't—so you play the aggression, the intimidation. Good for nothing but the shirk and the gripe, the bitch and the moan. And the guilt: you chained us, man, out from the jungles; you, the White Man, done it. How long, Lord? How long the bitch and moan? How long the guilt? *I didn't steal nothing. I a genius, boy. I earn everything I got. Earned it, son, up from nothing.*

Gold Tooth was still behind him, touching him, grabbing—yes, grabbing at one of his rings, it must be! Elvis turned around again, and again, so fast the tooth blurred, looked like a string of molten gold lassoing him, hog-tying him. He looked outside. Channa had left and the limo was gone again. Gone. Was he actually left here alone? (And where was he exactly?) *No way out.*

Elvis patted his hip, then above. There it was: the Colt. This is why it was necessary, why you needed to be armed nowadays, why this state of the world demanded it. He reached inside his cape, unsnapped the top of the holster, slipped the gun out and dropped it to his side. He could see the crowd step back toward the street. Now there was room, there was space. Hell yes!! Elvis would step outside and lift the gun over his head, the long barrel catching the sun, glistening; and the crowd would run down the sidewalk away from him in all directions, some this way, others that, some across the street, trampling on top of one another, Danny with them.

Suddenly he felt another poke from behind. Turning around Elvis saw the colored kid in the army uniform, crisp and official-looking, right in front of him. The kid had one arm, Elvis now noticed, and now he moved toward him, his fist clenched. Elvis grabbed his gun tighter; ready to pull it and aim, but the kid moved slowly, smiling slightly at him. Elvis looked down at the boy's hand, which was now opened in front of him. In it was a twenty-dollar bill.

"Here," the kid said. "Take it."

2 2

THE EARRING

IT HAD BEEN HOURS SINCE Sharon Teele had watched Sour Honey lead Elvis away from her, through the airport terminal, and the two of them disappeared behind the security door, arms interlinked. Sharon had wiped away her tears, repainted her mascara, and then came a rush of pre-Christmas traffic: college kids who didn't go to Vietnam going home to see their parents, couples, families reuniting, everyone leaving to join their families, loved ones, everyone had loved ones . . . on the other end of the trip there would be crying embraces at the airport. . . . What's the point? she thought. Her dear friend Wendy—God bless him—had tried to console her, but he was wrong. Wasn't no gods. Not down here. Not in Memphis.

Now her shift was over, and she left the ticket counter, began to walk down the corridor of the terminal. There were soldiers in front of her, returning home, or leaving home, lost either way; and then there were protesters, longhairs trashing the flag and the war and her and Hank, burning flags is what they wanted to do, patching their torn denim asses with it (some die for it, she'd said to Wendy one night—nursing her fifth gin, straight up but for a sliced lime—others fart on it); she saw them every day, outside the airport, the recruiting stations, chanting with their awful signs; they'd spit on Hank if they had the chance, all of them would, trashing this goddamned beautiful country.

Soon she was trotting down the hall of the terminal. First she thought she was following Elvis, a ghostlike image of him walking away from her, and Elvis, hearing her approach, began to run, so she ran, but she was in heels so he gained ground ahead of her, she ran faster, and as she ran she spoke to him, quiet but he heard her, she knew that he heard every word: *Why are you leaving me, Elvis?*

she said. *Why aren't you coming back from Vietnam? People are always leaving me; it's me, it's not them, it's got to be me. Why did you go and get killed? We never even had that little girl we wanted, never bought our house, never got started, not really. And I'm alone now. So alone.*

She stopped running and when she looked back up Elvis had vanished and in his place, as close as Elvis had been just hours ago, stood a girl, a teenager she looked like, with stringy blond hair, and dangling to her neck were round pendulous earrings, circles with huge silver peace signs in them. She wore a tie-dyed shirt hanging so low it was like a skirt, and the design on it was also a peace sign, with a white dove painted above, and it came to Sharon that the girl was just one big peace sign, the symbol turned human in some dreamlike transformation she did not understand, yet took on faith.

The girl held a daisy in one hand, a soft smile on her face.

"I saw Him too," she said. Sharon thought she said it. Then she handed Sharon the flower. "Peace," she said.

It was then that Sharon leapt at her, choking the girl's neck as she tackled her to the floor, grabbed with her teeth the silver peace sign hanging down before her eyes and, biting hard as she could, pulled the earring down, ripping it through the fleshy part of her lobe and off her right ear.

2 3

LUNCH WITH FRIENDS

COLONEL ALEX SITORSKI'S HEAD was turned downward so that his eyes saw only a thick green mush, which to him was a mosquito-infested, leech-filled swamp. His son was slopping knee-deep in the oozing mire as it sucked him down like a vacuum, embedding each foot at the bottom. In this scene Alex Sitorski was out of harm's way, circling overhead above the muck in some sort of flying cement mixer, trying to lift the boy to safety, but the helicopter poured cement down on Junior—Sitorski was powerless to stop it—banging down on his head like a hammer, burying him deeper.

Actually he was gazing down at a bowl of split pea soup, across the table from his friend, Max Sharpe. Try as he might, Alex Sitorski could not believe that he would actually be seeing his son in just a few hours. And he didn't have a clue what to say to him.

Sitorski shook his head, trying to stir the vision out of it, then dug his spoon into the soup. Tried to make sense of the words that Sharpe kept firing at him, carbine after carbine. In the two years they had known each other, he had never seen Sharpe so excited. But then, he couldn't remember when they had last had lunch; Sharpe's invitation had come out of the blue today, after his briefing at the White House.

"—and as I see it, this 'High on Life' plan can carry the party for years," Sharpe was saying. "It's a war on values, see: we have them, they don't. All we need"—Sharpe stuffed a hamburger into his mouth and chomped down, crudely oozing a thick mayonnaise sauce out the sides of the bun—"is a messenger. People gotta"—chomp—"focus on some"—wiping with a napkin, which only spread the sauce down his chin—"thing other than this war. Gotta be upbeat."

Sharpe placed the burger down, looked at his friend. He hoped that Ehrlichman was wrong about the leak; had even flirted with the idea of hinting to Sitorski that he was under suspicion, but thought better. After all, the President had a right to know what was going on around him, in his army, in his White House. And that was all Nixon wanted: information. Lawyers used detectives all the time; Sharpe had done so himself. Truth was nothing to be afraid of.

"See, Alex," Sharpe said, "the war on drugs is just the beginning, the first battle. You know the key to the '72 campaign is how we get the Wallace vote; we can't get by with forty-three percent again. So we need to capture that sector. Now, who are they? Anti–civil rights, sure; that's fundamental. But even if they're against the war, they're more against the people who are against the war. Their moral superiority, for one. And they think maybe the hippies are having too much fun, this 'stay high all the time' business. They want it made official, once and for all: we're right, they're wrong. So we do. 'High on Life.'"

Sharpe stopped. Tried to analyze Sitorski's expression.

"Uh huh," Alex Sitorski said.

Sitorski wasn't really listening. He felt weak, and thought food might help. He sipped some wine, though he never drank during the day, then ordered another glass. He wasn't interested in politics much, anyway.

Then, suddenly, the cement mixer–helicopter Sitorski was captaining plunged into his bowl, crashing down on his son, who was now drowning in the thick, gagging soup. Sitorski had dropped his spoon.

"HEY!" A dot of soup, round as a bullet hole, hit Sharpe on the forehead. "What's with you?"

"Nothing." Soup had coated Sitorski's glasses, so he took them off, wet his napkin in his water glass and began to clean them. "Sorry, Max. I'm tired. Haven't been able to sleep much lately." Without his glasses, the world was a blur, revealing only the vaguest outlines of figures, all faceless. Sharpe's head was just an empty oval topped with hair, without eyes, nose or mouth. Yet the noise—the words—continued to emanate from him.

"You need a girl, Alex," the blur said. "What's it been—two years since Elena left? It's about time, don't you think?"

Seeing the indistinguishable blur across the table from him, Sitorski began to feel that he, too, was faceless. The sensation seemed appropriate. He decided to keep his glasses off.

"Maybe you're right, Max. But I'm just not interested now. The family, we may be getting together again."

"Elena's coming back? I didn't know."

"Not Elena, not yet anyway. Now it's just Al Junior." *Where did that idea— that his family was reuniting—come from?* Maybe it was the blurred vision. Anonymity brought with it freedom; creating whole lives, artificial and fictive, was easy. "He's coming tonight, in fact. I didn't expect it, but Elena called last week."

"And Elena's visiting later?"

For an instant there was the vision: Elena at the airport with him, he holding her in his arms as they waited, together, for Junior to return home. That was the way it should have been. Instead of her meeting the kid in California, alone, and then him taking off, on the road, hearing only cursory words from Elena about the boy in the year since: "Give him time" (like he was still a kid), he was "getting by." His years in public relations convinced Sitorski that the words implied an opposite meaning. But when Elena described herself, how *she* was doing, there was a brightness and conviction that Sitorski sensed was real. (Once, when he asked, she said things were "groovy"; another time they were "cool.") Alex envisioned young long-haired lovers, a new community of friends. The vision wouldn't hold.

He put his glasses back on.

"No," he said. "But Junior, Junior's coming home."

"He's moving back here? With you?"

"Not exactly. For now it's just a visit."

Sitorski gazed back down at what was now, clearly, split pea soup.

"Alex," Sharpe said, "what else is up?"

"What do you mean?"

"At work."

"Well, there's this Calley trial—"

"Calley?"

"Right. The President seems to be interested in it."

He mentioned Calley on his own, Sharpe noted. *No prompting from me.*

"Calley. My Lai?"

"Yes. It was on the President's mind today. He asked me how he thought it would play. In Peoria."

"Peoria?" Sharpe said.

"Yes," Sitorski said.

Again: unprovoked.

"And what do you think?" Sharpe asked. "About, you know . . . Peoria?"

"About Calley? The court-martial?"

Sharpe nodded.

"I don't know. I've been trying to sort things out, actually, about this whole war, thinking about seeing Junior."

"And what are you thinking?"

Sitorski's mind began to drift again. This time brick walls popped into his vision. But instead of seeing just the walls, the images encapsulating the numbers of the dead, this time he saw, standing outside the walls, the families of the dead: weeping, but with a hint of resentment . . . no, accusation, rage . . . as if blame, guilt, and he, Alex Sitorski, were somehow linked.

"I imagine what it must have been like," Sitorski said, "in My Lai. A young kid, trying to do his job. He's told it's not his role to question, to think on his own. From the first day of training we tell him that the whole system's based on obeying orders. And then Medina tells Calley to clear out the village, and Calley tells his boys that's what's to be done, all down the chain of command. But then there isn't any enemy fire, the Cong had left town and only the ones who couldn't fight remained. But who could know? Then there's a line that's crossed, a guy spots a girl, and they're all just guys, after all, away from home, and so—it may have begun as innocent fun—and then she has to be killed, and then that becomes what's done. Then things really get out of hand."

He paused, looked across the table, but Sharpe didn't say anything. He was studying his friend's face. Sitorski continued.

"And the bodies, you've seen pictures of the ditch where they threw the bodies? Girls, babies, old ladies, old men. Pigs, cattle. There were lines that were crossed, I know, but they were young, you know, they were all so young, and they were only doing what we asked of them. But now we say the blood is just on *their* hands, you know? That makes things easy."

Sitorski seemed on edge, Sharpe thought. Like a man on the verge of being caught. A guilty man.

"I don't know," Sitorski said. "I've been involved in this war since the beginning. It's been a long time. You get buried in the numbers and the strategy. You lose track of what it's about. And I wonder, about Junior, whether there was something more I should have done."

"And Calley?" Sharpe said. "Peoria?"

"I don't know," Sitorski said. "I'd rather not . . ."

"But Peoria, Alex. How do you think it will all play?"

Sitorski didn't say anything.

"You have"—Sharpe paused, leaned across the table, closer to Sitorski—"doubts?"

Sitorski looked back down at his soup.

"Yes," Alex Sitorski said. "I have doubts."

2 4

JUNIOR

AL JUNIOR WAS IN HIS mother's small apartment in West Los Angeles. Just called the airline to change his flight to Sunday, to give himself another day to work things out, then talk to the lawyer. Eyes closed now, his hands tightly clenched a rolled-up sheet of paper, strangling it in his hands.

It was a week ago that he had been walking home from a march when a guy in a suit tapped him on the shoulder and said, "Alexander Sitorski?" and before Junior could nod his head the man handed him the subpoena and told him he was under orders to appear in two weeks to testify at Lieutenant William Calley's court-martial trial in Fort Benning, Georgia.

The man was not in uniform but Al Sitorski, Junior, knew that he was military. It was the clipped voice he had not heard, the rigid bearing he had not seen since he had come back from Vietnam about a year earlier. *Try as you might, you can never leave them,* Junior thought. *No escape.*

He had stared at the subpoena then just as he did now. In the background he had heard the man speaking, rambling in a way that was no longer so official. Now that he had served him with the subpoena, his job, like a relay runner's, was over. The army had been looking for Junior for months now, the man said, had heard he had gone to Mexico for a while at first, got a report he was then in the Southwest somewhere, Arizona or New Mexico, but could not find him (the man himself had been there; could testify to the spring mud on those nameless roads, the dry canyons of Navajo country); then weeks ago some surveillance film spotted him in a march in L.A.; that surprised them, and the prosecutors weren't happy, Calley's defense lawyers could impeach him with his antiwar contacts, suggest he had a political ax to grind, the sort of cross-examination that hit home at a court-martial. And the man said more: the army would fly him from Washington to Georgia on Tuesday next (now three days away); the prosecutors would like to speak with him first; the man had worked with other witnesses and this was what they did. Get your story straight.

Al Junior had just stood there with the man as the other marchers peeled away from them, eyeing them suspiciously. The man seemed younger than Junior, an army kid with the pull to get a stateside job, an M.P. or legal intern or whatever he was (not that Junior didn't have that pull himself, if his father had wanted to use it). The man could not understand that these hippies, these marchers, were Junior's friends now. Had been anyway, until they saw him conversing now: smelling counteragent, spy. The man hadn't talked to anyone in a long time and his was a lonely job, though safe at least. Yes, he was very young, anyone who had not seen war was very young, and Al Junior, walking with him, felt old.

The man said he was still in high school when . . . it . . . had happened, back in March '68. It may have been wild in Vietnam, he said, but things were crazy back home too. Later that spring Martin Luther King was shot dead in Memphis, and rebellions erupted in Washington, Newark, Watts, and throughout the nation; President Johnson was taken on by peaceniks within his own party, and then he bowed out and Bobby Kennedy jumped in the race and everyone assumed Kennedy would win, beat McCarthy and Humphrey, then Nixon and anyone else, but then Bobby Kennedy met the wrong end of a bullet in California and Humphrey hung on to win the nomination with battles breaking out in the streets of Chicago, and Richard Nixon became the candidate for peace, George Wallace for those repulsed by it all, and Nixon won, and the war went on.

Not that this was news to Al Sitorski Junior. He had followed most of it from Vietnam. And there were subtleties there that Al Junior understood.

The man wanted to know what it was like, what he had seen and what he was going to testify to. How did he feel about testifying against his own commander? It was a difficult thing to do and witnesses reacted differently to the request. He had seen some drop the subpoena and run from him. Others resigned themselves to following the order, accepted their duty; some were happy to have the opportunity, had thanked him for the chance to tell all, to get it off their chests, and they had begun to testify right there in front of him. And one man had looked at him and wailed like a baby.

Al Junior said little. He had tried not to think about the war since he had gotten back, and traveling for the first months had accomplished that: new sights in
Mexico, a language he did not understand, though occasionally he had run into
other vets on the road. But since he had been staying with his mother in L.A. his
mind had been slipping back . . . he wondered why he had come back to the
States at all . . . but when he was handed the subpoena he felt it may have been
his destiny that he return; karma, as the Vietnamese, the monks, would say. He
would have to face what he had seen, what he had done, and it seemed important that he communicate something about it all . . . how to stop it from happening again. . . . The memories began to flood back to him and he emerged
briefly to hear a few words the man said toward the end: "witness preparation,"
"get story straight."

The man had suggested that Junior see a lawyer; he suggested this to all the
witnesses. They all insisted that they didn't need one, but still, it was recom-
mended. You never knew. The man gave him a list of L.A. attorneys with some
experience in court-martials; some even had counseled witnesses in the Calley
case. Then he left, and Junior had walked home, alone, with the subpoena in his
hands.

That was a week ago. Junior had called one of the lawyers, and though the lawyer
said he was busy and could not represent him at the trial on such short notice,
he could meet with him on Sunday night, which is why Junior decided to
change his flight: the lawyer would drive him to the airport on Sunday, and from
Washington he would fly on to Georgia Tuesday.

Since then Junior had stayed holed up in his mother's apartment mostly, the
small cramped place bringing him down. His mother had changed so much in
the two years since she had left his father, now much of her was unrecognizable:
rather than the doting mother he remembered when he left for Vietnam, she
looked the aging hippie, a slightly graying flower child. He didn't feel at home,
didn't feel comfortable talking about the testimony he was supposed to give. He
told her only that he would visit his father in Washington and was vague about
details.

Clenching the subpoena now . . . thinking about testifying, what it would be
like . . . he knew the defense would try to shake him, question his memory . . .
and yes, it all happened over two and a half years ago, but still he would have no

problems with the details. He would need no preparation in order to testify about what he saw Lieutenant William Calley do at My Lai 4 on March 16, 1968. But he could not imagine how he could ever get the story of the massacre straight.

Now, alone in his mother's apartment, he unrolled the paper and stared at it, not reading the words, not certain what he was going to do.

2 5

PALMER GETS INSTRUCTED

PALMER WILSON WAS OUTSIDE on the sidewalk, where he had stood since running out of Ray's Saloon at the command of the voice on the other end of the
line, he wasn't sure how many minutes earlier. His environment—the middle of
an Arctic wind tunnel, it felt like—would have bothered him, were it not for
what he was holding in his hand: his trusty flask, Joe M. II. The flask had saved
his life once, back in a shootout in Oakland in '68, on an *agent provocateur* gig.
Palmer had fired the first shots, to get things going, and a cop had shot back (how
was Palmer to know that he hadn't shot at a real Black Panther?), distracting
Palmer from his target (Huey Newton was in point-blank range for God's sake,
a rifle, albeit unloaded, in hand), and the bullet that the cop fired headed for
Palmer's stomach, but lodged, magically, in the metal wall of the flask. Afterward
Palmer had it repaired and christened it Joe M. II, after the Senator, Joe
McCarthy. The idea—it was his father's, actually—was that when Palmer would
drink from it, the sweet whiskey that brought him solace would remind him of
the esteemed Wallingford's patron and idol, Joe McCarthy, and thus imbued
with the perspective of his father, his *weltanschauung* (as Wallingford himself
would put it), he would thus go about his tasks as an FBI agent with the unques-
tioning certainty that he was no less essential than a Roman sentry on night duty
intently watching for Huns, while the Emperor Nero was bent on emulating, not
Alexander, but Paganini.

   That was the idea. But its execution? That was something else again.

   He unscrewed the cap and sipped a nip or two of Jack.

   Then the pay phone rang. Palmer stepped in the booth and picked it up.

   "Palmer Wilson, Federal Bureau of Investig—"

"I know who you are, Palmer." It was the voice that had ordered him here, from Ray's. "This is Finlator."

"Yes sir, Mr. Finlat—"

"I have work for you, Palmer."

"I'm ready."

"Are you certain? You have failed so often in the past—"

"I know sir—"

"—but we are forgiving. Not stupid, but we will give you this chance to redeem yourself."

"Thank you," Palmer said.

"You have a job. Pictures of your quarry will be provided."

Palmer waited for the photos to fall from the sky into his hands. He had heard of such efficiency in the Bureau.

"There is a Monday deadline, Palmer. That is not a problem."

Palmer wasn't sure if that was a question or not.

"No," Palmer said.

"Your quarry does not suspect. He has a physical handicap. A frustrated member of the underclass. You understand frustration. You, Palmer, must understand what it means to be unable to accomplish."

Again Palmer wasn't sure if he was being asked a question. This time he said nothing.

"The fires are already there in your quarry, Palmer. The proclivities, the anger. Your job is to stoke those latent forces, encourage them. Give him the opportunity. A simple *agent provocateur* maneuver. He'll play along. Understand?"

"Yes," Palmer lied.

"His name is Ben Rollins and he must be arrested by Monday. If the first route fails, a setup will do—you will be given the materials to accomplish a setup—but that is only a last resort. But you must bring him in by Monday. Understand?"

"Uh huh."

"Are you getting all this, Palmer?"

Palmer nodded his head, but he was not in a position to give his boss a verbal response. He was too busy unscrewing Joe M. II, taking another gulp.

2 6

TOMMY

IT WAS PAST FIVE o'clock now.

For five hours Bo had called around the country. Tried friends in Memphis, Tupelo, Las Vegas hotels—front desks and bellmen—and made a dent in the list of girls to whom Elvis had returned for seconds. Had anyone seen Elvis? Heard from him? Any ideas, then? No, he wouldn't explain why he was calling. Nothing's wrong at Graceland. But by the way, if you hear anything . . .

No luck.

The clues Bo *had* come up with scared the hell out of him. There was that photo with "Am I? Am I?" written on it; at least Bo knew what Elvis meant by that one. It was one of Elvis's favorite stories: the first night Dewey Phillips had played him on Memphis radio, back in 1954, some folks listening thought Elvis was black as Chuck Berry, and some convinced themselves of it, so when they saw him later, this far-out, funky dude with clothes off the rack from Beale Street, they began to wonder, and Elvis heard them say (or thought he did anyway): "Is he? Is he?" And so Elvis began to ask himself: "Am I? Am I?" Bo had always taken the story as a throwaway, no meaning behind it at all, but now, with Elvis's graffiti and the picture colored in, it seemed like a message.

That wasn't all that scared Bo. There had been an anger building up in Elvis recently, more time spent looking inward and coming out depressed, frustrated; the onstage jokes about himself more biting ("Used to remember the words," "Hope I don't split this suit") and more rambling mid-song about his spiritual books.

And there were the guns: Bo saw that Elvis's safe was open, and there were empty places on the rack.

And the pills: Dr. Nick had delivered a new set of prescriptions in the past day or so, and none were left.

And then that "Avichi" business that he'd circled in his book: Bo didn't have a clue what E was thinking there.

Besides Memphis and Vegas, Elvis's main connections were in L.A., so now Bo focused on the coast. He started by calling Tommy Shelton in L.A. Bo had a feeling about Tommy.

Tommy had always been a little different than the other guys at Graceland. A free-thinker liberal type and a Unitarian to boot (maybe it was Congregationalist, but did that make a difference to Elvis?), none of which Elvis would usually stand for, but with Tommy he got a kick out of it, liked tangling minds with the enemy, Bo supposed, the to-and-fro. Then Tommy had left to try to make his way in Hollywood and Elvis had rubbed Bo's and Tubby's noses in Tommy Shelton stories ever since, the companion they could never be. That was what loyalty was worth.

The line picked up.

"Hello?"

"Tommy? It's Bo. Bo Price? Over in Graceland."

"Had to be you," Tommy said. "We don't have any Bo's here in Hollywood."

"And Sidney Potty-eh don't hang at Wendy's. So there."

"The beer's just as cold out west, Bo," Tommy said. "And we don't have flies, grits, or bigots. Kinda nice that way."

"Good ole Tommy. You always were pink around the gills. How you makin' it out there?"

"Getting by, Bo. Got some editing work at Paramount and—"

"Heard about that. And the babes? Are they like I remember?"

"Yeah, Bo." Tommy hesitated. "Just like you remember."

"By the way," Bo said, "mind if I talk to Elvis a minute?"

"Elvis? He's in town?"

"Oh hell, I'm sorry, Tommy. Tubby had written 'Tommy' on this calendar here and I just figured—"

"Something's up, Bo?"

"No, Tommy, it's just Tubby's damned sloppy chicken scrawl. Can't read a word of it."

"You don't know where Elvis is?" Tommy laughed. "He's gone AWOL?"

"AWOL? A few months in Fruitywood and you been smokin' that wacky tobaccy? I just—hell, I got my days screwed up in my calendar is all."

"My, my." Tommy was still laughing. "The Colonel must be out of his mind. He knows, doesn't he?"

"I gotta get off the line, Tommy. Don't tell anyone I called, all right? You remember how it is. E's supposed to have this surprise gig in L.A.—it must be next month; I thought it was today—and you know the Colonel, the press . . ."

"Sure, Bo. Be good."

In his apartment in Los Angeles, Tommy Shelton put down the phone. He strolled out to the patio, then immersed himself, slowly, into the hot tub. Just on the coast for a few months but Tommy already knew he would never make it in front of the camera. At least he was in the business, and there were worse things than editing. Yes, it was a Saturday, and in another hour he would have to go back to work, but he had some time to himself. And at least now it was his own time.

He knew how Bo must be feeling. They went a long ways back: he had played football with Bo and Tubby back in high school, when Elvis was just some wild-looking weirdo, and then Tommy went off to college and Elvis was just driving a truck back in Memphis, and that was the way life was going to be, right? Until Elvis, well, became Elvis, and then everyone's lives just stopped. Bo and Tubby and Tommy were summoned back home, enlisted as soldiers in the Elvis army, paid volunteers for the cause. The cause being whateverthehell Elvis Presley decided was the cause. Which is why, in a nutshell, Tommy Shelton had left all that.

He had tried to put it all out of his mind since moving to L.A., but nothing's that easy, and Elvis always seemed to crawl back into his life, try as Tommy might to escape him.

Now he eased his head under the water of the hot tub. Repeated to himself, over and over: Left all that. For damn sure.

2 7

BACK AT THE HOTEL

ELVIS COULD SEE HIMSELF, faintly, in the tinfoil the hotel folks had taped on the windows, just as he'd commanded them to. Must have been the creases in the foil that made his face seem old and wrinkled. And gilded in silver as it was, his reflection looked like a death mask. Some ancient god-king.

He was on his canopied poster bed in his three-room suite on the fifth floor of the Washington Hotel. Room service had come and gone already, leaving one hell of a spread: a cart stuffed with four hamburgers, three bags of potato chips, a stack of grilled peanut butter and banana sandwiches (he hadn't even asked for them), a half-gallon tub of chocolate fudge ice cream, eggs (scrambled and over easy), grits, a plate of biscuits with a trough of country gravy on the side, a cooler full of Cokes and beer. Money was no longer a problem; these were decent folk—not quite dumb as an ox on the wrong end of the slaughterhouse. Not that Elvis even had a dollar left from that twenty after the doughnut man was paid, but his credit was good here, and that driver didn't demand cash, said Elvis's word was fine with him. (Strange, but those were the words he used, too: "All I need is your word.")

Food was what Elvis had really been missing, why things weren't quite right since he'd touched down in Washington. But that was all behind him now. Already inhaled the burgers, sandwiches, and chips. Popped an egg yolk and coated the grits with it, then shoveled those in too. And that's not counting the doughnuts he ate in the limo. He unfastened his holsters, laid out his guns, his .45, his .38, the Luger, removed the retractable six-inch blade from the thin leather belt 'round his right calf, and lay back.

The tinfoil did its job, keeping the sun out, giving the room a dimness that could be any hour. Closed his eyes.

Content.

And alone.

Bored.

What do we do now, Bo? Got an encore in mind?

He almost said it out loud, like he was holding court in Graceland, the guys gathered 'round the foot of the bed.

Read to me, Bo. That bit about the Masters walkin' amongst us. Channa driving Siddhartha into town soest he seest the livin' and the dyin', what it's like out there beyond the castle walls. And Yea he shall become Enlightened, so Becomest the Buddha, Blavatsky, and Jesus hisself, Praise Be. Read me about Avichi, theosophic Hell. Wash me in the spiritual words.

The Lincoln statue he had passed flashed in his head and Elvis saw himself etched in stone, big as Lincoln, bigger even: sitting thronelike, thick folds of a jewel-encrusted cape on his lap, a sweaty scarf wrapped 'round his neck . . . a vast Elvis memorial: *"Truck driver to millionaire . . . multimillionaire . . . movie star, singer extraordinaire . . . girls fainting from ecstasy . . . friend to all, lover to many . . . never forgot his roots . . . embodiment of the American Dream . . ."*

That was good: he would have to remember it for his speech to the Jaycees.

But Bo, it's scary out here beyond the walls. Get me the right badge and then tell me I couldn't pull a Bond/Clint Eastwood/John Wayne all-in-one-good-guys rebellion out here on the streets. Ain't that right, Bo? And Bo nods yes, and Tubby nods yes, and . . . hell, even Priscilla, if she were around. Which she wouldn't be.

Here for a reason.

Right.

He picked up the telephone, asked the front desk to ring up the FBI, Bureau of Dangerous Drugs, John Finlator's office. Waited for them to patch the call through and then there wasn't an answer. No, the hotel did not have access to any private numbers for Finlator, the FBI, and certainly not for Director Hoover. Besides, the squeaky voice on the line insisted, it was Saturday, and after five, so all offices would be closed. Yes, the clerk knew who he was speaking to. He was fully aware who Elvis Presley was. No, he didn't know exactly how many records Elvis had sold, but yes, he knew it was quite a lot. Millions, he agreed. Ten million Elvis fans can't be—hell, a hundred million—but that wasn't the point. The point was that the Federal Bureau of Investigation was not going to open up on a late Saturday afternoon simply because the world's most popular singer and entertainer had happened to arrive in Washington, D.C., at that time and wanted in. They—the Washington Hotel—couldn't help him.

Elvis slammed the phone down.

If I can't get my badge, then why in hell did everybody nod yes?!

He got up, walked across the room, turned the television on, but kept the sound off, then sat back down on the bed. President Nixon was on the tube, then some one-armed colored bastard in a uniform took a medal from him and tossed it away as the President flinched. The Negro looked familiar, and now he remembered from where: the doughnut shop. Then the image flashed to troops in Vietnam, then protesters, cops with nightsticks teaching some lessons.

Tommy Shelton wouldn't have nodded yes. Good ole Tommy didn't take guff from nobody. I mean, you don't call it lovin' from a whore, do you? So who could call any of the other guys real friends—Bo, Tubby, Vernon, Priscilla. . . .

The idea of a quest wafted into his head again. Now he saw it as an American quest, a coming to terms and an understanding of the nation. *Just exactly where are we now, and where are we goin'? America, I mean.* Somewhere in its midst the submerged truth would reveal itself to him. Out there in the plains was the answer.

And the question.

Sure thing.

He picked the phone up again, leafed through a palm-sized telephone book he'd kept in his cape pocket, asked to be patched to an outside line. On television now there was a parade of his enemies: Jane Fonda, the Beatles, Abbie Hoffman, Eldridge Cleaver in black power salute. A special on Vietnam; another goddamned special. Ho Chi Minh might as well run all the goddamned networks.

"Allo," a solicitous French voice said on the other end of the line.

"Is Monsieur Flambeau there?" Elvis said, trying to make his voice French as he could, to take away the twang.

"May I ask who is calling?"

"Lawnfont," Elvis said, breaking into out-and-out laughter just about. "Ricard Lawnfont."

"This is Monsieur Flambeau speaking." Again the French voice, courtly and uppity. Elvis envisioned the speaker as the viewing public in movie- and televisionland knew him: Maurice Flambeau, the perfect French dandy, languishing on a chaise with a gold-tipped cigarette holder while he took a sip of Chablis.

"You alone?" Elvis said.

"Why yes."

"Maurice?" Elvis lapsed back into his everyday voice, though he still whispered. "It's me. Elvis."

"Elvis. Why, it is so wonderful to hear from you."

"Maurice, I'm in Washington."

"Zoot alors! What are you—?"

"I can't tell you, not now at least. But I think I'll be going to L.A. tonight."

"When?"

"I don't know yet. Call the airport and ask them. Actually, while you're at it, book me a seat on the next flight. American. I like those boys."

"Why of course, but—"

"I'll fill you in later, Maurice. But this is hush-hush. You never heard from me. Got it?"

"*Oui, certainement,* if you—"

"And the name's not Elvis. It's Burrows. Colonel Jon."

Next he called Tommy Shelton. Tommy was out, so he told the front desk to keep trying and tell Tommy to meet him at the airport, and keep it quiet. Then he told them to get a limo to take him to the airport. Like now.

He lay back, closed his eyes. Time, and the food he had eaten, had cut the effect of the pills, but he still felt a hint of them in his blood, shaking up his wiring enough to keep him awake, though he was so exhausted he could sleep forever.

Walked across the room to the desk, picked up a pen, some hotel stationery, and lay back down on the bed.

Dear Jaycees, fellow honorees, ladies and gentlemen, he wrote. *I humbly accept your award—citation.* He crossed the whole sentence out. *I am honored to be named one of the outstanding young men in America. I feel I have been blessed, throughout my life. Whether in music, television, or movies.* Movies? What the hell was so blessed about my movies? Besides being plain blessed awful. Elvis was never gonna be no Brando, no Dean. That was the Colonel. And that was L.A.

Oh, Channa, that damned driver, was right. He would never again be mistaken for colored. Had to work to show struggle in your soul nowadays . . . and he could not go back, he could only call up faint strains of his roots, so strained that it mocked what he once had been. . . . So what was left?

There was the money. And there was the shell: there was Elvis.

And, as the Beatles would say: Fuck Elvis.

He looked down at his speech and crossed out what he had written.

Picked up the phone again, dialed Maurice.

"Maurice. I ain't goin'."

"But Elvis, I have called the airlines, and everything—"

"They ruined me, Maurice. They boiled me up and wrung me dry. I can't go back there."

"'They'? Elvis, I am not certain if I—"

"I can't go back. I can't and I won't."

And he slammed down the phone.

On the television now was Tom Jones, crooning in front of some oohing-aahing middle-aged ladies—that was Elvis's audience now too; he'd have to admit it—and Elvis knew damned well that was a toilet paper roll down his pants. He picked up his .38 from the bed and fired at the television. The screen smashed and the tube, inside, blew up; Elvis saw the spark.

Looked back down at the stationery.

Dear Jaycees, he wrote. *I used to be a talented guy. I used to be a genius. Magic there. Once I could have been James Dean. Better even. James Dean was outstanding. So was Brando. Tom Jones is a piece of shit. So's Robert Goulet. Neither of them got a real set of balls between them.*

Then the phone rang. It was the weasel from the front desk.

No, Elvis said, the noise they heard was nothing. To hell he'd try to keep quiet! He was Elvis! The cheap-ass television blew up on him was all. No, they could wait to change it; he wanted to be alone. Yes, of course he still wanted the limo; he was going to the airport, wasn't he? No, he wasn't checking out; he'd be back. Just had some business to take care of on the coast. The driver'd be up to take him? Well, fine then. And get him a television set that won't blow up all to hell this time.

He hung up without putting down the phone, then dialed again.

"Maurice," he said. "I changed my mind."

PART TWO

Saturday Night

WASHINGTON TO L.A.

2 8

TUBBY

BACK IN MEMPHIS, Tubby Grove was wandering the hospitals, checking out the emergency rooms, then the intake desks for admissions.

He was going to the hospitals, because that is what his boss, Bo, told him to do. Which is what Colonel Parker, Tubby figured, had told Bo to do. Which was what Elvis paid the Colonel to do . . . beyond which only the good Lord knew. . . . 'Course, the name Tubby Grove was never mentioned in this chain of command, not unless someone fucked up the works, or Bo needed a scapegoat. . . . Yes, to answer the question on his mind at the moment, on the Graceland food chain Tubby Grove was but a tadpole.

But ah hell, it was a living—now he imagined the ever-present voice of the Colonel reminding him: a job as bodyguard for Elvis Presley churned dollars. It did that. No, Tubby hadn't taken three correspondence courses—college level—like his boss, Bo. Yes, little ole worthless Tubby Grove would more than likely be dining in soup kitchens off Beale Street if it weren't for that overgrown, overpaid baby Elvis Aron. And yes, his genius carnival hawker front man, the good Colonel Tom Parker himself: Tubby bent to kiss his ring too.

So while Bo manned the pool table back home (the bosses always have it so tough, don't they?), and the Colonel analyzed things poolside (indoors) not even in the state, and Vern did his usual (nothing), and Priscilla even less (cooling her hot pants on the side), Tubby was driving all over Memphis. He was no nuclear scientist, but Tubby Grove knew this much: shit rolled downhill.

As he drove from emergency room to emergency room throughout the afternoon and into early evening, Tubby ruminated on the sheer drudgery of his tasks, the stark inequities of the social structure in which he worked, sparking the tiny embers of ambition in his gut, leading him to the conclusion that if he did this job right, the Colonel just might reward him by leapfrogging him over his ever-bossing buddy Bo to a higher tier of the Graceland hierarchy. Though that isn't how Tubby expressed these thoughts to himself. Shit rolling downhill was more like it.

He had to be discreet, Bo told him that was key, so he had been asking nurses for a "Jon Burrows" (a code name the Colonel often used for Elvis when checking him in at a hotel front desk), which is what he did now, at his fifth hospital of the day.

"What does your friend look like?" the nurse at the desk asked, a brunette fat as the *Hindenburg* or, for that matter, Gladys—rest in peace—Presley.

"To be honest with you, ma'am," Tubby said, "he's got the damnedest resemblance to Elvis Presley that you ever saw."

The nurse pinched a chunk of fat on her cheek, between her thumb and finger.

"Young Elvis," she said, staring at Tubby dead on, expressionless, "or the way he looks now?"

Tubby felt he should slap her—wars were started over this kind of thing—but he didn't. What he did was laugh, a little coughlike guffaw at first, then, when Miss Hindenburg joined in, a rollicking, belly-bursting shriek of hysterics, terrifying in resonance, one bourbon away from tears, laughter that reached the soul, the dark bottom of things.

Tubby tried to answer the nurse a few times, but each attempt was aborted by another convulsion, erupting like vomit deep in his gut.

"Either way," Miss Hindenburg said finally, getting back to business, "we haven't seen him."

Suddenly, Tubby thought he might cry. After all, Elvis could be hurt, lost . . . dead. Admit it, Elvis could be dead right now. Elvis Presley. *Step back for a minute and think about that, will you, Tubby Grove?* And laughing at him, mocking him . . . *aren't you, in a sense, asking for the worst? Hell, if he could see you, he'd . . . he'd cut you out of his will for sure,* but there was more than that. Money couldn't be the only thing. *Could it?*

"Tubby! Where's your head, boy?"

He looked up and there was Sergeant Billy Ray Briggs, Memphis Police Department. A good old boy, heart big enough to begin to make up for some awful slow wits, Billy Ray fawned over Elvis even more than the sheriff did; he'd let Elvis take the wheel of his squad car to lead a chase or two, sirens blaring, even when there wasn't a suspect. (Which was where the sheriff drew the line; only Elvis's personal intervention, and a personal check from Elvis to the sheriff—intended, ostensibly, for the Boys Club—had saved Billy Ray from suspension.)

"I said, Tubby, what the hell you doing here?"

Billy Ray reached his right hand out toward Tubby to shake, but Tubby focused on Billy's left hand which he was lifting in the air, shoulder high. Around his wrist was a handcuff, from which dangled, in the air like a side of beef, a young woman. Both of her wrists were handcuffed, and a short chain attached her to the cuff around Billy Ray's left hand. The girl looked familiar, and Tubby couldn't help but think she was just Elvis's type; if he'd seen her when he was making the rounds of an evening, she would get an invitation to Graceland, most certainly. Instinct, ingrained from long, repetitive experience, almost compelled him to invite her now, except that Elvis liked them lively. This girl was limp as a chili-soaked noodle.

"Just checking up on a friend," Tubby said.

"King OK is he?"

"Sure," Tubby said. "Why? You haven't heard anything"—Tubby eyed Billy Ray—"have you?"

"No, why?"

"Oh, nothin'."

Tubby glanced down at the girl.

"She's something, isn't she?" Billy Ray said, pulling his handcuff up again so the girl's arms straightened up. "Damn near pulled a girl's ear off. Wouldn't think she could do it from looking at her. Grabbed an earring and ripped it straight through the lobe. Poor little hippie girl, but cute as a button; just checked her in. Can they sew lobes back on? Anyway, what do you say your friend's name is? One you're checking out?"

"Friend?" Tubby thought a moment. "Oh, right. That'd be Jon Burrows. Bona fide hero over in Vietnam, I tell you."

"Burrows?" the girl whispered.

Billy Ray's left hand suddenly dropped to his side, causing the girl to collapse to the floor with a thud.

"Now you're talkin'?" Billy Ray said, then turned to Tubby. "First word she's said since I picked her up at the airport."

The girl rolled over on her back, lay on the floor. Billy Ray and Tubby knelt down beside her.

"Colonel Jon Burrows?" she said.

Billy Ray and Tubby turned to each other, Billy Ray still in shock that his diagnosis of muteness since birth was inaccurate, Tubby wondering what the hell the girl knew.

"That's right," Tubby said.

"You know Tubby's friend, sweetheart?" Billy Ray asked.

She whispered again, too quiet for the two to hear, so they leaned close to her and turned their ears toward her mouth.

"Whatcha say?" asked Tubby.

And Sharon Teele repeated: "He's not a colonel. He's Elvis."

2 9

SITORSKI HOME

ALEX SITORSKI WAS CLEANING up his apartment, getting it ready. Had his own Christmas tree, a plastic one he had bought on his way home from the White House this afternoon, then put it together in the living area and tossed a few clumps of silver tinsel on the branches. No point wrapping a string of lights around it—the thing was so small and he had forgotten to buy any ornaments— but he did have a Nativity scene, which he set out on a white cotton sheet below. Al Junior had never been to his apartment—he had been in Vietnam when Elena left and they sold the house—and Sitorski wanted it understood that he was getting by. It was a small place, a one-bedroom apartment in a decent complex, with a small screened patio outside where he planned to serve dinner to Junior tonight, if it wasn't too cold. *Decent* was the word Junior would use to describe the place. Comfortable. After Christmas the boy would go back and tell Elena that he was happy, had a full life. Would probably welcome a visit from her, if he happened to mention it, but wouldn't miss her if she didn't. He didn't want to seem pitiful, after all. He didn't need anyone's pity. Didn't want any.

In his bedroom now, Alex Sitorski picked up the pictures he kept beside his bed. It was an old picture he now held, showing Al Junior as a skinny, gap-toothed kid with an oversized baseball cap on his head, a bat lying across his bended knee. The kid was rangy, tall and wiry ever since he shot up like a sprout in sixth grade. Junior's slightness created a vulnerability, Alex had always felt, an aura of weakness. Which was why Sitorski had driven him to play ball, for the boy's own good, because it would make him seem strong and think of himself as strong and then he would *be* strong and strength was something you needed to get by, to get by and win. And though their relationship was a little strained—

yes—at times—at least they were able to talk through their problems by talking around them, by talking baseball: scare the batter with a fastball whistled under his chin, then fool him with a curve. The lessons sunk in. Lessons having nothing to do with baseball.

Sitorski picked up another picture, a more recent one that Elena had sent him, taken in Vietnam. The change was obvious; for the first time the kid had real arms, biceps bursting through his gray army-issue T-shirt. A toughness to him, his face like a hide, crouching by the fire in camp, the flame of his lighter almost singeing his face as he lit a cigarette. The kid was doing his best to become a man, quick as he could. Probably too quick, a little false bravado mixed in, but it was better than not changing at all. War's tough; you need some mental armor to take with you.

They had not spoken since before Junior had left for Vietnam, back in '67. In high school the boy had questioned the war at times, but had never gone over to the antiwar side, which Alex took as a personal victory. But even the night before he left, when they had last spoken, Junior was uncertain. He had asked his father why, why were they fighting? He wanted Alex to tell him, treat him like an infant and explain the war to him. So Alex had taken a deep breath, sitting outside in the family's patio in Arlington, and pulled out a Marlboro, offered Junior one—all a stalling tactic, he knew, a chance to sort his thoughts out.

"You have to understand history," Alex Sitorski began. "Throughout history, civilizations have fallen victim to ideas. Today the threat—the idea that threatens to overtake us—is Communism. It wasn't taken seriously, and then it took over Russia. That vast nation, see it on the globe, turned red from the European border to Siberia."

"Yeah," Junior said, his eighteen-year-old skin smooth, just a boy, "so?"

"That was just the beginning. Then in Europe: half of Germany, Poland, Romania, Czechoslovakia—"

"I know all that, but—"

"China! A quarter of the world's population right there. And still some wouldn't take it seriously, the power of the idea, of Communism. They saw only our strength, not our weakness. And now Southeast Asia—"

"Dad, I know all that. But so what?"

"FREEDOM, that's what. We have it. They don't. That's why all these protesters can create the spectacles they do—and I don't begrudge them for it, but

I do begrudge that they don't appreciate that the Vietnamese don't have it, only in America, and that's why they have to fight for that freedom."

"But there's no freedom there, Dad. And the poverty—"

"You're missing the point. You see, Communism spreads to the weak and hungry first, like a virus. They're the most desperate for easy answers; they'll swap liberty for whatever comes next. But the world's connected. Once countries begin to fall, one by one, the momentum of the last conquest bears on the next. The image is important, so listen. The collapse of a chain of dominoes is inevitable, once it begins. So, you can't say that when the domino halfway across the table from you falls that that is of no concern. Once the chain reaction begins . . ."

Sitorski let the sentence trail off, hoping that somewhere in the cloud of cigarette smoke he had just exhaled his boy saw the same vision he did: the towering domino up north—the Soviet Union—falling, causing smaller pieces in Eastern Europe to topple, then the huge Chinese piece, creating ripples in North Korea—a separate fall in Cuba; so close to America that the wind led us to quiver a bit—North Vietnam, then South Vietnam, setting off another sequence of dominoes collapsing on dominoes, column upon column, not in a well-ordered line but with chaotic pileups in the middle as lines converged . . . on America.

"And that's the tamest scenario," he continued. "More likely, if the Russians gain enough confidence they won't wait that long. They'll start the ultimate battle. Then the fighting won't be in Vietnam, or even Cuba. It'll be in New York City. Washington. Arlington, Virginia."

"But Dad," Junior said, "why don't the Vietnamese fight this themselves?"

"Because it's your job," Sitorski said, "all of ours. It's been mine—still is—and now you've got a role in it. We're all in it together. We have to help each other."

Alex Sitorski looked up at his son's face, and saw in his eyes that the vision wasn't there for him. Junior's eyes had lost their expectant hopefulness, and now were glassy. He was scared. Looking up at his father—just returned from work late that day, Alex was still in full uniform—realizing that he had given the best explanation he could come up with, the boy began to shake. Then sob.

"Is that why, Dad?" he said. "Is that it?"

A lifetime in the military, the Cold War and all its battles, and on that day, three years ago, Alex Sitorski felt as if his son had just asked him why thunderbolts fall from the sky, who makes the clouds move—things parents, certainly Alex Sitorski, should know. It struck him then—a glancing, temporary insight; it didn't stick—that he was answering his son with myths; that the story of the inevitability of Communism, the domino theory, might make as much sense, and was as verifiable in fact, as ancient tales long discredited. Yet he continued. It was the only story he knew.

Now he put the pictures away, walked out of the bedroom into the small space that served as his living room, dining room, and den. There was a counter bar that cordoned off the room from the kitchen, and on it rested the telephone. Alone in the room; just him and the telephone. (After Elena had taken the television with her when she moved out he had refused to buy another, subscribing to the belief that had taken hold throughout much of the Pentagon that it was dangerous to watch media coverage of the war. Bloody images wrenched out of all context and meaning—an American soldier being dragged through the mud, say, or zipped into a body bag—appeared, on TV, to be isolated incidents of chaotic violence. Even a career army man could not help but be sucked into television's self-contained vision of the war. The change in Elena proved, to Sitorski, the power of those images.)

There was still the stereo and radio, and now, in a desperate attempt to go back in time, to the '50s when his boy was young and his wife was in love with him and both were at home, he stacked on the turntable a pile of old Elvis Presley records, first "Tryin' to Get to You."

Then the telephone pulled him toward it. It happened often: alone after a solitary day of reviewing cables, recon photos, casualty totals, and field accounts of the war, he would reach for the telephone just to hear a voice—an operator, a secretary at work. And Elena, of course Elena. (Though he would have to exercise restraint there; she had not forgotten that bad stretch just after she moved out when he called her constantly, at odd hours, made worse by the three-hour time difference between them.) He finished off the glass of Jim Beam he had been drinking, sat down on the stool, picked up the telephone and dialed. He knew the number by heart.

"Hello." Her voice shocked him, as it often did. Hard to believe she was just seconds away on the other end of a telephone line.

"Hi, Elena."

"Oh, Alex." She sounded distracted, a little preoccupied. More vulnerable than usual.

"How are you doing? Everything OK?"

"Oh, fine. You know, the money's tight. Especially with Al here. It's tough enough with just me."

"Both of you? He's coming here, isn't he?"

"I meant when he comes back, Alex. You know he's only coming for a visit, and—"

"He's staying for Christmas. The boy's at least staying here for Christmas. You said that—"

"I know, Alex, but it's up to him. You should be happy he's visiting at all; I thought he was going to stay here until last week when he changed his mind all of the sudden. I don't know why." Then she whispered, "I'm worried about him."

"He's OK, isn't he?"

"Physically, yeah. But he's not himself."

"What's that mean? He's been back for over a year. He's been traveling so much, he's probably tired. It takes a little while, I know, but it's time that he dove back in—"

"It's not that simple, Alex. Let's not argue about it now. Just see for yourself. Then we'll talk."

"All right." He took a breath. "I just wanted to make sure he got on the plane all right. He'll still be at National at eight?"

"Oh, I was going to call you about that. He decided to leave Sunday. He should be in at National Monday morning. He's taking the red-eye. American."

"Not tonight? Whose—?" Sitorski stood up, gripping the base of the phone, ready to slam the whole damned thing down to the floor.

"Look, Alex, I said I don't want to argue. It was Al's idea; I don't know what he's doing. I didn't—well, here he is."

Then there was silence on the line.

He gazed out the window. More cold wind had blown into town, ridding the city of the last of the unseasonably warm spell that had passed through in the morning. Outside, couples were bundling together, friends of his and, formerly, Elena's too. *Why do you blame me for the war?* he suddenly wanted to ask Elena. *These people, out there, they know that life goes on. War's a necessary endeavor. Junior understood that.*

"Dad?"

"Junior? That you?" A stupid thing to say, but he meant it; it had been so long.

"Mom told you I'll be there tomorrow, didn't she? Monday morning, I guess. That's OK, isn't it?"

"Sure it is."

"I just had some things I had to get done here and—you know how it is."

"Right."

"I'm looking forward to it, to talking—over there, I mean, the war, there are some things, you've got to understand, you know?"

The boy was rushing, as if time were something rare and precious. Slow down, he wanted to say. *Take it easy, kid.*

"Sure, fine. I'll see you Monday. I hope I can recognize you."

The kid laughed nervously, a coughing chuckle.

"I hope so too, Dad," he said. "See you then," and he hung up.

3 0

OVER WESTERN SKIES

As he peered out of the airplane window Elvis could see clouds, soft pillows of cotton that he appeared to be cutting through, flying. He knew that he was moving fast, devouring states underneath him as he flew westward, and yet he sensed that he was not moving at all, that he had stagnated; it was only the ground beneath him that moved, like a Hollywood prop, a backdrop of small towns spinning fast before the camera as the foreground remained fixed to capture the illusion of travel. Stuck in space and time, inert for years as the world passed him by, leaving him behind.

He tried to let his mind float, back to his early days, not just think back but actually drift back in time, time travel. His eyes closed, he felt himself floating through the clouds, but the reds screwed things up again, so the best he could do was drift for a few minutes, then snap out of it, then drift again. Which left him waking from his sporadic meditations with clues of what was on his mind, what was at the bottom of his quest.

Each cloud was a different image of himself, at different times, and all he had to do was find the right one and ride it. *A superhero,* he thought, *a blessed man, has powers. Conquered tougher elements than Time, yes sir.* Drift, drift, drift.

Loss was the word he kept emerging with. Change, and loss.

Where the hell were the Beatles, Jimi Hendrix, Mick Jagger and his woman lips and Rolling Stones when Elvis had shaken things up to create the world? Hiding in the caves while Elvis secured the area, disarmed and disabled the enemy . . . and now with the battle over, the threat no more, they emerged to claim victory; and the kids, barefoot, beaded, and chanting like Indian tribes, emerged too to worship the new breed. . . . Love is like that: fickle, impermanent. Even gods ride the vicissitudes of the pop charts. One-hit wonders, really, in the great scheme of things.

He reached into his pants pockets, felt for a photo he'd wanted to bring with him, not certain what it was—he didn't remember—but he knew that it was important, that it had something to do with this quest: a clue, an important one. Opened his eyes.

A stewardess was seated beside him, staring at him. Her tongue slipped out of her half-open mouth and rolled slowly across her upper lip. Then she popped her index finger into her mouth, sucked on the tip, and let out a girlish giggle.

"Dreaming, Mr. Presley?" the stewardess said.

"Am I?" Elvis said, and a switch was pulled down in his brain as he remembered what it was he had left behind in Graceland; it was in the top drawer of his bedside table. "Am I?"

3 1

ANGELINA

ALEX SITORSKI KNEW HE didn't belong in a bar like Ray's Saloon. There were sections of Washington to avoid and this was one of them, but now that he had drunk he wasn't sure how many bourbons, rudimentary principles of self-preservation escaped him.

So here he was: burned-out teenaged girls stripping before him as the night lapsed into early morning, gyrating onstage, legs straddling the poles on either side of the dance floor, all to the Elvis Presley tunes he loved—"It's Now or Never" was now playing—and each new girl was introduced by a pathetic Elvis impersonator, identifiable as Elvis only by the black hair greased over his head and the exaggerated snarl of his upper lip. The scene depressed the hell out of him, but at least it got his mind off Al Junior, and the fact that he would not see him tonight.

Lord knew what Elena had told him, how she'd turned the boy against him. So the boy was avoiding him now, of course he was. Blamed him. As if his father had personally requested that he serve with William Calley, Ernesto Medina, and directed his company to stomp through the South Vietnamese countryside to a hamlet the army would later call My Lai 4, and once there massacre every living soul they found: man, woman, boy, girl, child, dog. Pigs, even. Cattle. As if Colonel Alex Sitorski, Sr., ordered his son to help dig a ditch where the bodies were thrown, as if he equipped the troops with Zippo lighters to burn down the huts, urged them to rape the young girls, then poke their bayonet blades into their cunts, then kill them, toss them in the trench . . . and though there were reasons, damned good ones, to do what they did, they were reasons no one would ever understand (or admit they understood), and so the boys had to lie about the massacre afterward, say they had faced enemy fire though they hadn't . . . they would be found out and that would only wrap innuendo around the whole event, magnify it into something you could never live down, never forget, not a nineteen-year-old kid on his own for the first time, alone, alone, alone. As if it was all the work of Colonel Alex Sitorski. *See what the boy's made of. If he's got the belly for the business. Stomach for the fight.* He'll need it in this godawful doom-ridden world.

Sitorski leaned his head down, picked up his glass (it had become a ritual: think of the boy, the war, My Lai, drink a shot, order another; think of himself, his wars, drink a shot . . .), but this time his forehead dropped smack down against the hard edge of the shot glass as he raised it. Angry at himself for the drunken stupidity of the maneuver, he slapped himself in the head hard as he could with the bony base of his palm.

Onstage, Angelina was looking straight ahead at a customer, some drunk at a table. Past two in the morning now, past three, she wasn't sure, but she knew soon her shift would be over. Maybe Ben would come by, grab her off the stage and take her from here. She hadn't seen him since last night. Which wasn't unusual. Ever since he had returned from Vietnam he would go off like that, for days sometimes. It was another good thing lost.

Now she was cold, though just a minute before the lights had made sweat pour down her forehead like she'd just taken the last turn of the 880 in a track meet back in high school, the finish line straight ahead, hers and hers alone. She could see it now (when she was onstage it helped to think back, drift), and even if she were a stride or two behind in the homestretch she knew that the finish line read like a banner: "Angie Rollins, This Is Yours, Baby!" It was a year ago, but it was yesterday, that exhilarating rush. . . . It was a feeling she tried to hold on to, the way she had run track, the way Ben had played ball. You choose a path and you work it hard, hope things turn out for you. Though they don't, on 14th Street they sure as hell don't. One day, Ben told her back then, things are gonna change. The race doesn't end on some school track, see, one day we rise out of this life. . . . And when he got back he couldn't understand how she had lost it all so fast, how hard it was to get by, the drugs there and Ben nowhere. Maybe it was better for him to go off on his own path, not worry about looking after her anymore. . . . She would get by, nothing more. . . . It was cold and the sweat had dried salty lines on her cheeks.

Sitorski looked down to finish his bourbon, and when he turned back the girl had moved to the other end of the stage and was looking the opposite way at some drunk executive. The drunk stood up, glanced at Sitorski as he walked to the bar. Sitorski thought he'd seen the man's face before, though he wasn't sure where.

He left his table, took a seat at the bar. Ordered another.

"Tell me, please," Palmer Wilson said to Ray, who was behind the bar, trying not to listen, "how many people did that Calley guy kill exactly? And now tell me, what's the difference between us and Ho's boys? Doesn't this My Lai business solve that one, once and for all?"

If Alex Sitorski had heard the first question the man sitting beside him had asked, he could have provided an answer with more precision than any officer in the entire United States military. But he didn't. All he heard was the last two questions.

He turned toward Palmer, nudging him as he did.

"Seems there's a lot you don't understand," Sitorski said.

Palmer turned to Sitorski. Palmer wasn't used to hearing responses to his questions; years of silence from Ray, his constant audience, had convinced him that his questions were rhetorical, nothing more. But now he was scared. He looked Sitorski up and down. The crew cut, the rigor mortis–like bearing. An Army officer. Had to be.

Palmer tried to look as menacing as he could. Downed his bourbon—a double—slammed it on the bar and Ray poured him another. Thought some more.

On the jukebox Elvis had been singing "Paralyzed," but now "I'll Be Home on Christmas Day" was on.

Angie's shift was over. She scanned the crowd again for Ben but he was nowhere. She ran off the stage, and hurriedly slipped off her wig, put on her pantsuit and coat.

Sitorski wasn't angry, not at Palmer Wilson anyway. Now his mind was back on Junior coming home. He had seen the photos of My Lai, the path leading out of the village lined with bodies gunned down trying to flee, the ditch filled with more bodies. Imagined Junior amidst it all, watching the mad circus around him. The shootings, the burnings, the screams and cries.

Something short and snappy was in order, Palmer knew that much. He tried to summon up his FBI training, but little cut through the wall of whiskey.

"What's a little massacre between friends?" Palmer said, finally.

Sitorski looked over quizzically, didn't say anything.

Suddenly Sitorski thought he was going to be sick. Stepped off his stool, walked toward the door.

Still wary that he might take a swing at him, Palmer turned to watch. He saw Alex Sitorski stagger out of the bar, trip, and land, headfirst, on the sidewalk.

The Lord of Dumb Luck, Palmer Wilson said to himself. God bless him.

3 2

MAURICE

ELVIS LOOKED BLOODY AWFUL. And it wasn't just the fact that Maurice Flambeau was not used to staying up until one-thirty in the morning, so everyone looked to him (as Americans might put it) a little worse for wear, or as he, a full-blooded Frenchman, preferred, *comme merde*. No: even with American Airlines stewardesses (whom he assumed red-blooded heterosexual males would consider appealing) hanging on either arm, Elvis Presley looked far from his best when he stepped off the airplane at Los Angeles International Airport.

Maurice was standing just outside the terminal as he watched from some hundred feet away, but even from that distance he noticed that Elvis's entire face was puffy, the cheeks inflated like an engorged squirrel's; red blotches covered his neck; and those huge sunglasses, bloody ridiculous at any hour, looked especially so now, in the darkness. How tragic that the algae-green tint of the lenses kept the keys to the King's soul a mystery that, Maurice feared, would eternally be shrouded from him. What tasteless simpleton would allow Elvis to hide those searing X-ray eyes, eyes that said, "I love you," and to which Maurice Flambeau, gazing at them on album covers in the privacy of his home in West L.A., just hours ago, whispered back, "And I love you, too, Elvis. You know I do." (Priscilla, Maurice knew, was the gauche simpleton, bereft of all breeding and gentility; Maurice would never garb Elvis thusly, had he the opportunity and proximity.)

In his Hollywood years Elvis had taken a liking to Maurice (the last name, Flambeau, had been given by Elvis alone) though they had always just socialized *en masse*, when handfuls of actors—actresses, mostly—congregated at the Los Angeles watering hole *du jour*, the chic *ristorante de la semaine*. In such crowds Maurice would keep his true feelings in check, but now he assumed (though Elvis had been unclear on the phone) Elvis would be staying at his apartment. So they would, finally, be together. Alone.

Elvis had sounded odd, troubled, calling him as he did a number of times in succession, to make plans, cancel them, then reinstate them. Maurice assumed that there was trouble in paradise—ha ha!—with Miss Pris. He knew the story: *"Maurice, I don't feel the same attraction toward her that I used to. In fact, I ain't sure if I ever been plum intended for her. Felt I had to call you, Maurice. Felt you'd understand."* Oh, Maurice understood, without Elvis saying a word.

Oh, he was awful all right.

Elvis was just a few feet away from him now. He saw Maurice, or appeared to, for the first time. Maurice's mouth fell open.

Maurice had intended to yell, but rather than hear a melodious "Elvis," he heard a raucous "ELLLVVEEESSS!"—a cacophony of vile bellows that must have originated from some primordial swamp in Wachtach, Alabama; Boodleloxi, Mississippi; or Godhelpusall, Kentucky. *Mon Dieu!* Speak of awful.

Maurice turned around and then saw who—what!—had emitted the squawk: a hulking behemoth of a man who was walking onto the tarmac and now shook hands with Elvis.

"Tmmmy," Elvis whispered, slurring his lips downward. Elvis's body seemed limp, the girls apparently holding him up on either side.

"You look like crap," the behemoth said, and this, Maurice was certain, was uttered exclusively by the interloper.

Elvis smiled. His hair was disheveled, his suit crumpled and spotted with stains. And, up close now, Maurice saw that not only were his cheeks puffy but Elvis's skin was as white as his high-collared shirt had been, Maurice assumed, at the start of the week, and there was a soft fattiness under his chin, the makings of a hefty set of jowls. Charles Laughton as a very young man.

"What the hell is this?" the behemoth said, snatching a small red bag from Elvis, the size of a lady's handbag, emblazoned with an American Airlines logo.

"Toothpaste and stuff," Elvis muttered. "You need it for traveling."

"Lord, Elvis. This all you brought with you?"

Elvis shrugged. Behind him one of the stewardesses, the brunette, lifted up his valise. Then Maurice took a step forward, cleared his throat, and put out his hand: "Elllvis," he said. *"Excusez-moi* for speaking, but you look superb."

Elvis shook Maurice's hand, laughed as he stepped ahead of the stewardesses, then put an arm around Tommy Shelton (the behemoth) and another around Maurice Flambeau.

"No, Maurice," Elvis said, shaking his head. "Ole Tommy's right. I look like a dropped turd."

Then Maurice called the doctor, as Tommy told him to. Then Maurice drove Elvis (and Tommy and the girls) away from the airport, as Tommy told him to. Then they didn't even go to Maurice's apartment (despite the fact that he had fixed it up just as he knew Elvis would like, stocked with peanut butter, bananas, and loaves of Wonder bread), because they were going to Tommy's place in the hills, Tommy said. Tommy, that brazen cowboy-booted behemoth. And the girls. It was all the behemoth and the bimbos.

When they arrived at Tommy's place—no mansion, just a small rambler, the sort of overpriced *faux* exclusive enclave one would expect some uncouth hillbilly to be hoodwinked into buying—Maurice said he had to go back home.

"Must rise with the birds," Maurice said. "But we shall speak very soon, Elvis?"

Elvis was half asleep at the time, and didn't respond.

"Tough luck, Maurice," Tommy belched at him. The behemoth had gotten out of the car and was holding Elvis under the arms, had him half dragged out of the back seat. "You grab his legs."

So Maurice got out from behind the wheel and walked around to the other side of the car. Then he held his arms out, bent at the elbows, to create a seat, a soft passage on which Elvis's rear, then thighs, then calves landed—all absolutely necessary, Maurice was ready to explain if asked, to keep Elvis pristine above the pavement as he was removed from the car. Finally, Maurice stepped back and grabbed Elvis's ankles with each hand, Tommy still holding the armpits, and the men carried him, suspended in air, toward the house.

It was a long walk up the winding stone path to the house. To avoid the glare of the hillbilly hulk, Maurice looked down where his eyes, as chance would have it, met a welcome, most welcome, sight. Not that there was much to see; in Elvis's soporific state, *le saucisson de* Elvis—poor fellow—was limp. But still, it got Maurice thinking. A spurt of blood pranced through his loins like a doe in the woods.

Elvis slipped out of his grasp, but Maurice caught his feet just before they fell to the ground.

"Need," Maurice tried to say, but the sounds were guttural groans, "to change my grip."

Then he shimmied up in between Elvis's legs, which were spread apart on either side of him, until his arms hugged the thickest, most luscious portions of his thighs, and Maurice's belly was pressed up and rubbing against the intersection.

"There," Maurice said, and let out a deep breath. "That's better."

After they reached the house and laid Elvis in bed upstairs, Elvis didn't even say good-bye; not a word, in fact. Neither did Tommy. Only one of the girls, the dreadful blonde, who had batted her eyes at Maurice throughout the ordeal (having scooted across the front seat during the trip from the airport, forcing Maurice to edge away toward the door as he drove), asked him: "You in pictures?"

Saturday night, and again he was alone. Being homosexual wasn't easy in December 1970. Not even in Hollywood.

All the way home Maurice cried so hard he could barely see the road in front of him. When he got inside of his apartment, alone in his bathtub (but for a bottle of Beefeater's gin), blasting Elvis crooning "Are You Lonesome Tonight?" he seriously considered, for what was far from the first time, whether he just might as well kill himself.

3 3

LIGHTS OUT

THE DOCTOR WAS NOT Dr. Nick; it was nobody Elvis had ever seen before, just some tall, dark-skinned Indian in a white jacket who was standing over him while pointing a needle. Where he was, who the doctor was, and why the image of Little Elvis had just cropped up in his head were questions to which Elvis did not have a clue.

"This will assist you to sleep," the doctor said, in a clipped voice, a touch British, but with a high pitch, smiling as he held up the syringe.

"Lord, Elvis, you got to take better care of yourself."

Elvis didn't see who spoke at first, though the voice was vaguely familiar. Then the face appeared, a big smiling head: Tommy. Tommy Shelton.

"Where's—?"

"You're at my place, E. You slept from the airport. Your friend, the French dude, he left a while ago. Sends his regards though."

The doctor held Elvis's forearm firmly with one hand, leaning over with the needle in the other.

"Doc says you got some reaction, that's what's making you all puffy. The shot'll bring it down, and help you sleep besides."

Elvis scooted up in bed, away from the needle.

"I don't do drugs, you know. You know I don't."

"No drugs," the doctor said. "Medications."

And the needle poked under the skin of his forearm; Elvis squirmed with the initial jolt of pain so Tommy grabbed his other arm with one hand, held his chest down against the bed with the other, and the doctor jammed the needle in still farther, then pushed the end of the syringe down so Elvis could see, through the translucent plastic tube, its contents disappear inside of him.

"Now you sleep," the doctor said.

Tommy picked up a telephone from the bedside table.

"And I'll call Bo and the Colonel."

"NO!" Elvis wrenched his arm up, sending the needle—its point still lodged in the skin as the doctor was slipping it out—flying across the room, in between the doctor and Tommy, then grabbed the base of the telephone and tossed it to the floor.

"OK, then," Tommy said, "I just thought, given your—I mean—they'll be worried is all."

"I said no!" Suddenly, he began to feel weak; his eyelids drooped down, and his arm dropped off the side of the bed. "An' I meant it. Too."

"OK," Tommy said. He picked up the phone from the floor, tucked it underneath the bed. Elvis could see the doctor whisper something to Tommy, signal him toward the door with a finger. "I didn't know it meant so much to you."

"It does," Elvis thought he said, though he wasn't sure; suddenly so drained of strength, he didn't know if he had the energy to move his jaw up and down. "This here's a hush-hush deal."

Then the lights went out.

3 4

SHARPE AT WORK

ON THE OTHER SIDE of the nation, in the White House, Max Sharpe was still at work. Sharpe's office was across the street in the Old Executive Building, but Ehrlichman permitted him to use a carrel in the White House during off hours, a small office recently vacated by a victim of Nixonian rage (an embarrassing *Washington Post* story on the Cambodian incursion whose source, an unnamed "high-ranking official in the Administration," was never found, but was suspected by the President). Sharpe felt that if he made use of the office before it was reassigned, the laws of bureaucratic adverse possession might take effect, entitling him to the space.

Sharpe was working on his Get High on Life campaign. After some brainstorming earlier in the evening (into the early morning now), he had decided that what the plan really needed was a showcase, some dramatic event to kick it off. After all, as Ehrlichman had taught him, in politics reality was what the media presented. Or, as they liked to say in the White House, "Truth is what you get away with." (Since joining the White House staff Sharpe had heard innumerable variants of that adage: "Politics is what you get away with"; "Reality is what you get away with"; and even, "Victory goes to him who gets away with the most." Thoughts to meditate on, indeed.)

Tonight he had typed out yet another preliminary draft of another memo setting forth his HOLE plan, and now he pulled out a page from his typewriter and read it:

The problem is critical: As of December 14, 1970, 1,022 people died this year in New York alone from narcotic-related deaths. Two of youth's folk heroes, Jimi Hendrix and Janis Joplin, died recently within a period of two weeks reportedly from drug-related causes. Their deaths are a sharp reminder of how the rock music culture has been linked to the drug subculture. This subculture, as we know, is inexorably linked with the antiwar movement, the "anti-Establishment" movement, the hippies, the yippies, the SDSers, the Black Panthers, etc., and ultimately, of course, the Communists. More to the point, THESE FORCES ARE VEHEMENTLY AGAINST THE POLICIES OF THIS ADMINISTRATION. Although we know that their numbers are relatively small, when magnified by the left-leaning media, their voices have gained undue volume and influence. Therefore, they cannot be underestimated when planning for the 1972 election.

You are aware that the average American family has four radio sets; 98 percent of the young people between 12 and 17 listen to radio. Between the time a child is born and he leaves high school, it is estimated he watches between 15,000 and 20,000 hours of television. That is more time than he spends in the classroom. We have no control over the media to which our children are subjected AND MANY ARE HOSTILE TO OUR POLICIES AND MESSAGE.

THIS IS A

CULTURAL WAR.

HOLE will quell the threat posed by these forces by redirecting them. We will replace the leaders of this movement with new leaders, leaders who are friendly with this Administration, and who can be trusted to put forward OUR MESSAGE, creating a Pied Piper effect, in which we replace their piper with one of our own. Particularly if we can co-opt one of the heroes of the rock music culture to our cause, the people will follow.

The Pied Piper business might be a bit overblown—better switch to a football analogy in the final draft—but besides that, the memo was shaping up.

And Sharpe knew from whence he was speaking. Why, even now, while he had typed this draft, the transistor radio in his office had played "Me and Bobby McGee" and "Hey Joe." (To be honest, before the DJ had mentioned it, Sharpe wasn't certain that Joplin and Hendrix were dead.) And now he had Simon and Garfunkel cranked up: "Scarborough Fair" (or was it "Parsley, Sage, Rosemary and Thyme"?); whatever its name was, it was the "funky" version with Garfunkel (or was it Simon?) reading news stories about the war in the background. Oh, when it came to the hip rock and roll scene, Max Sharpe had credibility, all right.

Sharpe lit another cigarette, cranked up the volume on the radio a bit more, kicked his feet up on his desk. Picked up the memo, and another song came on—"Feelin' Groovy"—and though it was past two in the morning, Saturday night, and he was alone, it was perfect. He closed his eyes and listened.

The song, he felt, said it all. It was the key to HOLE, to capturing the youth movement. You had to make the war *cool*. It had to be *groovy* to go off and fight Commies. Imagine "Scarborough Fair," but with Garfunkel reading stories of Viet Cong atrocities in the background, tales of welfare fraud and abuse, gut-wrenching crime stories—"Negro rapes white suburban cheerleader" sort of thing. Have some Jimi Hendrix progeny call Ho Chi Minh "master of the new slavery." John Lennon was a lost cause, but Paul McCartney might be interested, or one of those other Beatles. Bumper stickers with GROOVE WITH DICK 'N' SPIRO; HENRY K. MAKES MY DAY!; HO BE THE MAN. And HOLE, the brainchild of Maximillian Sharpe, Jr., would weave all of these mini-campaigns together to form a tapestry, a flag emblematic of the war on values.

Sharpe laughed to himself, kicked his feet off the desk; certain he was alone, yelled "Hot damn!" and turned around to crank up the radio still louder. But then he stopped short, just before he ran head-on into the hunched, peering face of Richard Nixon.

3 5

ELENA

"I VOTED FOR NIXON, can you believe it? And there I was in L.A., burning all of my bras in the street!"

Elena Sitorski was laughing, sucking a joint deep into her lungs, and Al Junior tried to laugh with her.

"It was like a ritual," she went on. "There were people lining each side of the sidewalk, carrying all sorts of signs: women's lib, against the war, some far-out stuff. At the end was a platform where a bonfire was burning, and each of us walked down the aisle toward it, knelt down, said a prayer or a speech or anything we felt like. And then we dropped our stuff on the fire. We called it a purging. We would burn away what we wanted to destroy about our past, about ourselves, things that had been a part of us but we wanted to get rid of. Some guys burned draft cards, or war medals, and some of us burned marriage licenses, high school yearbook photos, cheerleader outfits. And I burned all my bras. Not much imagination, I know, but living with your father all those years, I guess I got a little conservative."

She laughed until the embers of her joint reached the tips of her fingers, then dropped what remained on top of the cone of incense that was burning in an ashtray on the table between them. Then she walked over to the kitchen. Since Junior had left home she had gotten a perm, frizzing her naturally wavy blond hair, and had lost weight, all of which made her look younger than her forty years. More than that, the fire in her eyes, the vigorous spark in her voice made her seem younger still. It made Al Junior feel old and stodgy. Like his father.

On the stereo the Beatles were singing "Within You Without You" ("We were talking, about the space between us all"), and the room was filled with smoke from the joint and the incense, choking him. A strange place, here in L.A. with his mother, neither at home anymore.

Elena turned around from the refrigerator with a bottle of wine in her hand. "Want some? It's Chardonnay. Not great, but what are you going to do?"

He shook his head.

She poured herself a glass, then walked into the living room, to the wall unit where the stereo was. Before the Beatles, Grace Slick had sung "Plastic Fantastic Lover," before that, the Doors, a Joan Baez album, more Beatles (The White Album: "The children asked him if to kill was not a sin"), and Bob Dylan. Now Elena picked up the stack of albums and flipped them over, then stopped just before putting them on the turntable.

"Wait a minute. I just want to play one song." She knelt down and pulled out another album, put it on the bottom of the stack, then placed them all on the spindle. "Remember this?"

It was Elvis, an old album from the '50s. His voice young, deep, undulating the words.

"I used to love this stuff," Elena said. "Your dad wouldn't get near a dance floor, so I'd dance with my girlfriends." She danced back toward the table, holding herself, spinning, singing along.

> When the night grows cold, and I want to hold you
> Baby don't say don't.

She sat back down as the song finished.

"Have you listened to the stuff Elvis is singing now?" she said. "What junk. And he looks terrible. Maybe I was better off marrying your father." She laughed, but this time Al Junior didn't join her. "But then, your father likes the crap he's singing now more than the old stuff. So there you have it."

The next record dropped, and they were quiet for a while, just listening to the music. Soon the Beatles were singing "Blackbird."

"I'm glad you're happy . . . now," Junior said, finally.

"Thanks. So am I." Elena sipped her wine.

"No, really. So much has changed, you know, everything—and so fast—it's hard to find a way to fit in. It just seems you've found something here."

The boy was still nervous, she could see, still staring at the label on the beer he had finished half an hour ago. Always had been a shy kid, reserved and seri-

ous like his father, but since he had come back from the war there was a strange-
ness to him, too. Not that that was surprising, having gone through what he had.
At any age, but at his age especially.

"I'm sorry we haven't gotten to talk much since you've come home," she said.
"I'm not complaining, it's just that I've missed you. You were away, and then you
come back and you're traveling. It's like you're avoiding us—"

"I'm not. I just needed to get away for a while."

"I haven't even heard where you went to."

"All over. When I got back I just wanted to move, you know? So I took off,
bought a cheap car and just drove back and forth across the country. I went
down to the South, I'd never been there before, then up to New England, then
to Canada. There's a lot of exciting things happening, like you were saying, a lot
of good energy, but there's a lot of meanness out there too. I didn't feel like I
belonged in any of it. That isn't what I was looking for. I just needed to work
things out. So I kept moving. It's not like there's someone somewhere that can
work things out for me. There isn't. Finally I went down to Mexico, then
Arizona, Indian country. I didn't understand the language there, which was fine.
Just what I needed."

Elena watched as he puffed his cigarette. Nervous, looking down at the floor,
at the label of his empty beer bottle, not at her.

"You know, you probably need someone to talk to," she said. "To work things
out, like you said. It doesn't have to be me, maybe it shouldn't be me, but—"

"You mean a shrink?"

"No, I just—I mean, your father, he keeps it all bottled up inside of him, you
know, and I don't think that's the best way to deal with it. And I know someone
here. Maybe when you get back from seeing your father?"

He shook his head.

"I—I'm not sure when I'm coming back," he said. "I don't know what I'm
going to do right now."

"I know that after I left your father I, uh, talked to someone, and it helped."

"Mom, I don't want to hear—"

"No, I want to tell you. I was able to figure everything out finally. It was like
I'd missed out on life for twenty years. Not that I regret it; I don't regret a minute
of our life with you. That was everything to me. But that was just it: that was
everything. I didn't have any life for myself. I didn't grow at all, I didn't nurture
myself. Your father wasn't there much when the war got . . . more involved.

Always working late. It was tough. But when I came out here I just felt like I'd walked out of a cocoon, that I was a butterfly, floating about, seeing the world for the first time. And in the summer of '69, that was something to see."

Elena tugged at the peace sign medallion that hung around her neck, then spun it around. Al Junior had made it for her in shop class in school: his greatest act of rebellion against Alex. The teacher had wanted him kicked out of class for making it and Elena had gone to the school and convinced the principal that Colonel Sitorski's son had a right to express himself. She then asked if the teacher could write for her, a hundred times on the blackboard, "In America, we have the First Amendment that guarantees freedom of expression." The principal suggested that her husband might be better suited to deal with her son's problems in the future.

"Why do you have to leave all of the sudden, anyway?" she said. "I thought we could spend Christmas together."

"I just have to go," he said. There were things you kept from her. "I'll see Dad. I'm not sure what next."

Then he stood up and looked down on her. He seemed tall—menacing—not her child—and his movement was so sudden it seemed violent.

"Why did you leave?" he said.

"What does that have to do with anything?" Elena said.

"Why did you leave him? Did you ever love him, Mom?" He fired the questions at her. "Were you ever happy?"

"Of course I loved him. We just grew apart. That happens."

"And so it was just a coincidence that you left him after I left home? Is that what you're saying?"

"I didn't say that."

"Then it was me."

"Yes, in a way. But only in a way." Elena got up from the table and walked back to the refrigerator, though there was nothing in there that she wanted, that she needed.

"What way?" He walked toward her, cordoning her off in the kitchen.

"It was your father. But it wasn't all your father." She looked at him. She didn't want to talk about leaving Alex, those horrible weeks when she finally learned about the massacre, when she found out that it had happened months before but that Alex hadn't told her. And then when he told her why he hadn't told her. "It was Vietnam."

"What do you mean?"

"I blamed your father." She walked slowly back from the refrigerator, then sat back down at the table. "I thought he pressured you into going. I know he did. Then I was afraid for you, and I blamed it on him. He could have pulled some strings, kept you—I mean, there was more to it, there were a lot of other reasons I wasn't happy, but that was what made me leave."

"But you didn't leave until later, after I'd been over awhile." Junior was confused and he showed it, his speech now quieter, uncertain. "What else was there? What did you blame him for?"

You spend lives talking around things, Elena thought, *leaving what's important unsaid.*

"We know, Al. I know you want to put it past you, but I know. Your father didn't tell me at first and then when I found out I guess it all came to a head, everything, and then I left him. But I know. We both know."

"You know what?"

"We know about My Lai."

3 6

SITORSKI HITS THE WALL

IF ONLY THE SIDEWALK would stop rocking, Alex Sitorski thought, lying face down on the concrete, then he could get up. He tried to stand, but the buildings darted away as he leaned against them and he collapsed back down with a thud. Got up again and, still unsteady, after a few steps did a full pirouette as his right hand slipped from the building, he tried to catch it again with his left but that slipped too and his legs crossed and, like Gene Kelly in the rain, he came full circle; the wall was now spinning, forming a circle of brick all around him, deep as a well they might have used for graves in My Lai, he guessed, trying quickly to hide the bodies fast as they could (though they hadn't, he knew; there was a ditch where Calley and his boys tossed the bodies), but the thoughts passed too quickly as the wall encircled him as he spun around. He tried to lull the world to stop rotating so fast around him, but it wouldn't; he—it—only spun faster, and now he could no longer control himself or stop. His revolution went awry, no longer the perfect circle, and as he swung out of orbit he saw the wall of the building race toward him, head-on, and he smashed into it, forehead first, fast and solid into the brick.

Angie had just stepped out of Ray's Saloon. She wasn't the only one on the street who saw the man run his head into the wall. Most every girl on the sidewalk glanced his way, keeping one eye on the cars slowing down and the other on him and the few other stragglers making their way up 14th, potential customers heading toward them. Even before he hit the wall a number of the girls were staring at him, some laughing hard. On the far side of Saturday night nearer to Sunday morning you took humor where you found it, magnified it out and ran with it.

And a clean-cut white guy trying his damnedest to ram his head into a brick wall, missing, and finally hitting it? That was funny.

Angie saw the man's head bounce off the wall, sending him staggering backward as if from a Joe Frazier left hook, and she glanced around quickly to see if somebody would make a move toward him to help, but no one did—the girls stepped away, and so did the guys: pimps, dealers, johns, stragglers—so she ran toward him, habit making her crouch first, touching her hand on the pavement, then springing up with the fire of the starter pistol; her head bobbed up and she saw the man's legs buckle and then he was falling backward toward the pavement, and her thigh muscles clenched, sprang to life, to their old, newfound power; he was limp, falling, the back of his head inches from the sidewalk when she reached him, Angie did, reached her hands low as if she were diving for the finish line, but this time she turned her palms up and slipped them under the back of the man's head so it landed on her soft hands and bounced off them as it hit, then settled, safely, down onto them.

He lay flat on his back on the sidewalk. Angie cradled his head in her arms. She parted his hair to examine the bruise underneath but it quickly covered itself with blood, which she wiped away, so now her hands were engulfed in it, a thin layer of red watercolors, like a child's.

Sitorski lay there; he wasn't certain how long. *The monks used to beat themselves too.* He used to take Junior to church and the boy was fascinated by religion and ritual, the ceremonies, he would study them, not take it on faith but reflect, analyze, *but that is not how you approach things,* that was what he tried to tell the boy, *some things you allow yourself to believe in because that is how you get by in this world.* He wasn't sure whether he had put it that clearly. When they met again he would be clear.

The monks used to beat themselves, he knew that and Junior learned that and now it just came to him that *centuries ago there were fathers and sons and there were wars and they needed to punish themselves for their transgressions.*

He saw himself falling backward, imagined the back of his head splitting open like an egg on the edge of the curb, but at the last instant a cushiony cloud had rushed below him, swept him up like an angel and laid him down, gently. And he wondered, *If this was not his punishment, what would be?*

Then he heard a piercing ring that grew closer and he realized it was a police siren, and finally he heard a screech of car brakes inches from his head with the siren on top of him. Car doors slammed and heavy feet pounded above him.

"Angie Rollins," he heard a voice say, "you know better than to do your business on the sidewalk, don'tcha?"

"Beating on your johns?" another said. "That's no way to get repeat customers."

Sitorski opened his eyes then, looked up. Two cops: a white one standing over him, and a black one now crouching down beside him and the girl.

"He OK?" the black one said. His face so close it seemed exaggerated in size.

"He's—" the girl began.

"I'm fine, Officer," Sitorski said, trying hard not to slur any words. Actually, he felt sobered up a bit. "I . . . slipped, and this young lady . . . she caught me."

He turned to the girl for the first time. She was young, Al Junior's age, and beautiful with her dark skin, short-cropped Afro, slanty eyes that seemed older, well worn, firing away at him. Her face was the face he saw in the bar.

"Hey Angie, we've heard some talk," the white one said. "Seems your brother's got himself into some trouble."

"You never could get anything on Ben," she said. "He's too good."

"Can't take you people anywhere," the white cop said, and the black cop cut him a glare. "Can't even say thank you to the President?"

"That *was* good metal he threw away," the black cop said. "Probably a night's worth of horse if you could have sold it on the street." The cops turned to each other and laughed.

The black cop put one of Sitorski's arms around his neck, the girl took the other, and together they lifted him to his feet. Once up his knees buckled, but the cop caught him and steadied him.

"C'mon, let's go," the white cop said. "I'm not bringing in some lousy drunken john at this hour." He looked down, and Sitorski was certain he was about to be spit on. "Let God sort 'em out."

3 7

SPIRITS IN THE PARK

"YOU KNOW HOW there are some things that happened over there that you never forget, never will?" Ben Rollins said.

He was in Lafayette Park, sitting under the stars. Lester, lying on his back beside him, nodded his head.

"Well, I remember huddling in this bunker we'd made for ourselves, a wall of dirt and trees and some such shit, waiting for Charlie to shoot himself out. So we're keeping quiet for a while, just hanging out. And there's this radio. You see, a few weeks before there was this white dude, Goldie we called him. One of those guys that, soon as he shows up you say, The man is history. We're takin' side bets on when, not if, dig? Never wants to hurt a fly, understand? He sees a brother, first thing he does is walk up to him and shake his hand. Which is cool, but no way this man's gonna pull a trigger on Charlie when he has to. So first day Charlie lays some shit on us and we're waiting for the shooting to stop, for them to come close, be patient, let Charlie think he's gonna win this fucking battle when all he's doing is shootin' the air and his own fucking jungle, wasting ammo till we blow him away. So we're waiting and Goldie just stands up, and I'm pulling him down by the boots, but he walks right out of the bunker, right toward Charlie, and the next thing we hear more shots and then there's a hell of a blast, and no more steps, and we all know Goldie's stepped on a mine. And Charlie hears it and charges after us and we blow him all to shit, screaming, 'This one's for Goldie!' while I'm shooting like one crazy sonofabitch.

"So jump to weeks later, and this radio we've got, it was Goldie's, but now it's like community property. And we're in a bunker just like the one Goldie walked out of. Charlie's a ways off, and me and some brothers are blasting Jimi, wailing

144

away on 'Machine Gun' on the radio, and then in the middle of some wild riff some white motherfuckers snatch it and change the goddamned station—in the middle of fucking 'Machine Gun,' dig?!—and they get some Frank Sinatra or Elvis on, some bullshit. And I say, 'What the fuck do you boys think you're doin'?' but not that polite, understand, and they say, 'No nigger uses language like that to me, boy,' and I say, 'Well, Benjamin Rollins do,' and before you know it we're fighting, wrestling and punching in this narrow-ass bunker, black on white, over the goddamned radio. I grab it and switch it to Jimi, and he grabs it back and we get Elvis, then someone else grabs it, and finally the captain comes in and he says the radio was Goldie's so he guesses he left it for the white boys.

"A few hours later we begin shooting at Charlie, and I snatched that radio and threw it far as I've ever thrown anything. The damned thing probably landed in Ho Chi Minh's lap, played Vietnamese folk songs ever since!

"So what got me thinking of that was this afternoon, over at Danny's I run into this fat old guy, thinks he's Elvis Presley. Saddest thing you ever saw. Got me thinking of old Goldie."

Ben lay flat on his back. Lester had remained still and quiet during Ben's entire speech, watching the word pictures play out on the screen in his mind. Ben could do that, Lester thought: make a movie with his words.

"Look at the fucking stars," Lester said a good minute later, turning toward Ben. "And the moon. The motherfucking moon."

The radio was playing more Hendrix now; the DJ announced that it was three months and a day since Jimi had passed on, so he would be playing his music through the night. "Electric Ladyland" came on.

"Feel all right about the medal, Ben?" Lester said.

"I didn't want the damn thing," Ben said.

"Check it out," Sunshine said. He was a comrade, a white hippie with a red-haired Afro bigger than Lester's. "The moon's like a big klieg light. It's lighting up a movie shoot of this wild show down here." He puffed deep on a joint, then blew the smoke into the air. "It's like Jerry Rubin says: 'The revolution will be televised.'"

"That's true, man," Lester said, taking the joint from Sunshine. "There'll be film crews on the front lines."

"Lester man," Ben said, "you're the one brother I know more into Jerry Rubin and Abbie Hoffman than Bobby Seale or Malcolm."

"I'm telling you, Ben, that's the future, man. Those bastards are smart. They understand things. See, it's all theater. That's all it is. Tricky Dick understands that, Uncle Ho digs it, Che for damned sure did. And we better too if we want to shake things up; otherwise we're just spinning wheels. Now you want to hear a real yip?" Lester tapped the white kid on the leg. "Yo, Sunshine. Take a load off. Tricky Dick's gotta be in bed now. Take five and hang with us."

Sunshine had been pounding Lester's drum every few seconds, but now he crouched down beside Lester and Ben.

"I don't know about that, Les," Sunshine said. "Dick keeps some weird hours, man. Wanders the streets and shit, all hours. Four, five in the morning, he doesn't care. Makes no difference to him. He doesn't need sleep like you and me. The man is not human. He's an evil spirit. Just when you think you're safe he'll be there, lurking in the fucking shadows, ear to the wall, calling in the pigs."

"You don't be dropping acid when you're on drum duty, my man," Lester said. "You do that shit in Vietnam, but *this* war's a serious business. Our soldiers best come to battle with clear heads, dig?" He took another drag, then offered the joint to Ben, who waved his hand, declining.

"I'm serious, man. I seen him." Sunshine angled the drum down so its top was in his lap and he could still beat it while he crouched down. "I saw him at the Lincoln Memorial a few months ago. It's about this time at night, and a bunch of us are just hanging, tokin' and rappin', waiting for a big protest the next day. And we're talking about how there've been these evil spirits, dig, coursing through history, and that whenever the people get their shit together to realize the Dream, that old evil spirit rises up and strikes 'em down. Check out Abe Lincoln—remember, we're right underneath the statue of old Abe while we're saying all this, practically in his lap—and the Weathermen: before they can use their bombs, what happens? They blow themselves up, and the ones that survive deep-six. And then there's all the soul mates in jail, Bobby, Abbie. And Martin and Malcolm and JFK and RFK and Jimi and Janis. One of us says it's a curse from Columbus, the pilgrims, stealin' from the Indians. Then we revved it up with slavery, and we've infected the wound over and over since then. We keep paying for our sins, dig? The curse, it keeps holding us back. It's the spirit, man.

"And I'm saying the spirit's taken on many forms. Now it's Tricky Dick. I tell you, if RFK hadn't been shot we'd be out of this war. How many of our own boys we killed over there? And for what? Tell me one goddamned thing in Vietnam worth that? But who benefits most from Bobby being shot down? The trickster. Even JFK: he beats the trickster in '60 and then look what happens to him."

"And Sunshine," Ben said, "how many hits did you say you did that night?"

"I'm serious, man. Dig it: we're saying all this, and I've just said the words 'Tricky Dick is the evil spirit to end all spirits' when suddenly he appears, right there under Abe Lincoln, right in the midst of us all. Nixon himself, with just a couple of his good Germans, and he walks right up to us. And we're all just standing there saying, 'Shiiiiiittttttt.'"

"He's shitting," Ben said, turning to Lester. "Isn't he?"

"No, this I know, Ben," Lester said. "This shit is true."

"It was, man," Sunshine continued. "I'm telling you, Tricky Dick himself was this close to me. If I had a gun I could have shot him dead like that. I could have offed him with a knife even, or slammed his head down against the steps, killed him that way. I've thought about that a lot since then, and we've talked about it, a bunch of us who were there, and we've all thought the same thing. How many lives could we have saved by killing that man? Tens, hundreds of thousands, easy. That's justified, isn't it? But the thing of it is, even if that happened today, and I knew he was coming, I don't think I'd be able to do it. I'd want to, and I'd know it wasn't wrong, but I wouldn't be able to pull the trigger. And I think the trickster knew that. That's why he walked right up to us. It takes a killer to know one, I guess."

"Now if one of the Panthers was there," Lester said, "and I'm not saying they're right, understand, but Eldridge or Huey would have blown that evil bastard away in an instant."

"And we'd have President Agnew then," Ben said, laughing.

"Then they'd blow him away too."

"But it never would have happened," Sunshine said. "See, only enemies of the evil spirit get shot down in this country. Or maybe the evil spirits are the only ones who have what it takes to kill. Or maybe the spirit protects his own."

"It's like I say," Lester said, "you elect your god with what's inside you. Today an evil god rules, and the only way we're going to change things is to start from within; that's the only way you overthrow a god. You stop believing in him, cast him away, accept another. When we do that, Nixon will fall. Then the good will rule in this land and above it."

Lester took a deep drag, then flicked the end of the joint high up in the air, and the three watched the sparks rise against the still dark sky, then fall, like a shooting star, against the backdrop of the White House.

"Like Goldie?" Ben said.

"Maybe."

"Because," Ben said, looking up at Sunshine, then at Lester, "I think about that scene with Goldie a lot now. Like one of those dreams that keep coming back to you, so you think about it, break it down. Maybe he was there when we were fighting over the radio, helping us switch the dial."

"But what about Elvis?" Sunshine said.

"What?"

"Why was Elvis playing on the radio, when the white guys took it? What's it mean? See, I think Elvis is one of those souls that got taken over by the evil spirits. He came on, at the beginning, as a force for the Dream, dig? But when he came back from the army, it was like they'd replaced his soul with something else."

"White boys and the cult of the King," Lester said, and he laughed. "King of Kings."

"No, dig it," Sunshine said. "When Elvis was front and center he shook everything all to hell. Scared the shit out of the order. Folks gathered up the kids and headed deep for the 'burbs, but it didn't do any good; he was still there, on the TV, radio, in the music stores. That's when the revolution really started, you know, when kids were getting together, breaking down the walls. Like Lennon says: 'Before Elvis, there was nothing.' A spirit, dig? But good. But now? Now where the hell is he?"

WENDY'S

AT THAT MOMENT, in Wendy's Chili and BBQ Tavern in Memphis, affixed to a bar stool that might as well have been endowed by his once ever-present and oppressing, now nowhere present and disappearing, Lord and Master, sat the rear end of the King's jack-of-all-errands and scut work, childhood buddy of Elvis's chief bodyguard (oh, Bo would never let him forget who was *the chief!*): Tubby Grove. Wendy's was a small, hole-in-the-wall joint, sawdust floors and a jukebox just off I-40 before the bridge into Arkansas, and it was open all hours, which was essential for Tubby since with Elvis's schedule he could never be certain when he'd have a spare moment to sneak out of Graceland for just a beer or two, a bowl of chili—maybe some ribs. (*"I pay for your time,"* Elvis would point out more than he needed, *"I'll give you some back when I choose!"*)

In most bars in Memphis hippie music was as welcome as the trash who sang it, but at Wendy's things were a little more—well—loose. In the jukebox there was Elvis (a mix of Sun sessions, recent stuff, gospel and now, given the season, "Blue Christmas," "Merry Christmas, Baby," and "The First Noel"), but there were also a few current rock 'n' roll tunes. Now Creedence Clearwater Revival's "Fortunate Son" was blaring.

Tubby was at the bar, nursing a Schlitz (or rather, he thought to himself, the beer was nursing him), chain-smoking Marlboros. Just finished his second bowl of the Fireman's Special (a jalapeño soup with a sprinkling of beans), rubbing his TCB pendant between his fingers, singing to himself (silently, in his head) along with the music: "Some folks are born / Silver spoon in hand / Lord don't they help themselves." The CCR tune had been his selection. Though he certainly wouldn't admit it to his boss (were he around and asking), on a night like this Tubby wanted to hear John Fogerty, the Doors, Jefferson Airplane, or even the Beatles. Anything but Elvis.

After this beer he would call Bo back at Graceland, break the news that he hadn't found Elvis. (He had sworn he'd call three beers ago, but now he meant business.) Some chick was a possible lead, and Tubby thought he'd try to see her later, when Billy Ray left the hospital, but Tubby had decided he'd underplay that one to Bo. If the girl did know something, Tubby figured he should be the man to give the Colonel the news. No reason for Bo to get the credit.

Not that he could imagine good news coming, not in the near future anyway. Tubby hated to mention it to himself—all night he had tried to force the idea from floating into the forefront of his brain, but now the beer had washed over the restraining walls—but if Elvis was . . . if he . . . wasn't coming back, then Tubby would be one of the first to be let go. To be a bodyguard you needed a body to guard. No Einstein, but Tubby Grove knew that much.

"It ain't me," Tubby sang now out loud, "it ain't me, I ain't no millionaire's son. It ain't me, it ain't me; I ain't no fortunate one. . . ."

"Hippie crap," a voice said, suddenly. The sound stopped Tubby dead in his thoughts. "Who's the Commie-symp playin' that shit?"

Before looking down to the end of the bar where he knew the speaker was sitting, Tubby looked straight ahead for confirmation, and the owner and bartender of the joint, Wendell Augustine Root (a Brit who had settled down in Memphis for some reason Tubby could never figure, and who, for reasons even more peculiar, preferred to be called Wendy), removed the slim, golden cigarette holder from his lips with a flourish, laid it down in the Elvis Presley ashtray on the bar, and nodded his head to the left. Yes, the gesture said, it was him. And he meant you.

"Who 'ain't no military son'?" the voice continued, belching out the words. "Who ain't gonna raise the flag?"

Even with the light dim and thick smoke enshrouding the place, Tubby knew who the figure down at the end of the bar was. But Tubby figured it was safer not to look; maybe Arnell Greenaway would let it pass, forget the lyrics of the song Tubby had played soon as he downed his next shot.

But even Arnell would figure it had to be Tubby who had pumped the jukebox full of quarters a good half hour ago, and it was all Grace Slick, Janis Joplin, Jim Morrison, the Beatles, and Fogerty ever since. No one else was at Wendy's.

Tubby grabbed the neck of his beer bottle, snuck a glance to see if Arnell was coming his way.

"Jungle music," Arnell went on. "Beat the drums for the hippies and the niggers why don't you?"

"Nelly, CCR's some good ole boys"—Tubby tried to say it laughing—"John Fogerty—he's white as you and me."

But Arnell wasn't laughing. Not even close.

"Watch who you callin' white." Arnell burped as he spoke, wafting a cloud of beer belch Tubby's way. "Don't you piss on my flag. Ain't that right, Wendy?"

Wendy nodded, smiled nervously. He had heard it all before.

Standing behind the bar, Wendy had been scrawling in his notepad, jotting down ideas for the book on which he had worked since he was tossed out of Oxford over a decade before. The manuscript was to be an all-encompassing History of Our Times, a compendium of cultural commentaries, analyses, and rantings, fiction and fact, philosophy, history, and modern myths, all in a jumble. Tonight he had been focusing on one strand of the work (a surrealistic-fantasy-satire version of his own life) in which he hypothesized a new religion (for lack of a better term) in which modern heroes (from pop culture, politics, etcetera) would be worshipped (or reviled) as heroes, saints, gods, and devils, and in which people could create their own Bible, out of whatever hodgepodge of stories they chose. In the book the central hero of Wendy's faith was Elvis Presley, and the Chili and BBQ Tavern was a temple, subtly infused with Elvis's spirit. The idea of the new religion, Wendy had just written, was theologically sound (Eton and Oxford had taught him that much), but its economics (without governmental imprimatur qualifying the bar for charitable deductions) were less so. He chuckled to himself, wondered if his readers would appreciate the incisive satire of the parable: religion failing for lack of dollars alone.

"Now Wendy here is white as the President," Arnell said. "White as Governor Faubus. White as George Wallace hisself."

While Arnell swilled another shot, then chased it with a beer, Tubby thought for a moment. In comparison to Arnell, he felt sober, clearness of thought being a relative thing, absolutes few on a beer-sodden Saturday night/Sunday morning at Wendy's.

(Wendy, putting his manuscript down and now drying off a beer glass, thought much the same thing, but put it to himself thusly: Einstein, that chap had something there, didn't he?)

Tubby—again, no genius—at least knew his math: Arnell's three-hundred-plus pounds was greater than his two-fifty; six-foot-four beats six-one. And with three brawls a week minimum for practice, Arnell better know how to toss you out of a window. The only hope was that Arnell would calm down or collapse on the bar in a drunken heap before they got to fighting.

But then Tubby heard a new record drop in the jukebox: Jimi Hendrix of all things, transforming "The Star Spangled Banner" into a chaotic pileup of feedback and electric screeches, and then he remembered the songs he had selected afterward only got worse: Jefferson Airplane's "Volunteers" (he imagined Arnell's face when Grace Slick sang, "See the people on the street? Wanta revolution?"), then Bob Dylan, the Doors, then more CCR, "Run Through the Jungle" and "Bad Moon Rising." Tubby didn't even like the stuff—he just chose them to rile Elvis, wherever he was—but Arnell would never believe that.

(Wendy's thoughts were also focused on the songs: music, he noted, served as a leitmotif to the scene, almost Wagnerian in depth.)

"We're all white here, Arnell," Tubby said, as the anthem, under Hendrix's direction, became unrecognizable. "All brothers, ain't we? Like Elvis says to me just the other day, 'Tubby, ain't that Arnell the whitest man this side of the Gulf of Mexico?' And I say—"

"Don't you bring your Lord and Master into this one, boy. He started us on this whole mess anyway."

"What the hell, Nelly." Tubby looked across the bar for help, but Wendy just looked away, served Arnell up another boilermaker. "I don't even know what you're talkin' about."

"You sure as hell do. Played that nigger music, and he sung it like one too, flailin' all about like some damned ape with his thing hangin' out his fly just about. And now look: the niggers 'emselves followed him right on stage, and we got girls hangin' and gropin' 'em, front of God and everyone." Arnell tossed down another shot, then chased it with a beer. "Damn."

(Wendy was thinking that Arnell had a point there too. In fact, Wendy had explained it in a chapter of his all-encompassing History: Elvis had served as a Trojan horse [as it were] bringing black music across the color lines of 1950s America, eventually blowing up the walls. . . . Arnell, in his own misguided way, was right. Though as to whether the effects of Elvis Presley were favorable or not—well, there Wendy parted company with the Yank rather drastically. . . .)

"And so now you got the protesters out there," Arnell went on, "burning the flag and so they tie the fightin' man's arms so he gets all shot to hell by the Reds. All began with that nigger music. Have your Elvis explain that to Rich, next time you see him."

(Arnell, Wendy knew, meant the next time Tubby saw Elvis, not Rich. Rich was Arnell's brother. Rich was dead, killed in Vietnam.)

"Nelly," Tubby said, "I KNOW Elvis! He's even met Governor Wallace himself, more than once. You ever met Wallace?"

From his corner of the bar, Arnell cut a glance at Tubby, stayed quiet.

"Ever met the Vice President?" Tubby went on. "Elvis has. And he talked with some John Birchers just the other day, 'bout some security problems we been havin'! Don't tell me about Elvis Presley!"

Arnell had lost a step, Tubby could see.

"Well," Arnell's voice was a little shaky, "what about this music you been playin' here? I ain't been hearin' any of your precious Elvis."

In fact, Bob Dylan was now singing "Of war and peace, the truth just twists, its curfew gull just glides." Tubby didn't know what to say about that one; he didn't have a clue what it meant. "And the princess and the prince," Dylan went on, "discuss what's real and what is not." That didn't help either.

Tubby pulled a dollar out of his pocket and slapped it down on the bar.

"Wendy, set my friend up," he said, and then he winked at Arnell. "Elvis is buyin'." Tubby lifted his glass up to toast Arnell from a distance. "Lord, Nell, it's only music."

Tubby looked at his watch. Past three. He got up from his stool and walked to the pay phone to call Bo, shaking his head all the while.

Wendy poured Arnell another beer.

Only music, Wendy said to himself. My ass.

3 9

PRATFALL

PALMER WILSON WAS LYING on his side in an alley on O Street, just off 14th, the former site of his pants seat set firmly within the ragged end of a rusty garbage can. From where he lay he could see streetlights, though the neon sign advertising Ray's Saloon had just cut off. An hour or so after he peeked outside to watch one of the strippers escort the guy who had staggered out the door, Palmer slipped out of the bar. Sometime later he too had fallen, his pants caught the top of the can, which tore them straight through to the flesh, so he could feel the cold wind, and then, as he rolled with the can, the putrid blend of sewage residue, water, and chunks of half-melted ice sloshed forward. His elbows were scraped and sore, his hips banged and bruised, his skull reverberating with the thunderous timbre of a Tibetan gong, but most of all it was the iciness of his ass that struck him now.

At least his lips were affixed to the warm mouth of Joe M. II, from which Palmer was sucking like an infant. Woozy with drink, he put away his flask and imagined himself, not as Wallingford Wilson (in Palmer's mind, his father was never Dad, or even Wally), nor Joe McCarthy nor J. Edgar Hoover nor Whittaker Chambers nor Barry Goldwater nor John Finlator nor Richard Nixon, and certainly not, if he happened to be in ancient Rome, a straight sober sentry at attention. No. Palmer closed his eyes and imagined himself as Charlie Chaplin. Harpo Marx. Buster Keaton.

He was a fool.

This was funny.

Ben Rollins had woken up minutes before, in Lafayette Park, and now he was walking up 14th Street. Sunday was like this, more often than not, since he'd gotten back from 'Nam; you stayed up most of the night Saturday bullshitting, while Angie took care of business . . . then slept through the next day. The rest of the week was a struggle to find some middle ground. Then Saturday rolled in again.

Hanging out with Lester and Sunshine had gotten his mind off the afternoon at the White House, the deal with the medal and Nixon. Which was fine; in fact, was the point. Lester didn't rub it in either. Lester was like that. Cool.

His friends had got him thinking about the future. The disability checks and work at Danny's were enough to get by on, but that isn't what he wanted. School, maybe: there was a lot to learn. Maybe politics, in one form or another. Take on the Nixons of the world. Lester had a point. Sunshine, too.

He turned right on O Street, heading east.

What did I ever do to the Lord of Dumb Luck, Palmer thought to himself, to deserve such blessed fortune? He could see the photograph he was holding in his hand (he wasn't certain how he had gotten the picture), and he could see the face of the man walking toward him. They were the same: his quarry, Ben Rollins, paying as much mind to the alley to his right as Palmer might to the stock portfolio of wise Wallingford Wilson. Palmer pulled out the other sheet of paper from his pocket, the instructions he had jotted down a lifetime ago, when he spoke to his boss, John Finlator. The ink blurry, illegible; his memory of the conversation dim. Something about *agents provocateurs*, a phrase he loved, though didn't quite understand. (Did the agent do the provoking or was he provoked?) Or was it a setup job? . . . Anyway he had work to do.

The quarry was walking on Palmer's side of the street; it would pass just a foot or so in front of him any second. The street was quiet and empty. As it should be, Palmer thought. A man alone with his quarry.

Palmer shimmied out of the garbage can, then grabbed the edges of the open side and lay down on the pavement, feigning sleep. The rest had done him good, and the cold air reinvigorated him. Oh, Palmer felt fine, stealthy as a tiger, sly as Hoover himself. Lying in wait for his quarry, he felt his biceps rise, his fists tighten their hold on the sides of the can like a vise, his thighs pumping in vigorous, preparatory thrusts . . . though his head was still victim to those gong-bearing Tibetans. He let go of the can and pulled out Joe M. II, opened it. Empty. He lifted the flask over his head and shook it; only a drop trickled down, hung on the lip like an Acapulcoan cliff diver, then plunged onto his tongue, outstretched and waiting below.

When he looked up from the flask, the quarry was gone. Palmer stood up and looked toward 14th Street, then the other way. There he was. Still walking, now past him, halfway to the far corner, near 13th Street. Palmer grabbed the garbage can, but the top rolled off and hit the pavement, clamored like a cymbal, and he ran down the street, full speed.

Ben heard the clatter and turned around, saw a bum run toward him, waddling more like it, his arms outstretched around a huge metal garbage can that seemed as big as he was. Ben figured the man was crazy, maybe just running blindly ahead, but as he got closer the bum's eyes seemed to fix on him. Ben waited, prepared to dodge one way or the other, but when the man got closer, he took off into the air; Ben wasn't sure if he had fallen or if he intended to leap forward with the can. Ben stepped aside and the bum landed on top of the can, then rolled off it, onto the sidewalk. Ben couldn't help but feel sorry for him. Then the bum got up, turned around to pick the can back up, and Ben saw that the man's entire butt was bare, bleeding around the edges, exposed through a huge hole in the seat of his pants.

When Palmer regained control of the can and turned back around, he saw his quarry staring at him. His timing could not have been more perfect if J. Edgar Hoover himself had timed and choreographed it. The fall had drawn Ben's attention to him.

"Pssssst," Palmer hissed. Waved Ben to come closer.

Ben walked a few steps toward him.

"Need to talk to you, brother," Palmer said. What he thought he recalled from Finlator's instructions played in his head like an eight-track tape: *agent provocateur* job. "Got a job you'd be interested in. The Pentagon, blown sky high. You'd like that, wouldn't you?"

Ben took a step back. The whiskey smell emanating from the bum was strong enough to overpower the stench of garbage in the alley.

"You've got the wrong guy," Ben said.

"I'm serious! We got it all worked out!"

"No thanks." Ben turned around, began to walk away.

Which left Palmer no alternative; none that came to mind, anyway. He pulled out one of the plastic bags that one of Finlator's men had given him (was it to be used as *payment* or *payback*?), ran toward Ben full speed and, before the quarry could turn around, hit him with the bags, clenching his fist so the clear plastic covers burst. A cloud of white powder erupted, and Palmer spread it on Ben's pants, his hair, inside his pockets.

"Dig?!" Palmer yelled, patting the powder, fanning it all over Ben. "Dig?!"

Then he ran, leaving Ben Rollins alone in the alley, puzzled, dusting himself off, without a clue that the powder that now covered his clothes, and underneath, and in his pockets, was heroin of the purest grade.

4 0

NIXON UNDER THE STARS

"MAX SHARPE."

The room was so small that simply by turning around to reach the radio behind him on the bookcase, Sharpe had almost collided with him. That is, with the leader of the Free World. Conservative politician extraordinaire. A mythic figure in Max Sharpe's political consciousness: Richard Nixon.

The two had never spoken before.

He (capital *H*) couldn't know his (submicroscopic *h*) name. In fact, now that Sharpe (mouth frozen like a dining Pompeiian) looked at Nixon, it was clear that the President was just reading the name tag that Sharpe had taped outside of the door to the office. But still: now He knew his name.

Sharpe tried to speak—moved his jaws up and down, up and down—but nothing came out, only teeth-chattering terror. Moses trying not to drop the stone tablets: that sort of thing.

"Ba ba ba, ba ba ba ba ba," the President said. It took a moment for Sharpe to decipher what he was saying or, rather, singing; Nixon was doing his best to sing along with Simon and Garfunkel.

"'Life I love you, all is groovy'?" Nixon said, slowly and uncertainly, like a tourist translating. "That's what the hippies listen to, huh?"

"Yes, Mr. President." Sharpe, still looking at Nixon, reached blindly to turn the volume down on the radio, which was now, he realized, quite loud. Thundering. "Exactly, sir." But he hit the wrong dial, accidentally turned the channel so the decibel level remained the same, only the song changed to the Doors, Jim Morrison singing, "THERE'S A KILLER OUT ALONE, THERE'S A KILLER OUT ALONE. . . ."

"Wild," the President said. "Groo-vy?"

"Yes, Mr. President." Sharpe's hand madly groped about the transistor, spinning every dial he could feel. Now Grace Slick screamed, "REMEMBER WHAT THE DORMOUSE SAID! FEED YOUR HEAD!" and Sharpe smiled at Nixon as he reached, still groping; then Country Joe McDonald sang, "IT'S ONE, TWO, THREE, WHAT ARE WE FIGHTING FOR? DON'T ASK ME I DON'T GIVE A DAMN! NEXT STOP IS VIETNAM. . . ."

"Hippie talk," Sharpe said, "that's all it is. Drug-induced"—finally he hit the right dial, and the music stopped—"GOBBLEDEEGOOK!!!!!"

The President took a step away from him. Sharpe hadn't realized he'd been screaming until it was too late. His last "gook" echoed down the hallway in the West Wing, through the central foyer, up the stairs to, Sharpe imagined, the residential section, awakening Pat and the kids.

The President poked his head back into the office, holding his chin with one hand, an elbow with the other, then poked out like an unshaven ostrich. The more Nixon stayed there, perched in the doorway, the more Sharpe realized that it was he who held the upper social hand, that Nixon was so uncomfortable with ordinary social relations that there was no reason to be frightened.

"Burning the midnight oil?" Nixon said.

"Yes," Sharpe said. "Exactly, sir. In fact, I was working on this"—he grabbed his memo from the desk—"the Get High on Life campaign. I think it's just what we—you—us—need, in '72, I mean. It's a—well, you can see—I call it HOLE—military acronym—maybe John—Mr. Ehrlichman mentioned it?"

The President paused for a moment, muttered, "HOLE?" then seemed to ponder the word. He didn't look at the memo Sharpe was holding out for him.

"This Calley business," Nixon said, finally. "The trial and—oh, it's tough. A tough fucking business."

Sharpe nodded in agreement.

High on Life would have to wait.

"Yes, Mr. President sir," Sharpe said. "I want you to know that the, uh, Peoria problem is being taken care of. I'm working on the, the leakage. You recall . . . ?"

"Right." The President looked straight at Sharpe. Sharpe wasn't sure if he even knew that Sharpe was dealing with that . . . problem. "Of course."

"And that business in the Rose Garden," Sharpe said, "the Negro, the medal, the"—he made a throwing motion—"it's all well in hand." Sharpe wondered whether he should remind Nixon that he had selected Rollins for the ceremony.

Fall on his sword; that sort of thing. Thought better. "I'm handling it all, Mr. President."

"The one-armed boy?" Nixon said. Then he smiled. "Wonderful scene. Exposes the fucking ugliness we're dealing with. We offer them honor, and they turn it into disgrace. Perfect."

The President took a step away from the office, out into the hall. Then he said, "Have you ever seen the stars from the White House lawn?"

"No, Mr. President," Sharpe said. "I can't say that I have."

"The view," Nixon said, looking up at the ceiling, "extraordinary."

Nixon turned toward the end of the hall. Sharpe stepped out of the office to follow, but then Nixon pointed back to the office.

"That," the President said, "take it."

"The . . . ?" Sharpe hurriedly stepped back inside, looking at Nixon. Sharpe pointed to a briefing book on welfare reform, but the President shook his head; so he grabbed another—on crime—but that wasn't it, either. Then a few surveillance files on Muskie and Ted Kennedy. No, the President's interests lay elsewhere. "This?" Sharpe said, finally.

The President nodded yes and Sharpe picked up the small transistor radio, and followed Nixon as he walked down the hall, out the door.

The air outside was brisk, slapping the two men as they stood on the lawn, invigorating them. Once they had stepped outside, Secret Service men had hastily posted themselves along the fence, but they didn't spoil the view, the vastness of the White House lawn, brightly illuminated by the nearly full moon, the security lights emanating from the house, the fence, and the guard posts, and the radiant, flickering stars that appeared to dance before them as they stood, heads cocked upward, hands bracing their lower backs, gazing at the wondrous display that seemed, to Sharpe, to have been summoned solely as entertainment for the President and his entourage of choice. A dancing harem before the king. Wise men bearing jewels. Shoulders weary from the weight of the world, and then a brief respite.

"Look at it," the President said. His deep, gravelly voice carried across the lawn, though he did not speak loudly.

While the President paused the only sound that could be heard was a steady pounding of a not-too-distant drum, one thud after another in perfectly timed three-second intervals: thud—one-two-three—thud—one-two-three. Sharpe had heard it—who in the White House hadn't?—virtually every day, at almost every hour, a constant antiwar vigil. ("I'd offer the bastard a job to get him to stop," Pat Buchanan had said once, "but he's already got one, I'll bet: welfare queen.") But in the quiet of the late night the sound was louder than ever, a thundering boom.

The President breathed deeply, so deep that his stomach sucked in, his chest out. Nixon was still wearing his suit from the day, a dark blue pinstripe and white shirt with a red rep tie only slightly loosened around the collar. When he let his breath out he shook his arms, holding them out from his body, then shook his hands as if some spirit were wending its way out from the bottom of his diaphragm, to exit his body through the fingertips.

"Ahhhhhh . . ." Nixon looked down, then turned his head to the side, a quizzical expression. Hearing the drummer for the first time since they'd gone outside, Sharpe realized.

"He's persistent," the President said, "give him that. Steady resolve." He pounded his closed fist into his palm a few times. "It's tribal. Something African, from before they came over, to our country." Nixon banged his palm three more times, then stopped when he failed to keep a steady beat. "It's not all the young people. A few of them don't understand, the stakes I mean, what this war is about, but there are always a few bad apples. History will tell you that there are always a few bad apples. A rebellious element. Forces of chaos. I know they are out there, out to get me. I know they want to bring me down. They think they will bring me down. But they are wrong. They underestimate me. That is grave error. As any football coach will tell you that is error. And that is where they are wrong. In the underestimating."

Nixon glanced at Sharpe's face for an instant, then looked away.

"You're young, ambitious," Nixon went on. "A bright fellow." Sharpe thought it might be a question but, uncertain of the correct Nixonian answer, or if the query was rhetorical, remained quiet. "When I was about your age I was in Congress already, taking on Alger Hiss. To this day"—Nixon raised his voice—"you hear those liberals whining about that one, claiming Chambers was a liar, claiming this and that. The only time you'll ever hear a Jew stand up for a German, when Richard Nixon's on the other side. There was a hole in the line"—he weaved an outstretched hand before him—"daylight. I was never graced with great talent, no Kennedy money or good looks. But I saw an opening and I took it." He smiled, still looking straight ahead. "I can never respect them, the liberals. Not like the Russians. Brezhnev, Khrushchev, I can respect.

We need each other, we depend on each other, and we each understand that. The fucking liberals—Kennedy, Muskie, and such—they will never defeat us because there are certain fundamental truths they can never understand. They stand up with the Communists, the liberals do, but there's an opportunity for them there, and they fail to see it. The Russians and us would never destroy each other. We're like two fighters, holding each other up, punched out in the late rounds. If you see the Russians go down, Brezhnev or whoever, Richard Nixon will be next on the canvas. And I don't mean just myself. Without the Russians, who will we have? The Negroes? The Jews? No, they can help in a few quarters, but today, in America, there is only one enemy that will work on the electoral level, and that is the Communist. Without him, we turn on ourselves. But the fucking liberals—that's what they don't understand."

Nixon went quiet for a minute, then turned to look toward Sharpe, though not at him. He was looking at Sharpe's hands.

"Well," the President said, "let's hear it. The young people, let's hear what they're listening to."

It was the radio Nixon was looking at. Sharpe turned it on.

"I understand them, you know," Nixon said. "You were there, weren't you? That night with Lincoln?" Sharpe nodded his head. "You saw how I can relate to them."

On the radio Bob Dylan was singing, "It's a hard rain's a-gonna fall." Nixon turned away, to the other side of the lawn, and the two listened.

Oh what did you see, my blue-eyed son?
Oh what did you see, my darling young one?
I saw a new born baby with wild wolves all around it
I saw a highway of diamonds with nobody on it
I saw a black branch with blood that kept drippin'
I saw a room full of men with their hammers a-bleedin'.

The men listened to the radio for a while, no one speaking.

Then Nixon said quietly, to himself, "The radio would play."

"Sir?"

"I would drive Pat at nights," he went on. "She wanted to date and I was not the man to sweep her off her feet. Richard Nixon was never handed anything.

So I agreed to drive her; if she was to date, I would drive her back and forth. There were hours when she and her man of the evening would be dining, or at the movies, and I would be alone, waiting for them to finish. But the radio would play for me."

They were silent again, but for the radio, and Max Sharpe thought he saw tears well up in the eyes of Richard Nixon.

"They laughed at me—her date, Pat—I know they did. And in college, at Whittier, when I went out for the football team each year, and they ground me into the mud each practice, and then never let me on the team, I know they laughed at Richard Nixon. Four years, I scraped the mud off my face and took my position again, and got knocked down again, and there was more mud and I scraped it off and trotted back to the line. Four years, but I never got farther than the practice bench. My dad loved football, loved fighters. Men must be tough in this world, right?"

Nixon's eyes were closed now and, yes, there were tears rolling down either side of his turned-up nose, but his mouth was firm, determined.

"But who's laughing now? Who's laughing at Richard Nixon?"

The President breathed deep, wiped his face dry with his fingers, opened his eyes.

"There's nothing like the playoffs," Nixon said. "Just a week from now. Roger Staubach, and Hill." He smacked one clenched fist into an open palm. "And Brodie. But I don't see the Cowboys losing, with Staubach so cool and steady in the pocket, going deep with the bomb. Like Kennedy; John, I mean, not the young ones. The fucking bastard."

Nixon paused, then turned toward the White House.

"Two and a half million tons," he said. "More bombs than we dropped in all of World War II. That's what they tell me, the Pentagon folks, we've dropped just since I came in. That is what Calley understood. We are dealing here with history, the historical level, that grand plane of events. History will judge us, and she will judge us judiciously, with an eye across time. We're at a bend in the road, a historical bend in the road. A point where rules change. Absurd to act as if the ordinary rules apply up here. They can't and they don't. It will only lead to disaster if we act as if they do, as if we are bound by the petty laws of the moment. *Then* history will not be kind to us, I assure you. Calley understood that when the bombs will not do it, the rules of engagement have changed. He saw that, that bend in the road. Calley took the new route. Who are we to say—who is the *New York Times*, Sulzberger and fucking Cronkite and Rather and Ben Bradlee to say he was wrong."

In Nixon's periodic silences only the radio could be heard—Hendrix introducing "Machine Gun": "For all the soldiers fighting in Chicago, in San Francisco . . ."—and, in the background, the beating of the drum from Lafayette Park: thud—one-two-three—thud—one-two-three—thud.

"Hear me, son. Listen to me like a father. If you want to make it in this business, there are certain facts about history which you must understand," Nixon said. "For one, no great empire has ever thrived because of its friends. Think about that. Almost by necessity this is true. Any great empire frightens everyone outside the empire, including its so-called friends. Friends are temporary luxuries. Illusory and grossly overvalued. But enemies: the great empires all had them. The 'Other.' It is so much easier to unite people around the Other than friends. All this is lost on the liberals. Fear is the great motivator: I didn't say it first, but there it is. This is key—and I'm not just talking campaign strategy. Change is everywhere, with the Negroes, the drugs; girls want to go to school, work—become boys, men; crime. And Vietnam is not a winning hand for us—nothing for us to be ashamed of, you understand, or run away from—but nothing to put us front and center.

"So there are these fears. You go back to our list of enemies—the Panthers, the hippies, the anti-establishment types, as they call themselves. We have to convince the people—not convince them, they already know this, but remind them that those forces will take over if the fucking Democrats win. People want order. They realize that when you mix people together they turn on each other; we didn't make them that way—we don't claim to be the Lord Almighty; we don't claim that sort of blasphemy—and yet that's exactly what the fucking liberals are hell-bent on doing: mixing them all up together, tearing down the walls of the zoo. Now when you do that, can you claim surprise when the lion preys on the gazelle? Do you weep over the gored ox? People like to keep to themselves, each to their own kind. Now I want the Democrats painted with those enemies' colors, paint 'em black, so when people see Ted Kennedy or Muskie, or whoever the nominee is, they think: hippie fag, burning the flag, spitting on our soldiers. I want this so imbued in the American psyche that it no longer operates at the rational level—none of it: not why the enemies are enemies, not what the enemies have ever said or done, not what the connection is between them and Kennedy or McGovern or even Scoop Jackson—whoever. I want visceral reactions. Blood-boiling, instinctive rage."

Nixon had been speaking more and more rapidly, his face becoming more red, his voice louder, but now he stopped. He breathed deep and Sharpe turned the radio down so he would not miss a word. Silence took over the lawn for an instant. Sharpe stared with awe at the Master. When Nixon spoke again he spoke quietly.

"Now. While all of this is going on, while these primal concepts are soaking into the bloodstream, I want another, more obvious campaign. Something with the same message, you understand, but gentler. Something with a firm but smiling face, something the President himself could be associated with, but that would emerge from the people themselves. That is key. You have to understand that, as in battle, politics takes place on many levels simultaneously. All facets of the psyche must be accounted for. So, at the same instant that we make sure the voter satisfies his primal emotions—his fear, revenge, his self-preservation—we must provide him with cover, something that lets him believe that he is *not* acting out of fear, or out of hatred, but out of—I'll say it—love. Hit the fucking sanctimonious Dems where they live. Gives our men something to take into the coffee shops with them, to do battle with the saintly motherfuckers. With the fucking socialist-leaning press, drumming the conscience card day-in, day-out, this is essential. I will win."

The President paused, fixed his gaze into the darkness before him.

"My mother"—and now the President's voice lowered and almost cracked—"was a saint. A deeply religious woman. She would speak to me of the voice of the Creator. Faith, honesty above all. But with my father there was the rod and the switch." He paused, listened to a cold breeze pass through the White House grounds, out into Lafayette Park. "I will win. I will clean up the dirty streets and the dirty air and the dirty water, if that is what they want. But you can clean up all that and have sanitized clean cities, but no color, no warmth. No human qualities. The real problem is finding some meaning to life."

The President shook his head. It was cold and late but Richard Nixon seemed not to notice, immune to the elements and time. The President looked up at the sky and so, then, did Max Sharpe. He tried to see the stars as Richard Nixon saw them.

And so they both looked up at the beautiful vast American sky that, Max Sharpe was certain, Richard Nixon held in custody for the nation for four years, and almost certainly eight. No wonder the President's shoulders were hunched: a Herculean task to carry earth and sky, as protesters jeered him, spat on him, knowing that he, arms busy with earth and sky, weighty matters, could not defend himself, fight back. Oh, Richard Nixon was an easy target, with his sweaty forehead, his crooked ski-jump nose, those thick, arching brows that seemed fit for a Hollywood villain. Tricky Dick and all that: an undeserved reputation, surely, for slick maneuvers. Not that Richard Nixon never bent a law, or used a slick maneuver, but who could not, holding earth and sky, taking on Ho Chi Minh, Brezhnev, Mao, Castro, the Kennedy clan, the Negroes, and the hippies all at once? Necessity forced David, overmatched by Goliath, to become a trickster. Love, war. Earth, sky. Weighty matters, up there in the night sky and all around us, here on the White House lawn with the blessed President of the United States. Weighty matters indeed.

Then Nixon put his hand to his chin again, and began to walk toward the White House. The Secret Service scurried toward him from the outer fence, enclosing him in a loose half circle of protection. Sharpe took a last look at the flickering sky, then walked quickly so he could reach the door before the President and open it for him. But before they walked inside the President put his hand on Sharpe's shoulder and looked him in the eyes. Sharpe had no earthly idea what he was thinking, or even if he saw him.

"I just want to ask you one favor," the President said. "If I'm assassinated, I want you to have them play 'Dante's Inferno.' And have Lawrence Welk produce it."

4 1

BO AND THE COLONEL

"GOT MY BOY BACK, BO?"

It was almost morning. Colonel Tom Parker was beginning to wear on Bo Price.

"We're workin' on it, Colonel," Bo said.

He was in the sunken game room at Graceland now, shooting pool, phone clenched under his chin. He had been trying for a trick shot—hit all four walls, then the eight-ball—when Colonel Parker called. No luck there either, so far.

Bo set up the eight-ball again.

"I got Vern and Tubby on the road, and I've—"

"Means you got nothing. Don't bull a bull-thrower, boy. What that lard-ridden buddy of yours come up with?"

"Tubby?"

"What other lard you got in your brood?"

Only Tubby, Bo thought. A good guy to down beers with, but incompetent? Useless? Yes and yes. Bo figured Tubby had probably never left his bar stool at Wendy's all day, that he'd even made up the story about talking to a crazy girl who didn't know anything. But since Graceland was Bo's show, whatever Tubby did or didn't do ultimately fell on Bo, far as Colonel Tom Parker was concerned . . . so any way you looked at it, it wasn't going to do Bo Price any good to dump on Tubby.

"Matter of fact, Colonel, he got some leads."

"Leads? You got Sherlock Holmes on the job?" Bo could visualize the Colonel, feet up on his desk back home in Kentucky, teeth clenching a long cigar, chuckling. "Speak English, boy."

"Yeah, well, Colonel, who knows if it'll come to anything, but there's this girl, but the thing is she's in the hospital now, and none too coherent if you believe the doctors—"

"But you talked to her."

"Tubby did."

"And what did she say?"

"Well"—how do you tell the Colonel that Tubby labeled the girl so crazy he wouldn't ask her details?—"this girl, the doctors say she's nuts, truth be, so we can't—"

"*Can't?* Don't think I know that word. Ah, hell."

The Colonel fell silent for a few seconds, and Bo could hear him slam his cigar down, obliterating the stub.

"I was sure he'd be back by now," the Colonel said. "Figured he couldn't make it on the outside."

"No one did," Bo said. "Never done anything like this before."

"At least you got Graceland covered bow to stern." The Colonel chuckled. "At least we know your Lord and Savior's not home."

"Colonel, you know someone's got to be here. Now I've been on the phone—"

The Colonel paused, exhaled.

"Anyway, I was thinking," the Colonel said, now in a calm, reflective tone. "I'm not writing him off, mind you, but I'm just considering. I mean, we're in a business here. Now if we're farming corn and the weatherman says there's hard rain on the way, a chance that a flood'll wipe out the whole crop, even if the weatherman's word's as good as a Jew's, it's still something you've got to consider."

"You're saying Elvis is . . ." Bo mouthed the word, but his voice box refused to say it. "That he might not come back?"

"I'm not saying anything, understand, I'm just considering. Listen: when I was in the carnival, back in the old days, I had this hermaphrodite midget that was just pulling in the crowds like you wouldn't believe. This little guy was three feet, tops, and we had him dolled up with some real lifelike looking titties—sewed them onto his chest—and we glued some whiskers on him just to clinch the deal. Anyway, I'm raking in money in wheelbarrows on this guy—it's a wonder what people'll pay to see—so we're going good but then my little man—forget his name, hell of a trouper though—it turns out the needles infected him. Boy's got a fever, and the whiskers fall out. Then he gets this red ridge on his chest, two big red circles, and soon he's coated with these red lumps. In a few weeks he gets better, but his chest is ruined. So the Colonel thinks back to what his momma taught him, about lemons and lemonade, and it comes to me. I paint *the rest* of his body with red splotches, glue on some more lumps and now he's 'The Creature.' We move on to the next town and he's part of the show again. Never drew the same crowds as before, but what are you going to do?"

There was another pause and Bo thought for a minute. The Colonel was always showing off how smart he was supposed to be with his carnival stories, but Bo knew that even if his mind was no match for the Colonel's, he was smart enough to know that if Elvis was gone, there was still money to make with Colonel Tom Parker. The thing was to think like the Colonel.

Bo picked up his pool stick, lined up his shot at the cue ball. Elvis had taught Bo to believe in synchronistic effects, so as he failed to hit the eight-ball once again the idea crept into his head, with inescapable certainty, that Elvis could really be dead.

"So," Bo said, "if he's, uh, dead?"

"You got an idea, boy?"

"Well, I was just thinking." Bo placed the stick down on the pool table, thought for another second. "Maybe . . . we can sell tickets to the funeral?"

4 2

DREAMS

THE FLUID THE DOCTOR SHOT into Elvis's arm traveled through his veins directly into a gland in his brain (the name of which Elvis knew, honest he did, but it had plum vanished from his mind), akin to the one on which sodium pentothal, the truth serum of detective movie fame, operates. Except that this gland was the master of surrealistic truth, the gland that triggers dreams. As soon as the lights went out in the room at Tommy's place, and he lay his head down on the pillow, someone threw a switch illuminating the stage lights that lined the walls of his skull, and the show was on.

There was an ancient temple, one in which a world king sat and received favors for his corrupt rulings, dispensing a wicked, misguided justice. Elvis knew this was both the temple Samson had crashed down by karate-chopping the pillars, and the one Jesus had preached outside of, except that it also looked Tibetan, or was it ancient Egyptian? Hieroglyphics on the pillars said something about a show tonight being canceled, the International in Las Vegas was sorry to say, but the Beatles, Tom Jones, Pat Boone, and Robert Goulet would be substituting for the previously scheduled Elvis Presley. Billy Graham was at the dais, but he wasn't speaking; just mouthing words and nothing came out. The choir was an odd mix: Priscilla and Vernon were front and center; beside them were Bo, Tubby, and the boys; and behind them were George Wallace, James Bond, Superman, J. Edgar Hoover. Then he heard a voice say, "I've been blessed, I was the hero in the comic books. I was the hero," and he could see that he, Elvis, was at the dais, no longer Billy Graham, but his face was changing as he spoke, one publicity shot melting into another: a few years ago as Dr. John Carpenter in *Change of Habit*; to onstage in '55; his army crew cut; a fuller head of hair in an army uniform in *G.I. Blues*; his wedding with Priscilla in '67 in the midst of those Hollywood years; a country boy, fat-cheeked like his momma; then '53, singing behind the wheel of his truck in the day, picking on his guitar at night, finally saving enough to buy a one-song recording session. Someone wanted to crucify him, that would be the final dramatic act to this scene, but he didn't know who, or why. Colonel Parker now stood up from the back row of the choir, towering over the others as his vast trench coat covered the faces of Priscilla and little Lisa Marie. "You ain't no superhero, but look what I got you," and the Colonel pointed up and Elvis could now see that the temple had no roof, and the sky was twinkling with dollar bill stars, bright as the Vegas strip at midnight, driving in from the desert. There was a line of Negroes trying to get in; he recognized some from Beale Street; a man with a gold tooth, a one-armed kid in an army uniform, and singers: Junior Parker, Sleepy John Estes, Arthur Crudup, Smiley Lewis; some of those rhythm and blues boys: Little Richard, Fats Domino, Chuck Berry; and they were all leaping up into the night, trying like hell to catch even one bill, but they couldn't, the bills only teased them, floating down close to their reach; then, as they jumped, Elvis yanked them away, out of their grasp, and the Negroes were screaming, and the Colonel was laughing, and in the choir Governor Wallace yelled, "Good boy!" and so did Vice President Agnew who, he now saw, was also there, and Elvis, now in a white jeweled jumpsuit, was laughing too, but then he was crying, his younger self, arms around Junior Parker and James Cotton in Sam Phillips's studio back in Memphis, crying 'cause his buddies couldn't get the money and it was theirs. Then someone said "Go man, go!" and everyone outside forgot about the money, and some white businessmen were handing him an award onstage, saying he was the outstanding young man of all time. Things were fine.

Then the music faded away and he saw that at the very top of the temple rested a huge throne, and in it sat the President, resplendent in white robe, scepter, and crown. This was where things quickly repeated themselves, like takes in a movie shoot, each scene differing from the other only in minute details, primarily in the costume that he, Elvis, the Son of God, wore. Because first when he stood on the stage (which was at the bottom of a long stone staircase that led to the throne), he was black as Junior Parker; and he looked up at the throne and saw Governor Wallace and Lester Maddox, whispering in Nixon's ears just as Elvis noticed some angry black spirit take over him. *Make me like it used to be. Let me try this all over again.*

Cut.

Next scene: Elvis is standing at the bottom of the stairs, looking up, but he is back in the mid-'50s, swiveling his hips, and the girls everywhere are screaming, and King Nixon coughs up a vast gob of spit from deep within his bowels, then propels it out his throat and down the stairs, heading toward the young rebel, fast as a thunderbolt.

Cut.

Elvis looks up the stairs and opens his cape, flashing the inside which is lined with law enforcement badges. Director Hoover has a huge golden badge on his chest—the ultimate, a magic pass that opens every door, turns back time and lets him jump on an old image-cloud and ride it—and Elvis nods to him and asks, *Can I have one too?*

Cut.

Richard Nixon is in the White House now, and Elvis, in his purple velvet jumpsuit and cape, Elvis today, could lose a few pounds. It is evening and dollar bills are twinkling in the dark night sky, and somewhere out there, blocks away, Junior Parker is still leaping in vain for a single bill, jumping up and down for so long he's forgotten why he's doing it. And there are young people circling the White House, hissing at Elvis, so he changes shapes for them: long hair like John Lennon; an Afro like Billy Preston; a beard; then his old, young self. And while he's knocking on the door to the White House, he's still changing forms, as if his head was a roulette wheel, time spins that fast, and when Nixon opens the door, he doesn't have a clue why he's there, or what he's going to do.

PART THREE

Sunday

L.A. TO WASHINGTON

SHARPE'S MORNING

MAX SHARPE'S HEAD WAS STILL abuzz, his body light, adrift. Back at work on three hours' sleep, adrenaline had kicked in, creating what he knew to be natural opiates, which gave him the airy enthusiasm that now possessed him. (His left-leaning law school roommate had called such a sensation a "natural high," but Sharpe had no independent means to confirm or deny the comparison.) Ordinarily his lack of sleep and sustenance would sap his strength, but his experience last night had instilled within him a boundless energy. He was high—yes, he could use the term. High on life.

He, Max Sharpe, had been touched by the Master. He was chosen. Blessed.

Sharpe couldn't help but notice the parallels. Like Nixon, Sharpe was a young lawyer, ambitious, morally certain of the evil of Communism; and like Nixon he was smart, knew how to turn a hint of public sentiment into a political juggernaut. Could Sharpe groom himself for a run at Congress, in '74, say, then perhaps even the vice presidency in '76? It was a pipe dream, sure, but with the President's support, who knew . . . ? Max Sharpe had thought stranger thoughts.

It would be bad form for Sharpe to boast of his meeting with the President, but perhaps he could just drop that he had "run into" Nixon last night, casually as he could. Ehrlichman would be in the office, even this early on a Sunday.

He dialed up his boss and mentor.

"John? It's Max."

"Heard you and the Pres had a talk last night," Ehrlichman said.

Sharpe's next words caught in his throat. The news had been transmitted to the inner circle almost immediately, as if by magic. Such things were known to happen in the White House.

"We need to talk," Ehrlichman said. He sounded busy. "I need an update from you."

"But the President. What did he—?"

"Keep up the good work, Max." And Ehrlichman hung up.

Sharpe put down the phone. He still had time to edit a HOLE memo to lay out on Ehrlichman's desk for Monday morning: now was the perfect time to push the idea. Should he copy the President on it? Not yet.

Then the phone rang.

"Max Sharpe here."

"Line's secure?" a gruff voice said.

"What?"

"Is the line secure?"

"Who is this?"

"Your friend in the Bureau's friend—boss, really—"

Now Sharpe's lack of sleep was catching up with him, all of the sudden. He began to diagram the sentence on the paper before him: *friend in Bureau* on one side; *man on phone* on the other. But where was the friend of his . . . ?

"The black bag job?" the man whispered. "The army guy?"

"Oh right," Sharpe gasped. "Sitorski."

"Can't confirm or deny that last."

Sharpe had the sensation that he had been sleepwalking, and now, suddenly, he had awakened, not sure how he had ended up where he now was. It was coming back. Alex Sitorski, Ben Rollins: this is what he did.

"I love a cold shake," the man said. "Clears the mouth of cotton, if you get my—"

"Cotton—?"

"Mickey D's."

"I've got work," Sharpe said.

"I'll be there. Fourteenth and K."

And the phone clicked dead.

Sharpe scrawled next to his diagram: "McDonald's, 14th and K Streets," but his hand was shaking so much that even a second later he couldn't read what he had written.

4 4

SITORSKI'S MORNING

ALEX SITORSKI COULD HARDLY TELL from the cramped room that he woke up in, but the sun was up. Opening his eyes he saw that somehow a bed—narrow and single—had been wedged inside (where, in fact, he was lying), and a sink and a toilet jutted out from the opposite wall by the door. The sort of low-rent scene Elena would revel in, but to Sitorski it seemed only like the depressing, decaying room on the wrong side of Washington that in fact it was—though what side of town, he wasn't certain. He wasn't sure what time it was either—his watch was gone—and only the faint light leaking through the room's sole opaque window suggested that it was morning. The window faced a brick wall inches away, which made him feel as though the room was at the bottom of a deep well (bringing back vague memories of the night before). His memory of last night was that he had been trapped, had dropped off the edge of time and would never stop falling. But the night, impossible as it seemed, was now over.

To his right, curled up in a white sheet on the other side of the bed, was the girl, fast asleep, her face against the wall.

Trying to remember. A kaleidoscope of faces, images, bodies from the night before raced past him too fast to make sense of. The girl. He remembered her, if vaguely, on the street outside, and then some time later, inside a hallway, turning a key, guiding him in.

A bolt of pain shot through his head so he gripped his temples with one hand. Felt a cloth on his forehead. He stepped out of bed, careful not to wake up the girl. The only problem was that his head was embedded in a Daisy Cutter bomb, the vibrations of his steps killing the villagers. He staggered backward, braced himself on the bed.

"Whaaa . . . ?" It was the girl. She turned toward him, still wrapped in the sheets.

"Sorry," he whispered.

Looked at himself in the mirror on the wall.

There was a large red blot on the cloth, above his right temple. A classic soldier, bandaged up hastily by his buddies till the medics arrived. It was Junior.

Trade me for him, he thought. *Lord, swap us, please.*

"You OK?" In the mirror he could see the girl speaking, sitting up. "How's your head?"

She stripped off the sheet, tossed it on the floor. Now Sitorski saw that his clothes lay on the floor in a pile, with his watch tossed on top. The girl's clothes were next to them, topped with a pile of bills, singles and fives. The room was a puzzle, a mystery with clues that proved nothing.

His eyes followed the elegant curves of the girl's body. So early in the morning, and his head woozy, still he felt a rise in his penis.

"You smashed it up pretty good," the girl said. She leaned forward on the bed, picked up her clothes and the money. Sitorski quickly snatched up his boxers, stepped into them.

"It's Sunday?" he said.

"Uh huh."

He walked back to the mirror, turned the faucet on and splashed water on his face and hair.

"I'm seeing my boy today," he said, finally.

In the mirror, he saw the girl pull her shirt on, then the rest of her clothes.

He looked the girl in the face. No older than Junior.

She saw him staring at her in the mirror.

"I can't give you back the money," she said, "so don't—"

"I don't want the money."

He peeled off the cloth—it stung as it clung to the wound—and wet it in the sink. Then he wiped off the blood caked on his forehead. There was a bruise high on his temple but it was mostly covered by his hair.

She walked to the sink and Sitorski stepped away and sat on the bed while the girl splashed water on her face.

"I haven't seen him in a long time," he said. "He's been over in Vietnam."

"My brother was there, too," she said.

"He"—another sharp pain shot through Sitorski's temple—"came back?"

"Uh huh." She seemed uncertain.

"And everything's OK?"

The girl shrugged. "Things aren't the same if that's what you mean. Ben's got this problem, see. He thinks everything was supposed to stop when he was away." She laughed.

Sitorski stood up, pulled his pants on, put on his shirt. Then he sat back down on the bed.

"Maybe I don't want to see him," he said. "Maybe that's what last night was all about. I've thought about it, but I still don't know what to say to him."

He turned and saw the girl, Angelina, staring at him.

"Something'll come to you," she said. "Just don't expect miracles."

"You don't get it," he said. "You see, there was so much I could have done." The pain shot through his head again and he cringed. "And what makes it worse is that I *know*, I know everything. It's as if I've lived it, from behind some glass wall, while I've seen what he's seen, and what it's done to him."

She sat down on the bed beside him.

"No one's gonna cry for you, you know," she said.

4 5

WAR IS UNHEALTHY FOR CHILDREN AND OTHER LIVING THINGS

"Tommy, let me level with you."

It was Bo on the line again. This time Tommy Shelton really knew why he was calling.

"I've never seen anything like it," Bo said. "I'm tellin' you, Tommy, he just up and drove off. He's disappeared. Maybe it's nothing but a tantrum and he'll walk in the door right now, but some of these calls he's been getting lately sound serious—and you know the Colonel, and—sorry for goin' off like this but I been up all night. And maybe they *were* after him. And"—Bo paused—"maybe they got him."

"I wish I could help you, Bo," Tommy said, "really I do. But there's nothing I can say."

"Tommy, if I had a dollar for every time I heard that tonight . . . well, I'd be rich as Elvis."

"Bo?"

"Yeah, Tommy?"

"The night's over. It's morning."

As soon as he hung up the phone, Tommy checked the upstairs bedroom. Elvis was still sleeping.

Then he walked back down a couple of steps. Looking about, he thought: Got to keep Elvis out of here. With the shades drawn, and the beaded curtain closed, the room was dark, except that the fluorescent black lights on the ceiling colored everything a glowing blue: the velvet posters that lined the walls—peace signs, doves, MCCARTHY FOR PRESIDENT, WAR IS UNHEALTHY FOR CHILDREN AND OTHER LIVING THINGS—the oozing lava lamp, the vast fish tank/diorama along the back wall, and, of course, in the center like a shrine, a photo of the Kennedy boys, John and Bobby, huddling together in the White House with Martin Luther King Jr. If you could stop history at one moment and rewrite it from there, that was the moment for Tommy Shelton. What would have happened if they all—or any one of them—had lived.

"Tommy, it's good to see you, man."

The deep drawl shocked Tommy, gave him an old Memphis déjà vu. Elvis had parted the beaded curtain and was now stepping down into the sunken living room. Tommy watched as Elvis scanned the walls, from the velvet Hendrix poster on the far wall, to the lava lamp, the peace sign poster, and finally—he had forgotten it was there—the psychedelic Beatles poster.

"Holy shit," Elvis muttered. "What the hell's happened to you?"

Next Elvis looked for a chair. There were none, at least not as the term is conventionally defined: no legs with a hard back. There were certain insights Tommy had gained since he moved to L.A. and one was that centuries of hierarchically inclined furniture designers had created sitting implements that tended to isolate, stratify, and make rigid social environments, while bean bags, throw pillows, and futons created a formless cushioned world, soft, comfortable, and free, allowing unfettered interaction, an infinite variety of positions. . . .

Elvis wouldn't understand.

"Here." Tommy placed two large bean bags on top of each other and pressed the seat down, doing his best to give them some height and form.

Elvis sat down, slowly and hesitantly.

"You a hippie now?" Elvis said finally, still staring at the Beatles poster.

"I'm the same as I always was, E," Tommy said. "The same Tommy."

"You always did choose your own path," Elvis said.

"We had our differences, E."

"That's right. Because you got a backbone, Tommy. Bo, Vern, and Priscilla—you rent 'em is what you do. Don't even buy their loyalty, either. But you can't buy Tommy Shelton."

Which wasn't how Tommy remembered things at all. It wasn't until he moved to L.A. that he found the real Tommy . . . though now, with the sudden appearance of Elvis, he felt all that begin to recede. . . .

"Well, you know, E, now that you mention Bo, he gave me a call this morning. I was wondering why—"

"You didn't let on, did you?!"

"No, E. I didn't. Like I promised. But he's awful worried and he just wants—"

"Well, keep it that way. Last thing I need is those boys screwing everything up."

"Screw what up, Elvis? I mean, what are you—I mean you're more than welcome but—what are you doing here?"

"Tommy," Elvis said, standing up now, "man, I tell you, it's gotten real crazy since you left me. They're climbing over the walls at Graceland, calling in the middle of the night, *Presley's a dead man*, and man, I feel like one too, can't keep up this pace. Hippies, Yippies, Beatles, Bogs, and Bears—hell!—so I got some business down in Washington I got to take care of, figured I'd talk to the Feds, maybe Nixon. Try to work things out, they need me, you know." Elvis began pacing about the room. "Remember pulling over poor bastards back home, turnin' on the sirens and flashing 'em a badge, scarin' 'em straight, that sort of thing? Figured we could do it on a big scale, turn things around 'fore this country goes all to hell, that bastard Lennon leadin' the kids off a cliff, know what I mean?"

Tommy spun around on his bean bag, watching Elvis walk around the room, checking out the posters. Tommy had found a bathrobe under the futon, and now he slipped it on and stood up.

"I don't get it," Tommy said. "Why aren't you in Washington then?"

"Well that's just it. I was there, but I needed to regroup. Things were moving too fast. All out of control. And besides, I need some help."

"Why not Bo, or Tubby—?"

"HELL, Tommy! That's half the problem right there. I could *hire* anyone for this job. I need volunteers!"

"Why me?"

"Like I said," Elvis said, "you always were a brainy one. Now go call Maurice—he's got a limo service—here's the number"—handing him a card. "We got to get to the airport."

"But you just hit town. And—wait a minute—*we?*"

"That's right. You and me, we got things to do in Washington."

"Elvis, I can't just pick up and leave. I've got work tomorrow, for one thing."

"Don't worry about it. How much cash do you need?"

"It's not the money. I've got a job. I'm supposed to—"

"I'll talk to those boys for you. I gave you the damned job, didn't I? I'll let you keep it."

"But I've got things to do. They rely on me. I can't just not show up."

Elvis stepped toward Tommy, stood facing him. Stared him in the eyes. Tommy stared back, and he saw that Elvis couldn't focus, that his vision stopped somewhere in the air between them, then turned back into himself, as if he was hypnotized, looking inward or maybe not at all. Then his eyelids drooped down, and his head wavered forward, unsteady.

"Let me call Bo and tell him you're here," Tommy said. "He can pick you up, and the two of you can go to Washington together."

"No!" Elvis said, snapping his head awake. "That's not gonna happen."

Tommy didn't say anything.

"We're going to Washington, Tommy. You see, I got myself a quest."

4 6

THE PRIEST

TWO HUNDRED AND FIFTY DOLLARS was what it had taken. That was the price that, after three rounds of bidding upward against himself, it took for Dr. R. Sherwood Sloan to suspend the visiting rules of the Psychiatric Unit at St. Jude's Hospital in Memphis and allow Tubby Grove to visit Sharon Teele alone in her room. Not only did the rules have to be suspended, but the three patients sharing her room had to be temporarily . . . relocated. To the hallway. No other rooms were available.

"No refunds," the doctor told Tubby, pocketing the money. "And I warned you. She hasn't made much sense."

Tubby was now standing in front of the girl's bed. Still asleep, her body turning, fists clenching the sheets.

A looker: the girl was that much. Tubby thought maybe he'd seen her before. Maybe at Wendy's.

Her eyes opened.

"Ma'am," Tubby said, "you and me gotta talk."

She looked straight ahead, as if Tubby was invisible.

"Sharon? That's your name, right? I'm Tubby."

Nothing.

"You work at the airport, right?"

Still nothing.

Tubby leaned over and clapped his hands in front of her nose. She blinked, but still didn't look at him.

"Ma'am." Tubby grabbed her shoulders and shook her, then held her chin and yanked it toward him. "Listen! You say you know Elvis Presley?"

Her eyes lit up.

"Elvis?" she said.

"Yeah. Now, it's not like he's missing or anything, or that we don't know where he is"—now her eyes were following him, transfixed on Tubby's mouth—"it's not that at all, it's just that we have to, uh, investigate, yeah, occasionally we're supposed to investigate where he's been just to prepare in case, uh, in case he walks out the door, or something happens to him really, you know? It's what we call a precaution. Understand?"

She didn't answer. In fact, it wasn't clear whether she'd understood a word Tubby had said.

"So, what I'm getting at is, did you see Elvis yesterday? At the airport. Or any-where else."

The girl's head nodded down, then up.

"You did?! You saw him?!"

Another slight nod.

"At the airport?"

"Uh huh."

"Elvis took a flight?"

"Uh huh."

"Where—where did he go?!"

"Uh huh." She smiled, nodded slightly. Tubby paused, and the girl nodded again.

The girl was quiet for a while, then smiled even more.

"Elvis loves me," she said.

"I'm sure he does, lady. Elvis loves all his fans. And that's why I need to know where he went off to."

He grabbed her shoulders again. Her arms were limp, her body giving no resistance, light as air.

"I'll give you one more chance. Where did Elvis go?"

Just then the door opened.

Tubby let go of the girl's shoulders and turned around. A priest walked into the room.

"Oh, I'm sorry," the priest said. Clean-cut, younger than Tubby. "I'm not interrupting . . . ?"

"No, Father," Tubby said. Tubby pointed from himself to the girl, suggesting something familial between them. "Sis and I were just . . . you know?" Tubby clasped Sharon's hand.

The priest walked to the bedside, positioned himself between Tubby and Sharon. Tubby never had had much use for church types. What was a strapping young fellow doing signing his crotch away to the Lord?

"But Mrs. Teele said there was only a sister," the priest said.

"Sis? Oh, that's just my name for her. We're married, for God's sake." He lifted the girl's hand and the priest's eyes looked down, and Tubby's followed. *Thank you, Lord.* The girl wore a ring.

The priest frowned, moved closer to the girl.

"I know about her husband," the priest whispered to Tubby. "You don't look like you've been to Vietnam." The comment was addressed directly to Tubby's belly, which was drooping over his belt. "And you look alive to me." The priest peeled Tubby's hand off Sharon's, then tossed it down. "Physically, anyway."

Then the priest mumbled to himself in some language Tubby didn't understand, then did his kiss-the-crucifix thing, bending over the girl.

"Sharon, your husband—your *real* husband—was saved," the priest said. "I want you to know that he had accepted Jesus as his Lord and salvation. I spoke to him before he left. The Lord welcomed a man like Hank. You realize that, don't you?"

"Uh huh." She was back to her slight nods. Tubby could see that the girl's head was now slowly turning away from the priest, phasing out.

"Now look, Father," Tubby said, "I don't care what the doctor told you, but I've got to talk to my wife here. Alone. When we're finished, you'll be more than able to—"

The priest kept looking at Sharon, but with his left hand shoved Tubby in the chest.

"Have *you* been saved, Sharon?" he said.

"Uh huh," she said.

"Now, Father," Tubby said, "I'm sure Elvis can make a contribution to your parish—"

The priest shoved Tubby again, harder, so he staggered back from the bed. "Hey!"

"Then you know, Sharon, that Jesus loves you, and Jesus—"

"No," she said, "Elvis loves me."

"Elvis?" The priest turned to Tubby, who was beside the bed again.

"Elvis," Sharon went on, "cares for me. He looks out for me. He freed me from—"

"No, Sharon," the priest said, "even Mr. Presley accepts Jesus—"

She turned to the priest, her eyes fiery.

"Elvis says it's natural," she said. She was smiling now, staring at the priest as he wiped his brow with a handkerchief. "Elvis says it's beautiful."

Tubby smiled, patted the priest on the shoulder and shoved him to the side, then sidled in closer to Sharon. The priest stepped back to the foot of the bed.

"That's right, girl," Tubby said, "exactly what you say. And what Elvis wants you to do now is to tell me where he is, OK?"

But the girl seemed oblivious to her visitors.

"Jesus told Hank to go to Vietnam," Sharon said. "And he killed him."

Tubby was looking at the girl, so all he saw was her wince as the gob of spit hit her in the eye. When he turned around the door was swinging, and the priest had run out.

4 7

THE SHAKE

"You're overdressed," the man said. He had just poked Sharpe in the back, then pulled him down to a seat at a table next to him, toward the back of the McDonald's. Sharpe was wearing his usual Sunday apparel: pressed khakis, blue blazer, white Oxford shirt, a new red rep tie, but compared to what the man to whom he was talking had on, Sharpe was dressed for a state dinner; the man was wearing innumerable layers of ratty old shirts, sweaters, and coats, with varying shades of dirt and mud encrusted in cakes on the elbows, back, and shoulders.

"Where I work, this isn't much," Sharpe said, then leaned over and said, firmly and curtly, "I work at the White House, you know."

"Down *there*," the man said, in the same gruff whisper he had used on the phone, then grabbed Sharpe by the shoulders and turned him around so the two were facing away from each other, back to back. "Now get some food and sit down."

Speaking with his back to Sharpe the man looked crazy, and his ragged clothes magnified the effect. Which, Sharpe supposed, was exactly the point. Finlator had told him Ronnie Bonnard was a master.

"Right there," the man said, without pointing. He lifted his milk shake and drank, leaving a chocolate mustache over his fake whiskers. While Sharpe waited on line for his own milk shake and fries he could hear the man muttering to himself.

"—and so we got a real head case here," the man said as soon as Sharpe sat back down behind him. "Don't turn around that should be obvious to you just look straight ahead and listen." He gulped some more of the shake. "Ray Kroc knows how to make a milk shake. You hear kids bitch about a guy with money but I'd like to see them contribute something like that to civilization something lasting as the McDonald's chocolate shake you won't see the likes of it again."

"I'm busy," Sharpe said. "I don't have all day, Mr.—"

"No names," Bonnard whispered. "I drink a shake, I'm The Shake. A burger, The Burger. Are-what-you-eat code."

"OK," Sharpe said.

"I gots me the virus!" Bonnard—now The Shake—screamed, all of the sudden. "The bugs'll jump on you, yes they will!"

Sharpe turned around to look at him. A large colored woman had placed her tray at Bonnard's table but now she picked it up and scurried away.

"You don't converse," The Shake whispered, still staring ahead, away from Sharpe. "You listen. In thirty seconds, take note. And when I'm through you wait thirty seconds, then ask what you like. Thirty seconds. Count 'em."

Sharpe sipped his milk shake and looked at his watch, but immediately The Fry began to speak.

"The bastard Nixon in the White House first there's the 'Nam wasn't that enough apparently not no there's Cambodia there's Laos there's Cambodia—all we are saying is give peace a chance—but the Weathermen blow themselves up now and—how many dead at Kent State at Khe Sanh at My Lai at Altamont at Memphis who are the citizens of Woodstock Nation?—Tune in Turn on—the Cowboys'll take the Super Bowl who can stop Staubach you tell me—"

He went on, not getting anywhere, as far as Sharpe could make out, just aimless babbling, until the thirty seconds were up. Then the nature of his talk changed.

"—that man you wanted us to check out the Colonel a real oddball go figure a straight arrow like that heads down to 14th Street then goes on a drunk at some strip bar down the street a haven for whores Ray's Saloon really ties one on then slams his head into a wall looks like it's on purpose or it's a signal hard to believe it was just a fall coulda been though I'm telling you the guy had four sheets to the wind and a whore from the strip Angelina Rollins—we've ID'd her—picks him up, a couple of cops hassle—our men, to confirm the ID—but lets them go in Miss Rollins's custody so to speak and she takes him to her place and there they spend the night the shades were closed and we couldn't get any closer didn't have a bug in place so we can't know what was said and done though your imagination is good as mine Miss Rollins is one fine piece of twenty-some-year-old Negro ass no conclusion at this point but evidence points most likely to a delib-

erate pickup at a prearranged location that could involve drugs or some underground subversive activities perhaps intelligence sharing—note said Negress is
sister of one Ben Rollins subversive vet former high school star of gridiron and
tosser of White House medals with whom you are familiar—coincidence means
conspiracy—nasty business here—and tomorrow quarry Colonel seeing son
whose background's well known by you I'm sure—gives motive opportunity and
more you do the math the Black Panthers have ties to the Reds we all know that
and we know how all those types are tied in together either that or we got a real
nut case on the verge of a breakdown either way it's not a stable situation not a
man for top military work I'm sure you'll agree no confirm on the press leaks yet
but circumstantials are mounting let me stop there and that's where we are now
a new man's on him now next shift the phones and house are tapped too so that's
what I got now to background noise and then take thirty and you talk the goddamned longhairs look like girlies and you know they fight like 'em too thank
God they're burning their draft cards let Canada take 'em all love it and every
Commie from Cuba to Harvard Square and the People's Republic of California
leave it am I right am I right am I right. . . ."

The Shake droned on a little more, then wound down to a whisper, and
finally to a halt at the exact instant that Sharpe's watch showed that thirty seconds had passed.

The man who Bonnard had followed didn't sound like Alex Sitorski. Alex was
straight as they came: excess in no things. He only occasionally drank, and
Sharpe had never known Sitorski to hit strip joints. But then, Alex must have
missed Elena. . . . Going to prostitutes was possible too, though surprising. But
the idea that Sitorski was involved in some underground scheme, that he could
be selling drugs or be subversive, was unheard of. And ties with Rollins? Could
Sitorski have been involved?

"How certain are you?" Sharpe said. "Your conclusions, I mean. Sitorski and
Rollins."

"In our battle," The Shake said, "we have no room for vagaries. There is black
and there is white, and any shade between belongs in one camp or the other. I
would have imagined you understood that. What we have here is a white gone
over to the other side. He does not then become a gray. He becomes a black."

Max Sharpe thought for a moment, sipped his shake. *You can never know
what's in a mind, a heart, a soul.*

Exactly thirty seconds later he turned around. No one was at the table.

WASHINGTON SUNDAY MORNING

BEN ROLLINS WAS AT Danny's Doughnut Shop, doing his best to clean up the place. He had no problem with the work: Danny was giving him a start, his first job since he'd come home, and maybe he would do more in time. Besides, cleaning reminded him of being a kid, climbing all over his mom as she mopped and dusted some white folks' big house. The problem was that now when he tried to push a broom, the best he could do with his one arm was to drag it across his body, but when he reached for the dustpan he dropped the broom and the handle kicked up the dirt, and his feet did too, and then the dirt was where it had started. The best way to go about cleaning the floor, he decided, was to get on his knees and mop it. But even then, since he didn't have a hand to brace himself, his hand slid as he swirled the wet rag, and he fell, chest forward, onto the floor.

Collapsed on the wet floor, the image of his mother came back to him, as she must have looked on her last job. When she died he instantly was supposed to become Angie's father and brother, but he was just a kid. Now he felt like an old man, looking back on a lifetime. You went from high school to that wild unreal scene, Vietnam, and then they dropped you back home, and you were supposed to go on like it was the night after graduation and nothing had happened. But there was a lot missing in between, and he could never know what was missing.

For an instant his old dream came back to him, of taking Angie away and getting out of this place, starting fresh. But to do that you needed money. Real money.

Music suddenly blasted from outside—an old tune from school days: "People get ready, there's a train a-comin'." Curtis Mayfield. It was coming from a

Cadillac that slowly cruised by. Ben dropped his rag into the pail beside him, stood up. Dex was smiling at him from the back of the car, the windows cracked open so the music would announce his arrival. Dex's smile said, My offer's still good. How much money does he make in a day? Ben thought. Just one day. Ben looked back down, tried to act as though he didn't see anything. As the car drove on the music trailed away: "Picking up passengers, from coast to coast . . ."

The pail of dirty water was beneath him. Ben kicked it so the water splattered against the top of the front door, then dripped back down to the floor.

Palmer Wilson, who was watching from a phone booth across the street, put down his binoculars, and for a moment thought he might give up his cover and see what was the matter.

4 9

THE MONEY

ELVIS AND TOMMY WERE in the back seat of Maurice's limo now, driving through Beverly Hills. Elvis had asked Maurice to bring them to the airport, but Maurice thought he would cruise past some of the establishments where he and Elvis had shared company in the past, in hopes that it would rekindle emotional bonds.

"I still don't get it, Elvis," Tommy said, "why exactly do we have to go to Washington?"

"If J. Edgar Hoover asked you," Elvis said, "you'd just go along, right? Or President Nixon? Or Agnew?"

"Hell no, I wouldn't go" is what Tommy thought he would say to that bunch of crooks, just like he shouted at protests every other Sunday.

Tommy shook his head slightly.

"Well," Elvis said, "that's what I'm talking about. That level of things." He put his arm around Tommy's shoulders, whispered in his ear. "Trust me," he said.

Maurice gazed at the rearview mirror, saw Elvis's arm around Tommy's shoulders, and winced.

"How much cash you got anyway?" Tommy said. "I've just got a few bucks with me."

"I'm not sure," Elvis said. He was looking out the window, unconcerned.

"But Elvis, you're—we're—going across the country. We'll need some money, a few hundred at least—"

"Tommy, you deal with the money!" Elvis turned to him, handed over his wallet. "It was never about money. You weren't there at the beginning. I was on to something there, you know. Something good."

Elvis's eyes were glassy, distant. Then he turned away to look out the window again.

Tommy opened the wallet. There wasn't even a dime in it, only a few loose checks.

It was Sunday, so the banks were closed, but Tommy had a friend, Mario, who worked at the front desk at the Beverly Hills Hotel. So Maurice drove there and Mario agreed to cash Elvis's check for $500.

"It's all I could get," Tommy said, getting back in the car now, "but it should get us through. Here." Tommy handed the money over, but Elvis leaned away from him, faced the window again.

As they drove off Tommy tried again. After all, it was Elvis's check, Elvis's money.

"Take it," Tommy said, and dropped the bills—mostly tens, a fifty, a hundred, and a pile of singles—into Elvis's lap.

Elvis looked down and stared at them at first. Then, with one sudden motion, he grabbed the bills with both hands and tossed them at Tommy so they flew about the back of the limo, like falling leaves in a windstorm.

"I told you I don't want it!" Elvis screamed, batting the bills in the air. "Don't you get it?! I didn't do it for the money!!!"

5 0

ENTER THE COLONEL

Bo Price was in Elvis's bedroom back in Graceland, staring straight ahead at an awesome apparition: an extended stomach that could pummel him from across the room, a gilded cane in its hand that might as well have been loaded, a rounded forehead bald as a bullet.

"It's been a day and a half now, Bo," Colonel Tom Parker was saying. "A day and a half of you boys spinning wheels on my dime."

It was no apparition. The Colonel was here.

"So the Colonel's gotta do everybody's job, all down the line. I'll be singing songs soon enough."

The Colonel sat down on Elvis's bed, leaned on the duck-head stem of his cane. It had been a long day for Colonel Tom Parker: flying from his home in Kentucky to Las Vegas to reschedule Elvis's Christmas shows, then on to Memphis, touching base with Bo all the while.

"But Colonel," Bo said, "it's not like we've been sitting on our cheeks. We've been through the police stations, hotel desks . . . and Tubby's checked the hospitals. Elvis ain't been hurt, we know that."

"Lord!" The Colonel covered his face with his hands. "The man's dead far as we know, and this one thinks he just needed his tonsils out!"

"Now wait a minute, Colonel. I was just playin' with you when I thought— well, 'course it's crossed my mind—but a day and a half don't make a man dead. And we did get a lead. That girl? The one Tubby found?"

"Yeah?" the Colonel said.

"Well," Bo said, "it's not our fault she's crazy and the doctor won't let us talk to her. Tubby says in another week maybe—"

The Colonel shook his head, walked over to the bookcase next to Elvis's bed and, using his cane, poked through the books on the shelf: *Christ, The Godhead and You*; *Cheiro's Book of Numbers*; *Getting in Tune with the Cosmic Spirit*; *The Rosicrucian Cosmo-Conception*; *The First and Last Freedom*; *The Quest: Turn Back, Look In*; *Theosophical Writings*; a few copies of *The Impersonal Life*. Bo knew the titles by heart. In the past months Elvis had sat him and Tubby down and read whole chapters to them. And when the downers, or exhaustion, got the best of him, Bo would read to Elvis.

"He actually reads this crap?" the Colonel said.

"You know it, Colonel. We only brought about a thousand of them on the last tour. Lugged them all the way to San Diego—don't think they'd ever seen anything like it in Oklahoma. Thought Elvis musta been some Arab sheik or something. Heavy bastards, too. The books I mean."

"Any point behind it all?" the Colonel said, picking up *The Quest*. The two looked at the cover: there was an old Indian, his eyes closed, legs crossed in the yoga position, floating in clouds that had psychedelic designs on them. Behind him was a middle-aged man, and behind him a teenager, then a child, finally a baby, each emanation receding back behind the other, and each was a different race: white, Negro, Oriental.

"Well," Bo said, "you see"—pointing at the book cover—"that there's involution. Like evolution. Only it's *in*." The Colonel looked blankly at Bo, his mouth open. "That's what Elvis says."

Then the Colonel picked up *Theosophical Writings*, began leafing through it. "Avichi?! Now what the hell's that?"

"Well, Colonel, that's what the theosophists—that's Madame Blavatsky's folks—that's what they call hell. It's—let me see—a dream of neglected duties, and abused powers, and there's"—Bo leaned over and read the book over the Colonel's shoulder—"some ambitions thwarted and hopes denied and, uh, failure—that's another one. Actually, I'm not too sure about that one."

The Colonel put the book back on the shelf. Then he picked up a piece of the photo lying on Elvis's night table.

"'Am I? Am I?'" the Colonel said as he looked at the picture. "That sounding colored stuff never made sense to me. Egghead garbage, if anyone bothered to ask me, which they didn't, I only created him was all. He was the right guy at the right time and that's all there is to it. Timing's the only thing that ever made a star. That and luck. And a genius promotin' him."

The Colonel stared down at the photo a few seconds more, gazing hard at it, then wadded it up in a ball.

"Papers better not get a hold of this," the Colonel said. "Doesn't matter if he is dead."

Bo didn't say anything.

"Gurus and minstrel shows," the Colonel said. "'Avichi.' You fellas need to shoot him down once in a while, like I do. Keeps him in line. That or you lose control."

"Colonel," Bo said, "he *is* a grown man."

Colonel Parker handed the ball of paper to Bo.

"To hell he is," the Colonel said. He walked to the door. "Now let's give some third degree to that Mrs. Looney Bird Tubby's found."

5 1

JUNIOR AND THE LAWYER

"'QUESTION: WHERE WAS LIEUTENANT Calley?'" the lawyer said.

He and Al Junior were in the back seat of the lawyer's town car, his associate behind the wheel, driving on the freeway to Los Angeles International Airport. Everyone had names, but Junior didn't remember what they were.

He was listening as the lawyer read from a pile of papers in his hands.

"'Answer: There. Firing. Question: Where was his weapon? Answer: Pointing into the hole. Question: Did you have any conversation with Lieutenant Calley at that ditch? Answer: Yes. Question: What did he say? Answer: He asked me to use my machine gun. Question: At the ditch? Answer: Yes. Question: What did you say? Answer: I refused.'"

The lawyer looked up from the paper. Junior had no idea how old the man was: his face was young, but his hair was streaked gray, receded up the temples, and he had a tough, raspy voice. The man had told him that he was a veteran, too, army in Korea and the early days in Vietnam. He had the look of a man who had grown old fast.

"This is good. The witness saying he refused, I mean. But a little strident if you ask me. Opens up a whole line about the chain of command, where you draw the line, and Calley's lawyer—Lattimer—then he'll trot out a parade of horribles." The lawyer puffed his cigarette. "But the basics are fine. The witness saw what he saw, but he did nothing, nothing to implicate himself." He took another puff. "Now that's direct examination. You'll meet with the prosecutor or someone from his staff beforehand, he'll give you a heads up on the questions they'll ask and then you come on the stand and look the jurors in the eye and the two of you dance your dance, try not to step on each other's toes but don't be too smooth either or they'll sense it's rehearsed. That's why the prosecutors want you down there now, to prepare. They're in Christmas recess, so you won't need to testify immediately. Understand?"

"I guess," Junior said.

"You hear some testimony now, you'll get the hang of it. Lucky I was able to get a hold of it. By the way, you never heard this testimony. You say I showed you anything, you're a liar. Get it?"

Junior nodded his head.

"Now here's some cross, just to give you a quick picture. Calley's lawyer is grilling the guy on specifics, 'How many were dead in the ditch, how many did Calley kill, where was he, where was Calley?' Bam-bam-bam. Imagine Lattimer—the lawyer—up in your face, firing questions, looking for a slip, uncertainty, an opening, that he can pick up with a tweezers and rip the skin off." The lawyer took another puff from his cigarette. "Listen." The lawyer picked up the papers again and read: "'Were they firing single shot or automatic?' 'I haven't any idea. Meadlo and Lieutenant Calley were both firing into that hole. I saw people go into that hole and no one come out. That's all I know.' 'Well'— this is Lattimer talking—'you've changed your testimony, haven't you? Didn't you tell the Peers Committee in January 1970 that you never saw Calley push- ing people into that hole?' 'I'—this is the witness—'never paid it no mind. I just remembered now. I haven't changed my testimony. I remember Calley was pushing people into that hole. Over a period of time, you forget things and then you remember.'" The lawyer turned to Junior, took another puff and exhaled. The back of the car was getting filled with smoke. "That's not good. The witness was not adequately prepared and Lattimer can sense weakness. Draws blood. You have a story and you stick with it. But they don't have prior testimony from you, right?"

Junior nodded again. He could picture what the man was saying; it was a movie he was now watching, hardly listening to the words.

"Good, very good. They'll be dancing in the dark then, and that's no fun on cross. Lattimer can take all sorts of approaches with you. Did you smoke pot?"

"Some."

"That day?"

"No. I don't think so."

"How do you know? How are you sure? March 16, 1968, and now it's December 20, 1970, and you're certain?"

"I—"

"Don't answer." The lawyer held up his hand so the cigarette was just in front of Junior's eyes and he could feel the heat. "Just want you to think about that. Lattimer'll ask anything. Listen to what they did to Conti on cross." He picked up the papers. "'Didn't you threaten a woman, say you would kill her child if she refused to give you a blow job? Didn't you carry a woman half-nude on your shoulders and throw her down and say that she was too dirty to rape? Do you remember you went into a hootch and started to rape a woman and Lieutenant Calley told you to get out? Do you deny that occurred? Didn't you go around and tell members of your platoon about the number of times you'd raped Vietnamese women? You didn't like Lieutenant Calley, did you, Mr. Conti? Mr. Conti, isn't it a fact that you'd like to see Lieutenant Calley hanged?'" The lawyer shook his head and laughed. "Lord! Is that shit true about Conti? Don't answer that. Let me give you more direct. Another witness."

He puffed again, and Junior coughed on the smoke. It was thick and enveloping the lawyer so Junior was alone with the voice.

"'Then you gathered up people. Why?' 'That was my orders. It ain't my reason to say why.' 'When Lieutenant Calley came up and said, "Take care of these people," why did you continue to guard them?' 'I figured he maybe wanted to hold them for interrogation.' 'What did you do?' 'I held my M-16 on them.' 'Why?' 'Because they might attack.' 'They were children and babies?' 'Yes.' 'And they might attack? Children and babies?' 'They might have had a fully loaded grenade on them. The mothers might have throwed them at us.' 'Babies?' 'Yes.' 'Then why didn't you shoot them?' 'I didn't have no orders to kill them right then.' 'Why didn't you fire first when Lieutenant Calley said, "I want them dead"?' 'Because Lieutenant Calley started firing first. I don't know why I didn't fire first.' 'What were the people doing when Lieutenant Calley arrived?' 'They was sitting down.' 'The women, the children, and babies were sitting down?' 'Yes.' 'Did they attack you?' 'I assumed at every minute that they would counterbalance. I thought they had some sort of chain or a little string they had to give a little pull and they blow us up. Things like that.' 'What did you do?' 'I just watched them. I was scared all the time.' 'How many people did you take to the ditch?' 'Seven or eight people.' Blah, blah, blah." He skipped a few pages. "'Calley said, "We've got another job to do, Meadlo." Question: You said you were under emotional strain. Can you describe that strain? Answer: Just I was scared and frightened. 'At what?' 'At carrying out the orders.' 'Why?' 'Because nobody really wants to take a human being's life.'"

The lawyer tapped the paper with his finger, shook his head, continued.

"'But they were Viet Cong, weren't they?' 'Yes, they were Viet Cong.' 'And it was your job?' 'It was my job, yes.' 'What were the children in the ditch doing?' 'I don't know.' 'Were the babies in their mothers' arms?' 'I guess so.' 'And the babies moved to attack?' 'I expected at any moment they were about to make a counterbalance.' 'Had they made any move to attack?' 'No.' 'When you left the ditch, were any of the people standing?' 'Not that I remember.'"

Junior saw another puff of smoke blow out from the other side of the back seat, caught a glimpse of the lawyer behind it.

"Get the hang of it?"

"I think so," Junior said.

"On direct they'll ask for details, then lead up to what you saw Calley do, and then what orders he gave you. If you—did you shoot anyone there?" Then the lawyer flashed his hand up like a traffic cop. "Sorry. Don't answer that."

"It's all right," Junior said. "Just some animals. Pigs, cows."

"That's good," the lawyer said. "A lot of them say that. That's good. Here's more cross, another witness. Watch for the inconsistencies. You remember things that are not possible. Watch for that. Lattimer'll sense blood. Listen." He read from the paper again. "'Question: And what else have you remembered that you saw? Answer: I saw Meadlo crying. Question: From seventy-five yards away? Answer: Yes. Question: You saw tears in his eyes?' 'Yes.' 'From seventy-five yards, that's your estimate?' 'Yes, I saw tears in Meadlo's eyes.' 'He had on his helmet and his gear and you saw tears in his eyes?' 'Yes.' 'Do you remember anything else?' 'No.' 'Well, tell me, what was so remarkable about Meadlo that made you remember him?' 'He was firing and crying.' 'He was pointing his weapon away from you and yet you saw tears in his eyes?' 'Answer: Yes.'"

The lawyer put the papers down. They were quiet for a while.

"It's an interesting case," the lawyer said.

Junior tried to imagine what it would be like on the stand, reliving it all. It had been two and a half years, and he had spent so much time trying to forget that little inconsistencies would be unavoidable, and he would be up front about that with the prosecutors, tell them they could not expect a perfect witness out of him. But most of what he had seen he would never forget. Yes, the babies were in their mothers' arms in the ditch, and yes, they might have counterbalanced at any moment. In Vietnam, in My Lai especially, he could imagine a baby teething on a grenade, then tossing it, suddenly transformed into a midget Cong—or maybe not . . . a mother with a baby in her arms, crying on her knees in the ditch, *No VC, no VC.* Evil was so far out of the bottle that there was no bottle—only evil—and Junior had no idea how to put it back, but that is what he thought he now must do. *Put the evil back in the bottle.*

He knew exactly how someone could see tears from the back of a man's head, firing away at that ditch.

"I know some lawyers down at Fort Benning," the lawyer said. "You're getting there Tuesday?"

"Yes."

The car had reached the airport and Junior saw planes taking off, others landing. There were soldiers with their families, coming home and leaving and waiting for others to come home.

"I'll get someone to meet you at Fort Benning on Tuesday." The lawyer jotted down a note as he spoke. "You'll do fine. They might not even decide to call you; probably just want to see what you know. But just in case, and if things don't work out, if my friend's late or whatever, don't dare say a word to them until they give you immunity."

"I don't need immunity," Junior said. "And I don't need a lawyer. I have a statement to make. There are things I have to say. But I'm just not sure about this . . . this forum."

The lawyer parted the smoke with his hand, looked at him, puzzled.

"That's crazy," he said. "I know what you think. You don't need anything because you're innocent. Well, everyone's innocent. I make a very good living representing the very innocent. Doesn't matter to the prosecutors. People have this sense that guilt and innocence is some definite thing; you are or you aren't." The lawyer shook his head, blew more smoke that now covered his face. "No sir. Justice is one relative motherfucker."

5 2

LOST IN L.A.

"MAURICE," TOMMY SAID, "you got any idea where you're going?"

Maurice cut his eyes at Tommy through the rearview mirror, but that didn't change the fact that the brazen bucktoothed behemoth had a point, a point that had been lurking in the back of Maurice's mind for a good half hour now, a thought he had tried to suppress, hoped no one else would bring up (Elvis wouldn't: he'd been sulking ever since he'd tossed all that money up in the air), but there it was . . . Maurice had noticed, with horror, how the color of the human foliage outside had changed as they drove, from lily-white Beverly Hills to steadily darker crowds as they approached downtown L.A., to a brownish hue farther south (Mexican country), to, more recently as they neared the coast, a motley assortment of Negroes, whites, browns, reds, yellows, and all combinations imaginable . . . but no, to answer Tommy Shelton's question: Maurice Flambeau didn't have a clue where he was driving.

He had lost track when Elvis had tossed the money all over the back seat. Maurice had been listening to the spat, and felt all along that Tommy simply didn't understand Elvis. Of course Elvis wasn't interested in the money. It was appalling even to bring the subject up. The man was an artist—an *artiste!*—not some commercialized pawn! The hubris of sullying the King with the issue of dollars must have—to dabble in American colloquialisms—galled him.

Maurice had turned the speakers on in the back, and was stewing, stewing in sympathy with Elvis when he was supposed to take the LAX turnoff at Sepulveda Boulevard, but he had missed it, headed due south and . . . was trying to figure out where to make the next turn back to the airport when he found himself on the Pacific Coast Highway.

And now, while Maurice sulked and stewed and navigated . . . Elvis was singing. A gospel radio station was on, and Elvis was singing along.

Tempted and tried we're oft made to wonder
Why it should be thus all day along
While there are others living about us
Never molested, though in the wrong

"Crank it up, Maurice," Elvis said. It was Elvis on the radio, in a younger, deep-throated whisper, and it was Elvis singing along, his voice worn and rough, his pace slower, almost reciting the words rather than singing them, and now it was Elvis screaming, too. "Louder, Maurice! Louder!" So Maurice turned up the volume and, with the radio blasting, Elvis sang loud to be heard over it.

Farther along, we'll know more about it
Farther along, we'll understand why
Cheer up my brother, live in the sunshine
We'll understand it, all by and by.

Maurice wasn't singing along. He had discerned where they were—thought he had—and . . . then turned around—tried to—but was unable to maneuver back to the main road . . . so . . . now they were . . . well . . . here. According to the billboard (now that Maurice cranked the window open he could, in fact, smell the salt of the sea, hear waves), Redondo Beach.

"Maurice," Tommy said; the song had ended, and Elvis—and the radio— were quiet, "if there's an airport around here, you got some inside stuff I don't." He chuckled, in a mean, exasperated way.

At which point Maurice slammed on the brakes, sending Tommy flying up against the back of the driver's seat.

"You're just jealous!" he screamed.

"Jealous?!" The Frog was nuts, Tommy thought. "Of what?"

"Of me and Elvis," Maurice said. "You've been keeping him to yourself since he got here."

The Frenchman's face was turning red as his turtleneck ascot. The guy was serious.

In the rearview mirror now they both saw a police car, its red light flashing.

"Now you did it," Tommy said. "With the cops it's going to be front-page news that E's here in L.A. Elvis, I don't think we can keep you hidden anymore." Tommy turned to Elvis. "Elvis?"

But Elvis didn't respond. He couldn't.

He wasn't there.

ELVIS ON THE BEACH

ELVIS HAD STEPPED OUT of the limo once it screeched to a stop. Hearing Maurice and Tommy go at each other had reminded him of home, of Vern and Priscilla. He needed some air.

When Tommy caught up with him Elvis was on the beach, walking slowly toward the ocean. The surf was rough, waves crashing hard on the shore. Sun shining, but a steady breeze whipped along the water. Too cool for sunbathers, only a few stragglers were stretched out on the sand, a couple of bums combing for garbage, and a band of hippies frolicking in the water just ahead.

Tommy watched Elvis for a minute, saw him search his pockets, then drop something in his mouth, jiggle his head. During the years Tommy worked at Graceland, Elvis had just used pills to handle his schedule, carry him through a long night or wind him down afterward; but by the time Tommy left, the drugs had begun to take control, and the drugs began to alter him; not just his energy level, but his mood, his self. Without Tommy, well, Bo and Tubby weren't going to say no to Elvis, so then who would?

Tommy walked up behind him, slowly and quietly, and Elvis, gazing out at the water, didn't turn his back, but said, "Been a long couple of days. Need my medications."

"How did you—"

"Check out that cloud." Elvis pointed to the sky. "That big sucker, there."

There was only one cloud overhead, a crooked sliver that Tommy thought looked like a map of Vietnam.

"You know that picture, in the living room back home, from back in '55, with those girls screaming and all hell breaking loose?"

Tommy didn't even know which living room Elvis was talking about.

"I guess," he said.

"That's it," Elvis said. "That's me. Back in the old days."

Tommy looked again at the sky. He could almost make it out—the cloud had broken up a little now; a strand had shot off that could be a leg, or an arm—but no, he couldn't see it.

"Tommy, I shot a picture around here, remember? I think it was *Paradise* something or other . . . ? I don't know."

"I don't either. I—"

"You never watched my movies. I know, Tommy, they were crap. I know I know." Elvis was talking faster now. "Ten years I spent in front of some cardboard picture of this. And you're right: why watch 'em?"

"They were fun," Tommy said. "The Beatles have put out the same sort of—"

Elvis wiped his forehead with the back of his hand. "They want to bury me, man. Like old Elvis never was."

"That'll never happen, E," Tommy said. "Hell, they're breaking up already, and you're still here."

"I never told the President to fuck himself, Tommy," Elvis said, enforcing the point with a jabbing finger. "I never did that."

"I think you did, E. In your own way."

Elvis glared at Tommy. Then he smiled.

"Tommy, I love you, man. Tell Elvis to fuck himself, to his face. Gotta love a bastard like that." He laughed.

"I didn't mean it that way, E. I just—I mean, times change. You played the rebel for a while. Now it's their turn."

Elvis turned away, walked closer to the water, and Tommy followed. Elvis lifted a leg as a wave rolled underfoot, then slowly stepped down into the water. The water was up to his shins, and there ahead, deeper, the longhairs were splashing away. The hippie girls were naked, Tommy saw, their breasts bouncing up and down as they leapt.

"You were tired of me, weren't you, Tommy? That's why you left, right?"

"Not exact—"

"I know, I know, I know." Elvis kicked the water as he spoke. "Always the hassles, the all-night sessions, and the money's got to be spread around and everything kept quiet, you can't go out because it's Elvis, always, always. I know how you must have felt."

Tommy just watched Elvis, his body fidgeting, his patter getting faster and faster.

"But you can leave, you know, Tommy? You can do that."

Tommy nodded.

They were quiet for a while.

"What about Priscilla, E? You want to go back and see her?"

Elvis shook his head. "Nothing there anymore. And that's what I mean, things move so fast now, Tommy, all out of control." He turned to Tommy, his eyes full and watery. "How many years does love last, do you think? Ten years? That's probably about all you can bank on."

"But what about your girl?" Tommy asked. "It's Lisa, right?"

Elvis nodded. "Tommy, when your old man's done it all, what's she gonna do for an encore?"

Tommy didn't say anything. He felt a cool breeze and stuffed his hands deep in his pockets, found a joint there he didn't expect and pulled it out and lit it, cradling it in his hands, his back protecting the flame from the wind. He took a few deep drags, then handed it to Elvis. Elvis took it and smoked.

"Lost opportunities," Elvis muttered to himself. "Futile regrets, and ambitions thwarted, hopes denied. Powers abused. Ending in ultimate annihilation." Then he turned to Tommy. "Avichi," he said, answering a question Tommy hadn't asked. "Tommy, you ever read *The Impersonal Life*? I gave you a copy once, didn't I?"

"I think so, Elvis."

"'Cause what's got me thinking is," Elvis said, "well—a couple of things. There's that idea of the Masters, you know, how God has sent Masters down here on earth, a goodly number of 'em. He keeps on sending us down here, bringing messages, fighting His fights. To think that it all stopped with Jesus . . . well, that doesn't make much sense, does it? That the Lord would send down one Master and then ignore us for a couple thousand years?"

"No, Elvis, it sure don't."

"That's right, Tommy." Elvis looked out at the water now as he spoke. "So then, these Masters, you see, they're sent down, and folks flock to them, you see? They're sent to do great deeds." Now he looked at Tommy. "Understand what I'm saying?"

Tommy nodded.

Again they were quiet. Then Elvis took another drag from the joint.

"Tommy, you think I'm full of shit, don't you?"

"No, Elvis. I mean, I don't buy it all but—"

"There's hidden wisdoms, Tommy. Involution and evolution. I've seen bodies, Tommy, you know, I've held corpses in my hands and I sensed what was happening there, the travels, spirits leaving this world. The Buddhists got that one right: all this—we're just proceeding through the Hall of Ignorance, that's all it is."

"I'll buy that much," Tommy said.

Elvis chuckled.

"Tommy, you think there's a reason for everything?"

"I don't know. Haven't got that one figured out yet."

"OK, this trip then. Me being out here, with you."

"Actually, that's another one I haven't figured. You called from Washington, and now you just want to get back there, and I don't know why you wanted to go there in the first place."

"Everything's slipping out of control, Tommy. See, there *is* a reason for everything, and there's a reason why I was put here, why I was made who I am. I've got powers, Tommy, it's true, and I'm s'posed to use 'em. Maybe that's what this is all about. See, I've lost track, not sure what it was I was intended to do. Can't be to lead, 'cause who's followin'? So maybe I'll go it alone."

"And why do you want me to come?"

"'Cause I can't be alone."

Elvis took another puff, then flipped the joint into the water. He did it so quickly Tommy didn't have a chance to grab what was left.

Then he spoke again.

"It's Sunday, isn't it?"

"That's right," Tommy said.

"There was a time I used to go to church. When I could do that. When everyone wouldn't just about kill me when I stepped out, and when that was me, how I felt, too." He paused. "You know what Madame Blavatsky says? Only one voice: Jesus, Moses, and the Buddha. No reason to divide everyone up."

"She's got something there."

Elvis looked out at the water again. There were six hippies, three guys and three girls, all stark naked, and now they high-stepped over the waves, then ran onto the beach.

"Maybe I should have been a preacher. You know, I could clean those kids up. I've done it: laid down hands and there it was. Healed. Now I know some say it's not about powers, that it's just faith, but you need powers so others can have faith in you, right? I mean, tell me there weren't big things going on when they put me here." He turned to Tommy. "You have doubts?"

"Elvis, I have doubts about the Sermon on the Mount."

"Maybe you just never had it explained to you right," Elvis said. "Those priests are just mouthing the words, man. Check it out." And Elvis stepped forward, then turned around, facing Tommy, so the waves splashed against the back of his legs, and he began to speak, yelling like a preacher. "Whoa all ye motherfuckers, of kind thoughts and good deeds! Let me tell you what *really* went down in that Bible!" Elvis rubbed his hands together, like someone Up There had cranked up the dial. "Now Moses, that white-haired sonofabitch, comes running down from this big mountain. Now his damn hair had turned white because he had seen the Lord, and those things can happen when you see the Lord, yes sir! He came on down from the mountain, and how he got down was the burning bushes directed his ass on down! He's carrying these fucking stone tablets on his back and damn it if he didn't chisel some of those damned Commandments wrong, scared shitless as he was."

The hippies crouched down on the sand behind Tommy, towels draped around them.

"Now Jesus,' Elvis continued, "he was getting it on with Mary, the woman at the well—you know, Mary Magdalene. It ain't in the Bible, but it's true. She got stoned, but Jesus took care of her and they traveled around a lot together. She was cute, fourteen when he met her, but damn it if she didn't pass for legal with her makeup and eyelashes all done up, man, she was fine, and Jesus, you gotta know the girls are all crawling over him, he's the hottest thing that part of the world ever seen. So he picks up with Mary, but he's got an obligation, don't he? to minister to his flock (travelin' from town to town can get old fast, let me tell you), and sometimes Mary says, 'To hell with it' and the shit-ass hotel rooms and stays home in Memphis. Which is why Moses I gotta think got it ass backwards with those Commandments there 'cause tell me Jesus didn't have to bend a few now and again."

Elvis caught his breath for a second, then clapped his hands together.

"Now Jesus was just thirty-three or -four or something but he felt like he was eighty-two, living so hard and fast as he did. And—this is something the Bible doesn't let you in on at all—he began to doubt himself—Yes, saith the Lord!—

for Jesus knew that things were gettin' a little out of control, see, making a little too much out of his act 'cause he knew that the Lord had told him he was Master to those he could touch, and minister to, but after that he'd just be a page in a book, see, and then you're on your own. Which is cool, you know, because the Lord knew he'd just send another Master down to minister to the next bunch of folks, when Jesus got old. Jesus got no monopoly on the word a' God. He's not the only Master 'fore or since; he knew it and so did the Lord. Look at the Buddha. Madame Blavatsky. The President hisself! And, motherfuckers, look in front of you."

The hippies began to clap and hoot and Elvis seemed to see them for the first time, and Tommy clapped too. He hadn't heard one of Elvis's sermons in a long time.

Elvis paused. He looked up at the sky, glanced around. Only the sun was up there and it shone harsh and fierce in his eyes, blinding him. He closed his eyes, breathed deep. Suddenly he was very tired.

Tommy looked around him and there was Maurice, walking toward them from the road, the police car driving off behind him.

"Elvis," Maurice screamed, waving, "you will be late for de plane!"

Elvis looked at the hippies.

"What I'm saying is," he said quietly as he began to walk out of the water, toward the beach and the car, "at the end Jesus said he was old and of age. And he fell ass backwards in the dust."

5 4

PALMER AND THE SHOT

NOW IT WAS EVENING in Washington, and Palmer Wilson was back at Ray's Saloon, nursing his latest glass of Jack. Since he'd left the alley he had been unable to find his quarry. Palmer felt adrift.

At this instant he was pondering the whys and wherefores of his profession. Mnemonic techniques, for one: why associate a color with a number, then commit the colors to memory, instead of just remembering the phone numbers? And codes, signals. How do you detect the nuances of a handshake that might indicate Yes, No, the Job Is Off, the Job Is On, by the differing tensions of the grip, or whether the slight tug at the wrist went clockwise or counter? And then the Big Picture stuff. So what if Ted Kennedy danced till dawn with the daughter of the former king of Italy? Or if the Weathermen or the Black Panthers got blamed for hurling a stone at a Vietnam vet. That was just the top of Palmer's list of grievances that he was presenting—for lack of an audience who possessed any real power to change things—to Ray O'Reilly.

But Ray, who was washing a glass behind the bar, was pondering his own problems. If his constant customer had tapped out the monthly stipend he received from his daddy's trust fund—as Ray suspected—Ray would have to cut back expenses. Some dancers would be the first to go, and he dreaded breaking the news to Angie Rollins and the others. . . . At Ray's Saloon this Sunday evening, self-pity was all the rage.

Then the door opened, revealing what looked like Palmer's twin brother, had his father granted him such close companionship to traverse the burdens of this world, a fellow traveler wearing similar—if more convincing—ratty rags.

• • •

Ronnie Bonnard sat down at the bar. It had been a productive day for him. He had filled three rolls of film, two cassette tapes of dictation, three more from phone taps, and half a pad of notes, all on the Sitorski case. The taps were still on the phone, the bugs in the house. The information he had was enough to destroy a quarry of his level. Nixon's boys had been satisfied with far less, when they wanted to nail someone. The surveillance would be called off soon.

He glanced at the table behind him. There was the stupidest man to have ever graduated from the Academy, a blight on the Bureau. Palmer Wilson. The reason Bonnard had to visit this blighted dive, to see the man who had proven himself so incapable of fulfilling his simple tasks, was that Ronnie Bonnard had been summoned by their mutual boss, John Finlator, to finish his job, too.

"Ray," Palmer said, staring at the shot glass in his hand, "you haven't seen my flask around, have you?"

Ray didn't say anything.

"I've misplaced, at least since last night, old Joe M. II—well, it'll turn up." No response. "Anyway, Ray, let's say you didn't run this bar, what would you be?" Silence. "Me, I've always wanted to be a chef. The simple pleasures of season-ing a steak tartare, pungently, with a deft, subtle hand—that sort of thing. But Wallingford Wilson, you know." He downed his shot. "Life goes off course like that."

More silence.

"Anyway," Palmer continued, "I've got a little problem here—not the chef thing—but something maybe you can help me out on. You see, Finlator's got me in on a hush-hush *agent provocateur* job. Now to be honest with you, it's been a while since I had one of those, and the quarry wouldn't take the bait, so I shifted it to a setup, spread a little white powder around and then, well, I wasn't able to finish up with the *coup de*—the arrest. I was on to him again—well, Finlator gave me a tip—but still, there I was, on top of the quarry—and—" No response. "The point is, I could use a little background on how to approach this. There's a motivational problem, seems to me. For the quarry. Well, actually for me too—but—anyway. Ever happen to you?"

"Motivational problems?" Ray laughed as he put away another glass. "You got to be shitting me."

5 5

ELVIS AND JUNIOR

THE SCENE AT THE AIRPORT was smooth this time, the folks at American Airlines having gotten their act together, apparently. Once Maurice dropped them off, with Tommy's help Elvis was escorted on the plane without having to bother with security . . . or tickets . . . and now they were in the airplane, stewardesses hovering around Elvis, back and forth along the aisle, like vultures on carrion.

Elvis had realized he needed to change names again, at least for this leg of his flight. Anyone with a mind to could track the Burrows name to him; some would know that Colonel Parker used it himself; others would note the physical resemblance between "Burrows" and . . . well . . . Elvis; and once that was established, a few dollars spread around to the girls at American Airlines could find out where Elvis (Burrows) was going next, and then . . . they (who wasn't, or couldn't be, *they*?) could seize him, all for a ransom, a quick headline, some crazy political message . . . *assassination* (if Kennedys could be gunned down, surely Elvis could) . . . after all, anarchy was on the loose, wasn't it?

John Carpenter was the first name that came into Elvis's mind at the airport. He didn't realize until later where it had come from: it was his role in one of his last movies, *Change of Habit*, which made the move all the more inspired. The movie was a dog—the Colonel had never chosen a worse one for him—so there were few who sat through the awful thing who would remember his name. James Bond himself couldn't have done better. His path would be clear for at least another day or two.

Adrenaline had carried Elvis through the morning, but that had burned itself out. He closed his eyes, felt his head rock in slight, tight ovals, and realized how frayed his mind was, his brain cells a morass of tangled wires firing away, then shorting out in the swamp in which his brain sat: a dying battery and a starter shot to hell, all creating a grating screech when he turned the key to start thinking. *(Where had he left his car, anyway, yesterday morning?)*

The feeling of being on the plane, shuttling on without really knowing where he was going or why, gave him comfort, in a chaotic, confusing way. It reminded him of touring, moving so quickly from place to place that he had to give up attempting to keep track of where he was, only that he was on the road, he was Elvis Presley. . . . Fatigue took over, that and the fast rush of time; on the road all anchors were cut, so his mind, adrift, floated downstream, recalling memories, grabbing sensation, romance, and money (Lord, the money!). . . . Success had its own logic: the popularity that had delivered him from the drudging repetition of the workaday world propelled him into a chaotic abyss *(didn't heroes exist out of all time and convention?)*; things hadn't slowed down since, and somewhere, he now thought, he had lost track of where he wanted to go, who he wanted to be, and why.

In his back pocket Elvis found the American Airlines stationery on which he had started his letter a day ago, and he reread it, tore it up, got another sheet from the stewardess, and started again.

The parallels were clear to him: Elvis/America; under siege, at war. Used to be number one but no more. They were fat and old and tired but it wasn't their fault. And there was the Beatles, enemies in lockstep coming toward him, like Pied Pipers. Many levels here. A complex situation. Demanded some delicacy, undercover ops and a frontal assault and public relations all at once. But he was perfectly situated to infiltrate the enemy and destroy it. He would first make contact with the FBI. His Memphis contacts had mentioned a John Finlator to him, apparently well tuned to the layers of the struggle. And that would lead him promptly to Hoover, and then . . .

Nixon would understand.

Dear Mr. President, Elvis began. *First, I would like to introduce myself. I am Elvis Presley and admire you and have great respect for your office.*

He kept writing, his mind beginning to click into gear, things making some sense finally. Then he stood up, gave Little Elvis a pull, closed his eyes and kicked his fists out fast and straight: a warm-up Mr. Rhee had taught him.

When he opened his eyes, a young vet was before him, clean pressed army greens. It was Elvis, 1960 in Germany, with 'Cilla at fourteen, just a sweet girl. More signs. Things falling into place.

"You been to Vietnam?" Elvis said to the boy.

"Yes sir."

"Have a seat."

Elvis patted the empty aisle seat, and Junior sat down. Tommy had just stepped through the curtain, and Elvis handed him the letter he had been writing.

"Read this over," he said.

Tommy sat down on the other side of the aisle. It was a letter addressed to that evil bastard himself: Richard M. Nixon.

Elvis placed an arm around the boy.

"I'm Elvis Presley," he said softly. "That Carpenter business is code, is all."

The boy rubbed his eyes, decided he'd play along.

"It's safer that way," Elvis said. "But I don't need to talk to you about danger."

Elvis raised his glass and clinked it against the bottle before handing it to the boy.

"To victory," Elvis said.

The boy took a sip of the drink. Once in Vietnam he had seen Bob Hope at a USO show. He had sat far in the back, and a helicopter had flown in with wounded so he couldn't hear the words, so the comedian seemed like a marionette pantomiming on the stage. Looking at Elvis beside him now, he got the same feeling. Elvis's bushy sideburns edged halfway down his jaw and onto his puffy cheeks, his eyes narrow and squinty. *Nothing real here.*

"Things are pretty hairy over there, I'll bet," Elvis said.

The boy nodded his head slightly, glanced behind him.

"In Vietnam, I mean."

"Oh. Yeah."

"Well, we're behind you boys a hundred and ten percent," Elvis said. "Don't let the Beatles make you think all the young people are against you. There's just a bunch of lost kids, that's all. But we'll deal with them." He leaned over and whispered into the boy's ear. "That's why I'm going to Washington."

"Yeah?"

Elvis nodded. "You got family there?"

"My dad."

"Love your mother," Elvis said.

The boy didn't respond, and Elvis turned away to look out the window, and they were silent for a while.

"She was a big fan of yours," the boy said. "Just the other night she played me some of your old stuff."

The kid had underlined *old stuff* with a black Magic Marker, but Elvis let it pass.

"That right?"

"Yeah. My dad loved your music even more."

Elvis had no idea how old the kid's parents must be; he thought of himself as little older than the kid.

"Well, people were crazy back then." He gave an aw shucks shrug that made everything a joke: Elvis Presley, history.

"It's true," and now the boy could almost see the vague outlines of his father's face in front of him. "When my dad thinks of you I think he sees this perfect world that used to be. I was just a baby, and there wasn't this war." He stopped himself, caught his breath. "But that perfect world? It never was. That's what's so sad about him. And I think, deep down, he knows that."

Elvis's eyes seemed even more narrow, like his mind was drifting off somewhere.

"You're coming home for Christmas," Elvis said, finally. "I used to love it when I was a kid. My mom was a queen. I was her little prince on Christmas."

Elvis sniffed inside the scotch bottle. Smelled like Vernon.

"You get your daddy something nice, hear?"

The boy didn't say anything.

"You need money?" Elvis said. "That the problem?"

"No, really it's—"

"Tommy!" Elvis yelled.

Tommy leaned over into the aisle.

"Yeah, Elvis?"

"You got that money?"

"Sure."

"Well, let me have it."

"E, why do you need it now?"

"C'mon." Elvis reached his hand across the aisle, held his palm open. "Gimme."

"But, I mean, Elvis, you can get anything you want here without—"

Elvis glared at Tommy.

"How much?" Tommy reached in his pocket.

"All of it!"

"All—? But Elvis, this is all the spending money we've got."

"I SAID ALL OF IT!" Elvis reached an arm into the aisle. "That there's MY money. I don't have much anymore, but I got that. Now this young man," and he patted the boy on the shoulder, "has just done his duty to his country, understand? More than you'll ever know. He's coming home for Christmas to be with his dad." Elvis held his open palm out again. "C'mon now."

Tommy pulled out his wallet, then took out the bills. He looked at the soldier, but the boy's head was down in his hands, so only the top of his shaved dome was visible.

And Tommy laid the bills, all five hundred dollars, in the hand of Elvis, who tucked them into the jacket pocket of Al Sitorski Junior.

5 6

KIDNAPPED

"YOU'RE SURE THAT WAS her name, Bo?" said the Colonel.

They were at the nurses' station at St. Jude's Hospital.

"Yes, Colonel," said Bo.

"You hear that, girl?" barked the Colonel.

"Her name's Bo?" asked the head nurse.

"Her name's Teele. You heard the boy: Sharon Teele!"

"Teal? Like the color?"

"I don't know what it's *like!* It just is! Spell it, boy!"

Bo began to spell it, but the Colonel interrupted him.

"Hell, you've got her name right there."

"Well, I'll have to check, sir." The nurse looked down her list. "We have it organized by patient room, not by— Here." She looked up at the Colonel. "Found it. Now, you are . . . ?"

"I'm Colonel Tom Parker for God's sake! You ever heard of Elvis Presley?! Or don't you stay on the planet Earth much?"

The nurse glanced over at Bo.

"*That's* Elvis Presley?"

The Colonel kneaded his eyeballs with his knuckles.

Bo had been scanning the hall, looking for Tubby, when he saw Billy Ray Briggs strolling toward them, a bouquet of red roses in his arms.

"Billy Ray," Bo said, "what are you doing here?"

"I, uh, is Miss Teele . . . ?" Billy Ray pointed into the room at the end of the hall, trying to hide the roses behind his back. Out of his Memphis Police uniform, Billy Ray looked even younger and gawkier than usual. "I, uh, didn't finish questioning . . . ?"

"Teele, did you say?!" Bo said.

Bo raced down the hall, into the room behind Billy Ray. There were four beds inside. All empty.

"Billy Ray, you're sure Teele was in this one?"

He nodded.

"Colonel," Bo yelled down the hall, "she's gone!"

The Colonel grabbed the printout from the nurse.

"That Room Three-oh-six?" he said.

"Sure is, Colonel," Bo said.

The Colonel turned to the nurse, shot her a fierce glare.

"The doctors didn't discharge her," the nurse said.

"Then where the hell is she?"

"Actually," the nurse said, "now that you mention it, I did see someone with her about an hour ago who looked a little suspicious."

"Big burly guy?" Colonel Parker said.

She nodded.

"A tad slow?" Bo said.

"That's right," the nurse said. "Came by yesterday asking for a Colonel Burrows."

5 7

AN ANGEL

"SOMETHIN' I BEEN MEANING to ask you," Arnell Greenaway said. He was slumped over the bar at Wendy's Chili and BBQ Tavern in Memphis, his fifty-inch-plus buttocks firmly implanted on the stool in which he had spent over two thousand hours each of the past three years, over six thousand all told (Wendy, shaking another bottle of Tabasco into the chili pot, had run the numbers out himself), with the loose flabby cheeks of his ass hanging off the edges. Had been there every day, in fact, since he'd gotten the news that his younger brother, Rich, had been killed in Vietnam.

It was so late on Sunday night it was almost Monday morning, and Arnell was in a ponderous mood. A quizzical mood. A querying, questioning frame of mind. Arnell suddenly found the skeptical school of philosophers appealing; that is, in their ruthless pursuit of truth, their insistence on peeling away that last slim layer of the onion we call the Mysteries of Life to probe the inscrutable core . . . and answer the question that had plagued Arnell S. Greenaway (the S was for South: the side in the War of Northern Aggression) for well over half of his hours of alcohol-induced contemplation. (Not that Arnell would describe his state of mind in those words; that was Wendy's reading, and he might have added a little gloss.) What Arnell asked was this: "Why they call you Wendy, anyways?"

On the jukebox Wendy was playing nothing but Elvis: "Suspicious Minds," "In the Ghetto," and "There's Always Me" had just played, and now Elvis was crooning "Crying in the Chapel," and Wendy, listening, imagined the King on his knees, on some cliff, or a vast pasture . . . "I know the meaning of contentment," Elvis was singing, "Now I'm happy with the Lord." The winter's light began to stream through the side windows as if they were stained glass in a chapel, and though technically it was no longer Sunday, *this*—drinks at Wendy's Chili and BBQ Tavern, bonded in silent company—was church.

"I mean," Arnell continued, "I just don't know any guys called that particular . . . you know?"

Wendy had understood the question the first time.

"That what they call y'all back in Australia, or wherever it is you hail from?"

Wendy had survived the initial shock of the question without audibly gasping; now blood was beginning to course back into his face. He pondered whether to nod yes—about that Australian nonsense—but then thought better. To divert Arnell's attention, Wendy would recite from his manuscript—his all-encompassing History.

"Arnell, my dear fellow," Wendy began, "to answer that I will have to begin at the beginning. You are aware, are you not, that this bar was constructed, by Yours Truly himself, as a shrine for a new faith, a religion in the true sense of that term—not as it is abused nowadays, mind you, to mean—quoting Dylan—'social clubs in drag disguise.' Do we understand each other?"

(Wendy would have to edit this section of the book for it to gain mass appeal, though—then again—damn it!—the subtle satire would soar over the masses' heads in any event. Let it stand!)

Wendy continued. "The sacred relic of the aforementioned shrine—here doffing my hat to the Greeks—was a scarf upon which Elvis himself had perspired during a concert in San Diego. Now, during the construction of this establishment—specifically, the plumbing of the loo—I, serving as High Priest, with a ceremony and ritual worthy of Dionysus, wrapped the scarf around the piping feeding into the water supply. My intent being that the water from the sink, if one immersed one's head in it, would cause the wettened one to be *born again, Yea but in the likeness of Elvis.* Again, note here a doff of the multicultural cap."

Wendy saw that Arnell actually appeared to be listening, the glassy eyes denoting concentration, not slumber, and (not knowing that Arnell was, in fact, thinking of his brother, Rich, and wondering if he could have saved his life by volunteering for Vietnam) he poured Arnell another beer and a shot.

"Now," Wendy went on, "there was a small problem. And here the satirical skewers are sharp indeed, penetrating—if I can doff the cap this once in my own direction—to the very core of so-called religious practice. You see, the relic that contained the powers of transformation and salvation—the aforementioned scarf—was placed, accidentally—or was it? a quick doff to Freud—around the wrong pipes. Leaving us banging in frustration at the base of the sink, vainly attempting to dislodge that misplaced scarf, hoping—praying—that the water from the spigot be sanctified by the King. And there we are—not to put too fine a point on it—the relic real, potent, so close if only we could reach it, not knowing that the scarf, through no fault of our own, remains forever beyond our grasp."

Wendy studied Arnell, watched him drop his mug to the bar with a splash.

"Well lookee here!" Arnell yelled, turning toward the front door, which had just opened. "The fortunate son hisself, returning in the flesh!"

It was Tubby. He stepped inside, and both Wendy and Arnell noticed something different about him. And it wasn't the beaming smile on his face, or the fact that his cowboy boots were polished to a mirrorlike gleam that struck the two men as so strange, or that he was wearing a necktie (on it were fat jolly Santas, patting their bellies like—thought Wendy—Buddhas, or like—thought Arnell—Santa himself).

It was the bouquet of red roses Tubby clutched to his chest.

He held the front door of the tavern open as he peeked outside, whispering, "C'mon in now. Nobody's gonna hurt you."

Then Tubby sucked in his gut and let Sharon Teele creep slowly past him, Tubby patting her on the backside all the way, guiding her in.

Wendy thought the girl might wither away on the floor once she stepped into the light, she looked so frail, her steps slow and tentative as a woman three times her age. Having not seen Sharon in the past few days, Wendy had been worried about her. Thought maybe she had suffered . . . well . . . a setback of sorts, in dealing with Hank's death. But with her hair pulled back tight against her head, exposing her soft white skin, she still looked pretty, Wendy thought; if you were attracted to that sort of thing (women, Wendy meant), you'd most likely find her attractive.

Wendy gave the chili another stir, looked at Arnell who, it was obvious, was transfixed. Wendy didn't know what he was thinking, and he hoped it wasn't about the mystery behind his name.

It wasn't.

What Arnell was thinking was this: She's an angel. An angel from heaven.

BORN AGAIN

"IS ELVIS MEETING US HERE?" Sharon Teele said as she and Tubby sat down near the back of Wendy's, far as possible from Arnell, who, until they entered, had been the only customer.

"Now Sharon," Tubby said, "sweetheart, I told you you've gotta get off that horse now, or you'll wind up right back where you came from. Elvis can't meet up with us until you tell me where Elvis is at. Then I'll tell him where we're at and then we'll get ourselves someplace."

"But I thought you said—?"

"I said you be a good girl and Elvis'll come to visit. Now, you want to be a good girl, don'tcha?"

Sharon nodded her head, though she could only manage the tiniest motions. The medication the doctors had given her made her skull feel as if it was filled with cement.

"That's good. Now, first some meat on your bones is what you need." Tubby lifted his arm up, waved it at Wendy. "Wendy, couple of bowls over here, will you?! And beers for me and the lady. And put a little something special in for Sharon here, willya?" Tubby winked. "She's been sick and all."

"Sick," Sharon said.

Suddenly she felt a tickle in her throat, a quiver in her stomach. She was going to throw up, but she was able to stop it and swallow, the residue burning her throat as it went down. Had to be the medication; she hadn't eaten at the hospital, so nothing else was inside her.

"Gotta—ladies' room." She pointed to the back wall.

Wendy saw Sharon stagger up from her chair. He walked across the room with the drinks, set them down and caught her before she fell.

"Steady, girl," Wendy whispered in her ear. "Remember, the gods do walk among us."

If Arnell's eyes were summer sunlight, and a vast magnifying glass partitioned the seat where he was planted from Tubby and Sharon, Tubby Grove would have spontaneously combusted: Arnell's glare was that hard and fierce. The truth was, Arnell had had his eye on Sharon for months now, but he'd never tried anything on her out of respect for the fightin' man. Then, when word came down that the Cong had gotten old Hank, well, Sharon hadn't been around. And now that she was, that angel who'd floated back into Wendy's lighter than a butterfly . . . was with that Elvis hanger-on, that dumb lackey, Tubby. *All the hours the girl's been in here listening to Wendy's egghead babble, I never paid her no mind. Look where respect for the fightin' man gets me.* Arnell slammed down his beer, pounded the bar to have Wendy pour him another, and stomped into the men's room.

Which is where he now stood, in front of the mirror that hung on the wall over the sink.

He pounded the sink, then pounded it again and again. Then again. Then once more.

Then Arnell placed the stopper down in the bottom of the sink, turned the faucet on full bore, and dunked the top of his head, deep as it could go, into the water. The water was cold as dry ice; it grabbed the loose diaphanous skin encasing his brain and gave it a shake that dumped three years of boilermakers and dead cells out his ears; so cold the water burned, woke him to roots he'd long forgotten he ever had. He pulled his head out and shook, combed his hands through his thick hair, wetting it down. Scruffed his bushy sideburns out.

Not bad-looking there, Arnell, he thought. *Drop a hundred pounds or so and you could almost pass for Elvis hisself. Then that sweety pie, the little angel, would flock to you like a bee to honey.* In fact, looking at himself in the mirror now, Arnell imagined himself being Elvis. Imbued with his spirit.

Almost.

Who you kidding? Wake up, Arnell.

For one, Elvis knew what the hell he was doing, where he was going and why.

Arnell, you just sit on that round rear of yours all day, doing nothing and then making excuses for it.

Still, he felt strange.

Cast thyself in the waters (Arnell was born and raised a Baptist) *and Thou shalt be born again, praise God,* is how the preacher said it back when he'd go to church on a Sunday. But that isn't the way Arnell said it to himself now, before the sink.

Arnell embraced the sides of the sink and stuffed his head back down into the ice-cold water, fighting himself—the weak, wretched side of himself; the side, he admitted now, alone in these frigid reviving waters, that had taken over his soul three years ago, when Rich had been killed, when he'd tried to kill himself with drink and barroom brawls—keeping his head down for what he knew was his own good.

Sat on your ass for too long, Arnell. Alone with your ever-lovin' mug of beer, drinking away whatever money you can lay hands on, eating what's left over in chili. Bitching about the hippies. Bitching about the Negroes. Bitching about the women's libbers. The pot-smoking longhairs always picketing something. Bitching bitching bitching. Admit it, Arnell: you're only bitching 'cause you're afraid they're right. You don't really think the coloreds and the whoevers can't cut it. No: you know, deep down, they can cut it, maybe better than you. You're scared, buddy! Admit it! The hippies are right! Right about the war, too. You know it. The sad fact is we're gonna lose this war and lose it bad, so in the end Rich'll still be dead and we'll have nothing to show for it, just blood and bodies down the toilet of history. The blood is really on your hands, Arnell, for standing up and fighting so damned hard for this war, and you know it, deep down at the bottom of this cold ocean of a sink you know it, and that's why you hate with such rage, a rage that drills down to your core. 'Cause those hippies won't let you forget it.

He took his head out of the water, shook his hair out some more, then opened his eyes. Looked in the mirror.

Lord! Arnell thought, *whatever's in that water old Wendy'd better bottle and sell it.*

I look like the spitting image of Elvis.

Three feet away, if you burrowed straight through the mirror at which Arnell was gazing, through the wall of the men's room, into the ladies' room, through the mirror that faced him, you would see Sharon Teele staring straight ahead, looking in Arnell's direction. The medication was wearing off. Vomiting in the toilet just now had helped get it out of her system.

She still couldn't account for most of Saturday. The day was a blur to her: half dream, half washed-out memories. When the doctor told her that she had torn a girl's ear off it was news to her, though when he mentioned that the girl was wearing an earring with a peace sign on it Sharon had remembered something, a vague dreamlike image; she recalled grabbing a peace sign, though she remembered it as something huge and threatening. And when the doctor asked her if she knew that her husband was dead, that he'd been killed in Vietnam, she nodded yes, she knew, though she didn't. She'd forgotten that too.

Sharon didn't know why she had attacked the girl. Now, splashing cold water on her face from the sink, she remembered that when she did see the girl for the first time in the airport, she knew Hank was dead. But she had known for over a month. So that didn't explain anything. She had seen Elvis that day, and then Sour Honey had taken him away from her. That seemed important, though it didn't explain why she attacked the girl. There was a connection somewhere, she felt, between all of this, but Sharon was at a loss to know what it was. It seemed, to Sharon, that if only she could see Elvis again, he could solve this riddle for her, explain it all. Then everything would be better.

She dried her face with a paper towel, made sure the corners of her mouth were clean, no signs of vomit. Shook her hair dry. Then she stepped out of the bathroom.

Wendy had designed the tavern himself, and with no formal education in architecture, there were bound to be mistakes. Even Frank Lloyd Wright had a fly in the works on occasion: a slight tilt to the floor, a window that stuck. Wendy was no different. He never claimed to be.

And yes, Wendy knew that the bathroom doors could have been configured in a manner more conducive to the safety of patrons; knew that anyone who had the ill fortune to step out of the men's room an instant before a woman walked out of her, adjoining, bathroom, would more than likely, after taking one step toward the dining room, be hit in the head with the swinging door to the ladies' room. And yes, his lawyer *had* told him that he was now on sufficient notice of the problem that the next accident would likely be deemed to be caused not by mere negligence but by *reckless disregard* of an architectural defect that he had personally caused and of which he was fully aware, and that such *gross negli-*

gence and *wanton recklessness* could subject him to *punitive damages* for which he would be *personally liable*, and which his insurance would not cover. Yes, yes, he knew! The lawyers had drummed it all into his head so often he should have been awarded an honorary degree in the field of *Tortious Litigation*, with a special distinction in *Premises Liability*. But more pondersome matters weighed on Wendy's mind. Like the historic use of religion to promote hypocrisy and evil; the death of faith; the potential for a true morality; his fear that his homosexuality would be discovered and that would be the end of his life in Memphis; and his manuscript, the all-encompassing History of Our Times.

He never corrected the problem.

Still imbued with the spirit of Elvis, enlightened, in tune with himself and his surroundings as if truly born again, now resolved to dispose of his flaws like yesterday's chili and begin anew, afresh . . . in love . . . Arnell had just opened the door of the bathroom and taken half a step out when Sharon stepped out of the ladies' room, and swung open her door. While in the ladies' room Sharon too had worked herself up into something of a frenzy, and was talking to herself, swinging her head back and forth, and her eyes followed the path of the door as she slammed it open so, though she could do nothing about it—she couldn't catch the door fast enough to stop it; no one could—she saw Arnell's face.

The instant before the door hit him, her eyes bugged open wide and she let out a scream. What she screamed—in a bloodcurdling pitch, half question, half burst of recognition—was this:

"ELVIS?!"

PART FOUR

Monday Morning

WASHINGTON

5 9

MEETING PLANES

RONNIE BONNARD WAS LYING down on a couch in the American Airlines passenger lounge at National Airport. Even if you were Max Sharpe and had had coffee with him less than twenty-four hours earlier, or his boss, John Finlator, who saw him most every day, you would not have been able to recognize him. Even if the flowered housedress he was wearing didn't fool you, the blond wig certainly would have. And Colonel Alex Sitorski, who was far from certain that anyone was even following him, and who had not gotten a clear look at Bonnard in any of his disguises during the past two days, certainly couldn't make him out, even though the two men were seated in the same lounge, just a few feet away from each other.

Sitorski was waiting for his son, who was expected to arrive any minute.

Which Bonnard well knew. The tap on Sitorski's home phone had picked up a call late Saturday afternoon to the colonel's estranged wife, Elena, who had taken to calling herself by her maiden name of Rubin and was now living in Los Angeles. Since leaving her husband, she had consorted with a hornet's nest of counterculture types; she had, in fact, slept with a high officer of the Black Panther party, who happened to be an agent for the Bureau.

Finlator had told him last night that contacts from the Coast had reported information on the only son of Mrs. Sitorski and the colonel. Photos and tapes showed Al Junior with Panthers, Mobilization to End the War types, Veterans Against the War, hippies, Yippies; smoking marijuana, dropping acid, meditating. Junior bounced around from group to group, march to march, rally to rally. Never met up with the same crowd twice. The Bureau now had more than enough to warrant picking the kid up, shake him down for information—names, dates, maybe even pressure him into an undercover assignment. But the wiser course, said Finlator, was to sit back and let the kid dangle, let him turn his necktie into a noose.

He would leave the next day for Georgia, having been subpoenaed to testify for the prosecution at the army's court-martial trial against Lieutenant William Calley. Which, clearly, implicated the Peoria plan, Finlator was certain, and the quarry's knowledge thereof. Dumb luck was not a tenet of faith much followed in the Bureau.

Now Bonnard heard commotion. A plane had arrived, and the passengers were walking into the terminal. Had to be Junior's flight. And, indeed, there was the quarry, Colonel Alex Sitorski, standing up, rigid as all hell in his officer uniform. Who could know that his blood was still infused with alcohol from his Saturday night escapade? Or that he was a lousy whoremonger who had befriended the sister of an angry Negro veteran, who was himself a quarry? Who, other than Ronnie Bonnard, knew truth?

Colonel Sitorski walked slowly toward the crowd, then stopped. A young man, also in uniform, continued to walk toward him. That was Junior; Bonnard knew him from the pictures. In person the boy looked even more bizarre than he did in the photos; his shaved head gave him an otherworldly aura.

Bonnard got up from his post at the couch and, keeping an eye on the Sitorskis, positioned himself by the exit door.

The Sitorskis did an awkward double take—their steps uncoordinated, at odds with each other—and then their hands finally met, and they shook. They didn't try to hug, and the boy wouldn't let the colonel take his small bag. Apparently that was all the boy brought with him, suggesting a short trip. Keeping a distance apart from each other, the two walked through the lounge, toward the exit. Toward Bonnard.

As they neared, Bonnard shook out the long blond curls of his wig, began rattling a metal cup, jabbing it at passersby before they left the terminal. No one gave him anything until the Sitorskis reached him. Then the boy, Al Junior, stopped, looked Bonnard in the eye and, as Bonnard gazed down at the cup, shielding his face, the kid dropped a twenty-dollar bill in. Which was perfect, because the gift was so extraordinary that it didn't seem odd for Bonnard to then embrace the boy in a bear hug, so he couldn't notice when Ronnie Bonnard's hand slipped into his pocket.

6 0

THE LETTER

"SO?" ELVIS SAID. "What do you think?"

Tommy and Elvis were in the back seat of a limo, heading out of National Airport, toward Washington. When Elvis spoke Tommy opened his eyes, realized that he had nodded off for a moment. He hadn't slept at all during the flight.

"About what?" Tommy said.

"The letter!" Elvis pointed at Tommy's chest and Tommy patted the breast pocket of his shirt, pulled out the paper within it. Right: the letter. Elvis's letter to Tricky Dick.

"It's clear enough, isn't it?" Elvis said, and snatched the letter back from him.

Tommy recalled Elvis's rambling paranoid delusions from the days he worked at Graceland, and after reading the letter Tommy wondered if that had become Elvis's view of the world, and if it was the pills, or Elvis's isolation, or his company—Bo, Tubby, and the guys—or growing older that had led him here.

"Elvis," Tommy said, "it's perfect." The limo had crossed over the Potomac, and was now in the city. "What are you planning to do with it?"

"Tommy, for a college boy, you can be right stupid sometimes," Elvis said, chuckling to himself. Then he leaned back, looked up at Channa in the rearview mirror. "To the White House."

"The *White* House," Channa repeated.

"That's right," Elvis said, smiling.

"Here we are, Mr. Presley," Channa announced.

Elvis opened his eyes. The White House was in front of them.

"Where do you go in?" Elvis said. "Where do you go to see the President?"

"Elvis," Tommy said, "you can't just walk in unannounced."

"Well, where do I give him my letter?"

"There's a guard at the gate," Channa said. "Over there." He turned around toward Elvis. "I'll deliver it for you."

But before he could, Elvis opened the door and walked out.

The guard was inside of his kiosk when he saw the limo stop. He squinted his eyes, saw a man walking to the center of the front gate of the White House and—yes—the man was wearing a purple velvet suit, and what looked like a jewel-studded cape flying behind him, like a comic book superhero.

"Stay right there!" the guard yelled, one hand grabbing his holster as he jogged toward Elvis.

Elvis stopped, reached under his cape.

"ELVIS!" Tommy jumped out of the limo, ran toward him. He reached Elvis just before the guard did.

"STOP!" the guard said. "Both of you!"

Elvis slowly pulled his hand out from under the cape as the guard unsnapped his gun from his holster. The guard looked at Tommy, then at Elvis, then back at Tommy.

"Here," Elvis said, and handed the guard an envelope. "This goes straight to President Nixon himself, you understand."

The guard took the letter, puzzled.

"I'm Elvis Presley."

The guard looked down at the envelope. On it was written: *For the President Only. From Elvis Presley.*

"Make sure he gets it right away," Elvis said to the guard. "As I say in the letter, I'll be waiting at the hotel."

Elvis winked at the guard, and walked back to the limo.

Back in the limo, it struck Tommy that Elvis could have been arrested out there in front of the White House, or even killed. The next scene that flashed before his eyes was of Colonel Parker booming down at Tommy with a voice of quiet but tumultuous thunder: *You killed my boy, Shelton. The blood's on your hands.* Then the Colonel would inflict punishment on him, using methods that Tommy imagined would be medieval in their excruciating pain and brutality. . . .

"Elvis," Tommy said, "I've really got to call Graceland. Like I told you, I can't just take days off like this. I'll lose my job. And besides, you know they're all worried sick about you. Vernon and—"

"Vernon?" Elvis said, as he closed the door, and the limo began to drive off. "He won't notice I'm gone. Not as long as his paychecks keep coming in." Elvis was looking out the window again.

"What about Priscilla? You know she misses you."

"I don't even want to think who she's with."

"Elvis, that's not right and you know it. Besides, you wrote the President that Tubby'd be with you. Why don't I get him to come?"

Elvis looked up at the mirror, at Channa.

"To the hotel," Elvis said. "Let's drop Tommy off."

"Done," Channa said.

"I got some business to take care of, Tommy," Elvis said. "I need you to wait for the President to call."

"Elvis, the President isn't going to call you. Maybe he'll write you when you're back at Graceland but—"

"No, Tommy. President Nixon's a smart man. He'll call. Now go ahead and call Tubby. Tell him to meet us."

6 1

THE LETTER AND MAX SHARPE

MAX SHARPE WAS IN his office, reading the letter for the fourth time. Who could say with certainty what divine hand had delivered it to him, but it had been directed from the guard at the White House gate, through several levels of the security hierarchy, past additional layers of Executive Office bureaucracy, and . . . somehow . . . from Elvis's hands to Max Sharpe's eyes . . . here it was:

Dear Mr. President,

First, I would like to introduce myself. I am Elvis Presley and admire you and Have Great Respect for your office. I talked to Vice President Agnew in Palm Springs 3 weeks ago and expressed my concern for our country. The Drug Culture, the Hippie Elements, the SDS, Black Panthers, etc. do not consider me as their enemy or as they call it the Establishment. I call it America and I Love It. Sir, I can and will be of any service that I can to help the country out. I have no concerns or motives other than helping the country out. So I wish not to be given a title or an appointed position. I can and will do more good if I were made a Federal Agent at Large and I will help out by doing it my way through my communications with people of all ages.

First and foremost, I am an entertainer, but all I need is the Federal credentials. I am concerned about the problems that our country is faced with.

Sir, I am staying at the Washington Hotel, Room 505-506-507—I have 2 men who work with me by the name of Tommy Shelton and Tubby Grove. I am registered under the name of Jon Burrows. I will be here for as long as it takes to get the credentials of a Federal Agent. I have done an in-depth study of Drug Abuse and Communist Brainwashing Techniques and I am right in the middle of the whole thing where I can and will do the most good.

I am Glad to help just so long as it is kept very Private. I was nominated this coming year one of America's Ten Most Outstanding Young Men. That will be in January 18 in My Home Town of Memphis, Tennessee. I am sending you the short autobiography about myself so you can better understand this approach. I would Love to meet you just to say hello if you're not too busy.

Respectfully,

Elvis Presley

P.S. I believe that you Sir, were one of the Top Ten Outstanding Men of America also.

I have a personal gift for you which I would like to present to you and you can accept it or I will keep it for you until you can take it.

At the bottom of the letter Elvis had scrawled a long list of his private telephone numbers in Beverly Hills, Palm Springs, and Washington, and several in Memphis. He signed the letter:

PRIVATE
AND CONFIDENTIAL
UNDER THE NAME OF
JON BURROWS

The beauty of the thing, thought Max Sharpe. The glorious luck and the unrivaled beauty. *High on life,* he repeated to himself, and as he did he could hear Elvis singing those words on a soundstage far grander than the Republican convention had seen in Miami or had ever seen anywhere, a vast palatial stage that looked like Cecil B. DeMille doing Las Vegas . . . no . . . that looked like America . . . yes! . . . and in the middle of the vast stage of swaying amber wheat fields, of Little League baseball diamonds and Big Ten football stadia, of Billy Graham revival meetings . . . was Elvis Presley, singing—not dancing: his hips would be rigid, his costume regal but at the same time subdued, nothing too provocative—what would become the theme song of the President's 1972 reelection campaign, of the Republican Party, and an anthem for the nation itself. *Get high on life, America!* Elvis would sing. *Say No to drugs! Yes to life!* (Sharpe anticipated the skeptics' response: *How does Nixon define this "life"? Is Vietnam "life"? My Lai? Cambodia?* And he knew the answer to those skeptics: Sing louder. *High on life!* Sing it with the King!)

To get his ideas to the President he would have to scale the White House ladder, and with such time constraints, he needed to start at a high rung. A memo to Haldeman, delivered through Ehrlichman, was the ticket.

The memo wrote itself. Or rather, Max Sharpe was a mere medium, the corporeal entity that typed the words while the spirit of Nixonian political genius guided his hands, suggested the ideas, dictated words to him. In fact, from the moment Elvis's letter was revealed to him Sharpe became convinced that it had taken on mythic importance; that the meeting between Elvis and Nixon was predestined, marked a point at which synchronistic political forces of glacial size and scope would converge. With a little help from Max Sharpe, history was being made.

Sharpe left a message with Haldeman's secretary that Elvis demanded a meeting with the President, and that a memo explaining the importance of it would be forthcoming. Then, per their agreement, Sharpe typed the memo to Haldeman, addressed it from Dwight Chapin, but made sure that any eye experienced in the bureaucratic machinations of the Nixon White House would know that Max Sharpe's hand was behind it. He knew that H. R. Haldeman had just such an eye: in fact, the President's Chief of Staff possessed a matching set.

The memo read:

> Attached you will find a letter to the President from Elvis Presley. As you are aware, Presley showed up here this morning and has requested an appointment with the President. He states that he knows the President is very busy, but he would just like to say hello and present the President with a gift.
>
> As you are well aware, Presley was voted one of the ten outstanding young men for next year and that was based upon his work in the field of drugs. The thrust of Presley's letter is that he wants to become a "Federal agent at large" to work against the drug problem by communicating with people of all ages. He says that he is not a member of the establishment and that drug

culture types, the hippie elements, the SDS, and the Black Panthers are people with whom he can communicate since he is not part of the establishment.

I suggest that we do the following:

Sharpe stopped for a moment to survey his work. Now was the time to actualize the HOLE campaign. He would have to put this meeting in the context of the grand HOLE plan. He finished the memo, summarizing his concepts — while making sure not to be too self-aggrandizing. Sharpe considered demanding a full-scale meeting for Elvis and the President, something more akin to a head of state than a mere celebrity, but given the time pressures, he concluded that Open Hour was the best he could hope for. At least by scheduling Elvis's meeting at the end of Open Hour, the two (along with Sharpe himself, who planned to be there) would not have to be limited in the time they spent together. The President could always run over the scheduled time: Sharpe had seen prime ministers wait, frustrated and impatient, outside of the Oval Office, their long prescheduled meeting delayed because the President was entangled, not in some emergency in Vietnam, but with an analysis of the Redskins' upcoming game against Dallas. The end of Open Hour was just fine.

He ended the memo with:

Approve Presley coming in at end of Open Hour _____
Disapprove _____

The next battle was to make sure that Haldeman approved the meeting. Sharpe thought quickly — it was 8:25 when he completed the memo — and considered the bureaucratic weaponry at his disposal.

At 8:30 Ehrlichman and Haldeman would have their traditional Monday morning meeting before briefing the President on the day's schedule with Chapin. The last thing Sharpe wanted was for Elvis to be discussed there, before Sharpe had been able to place the event in the proper context. He could just imagine it: Haldeman would toss a few caustic barbs at the idea and Chapin would then quickly retreat, gratuitously stomping on Sharpe as he fled. One used meetings to affirm a *fait accompli*, give the predetermined a democratic stamp, nothing more. The idea would have to be approved before any meeting.

Sharpe called Ehrlichman, told his secretary he would be over in a minute.

Next, Sharpe ran down the hall to Ehrlichman's office, raced past the secretary's desk, slowing just as he reached the door. It was 8:30 exactly.

"Mr. Ehrlichman isn't in, Mr. Sharpe," his secretary said.

"Wha-wha-? Where—?" was all he could get out.

The secretary didn't say anything else, just pointed down the hall in a he-went-thataway pose.

So Sharpe ran off again. Ehrlichman was just around the corner, walking toward Haldeman's office.

"John," Sharpe panted, grabbing his boss and mentor by the shoulders, "we've got to talk."

"I've got a meeting with Bob," Ehrlichman said, tapping his watch. "We'll talk later, OK?"

"No," Sharpe said. "NOW!"

At which point Max Sharpe launched a furious flood of verbiage at Ehrlichman, right there in the hallway of the West Wing, two doors down from the Office of the Chief of Staff, within yards of the Oval Office, during which Sharpe explained, as best he could, about the Get High on Life campaign, its broad, vast meaning, its relation to the President's approval ratings, to the '72 reelection campaign, and beyond that, to the future of Republican politics for a generation—more!—and he explained his reasoning, the underlying Nixonian precepts: about the dark core of the American soul, that molten nucleus of prejudice, selfishness, and greed (where did that notion come from? Sharpe wasn't certain), and how, if that core was tapped, a political mine field could be reached, a rich vein of votes that ran beneath party line and label and that linked, in 1968 general election terms, the Wallace vote and the Nixon vote (Wallace's 14 percent and Nixon's 43+ percent) to form a solid 57+ percent majority, and how that vein could only be successfully mined if the voters were given emotional and psychic cover, a soft smiley face overlay to the ugliness that actually motivated them; what was essentially a negative vote—against them—would have to be cast as a positive one—for us—or—and here was the brilliance of the Get High on Life campaign!—for them! And that he, Max Sharpe, had earned this meeting! Remember Sitorski! Remember Ben Rollins! And all this—the entire campaign, the symphonic convergence of a solid electoral majority, for now and for all time!—would be accomplished with Elvis Presley acting as Master of Ceremonies, leading the chorus in song.

"You see, John," Sharpe concluded, "it's like the President told me! Dante's Inferno. But produced by Lawrence Welk!"

Sharpe was out of breath, and Ehrlichman examined him with a confused, discomforting look.

"Max, you've really got to get some sleep," Ehrlichman said.

Sharpe handed him the memo, with Elvis's letter clipped to the back.

"Get Bob to OK it!" Sharpe pleaded.

And Ehrlichman took the memo, then vanished inside of Haldeman's office.

The next two hours, back in his office in the Executive Office Building, waiting to receive word of whether the memo had been approved, Sharpe was in hell. The White House was heaven. Fifteenth Street, running between the two buildings, was whatever lay in between. Earth. Purgatory. This life.

Though Sharpe wasn't certain what he had said to Ehrlichman out there in the hallway before he gave him the memo, he sensed he had lost control of himself. That wasn't good. As Nixon would say: *Never get too high or too low. Moderation in all things. Including moderation itself.* Or was that said by Sharpe's old football coach, back in high school? He wasn't sure.

In any event, they were right. He had lost control.

He did need sleep. Nixon would say that great men didn't need sleep, but that didn't help. Maybe Max Sharpe was not a great man. He never asked to be. He only aspired to be near greatness.

He closed the door to his office, closed his eyes, but he couldn't sleep. Adrenaline, fear, and anticipation were pumping his blood too furiously. So he drank another cup of coffee, tried to contemplate the next step for the Get High on Life campaign.

The next thing he knew there was a knock on the door. He had fallen asleep, his head resting on his typewriter. When he opened his eyes he saw his secretary poke her head in and drop a large manila envelope on his desk. In his exhausted state, all Sharpe saw of her was her stumpy, age-spotted arm when it slipped through the crack of his doorway.

Sharpe rubbed his eyes, picked up the envelope. White House interoffice mail.

This is the old you, Max, he told himself, holding the envelope up to the light.

Remember you when. Then he opened it, pulled out the memo. His eyes raced to the blank lines at the bottom.

At the bottom, Haldeman had checked the line beside *Approve Presley coming in at end of Open Hour.*

He had approved the memo. He had approved it! Good old Ehrlichman had explained the genius of the Get High on Life campaign, and Haldeman had understood! President Nixon himself probably saw the genius of it!

Sharpe leaned back in his chair, glanced at the memo again. Now he noticed, at the very bottom, Haldeman had written a note in the margin. Next to the last paragraph, where Sharpe had suggested that *if the President wants to meet with some bright young people outside of the Government, Presley might be a perfect one to start with,* Haldeman had written, "You must be kidding."

6 2

THE PRESIDENT AND HIS MEN

"ANY MORE NEWS ON THAT My Lai . . ." Nixon waved his hand in circles, as if that would generate the missing word.

"Incident," Haldeman assisted.

"Yes," the President said, "the incident."

Nixon was slumped on the couch in the Oval Office, the back of his head resting on the cushions. Haldeman and Ehrlichman were seated in chairs on either side of him, with Chapin standing at the back of the room.

"Well, the campaign is in full swing," Haldeman said. "In fact, we've got a few groups coming in today to speak their piece in support of the good lieutenant. Who are they, Dwight?"

Chapin read from the schedule memo he was holding in front of him.

"Chicago Veterans for Calley are presenting you with a plaque commending you and Lieutenant Calley for 'heroic persistent steadfastness in defense of peace and freedom in the face of liberal opposition—'"

"Who wrote that one?" Ehrlichman said.

"I think Buchanan," Haldeman said, "I'm not sure."

"We could do with a few more editors over there in P.R.," Ehrlichman said. "Sometimes Pat gets carried away with the venom of the moment."

"No," Nixon said, "I like it. What else?"

"Let's see." Chapin looked back at his memo. "Polish Prisoners for Peace are bringing a statue of Calley for you to give to him."

"We commissioned a statue?" Ehrlichman asked.

"We found it in storage," Haldeman snapped. "Left over from Korea. Go on, Dwight."

"Well, there are the usual petitions. A group called Daughters of Orange County have one asking for Calley's immediate release and promotion. A few veterans will make impromptu comments about how Calley waged the war the only way that can bring us victory. Pat's written some real tear-jerking stuff for them. Powerful."

"Good," Nixon said. "And have someone say that the Democrats aren't giving me the chance to win. That they're tying my hands. But don't overdo it. There's that fine line between taking credit and dispensing blame. We can't lose sight of it."

"I'll tell Buchanan," Haldeman said.

"And the morality angle, the religious angle," Nixon said. "Do we have that covered?"

"Yes," Haldeman said. "We've talked with Billy Graham. He's visiting with you today, and he's agreed to speak to the press on the way in."

"Fine."

"Then there's Open Hour, Mr. President," Chapin said. "The usual routine: just act as if you're treating them seriously, like it's a real White House meeting with the President, and they'll go home happy."

Nixon nodded.

"And the leak?" the President said.

"The colonel?" Ehrlichman said. "It's taken care of. We got the goods on him. We'll bring him in today. Finish him up."

6 3

SITORSKIS' REUNION

"How are you doing?" Colonel Alex Sitorski said.

It wasn't the first time he had asked this of his son since picking him up from the airport, but he still hadn't gotten a straight answer. In the taxi to Arlington they had each floated awkward welcomes and small talk to the other, but neither had really listened, so they repeated the same questions and answers. It was a getting used to each other again, a thawing out. Alex said he was fine, the boy said Elena was fine, and that he, Junior, was fine. That was what was said.

Now they were at Sitorski's apartment, each holding a cup of coffee, standing outside on the small concrete patio. It was cold so their breath formed clouds that floated up between them. When the boy didn't say anything, Sitorski continued.

"I wanted to have a barbecue last night, like we used to. But you didn't come." Sitorski looked down at the small grill, the briquettes still stacked carefully in a pyramid, the can of lighter fluid beside it. It was the wrong thing to say, to blame the kid for making him wait so long to see him. *Focus on the present.* "It was too cold anyway."

The boy had taken off his cap and was rubbing his head nervously.

"When did you cut off your hair?" Sitorski said. The boy's skull was smooth as a billiard ball.

"Soon as I got back," Junior said. "I'd let it grow when I was traveling. The monks—the Buddhists—wear it like this. They're a small people—thin and wiry, you know; not much food—and in their robes, they look like they're floating. The baldness adds to it."

"I noticed that too," Sitorski said. "They're so small, we worried whether they could carry the heavy arms. They seem to be managing, though."

Sitorski meant it as a joke, but Junior just stared blankly at his father.

Morning now, so the sun was out there, somewhere, though it was hardly visible in the cold, cloudy sky. The boy looked good: bulging at the shoulders and chest; not the rangy kid who had left home three years ago.

"Got a cigarette?" Junior said. "I killed all mine on the plane."

Sitorski pulled out a pack of Marlboros, lit himself one, then handed the pack and a butane lighter to Junior, who was now sitting at the picnic table. The boy studied the lighter for a second, then lit a cigarette.

"First weapon I've touched since I've come home." Still holding the lighter, he seemed to smile for an instant. "Stupid bastards, with their goddamned straw roofs. If they knew we were coming, they should have built something more solid. Aluminum with a booby trap outside. But I guess we would have figured out a way around that too, wouldn't we?"

The kid was doing what he always did, trying to draw him into opposition. Sitorski restrained himself.

"I suppose so," he said.

The boy slowly blew a long line of smoke from his mouth.

"I think they have a mind-set that helps for a long fight," Junior said. "And their religion, their Buddhism. I studied it some in high school before I went over. The endlessness of life, of cycles. I mean, imagine if we believed that we would meet up with them again, that we're all really ghosts, you know, in this form just for this life. That we'll reappear in years to come. It would change things, wouldn't it? I mean, what would we say to them, if they came back? 'It was all for your own good. You gotta understand, we were trying to save you from the Russians. Them and the Chinese. Shoulda trusted us.'"

Junior flicked the lighter on again, watched the flames as they leapt upward, then shut it off, flashed a clipped smile at his father.

"See, I really think they are like ghosts, in a way," Junior said. "When you try to wipe out a people, they don't vanish that easy. They reappear, float about, always reminding you. Whispering: 'This is what you've become. Look at yourself in the mirror.'"

They were silent.

"You look fine," Sitorski said. "You're lucky. You did your job, came back. I know it wasn't easy, but still."

"Right," the boy said.

"And you shouldn't blame yourself. You didn't make the policy, or the rules."

"I'm not—"

"But you said 'what you've become.' I thought you were—"

"That isn't what I meant. I meant what *we've* become." The boy took another drag from his cigarette. "I know I did my job."

"Look," Sitorski said. He walked over and put his hand on his son's shoulder. "This isn't easy for me to say. But I'm proud of you."

Junior slid away from his father, then stood up, walked to the far edge of the patio. Looked out over the river, toward the city. Dropped his cigarette and stomped it into the concrete with his boot.

"You know about My Lai," the boy said.

"Yes. But it doesn't matter. Like I said—"

"You know, there was this ditch—"

"I know. I've—"

"—where most of the bodies were—"

"—seen the—"

"No!" Junior's voice carried and Sitorski winced, embarrassed and afraid that the sound would carry down the long gradual hill of concrete road and brick apartment buildings of Arlington, into Rosslyn, to the Pentagon, and out across the Potomac to the White House. "Listen. Before I went over you explained it all to me and you tried to convince me that there was some reason for all this, that it all made sense. Part of some natural order of things. You talked about good and evil, and freedom, as if that had something to do with what we were fighting. You always explained everything to me with such logic, such control. But let me tell you what it was really like. Let me try to."

Junior continued to look out toward the Potomac.

"There was this friend of mine, a quiet guy who hadn't done anything. He'd just watched Calley and the others when the killings began, but soon he began to feel out of place, like he didn't belong. Then, all of a sudden, he started firing everywhere. He cut throats, cut off hands, cut out tongues, scalped heads. Once he killed the first one the rest were easy. That's what he told me afterward. I know he was right." Junior lit another cigarette, then took a drag from it.

"We dug the ditch and Calley had us round up the villagers and throw them in, the ones that were still alive, shoot them, throw more in. There were clouds that would form, smoke, gunpowder, and dust, and then they'd float away. When a body would move, try to get up, the smoke would stir up again, and Calley or someone else would shoot until the rustling stopped and the smoke would rise up again and another cloud would pass. We all thought the last cloud had passed, when we saw some more rustling. No one had noticed, but a boy, couldn't have been more than two, crawled out of the ditch. Must be a miracle, I thought, how the bullets could have missed him. I watched the kid crawl toward us. It seemed like slow motion, like time was slowing to a stop. He crawled closer to Calley, and then Calley stepped toward him, leaned down and picked him up with both hands. No one knew what he would do next. We all waited. There's a sense you get sometimes that you're acting through your captain, and even with Calley sometimes I felt that. And I did then, we all did, standing back watching him holding the baby. He looked at the kid. Everyone was quiet. Then he tossed it—casual, like some trash he was throwing out—into the ditch, and he shot him, several times. Then he walked to the edge of the ditch just to make sure.

"I was stunned, for a minute, but then what he had done didn't seem strange at all. Because this war, it's strange. It's not against real enemies, not against anyone who might hurt us. It's against an idea, desires, what goes on in other people's minds."

Junior dropped his cigarette, let it smoke from the patio floor and lit another.

"But that baby, that isn't the image I can't get out of my head. After most of the village was gone, I'm supposed to be looking for survivors, and I came across this Buddhist monk. Shaved head, white robes, barefoot. He's kneeling in front of a hut that I suppose was the temple for the village. His eyes are closed and his head is bowed, forehead in the dust. I walk close to him and he doesn't budge. He doesn't even know I'm there. It's as if he's transported somewhere else. Like in the midst of all this slaughter, there was this small zone of peace he could close his eyes and visit. And I thought, God has abandoned us all, all except for this small corner of the planet, where this man has gone to. I wondered what the monk could be praying for, his whole village, his world, already destroyed. It was after Calley had killed the boy, so maybe his prayers had something to do with that. But I got the sense that he was praying for Calley. For us.

"A few minutes later a friend of mine stumbled upon us. I looked at him and shook my head and he knew that I wasn't going to shoot the monk. So he walked up to him, and the monk said, 'No Viet, no Viet,' but my friend wasn't listening.

He hit him with the butt of his rifle, knocked him over. Then he placed his gun against the back of the monk's head. Brains and blood spilled out on the dirt. Then he walked away."

Junior turned around and walked back to the picnic bench, toward Sitorski. They were quiet again.

"I know what you're saying," Sitorski said. "But you didn't participate. That's the difference."

"So that excuses everything, right? When I see those puffs of smoke, those ghosts, that's my defense? And you know, that's not even true." Junior paused, flicked the lighter on and off, his father watching him. "A week or so after the . . . after it happened, I was alone with Calley. Happened to be in the latrine at the same time. And I said to him, 'God will punish you. You know that, don't you?'"

"What did he say?"

"Nothing. He just stared at me, with this look like he knew a lot more about God than I ever would."

"You know there's a reason Calley's being court-martialed and you aren't. You're not a criminal."

"You don't understand. I *know* I was doing what I was supposed to do, what everyone wanted me to do. I know I'm no different than anyone else. But you see, that's just what gets to me. How did we get this way? When did there get to be so much evil?"

Junior's father said nothing.

"You know the story of the Buddha?" Junior said. "Siddhartha lived this sheltered life, and then his charioteer, Channa, takes him into the village. And there he sees disease, death. What he sees, really, is life, for the first time. Channa puts a mirror up to him, and he sees what life will subject him to. What transforms him into the Buddha is what he does with that simple, basic knowledge. He doesn't just accept it. He transforms it."

They were silent again.

Junior turned around to face his father.

"They've subpoenaed me to testify. At Calley's trial."

"I—" Sitorski stopped himself. "I didn't know. Your mother didn't—"

"I didn't tell her. I didn't want her to know."

"You should have told me. Maybe I could have done something."

"I wouldn't want you to. It's something I have to face. Not that I'm sure what I'll do because I'm not. I mean, there are things I have to say, that I want to say, but the trial— I just don't know."

"You'll testify. And everything will be fine."

"I don't know, Dad. I've seen what they're trying to do with Calley now, and I guess it's right, but it misses the point, you know?"

"You're scared. But you didn't do anything wrong. You didn't, you said you didn't. So there's nothing that can happen to you."

"I can testify to what I saw Calley do," Junior said. "And what he ordered the others to do, what we did on our own. I can do that. I have things to say, I have a statement to make. But the action, what happened there, on the surface, that wasn't what was important. It was the feeling. For a time there, everything was permitted, and you could feel the ugliness, that sensation take over all of us. The lawyers aren't interested in hearing about that. The way they look at me now, since I got back, they know about that feeling, that feeling that swept over everybody. And the thing is, it's not just us. I can see people shouting down the protesters, and I can see they've got the feeling too. It's like something bottled up in all of us, an ugliness, that's unleashed once the stopper is off the bottle. And I wonder how we can put it back inside the bottle."

They didn't say anything for a while. Junior blew smoke from his cigarette and it was getting colder so their breath created more smoke between them.

Then the phone rang, and Sitorski stepped inside to pick it up.

"Al? It's Walter."

"Who?" Sitorski was confused; needed time to adjust.

"Popkins."

Sitorski was looking outside, at Junior. The boy had turned his back on him but Alex thought that he could see him crying.

"You OK, Al?"

"Fine." Sitorski turned back around. "Yes."

"A little late, aren't you?"

Sitorski looked at his watch: past ten already. Yes, he was late.

"Something's come up," Popkins said.

"Walter, my boy's just come back from— Are you sure you couldn't . . . ?"

"Orders, Al. Nothing we can do."

"Just for today, if I could have a little time. I'll finish up in the evening."

"Sorry. We need you now. It's important."

Sitorski didn't say anything.

"We'll expect you. Drop by the White House first. The Oval Office. There's a briefing."

When Sitorski walked back outside to the patio, his son was gone.

6 4

THE SHOOTING

AS PALMER WILSON STROLLED UP 14th Street toward Ben Rollins's apartment, it struck him that he would never see Joe M. II again, and that, as the esteemed Wallingford would say, certain profound implications resulted therefrom. Not a matter of logic, this insight, which made it all the more powerful. The long view, a rationale for his professional life, would never be there for him. He questioned, even, if the Lord of Dumb Luck did indeed reign supreme in the cosmos.

And so, there he was. Adrift. Marionette with strings severed. Untethered astronaut. Empty as last night's bottle of Jack. He felt nothing.

Not even fear, though objectively looking at Palmer's situation, he should have. It was broad daylight; he was dressed in the uniform of the most detested and feared governmental entity within a much-detested and feared federal government, with FBI—BUREAU OF DANGEROUS DRUGS printed in bold, block letters on the back of his parka; he was white, and the Negroes who lived in the cramped, decrepit apartments beside, above, and below the apartment of Ben Rollins all understood with a certainty that needed no formal proof that the government of Richard Nixon and J. Edgar Hoover saw the nation as it did the world: a state of war, us against them, with Nixon, Hoover, and their compadres constituting the Us, and Negroes inextricably among the Thems. And they— Ben Rollins and those who lived here, near him—were right, and Palmer knew they were right. And it sickened him.

Ronnie Bonnard was in an apartment directly across the alley. He was lying on a bed, gazing out the window. The lights were out, but he could see straight through Ben Rollins's bedroom to the front door of his apartment. The door was in the exact center of his vision. He knew it was the exact center because Bonnard was looking through the high-powered scope of a rifle, and the front door was in the crosshairs.

Ben was asleep on the floor. He was dreaming, and in his dreams he was back in high school, playing football, running with the ball, except that he was older, as he was now, and he still had both arms. On the sideline he saw Angie, but he had stayed home and kept the streets from getting her so she was bright-eyed and clean, and there was the man he had given the money to at Danny's, the man who thought he was Elvis Presley, and he handed Ben a check, shouting, "You'll need this," as Ben ran, grabbing Angie. The money was a magic pass (he wondered if he'd inhaled some of the drugs he'd dusted off his clothes), but then a crowd amassed behind him and they were walking, not running, because it was no longer a game but a march, a celebration; but where they were going, he did not know. . . .

Then he heard the knock on the door. Tried to recapture the dream, but he couldn't; the pounding didn't stop.

"OPEN UP!" he heard.

Ben got up off the floor, quiet so Angie wouldn't wake up on the bed above him. Then he picked his army fatigues off the floor, pulled them on and buttoned them, and began walking slowly to the door.

Angie, too, had been dreaming, but now she was only half-dreaming, aware of her conscious thoughts. Just tonight, before they had gone to sleep, Ben had told her that he had gone to the White House, thrown away his medal. It hadn't sunk in at first, but while asleep she had imagined it all, and she saw him as a hero again, someone everyone looked up to. She hadn't thought of him that way in a long time.

She woke up. Saw Ben's blankets in a heap on the floor. Saw him standing, about to open the door.

Across the alley, Bonnard had cracked open the window, and now rested the rifle barrel on the bottom of the frame. He could see the back of Ben Rollins's head, his hand on the doorknob. The crosshaired target was just over his left shoulder.

•   •   •

Palmer saw the knob turn. He patted his belt; Joe M. II still wasn't there. The last and only time he had been faced with such a threat of danger was that time in Oakland with the Panthers when Joe M. had saved his life. His belly bare, the fear set in and then, quickly, a flash of thoughts: *To hell with Joe M. II. To hell with J. Edgar Hoover, John Finlator, Wallingford Wilson, the esteemed unloving bastard. To hell with agents provocateurs and setup jobs and black bag jobs the world over. To hell with them all.*

He had been holding his Magnum in one hand as he knocked on the door— "Guns drawn; no reason to take chances"—but now he leaned down to place it back in his holster. *Put away childish things.*

Ronnie Bonnard was waiting for a sound, his eye socket glued to the scope of his rifle. His plan was to start firing as soon as he heard a shot, from Palmer or Rollins. Make it sound like a chaos of gunplay ensued from both sides, and who knew what happened next. *The suspect, Benjamin Rollins, was informed that he was under arrest, drugs being on his person, and he must have reached for his gun and shot at the arresting officer, Palmer Wilson.* Standard procedure: Bonnard must have done it a hundred times. Never had he missed his quarry.

Angie assumed that the knock on the door would be for her, a john drunkenly confusing sex and love, a dealer offering a sweet exchange. Not someone she wanted Ben to see. Not that he didn't know, but you avoid those little run-ins, play them down. So Angie got up as soon as she saw Ben going to answer it. When he opened the door the first thing she saw was a white guy, in some official-looking uniform, with a gun in his hand, bent over. She jumped out of bed and ran to the door.

Where's his head? Bonnard thought. Bonnard swung the scope sideways but still didn't see his quarry's head—or anything else—when the door opened. He took his eye off the scope, trying his best to keep the rifle steady in position, then looked again. Still nothing. Then Palmer appeared, standing back up. But no gunshot.

Ben thought he recognized the guy from earlier in the weekend. Looked harm-less. Then Ben saw the gun and jerked toward it, but the man stuck his hand out, looked up at him with almost tearful eyes, and Ben could see he was putting the gun away, then tossed it behind him and held his empty hands up.

"He's got a gun!" Angie shouted as she ran toward Ben. Ben turned around once he heard her, and even Ronnie Bonnard, across the alley, heard a yell, though he couldn't make out the words.

A commotion'll have to do, Bonnard thought. *Suspect resisted arrest, leading to chaos, gunplay.* . . . He locked in again, the crosshairs of the scope dead on, above the eyebrow ridge.

Angie pounced toward the door, crouching out of the starting block, Ben and Palmer examining each other, cautious, and as Angie reached the doorway to tackle Ben, Bonnard pulled the trigger.

NOT GIRL HAPPY

BACK AT THE HOTEL, Tommy had tried telephoning Graceland for forty minutes but got no response, only a persistent, oblivious ring.

He had already called work, and the folks at Paramount weren't happy with him not showing up. Tossing Elvis's name out for cover only made matters worse, reminding the crew how he got the job in the first place. Even Elvis couldn't bail him out of this one. The truth was, to the folks Tommy worked with, Elvis Presley was a joke. Tommy had to get back to L.A., but he couldn't— wouldn't—abandon Elvis. So he had to get a hold of Bo or Tubby, someone who could take care of Elvis from here on out, someone to bring him home.

That uptight French limo driver. Maurice Flambeau was his name. Tommy knew that Maurice wouldn't want to help him, but it was worth a shot. He called L.A. information.

As he held the phone to his ear, Tommy watched the news on television. A number of citizens' groups were demanding to see President Nixon, to present him with petitions in support of Lieutenant William Calley.

"Calley's a hero," a fat white lady was saying to a reporter, the White House just over her shoulder in the background. Tommy thought he recognized her from the flight to D.C. "The only way we'll win this war is with soldiers like him, courageous folks not aiming to please the yellow bellies in the Congress, or the Jews and such in the press."

"Ma'am," the reporter said, "the army says that no one in the village was armed, and that even after Calley found this out, he and his soldiers continued to rape and kill—"

"That's what I'm talking about!" the lady yelled.

Other women, of similar girth, all in loud flowered dresses, surrounded the reporter and began to point their fingers at him, shouting.

"Whose side you on?!"

"Love it or leave it!"

Yes: the ladies were familiar.

Next, a representative of a World War II veterans group was interviewed to discuss his petition.

"Abbie Hoffman and those black power types are on the streets," the man said, "and an American hero's in jail. World's upside down as a cake."

"The only way we can defeat these . . . Orientals," another older vet said, "is like Calley done. We can't change them." The man gulped, caught his breath. "But we can kill them."

"Right," another said. "Now those politicians are trying to tie our boys' hands—"

As he dialed Maurice's number, Tommy could just imagine beer-swilling blowhards from Miami to Baton Rouge to San Diego, planted on bar stools or living room couches—folks whose wives loved Elvis when they were young and so was he, and loved him still—cheering Nixon and Calley with a passion more intense and fiery than any love. Tommy could picture the angry man on the bar stool, could see him: he was Arnell Greenaway, affixed to a stool on the far end of the bar at Wendy's back in Memphis. Probably hadn't budged an inch since Tommy had left for the Coast.

Tubby was probably still there, too.

Why the hell didn't he think of that before?

In his apartment in West Hollywood, Maurice Flambeau was naked, save for an open bathrobe. A tub of popcorn resting on his stomach, he was watching television: an Elvis movie, *Girl Happy*. As the phone rang Elvis was singing "Fort Lauderdale Chamber of Commerce."

"Any male in Fort Lauderdale," Elvis sang, "not pursu—ing a cute fe—male, will immediately land in jail."

"Allo?" Maurice droned, picking up the phone.

"Maurice," Tommy said. "This is Tommy Shelton."

"Oh."

"Remember me, from yesterday—"

Oui, oui. The behemoth. Maurice remembered.

Just then, the phone in another bedroom in the suite—Elvis's room—rang.

"Hold on a sec," Tommy said, and ran to answer it.

Just before he placed the call, Max Sharpe had found himself in a bind. He knew that protocol didn't permit him to dial Elvis—he would lose prestige by placing a call himself—but he didn't want to trust anyone else to do the job; not his secretary, and certainly not Dwight Chapin. He considered, for a moment, what his friend Gordon Liddy would do in such a situation, and concluded that deception was the way to go.

So he called the Washington Hotel himself, asked for Jon Burrows in a staged British voice. The man at the desk didn't understand him at first, so he modulated his tone slightly, and was patched through.

"'Lo?" a gruff, southern voice panted on the other line.

"Mr. Burrows, please," Sharpe said.

"Burrows?"

"This is Room Five-naught-five through Five-naught-seven?"

"Naught?"

"Five hundred and five through Five-hundred-seven," Sharpe barked.

"Right. But there's no—"

"Elvis Presley," Sharpe said, dropping the accent. "Is Mr. Presley there? This is the White House calling."

"This is the President?" Tommy said.

"Not quite," Sharpe said. "This is the office of Maximillian Sharpe."

"Maurice," Tommy said when he returned to the living room phone, "we're going to see Nixon around noon."

"I am not on the invitation list, I expect," said Maurice.

"No, sorry. But I need you to do something."

Silence on the other end.

"Maurice, *Elvis* needs you to do a favor."

"Oh, really?"

"Yes. You gotta call Memphis. A place called Wendy's."

6 6

THE WEDDING

IT WASN'T OFFICIAL—THAT IS, like the religion of which Wendell Augustine Root, a.k.a. Wendy, was a High Priest, it wasn't sanctioned by the state of Tennessee or any other governmental entity—but, nonetheless, Arnell Greenaway and Sharon Teele were to be married. Wendy was to perform the ceremony at his Chili and BBQ Tavern back in Memphis.

The two had been brought together by the spirit of Elvis himself. Both of them were convinced of it.

When Sharon crashed into him just outside of their respective bathrooms, Arnell was knocked out cold. Before this, the only time he had seen stars appear over an unconscious man's head was in cartoons, but this time he actually experienced the sensation. He felt he was transported into space, floating through the stars.

There wasn't no God up there. No gates of heaven. And the only angel he saw was when he opened his eyes and there was Sharon Teele, leaning over him. Then Sharon felt a large, heavy hand rest on her shoulder.

"Honey. This boy can help hisself up. Just drunk is all."

It was Tubby.

"Let's quit this joint."

Sharon's eyes were locked onto Arnell's, like some magnetic force—a power neither of them quite understood—held them to each other. Tubby pulled her up to her feet, and as she stood, Arnell's hand slipped through her fingers, flopped onto the floor, the limp flipper of a drunken walrus.

"We best be goin'," Tubby said, putting his arm around Sharon to lead her out. "I know a place. . . ."

Then the phone rang. Wendy picked it up.

"Allo," a hesitant French voice said on the other end, "but is there residing a, ahem, 'Tubby' Grove?"

Wendy laughed.

"I share your disdain for the southern monikers," Wendy said. "The chap's parents probably gave him a fine name, too, which he's chosen to waste. Pearls, swine, and all that."

Maurice Flambeau—the voice on the other end of the line—was tickled.

Maurice was tickled not only because the voice who picked up the phone appeared to be familiar with this particular Tubby, but because the voice had a charming, intelligent . . . European . . . lilt to it. For the first time since the brazen behemoth had commandeered Elvis from him, relegating Maurice to the status of mere chauffeur, Maurice smiled.

"Swine, *certainement*," Maurice said, "but speak of pearls! In the swamps of Memphis, no less! To whom do I have the pleasure of . . . ?"

"I prefer to be referred to as Wendy."

"And why, if I may?"

"Matters dealing with, shall we say, unconventional predilections and the like."

"And why Memphis?" Maurice said, an understanding wink in his voice that, he could sense, his companion understood.

"It's a long story."

"You may try me."

"It concerns a certain entertainer *nonpareil* who resides here," Wendy said. "One for whom I have a certain affection. To understand, one would have to be familiar with a rather all-encompassing History of Our Times, if you will, part account of antiquity, part hypothetical future."

"I have time," said Maurice, intrigued. "Speak. Please."

And speak Wendy did. He explained that it was not a sexual affection he had for Elvis—though it was, perhaps, partly that—but a religious and intellectual one. At Oxford, Wendy said, he had immersed himself in the study of religion and folklore, and discovered that there were certain immutable elements of the hero story that were as prevalent today as in the days of Zeus: heroes of the present order were worshipped because they defeated the kings—or gods or heroes—of the old order, and thereby ushered in the era in which their believ-ers lived. But once that hero story no longer rang true, once the story no longer represented the creation of the world in which present-day believers lived, then that hero became ripe for overthrow. The beliefs Wendy held dear—for exam-ple, freedom, self-expression, love unbounded by petty morality—were not rep-resented by the Trinity he had been raised to obey. Isn't God free of prejudice? Can it be a sin to love? His God, Wendy concluded, loved love of all types, and loved freedom, variety: no bigot He—if it was a He. His hero was Elvis.

All this Wendy explained to Maurice, in some detail.

"Brilliant," Maurice said. "Enlightening! And let me say, I share your philos-ophy to a T, down to your love of the King and, uh, the predilections you have, well, intimated. If you will pardon my forthrightness."

"Thank you," said Wendy. "And yes. As far as the pardon, it's not called for." Since moving to Memphis, no one had ever listened to his theories with such interest. Intellectual compadres were as rare as fellow devotees of his particular predilection. "But why did you call?"

"Oh," Maurice said. "I need to tell that 'Tubby' fellow to go to Washington. It appears that Elvis is there—*oui*, the man himself; I know him, you see—at the Washington Hotel. A certain Tommy Shelton—a brazen behemoth of a man—has accompanied him, and would like to be relieved of his duties. As to what other duties he might have . . . I say nothing more."

"I think you better talk to Tubby," Wendy said. "We can continue later, I trust? Tubby!"

So Tubby let go of Sharon, walked to the bar and picked up the phone. As he talked to Maurice, jotting down phone numbers and hotel rooms, the eyes of Arnell Greenaway and Sharon Teele once again locked. Then they began to speak to each other, and they didn't stop for the next fourteen hours, not even when Tubby, before rushing out the door, asked Sharon if she'd come with him, to meet Elvis hisself.

And then, when the sun came up on Monday morning, just a few short hours ago, Arnell and Sharon approached Wendy and asked whether he would marry them, which he agreed to do, on the spot.

The ceremony had just begun. Wendy was just about to give a few words before the final vows. He placed a hand on Arnell's shoulder, and another on Sharon's, and smiled down upon them.

Then Bo and the Colonel stormed into the bar.

6 7

THE REVEREND

MAX SHARPE WAS PANTING, breathless. After speaking to who he assumed to be Elvis's chief deputy, he had raced to Chapin's office, but Chapin was out, his secretary didn't know where; then to Ehrlichman's office, but was informed that he was with the President in the Rose Garden. So there he was now, outside on the walkway leading to the Rose Garden.

In the Garden, the Reverend Billy Graham was standing at the podium. The press corps was circled around him, and behind them a small crowd was seated—the same band of White House and RNC employees who had attended the veterans' awards ceremony on Saturday.

Sharpe scanned his eyes for his boss and mentor. Then he spotted him in front, near the press.

"John," Sharpe whispered loudly. "Psssstttt!"

Ehrlichman turned around.

"I've got to talk to you," Sharpe said. "About Elvis."

"Listen to this, Max," Ehrlichman whispered, walking toward him. "Peoria." He winked.

"Mrs. Nixon and the President were kind enough to invite me here for lunch," Reverend Graham was saying, "and my mother taught me to never keep a good host waiting." The crowd laughed, and the President—Sharpe now saw Nixon behind the Reverend—laughed too. "But first a few words, before I join my gracious hosts. In this Christmas season my thoughts turn, as I know do all of yours, to peace, in Vietnam and throughout the world. Now, about peace. We have heard a good deal of talk about the calls for withdrawal, immediate withdrawal from Vietnam, which some have called—I believe wrongly—pleas for 'peace.' Biblical truth would indicate that we will always have wars on the earth, until the coming of the Prince of Peace. Until then, our job is not to end war, but to ensure that the forces of good prevail. Which is what you, Mr. President, continue to do. And we thank you for it."

Then the President stepped up and shook hands with the Reverend. The President's press secretary, Ron Ziegler, stepped to the podium to ask if there were any questions for Graham.

"Brilliant," Ehrlichman whispered to Sharpe. "Those words will carry."

"John," Sharpe hissed. "I need to talk to you. It's important."

"Hold on," Ehrlichman said.

Ziegler pointed to Dan Rather, who now stood up.

"Reverend Graham," Rather said, "this display that we've just seen here today—"

Ron Ziegler stepped in front of Graham.

"Display?" he said.

"Yes," Rather continued, "the petitions to the President, the pro-Calley groups coming to see the President—it was clearly intended to suggest that the public is behind Lieutenant Calley, and would like to see the prosecution end—"

"Now first, Dan," the press secretary said, "the President and this administration intend to let justice take its course in the Calley case, like all others, and take it from there. At the same time, we will continue to listen to the voice of the people on all of their concerns. We will not castigate citizens who care deeply enough about their country that they spend their hard-earned dollars to fly three thousand miles to voice their opinions to the President. This President will continue to listen to the voice of America. And, further, let me note that Reverend Graham is not a member of this administration and is not speaking as such. He is a universally respected man of the cloth, an independent, leading voice of the religious heart of this nation."

Ziegler stepped back, leaving the podium to Billy Graham.

"Thank you, as always, for your help, Ron," Rather said. "As I was saying, Reverend Graham, particularly in light of the display we've seen here today in support of Lieutenant Calley, do you, as the"—Rather glanced at his notepad—"'leading voice of the religious heart of the nation,' consider that the massacre at My Lai was morally justifiable?"

Billy Graham paused for a moment. Then he spoke.

"We have all had our My Lais in one way or another," Graham said, "with a thoughtless word, an arrogant act, or a selfish deed. None of us, since Eve ate of the apple, is without sin."

"Reverend Graham," Rather said, "are you equating the massacre of five hundred innocent women and children with a thoughtless word?"

Before Graham could answer Ziegler stepped in front of him and announced that the session was over, but that Reverend Graham and the President would make themselves available for photos.

"Perfect," Ehrlichman said, chuckling. "Like we scripted it." Then he turned to Sharpe. "What's up?"

"It's Elvis."

"We've handled that. You got your photo op—"

"It's a meeting."

"Whatever. What's the problem?"

"The thing is, I've—we—called Elvis's hotel, but he wasn't there," Sharpe said. "Hopefully he'll be back soon, and he'll get here by noon, or twelve-thirty, but if he doesn't . . ."

Ehrlichman stared at Sharpe.

"Is that all? You're afraid Elvis might not show?"

Sharpe nodded yes.

"Who cares about Elvis?" said John Ehrlichman.

6 8

ELVIS AND FINLATOR

"Mr. FINLATOR SIR," ELVIS SAID, "let me tell you where this country's gone wrong."

Look in the mirror for starters, John Finlator said to himself.

Elvis was sitting in the visitors' rigid Victorian chair, facing Finlator, who had strategically positioned himself in the dominant North Carolina leather chair behind the desk. It had taken some doing to get Elvis sufficiently settled to seat himself: his legs were wound like springs. And now Elvis shot up again, began ambling about the room, poking his jewel-encrusted fingers at the pictures on the walls.

"That you and J. Edgar?" Elvis said. "Man, look at that piece! Winchester stopped makin' those machine gun jobs in the thirties, didn't they?"

"Actually," Finlator said, "they reissued them in '41, for the war. . . ."

"Dillinger's corpse! You had a hand in that deal? I know a thing or two about corpses, you know."

Oh, Finlator knew. He knew.

And on and on Elvis paced, stopped for an instant to look at a photo, his feet continuing to tap, around the room in fits of nervous energy. Since this morning—when Marge had taken a call from this . . . "King" . . . and after a few well-placed calls he was ordered to meet with him—Finlator had reviewed the FBI files on Presley, so he was certain that this unnatural energy was fueled by one part adrenaline, natural opiates emitted after an all-night session, and nine parts opiates of the artificial, illegal, type: according to Finlator's file on *The King*, a garden variety of uppers.

"Got that, Marge?" Finlator said, turning to his gap-mouthed secretary.

Marge had trailed Elvis into the office like a puppy and was now seated along the back wall, holding a pencil and pad, both of which she was presently incapable of using.

"The nation's problems," Finlator said, "coming up."

She nodded her head absentmindedly.

Elvis paused for an instant, squinted at Finlator.

"You want to hear it, or don't you?" Elvis said.

"Oh, I'm all ears." Finlator tapped the tobacco into his pipe, inhaled flame into the bowl.

"All right then. Well"—Elvis turned around to wink at Marge, then sat back down across from Finlator—"it's basically the young people that I'm concerned about. You know, the counterculture types, Panthers, Yippies, SDSers . . ."

Babble on, Elvis, Finlator thought, looking down at his watch. Might as well catch up on some work.

He opened an envelope on his desk he hadn't noticed before; Ronnie Bonnard must have had it couriered over. Pulled out the papers inside: a cover memo "Re: Colonel Alex Sitorski," with photos attached.

". . . Jane Fonda, the drugs, the Yippies—did I say that?"

Finlator nodded; began to read the memo. *Quarry seen fraternizing with known prostitute and stripper, one Angelina Rollins, sister of one Benjamin Rollins, local character, creator of disturbance at Rose Garden veterans' ceremony Saturday afternoon, hurling medal . . .*

Finlator stopped to analyze what he had read.

"Now I know you're the honcho on drugs," Elvis continued, "so I don't have to tell you about the drug problem. These young folks are impressionable, and they're just following their leaders, on all these . . . well, you know who's at the head of the parade, of course you do."

Finlator glanced at Elvis. His eyes said no, not a clue.

"These kids are following John Lennon and those long-haired boys from England now. Not like when I . . ."

Finlator glanced back down at the report. *Quarry spoke to estranged wife (now fraternizing with known Black Panthers, women's libbers, and hippies in Los Angeles area) Saturday afternoon. Lunched with Max Sharpe. Monday morning met son at airport. Son is Vietnam vet of My Lai 4 incident, subpoenaed to testify at Calley court-martial, traveled abroad since return to States, then fraternized with members of antiwar movement in California . . . Quarry's extensive knowl-*

edge of My Lai details . . . and note with interest Quarry's apparent refusal to pull strings to keep son out of front-line action . . . unlikely that these connections are result of mere coincidence. . . . Far-ranging conspiracy with tentacles in Pentagon, Panthers, antiwar movement, and perhaps WH itself likely . . .

". . . now in my line of work," Elvis went on, "I meet all types, all manner of depravity and drugs, I don't need to tell you I'm sure."

Oh, I've seen the files on those Graceland parties, Finlator thought. *Seen you watching from the couch while the lesbians go at it. Even seen photos of Little Elvis. Don't tell me about depravity.*

"You ever read Madame Blavatsky?"

Finlator shook his head no, still reading the report.

"The Secret Doctrine?"

No.

"The Inner Voice?"

Nuh huh.

"Remind me. I'll send you a copy. But let me give you an idea about what she's talking about, about my powers. I'm in Las Vegas the other month, after a show"—Elvis stood up now and began to walk quickly around the room—"and I get to talking with this comic, Ernie Charles, fast-talking Jewish guy in the Green Room, trying jokes when he breaks into tears all the sudden. Well I talk to him and he tells me 'Elvis, it's the drugs,' heroin, he's shaking and crying, telling me he needs a fix bad but he don't have the money could I loan him some. So I walk over to him, and I place one hand on his forehead and the other around his arm. 'Show me the marks,' I say to him, 'where you shot that shit into your veins.' And he does, on both arms, and I lay hands on 'em. And I'm think-ing all the while, and saying aloud—a feelin' comes over me—'Devils leave this man, leave him and he shall goeth in the path of righteousness, shall liveth in the straight and narrow way, praise be' and the rest. Then I remove my hands for a minute, and I cover his mouth then his ears then his eyes, and then I slap him hard on the forehead. And all the sudden, he stops shaking, stops crying, stops sweating. And he says, 'I'm cured. Elvis, I'm cured!'"

Elvis looked up at Finlator.

"And he was, was the thing. Never touched the stuff since. I done this a few times now." Elvis sat back down in the chair in front of Finlator's desk. "Now what I need is a badge. I've got a bunch of 'em, you know." He pulled one out, but Finlator motioned him to stop.

Finlator put the report down and looked up at Elvis.

"And the thing is, I need a real FBI one. One from you narcotics boys would just hit it. John O'Grady—you know him; used to work for you boys—told me you could get me one. I figure with an Agent-at-Large I could get around, really spread the word, make some change. I don't just mean healing, either. Me and my boys'll chase down poor bastards on the highway if they're not careful, just like James Bond."

"Let me make sure I understand this," Finlator said. "You want an FBI badge? You want to be an agent? Just like that."

Elvis nodded.

Finlator exhaled a long stream of smoke, then tapped out some tobacco into the American eagle ashtray on his desk.

"I'd like to help out the department, too," Elvis said. "What about $4,000? To buy some new guns for the boys in the field."

"Mr. Presley, I don't think you understand how we do business up here."

"I don't think *you* understand, Mr. Finlator."

Finlator looked back down at Bonnard's memo, but then it was pounded onto his desk, out of his hands, by a jewel-encrusted fist. He looked up and there was Elvis, sunglasses in hand.

"You don't think I'm serious, do you? You think I'm just some hick from Tupelo. Some white trash."

Finlator didn't say anything.

"I know what's going on out there," Elvis said. "I know what you're up against. Ask your boys in Memphis: I've got some calls lately, threats, serious ones, not sure from whom."

"I'm sure you have."

"Now listen," Elvis whispered in a husky voice, "I need a badge. A real FBI badge that I can flash at anyone and go anywhere with, anytime, so there's nothing nobody can do about it. I know how this works, I've seen Bond and all those boys, snap your fingers and you're anywhere, anytime. No one'll bother me when I want and then they'll be there when I need 'em. I know what that's like, that freedom. I remember it. I've seen the movies and I've been the heroes in the movies and I can be again. I know it." Elvis stopped. "Do you understand what sort of badge I'm talking about?"

Finlator kept his eyes on Elvis while he laid his pipe in the ashtray.

"It's not a badge you want," John Finlator said. "It's a magic pass."

Elvis didn't say anything, but Finlator thought he detected a nod.

"My powers are limited, Mr. Presley," Finlator went on. "Certain matters are beyond my control."

"Well," Elvis said, "then to hell with you. I need to talk to Hoover."

WEDDING INTERRUPTED

"WHERE IS SHE?" Colonel Parker yelled, wielding his cane like a machete as he stomped into Wendy's Chili and BBQ Tavern.

Sharon and Arnell were facing each other, holding hands just in front of the bar, Arnell garbed in a black leather jacket, upraised collar, greasy black hair tossed over his head, and Sharon in a short white dress. Wendy stood before them atop a chair, in a broad-lapelled white cotton suit, black shirt, purple, yellow, and pink psychedelic paisley tie. He was in mid-sermon when the Colonel and Bo barged in.

"You Sharon?" the Colonel screamed.

Sharon nodded.

"Well, what you done with my boy? Where you put him, you looney bird!"

"What the Colonel means is," Bo said, "where's Elvis?"

Arnell and Sharon looked at each other, then up to the sky.

"You killed him?!" The Colonel poked Sharon with his cane. "You looney bastards done away with my boy?!"

The Colonel lunged at Sharon, cane in hand, which prompted Arnell to step in front of her, fists clenched, which prompted Bo to lunge at the Colonel to stop him, arms outstretched, all of which prompted Wendy to scream, "NOBODY'S DONE ANYTHING TO ELVIS!"

Which prompted everyone to flinch backward, then freeze in their positions, forming a midfight tableau.

"Pardon me," Wendy said, now subdued. "Nobody *did* anything to Elvis."

"Well," the Colonel said, "where the hell is he then, Mrs. Looney Bird Teele?"

Arnell clenched his fist again, and stepped closer to the Colonel.

"You don't talk thataway to her," Arnell said. And he cocked his fist back and landed it hard across the Colonel's chin, sending him sprawling to the floor.

"And besides," Arnell said, stepping forward to deck Bo, "it's Mrs. Looney Bird Greenaway now."

7 0

TUBBY IN THE AIR

TUBBY GROVE WAS IN THE air, on an American Airlines flight to Washington, D.C. The plane had just taken off from Memphis, and already he had ordered two beers and an extra bag of peanuts.

He had come up with an angle to this Washington trip, a plan by which he could leapfrog over the hierarchically superior position of Bo into a more prominent, dominant rank in the Memphis Mafia. (Not that those were the words Tubby used to express it to himself.) It was the most ambitious thought Tubby Grove had ever had in his life.

The plan was that he would personally report back to Colonel Parker when he got to Washington, bypassing Bo, so that the credit for rescuing Elvis from otherwise certain death and/or disaster would fall solely to him. Hints would be dropped that Bo had discouraged Tubby from even looking into whether Elvis had flown out of town; suspicions would be planted, then watered. The Colonel would be forced to rethink things, about whether the right man was in charge of handling Elvis at home.

Tubby realized that Bo had given him the job with Elvis and that, besides, they were buddies. But opportunities like this didn't present themselves every day, and you had to take advantage of them when they did. Wasn't that what made America such a great country?

Isn't that what Elvis's life had taught him?

7 1

CHANNA AND ELVIS

FINLATOR, ELVIS THOUGHT. That bastard.

Elvis had just walked out of the FBI building. He looked up and the sun seared his eyes like a flame surging up from a barbecue grill, so now he saw only spots of white light that obscured his vision. It was only then that he realized that he was holding his sunglasses in his hands. He slipped them on and staggered against the side of the building.

Finlator doesn't know. Couldn't understand what he's dealing with. The man laughed at me.

Thinks I'm a joke. Over the hill.

Suddenly he felt exhausted. He let his back slide down and sat on the sidewalk. *Think I'll stay right here.*

When Elvis next opened his eyes, he was in the back of the limousine.

"Life's tough outside the gates, ain't it, King?" the driver said.

"Channa?" Elvis said.

"That's right."

Elvis dug into his pocket. No pills. Dug deeper. Still nothing. A sweat broke out across his forehead. Tried the other pants pocket, dug hard at the bottom. Now he felt something. Pulled his hand out and there was a red. Just one small pill, but still, it was something.

Popped it into his mouth.

Ahhhhhh.

He could feel his blood begin to perk again. But this time his head wasn't a tethered balloon: airplanes were taking off inside, engines blaring.

Elvis opened his eyes and there, just in front of him, was the huge plastic chocolate-covered doughnut outside of Danny's. When had he been there? Yesterday? The day before?

"Stop here," Elvis said. "Just be a minute."

This time there was no crowd, so Elvis could walk in undisturbed. The same colored man was behind the counter, the same white smock wrapped around him, a baker's hat on his head.

"You bring money this time, Mr. King?"

"That's what I'm here for," Elvis said. "That boy the other day, the one who bailed me out?"

Danny grimaced, said nothing.

"One arm . . ."

"That's right," Danny said. "Ben Rollins. Smartest kid, with the biggest heart you ever saw. Boy's a hero."

"He'll go a long ways," Elvis said. "In this country sky's the limit. Where is he?"

"Why you want to bother him now?"

"I want to thank him," Elvis said. "And pay him back."

7 2

PEORIA

"YOU DON'T UNDERSTAND," Sharpe said.

He was following his boss and mentor as Ehrlichman walked away behind Haldeman, who was behind the Secret Service men, who were behind Billy Graham and the President, all walking along the terrace into the White House, then down the hall.

The press conference had broken up.

"Elvis is rock 'n' roll," Sharpe said. "Rock 'n' roll is the counterculture. That's the heart of the opposition. If Elvis signs on with us, that's it. Endgame. The opposition is neutralized."

Ehrlichman stopped and turned around.

"Look, Max," he said, *"you* don't understand. I thought RN would have gotten this through to you the other night. Listen: you neutralize with information, with power. Like what you did with Sitorski."

"But John," Sharpe said, "what did I do with Alex—with Sitorski? I mean, I know what we found out, but what did he do?"

Ehrlichman stopped walking and looked at Sharpe.

"Max, I've already told you something about history, what it really is. Well, RN's—we've—realized some time ago that the, uh, history of Calley, of My Lai, was being distorted. It's an important point, and Ben Bradlee and his merry band were turning it into a murder story, wrenching it all out of context. Now RN went along at first, up front anyway, said he was outraged at what Calley did. Which was fine. Because the people have to lead. We need to follow the message that comes from, well, Peoria."

Ross Turnbull, the chief of White House security, walked by them in the hallway and saluted, and Ehrlichman nodded. When he passed, Ehrlichman walked into the bathroom, a few doors away. Sharpe followed him inside. Ehrlichman checked out the stalls, then leaned against the sink and went on.

"Listen," Ehrlichman said, his back to the mirrors, "the *truth* is that Calley was right, that he was fighting this war the only way it can be fought—fought *and won*. People have to come to understand that. They have to see My Lai from Calley's eyes; see that the enemy is everywhere, is nowhere; that the babies mothers hold could be disguising bombs or grenades, and so—yes!—the babies themselves might as well be grenades, and you can never tell until it is too late . . . and so the safer course is to act . . . preemptively."

Ehrlichman's eyes were growing more fiery, intense. He turned around and splashed water on his face, then stared at the mirror. "The *truth* is that the Cong respond only to fear, to terror. Bodies, the growing counts, are meaningless to the Asian mind—Westmoreland's right there—given their belief in transitory states, in reincarnation. *This life is but a fleeting presence, a stage, a step up the ladder,* you know. But terror, a sense that America has become unhinged and is now capable of anything—that RN himself is now feeding on the blood—*that's* a silver bullet into the Cong spirit. That will hit them where they live. Fuck their karma up, and good."

Ehrlichman paused again, caught his breath, still looking in the mirror.

"Now, if our plan—Peoria—works, if circumstances play out, the sweet center of the electorate will understand Calley. They will *become* Calley. The only problem, then, will be in tempering their rage, explaining to them why we should hold back at all in our attack, why the Bomb is not justified here. And this feeling, this spirit, Max, will stay, if Peoria takes hold. Even if we lose this war, all we need is another Cong. The spirit of Peoria will live on."

He turned around to face Sharpe.

"But we can deal with all that another time. The point is that Calley will emerge from this whole thing a hero, and if he is convicted, we'll be forced to bow to public pressure and release him, in some way or another, or if he is found innocent, stand behind the verdict with a wink that it was the right result. That justice was done."

Ehrlichman straightened his tie and took a step toward the door.

"Max, you had a job to do—in Peoria—and you did it, quickly and efficiently."

Ehrlichman opened the bathroom door and stepped out into the hall. Sharpe followed. Then, together, they walked in silence down the hall toward the Oval Office. When they reached the door, they saw Haldeman waving at Ehrlichman to come in.

"And as far as what you were saying, about that High on Life business, and Elvis Presley," Ehrlichman said, as he took a step toward the door. Then he whispered. "Defeat the enemy, and we defeat ourselves."

7 3

FUTURE AND PAST

CHANNA, THE DRIVER, HAD his right arm around Elvis's back, his hand cupped under Elvis's arm, holding him up. They had made it out of the limo, through the lobby, then into the elevator of the Washington Hotel. Now in the hallway on the fifth floor, Channa was carrying Elvis to his room.

Channa Stalls believed in the lightness of souls; that the soul of Elvis, his inner spirit, upon his death would lift like a cloud, a puff of smoke, from its temporary home in this world to travel into and occupy another body abode. Channa knew that since spirits did not travel until the moment of death, this would not occur with Elvis until almost seven years in the future. (Channa could also read the future like a comic strip.) He knew that in August 1977, sitting in his bathroom in Graceland at night, reading, Elvis would fall over onto the floor, and his spirit would lift up from his then-functionless body like a cloud, and drift . . . and what struck Channa now, as he lugged Elvis by the arm to the door of his hotel suite, trying desperately to reach his hand high enough to knock on the door, was this: How can a soul this heavy ever lift to the sky?

"Ah hell," Elvis said. "Just take me home. To Graceland."

"That's not possible," Channa said. "You still have more to see."

When Tommy opened the door a second later, Elvis was alone in the hallway.

"Elvis," Tommy said, "you won't believe this shit." Elvis staggered away from him, involuntarily backpedaling, so Tommy grabbed him and dragged him into the suite. "I'm telling you, you got to be careful with those pills."

"Don' worry," Elvis slurred. He collapsed on a couch. "We're goin' home,

Tommy. Had it with this town. You wouldn't believe that bastard Finlator. Wouldn't even give me a badge."

"To hell with him, man," Tommy said.

"The bastard much as spit on me."

"Don't worry about it, E. Just some tight-ass bureaucrat. You know those types."

"I don't think it was him, man," Elvis said. "I don't know, but I'd bet . . . ten, fifteen years ago, man, that wouldn't happen, you know? They'd be rolling out the carpet for me. What the hell's happened?"

"Elvis, fifteen years ago the FBI would have slapped cuffs on you if they could. You were dangerous back then." Tommy laughed. "Remember Florida? When they said they'd arrest you if you moved your hips?"

"That's right." Elvis smiled. "All they'd let me do is wiggle my damned finger," and he laughed, then began to wiggle his forefinger as he sang "The Battle Hymn of the Republic," his finger dancing along.

"Glory, glory Hallelujah! His truth"—the finger dipped—"is marching on!"

"You were a devil back then, E. That's what the Establishment guys thought, anyway."

"I *was*, wasn't I? Those boys were scared of me." Elvis shook his head. "Shoulda been, too."

"And Cardinal Spellman preaching against you. The *New York Times* and Walter Winchell, all of them up in arms, saying the world was going to end if you took over." Tommy laughed and Elvis laughed with him.

"Tommy, that's what I mean. That's just what I'm talking about. Who gives a damn about me now?"

"Well," Tommy said, "that bastard Nixon, for one."

"What do you mean?"

"That's what I was going to tell you. One of his flunkies called. The President wants to see you. Supposed to be at the White House by noon. That just gives us an hour. Tubby or Bo should be meeting us here, if they make it in time."

"Man, that'll show that Finlator." The thought perked Elvis up like a fresh vial of reds. "And John Lennon, too. See when he gets invited to meet the President."

"Elvis"—Tommy walked over to the couch, sat beside him—"I know what you're going to say, but I don't think you should see him."

"Who?"

"Nixon. The only reason that bastard'd want to see you is to use you for one reason or other. I mean—"

"Tommy," Elvis said, lifting his hand for silence, "hold it. We'll see who uses who."

7 4

JUNIOR IN THE PARK

EVEN THOUGH RONNIE BONNARD had put the Sitorski job to bed—completed the investigation, drafted the report, delivered copies to John Finlator and Max Sharpe—he wasn't finished.

Which is why he had returned to Sitorski's home in Arlington, listened in on the meeting with his son—the bugs in the house had not been removed—and was now following Sitorski's car over Key Bridge, into the city. Nearing the White House. And nearing the boy, Al Junior.

How did Bonnard know the boy was close? When he had embraced Junior at the airport he had dropped a radar sensor into his pocket. Which caused a light to blink now on the glass map below his dashboard, indicating the kid's present whereabouts.

As Bonnard followed Sitorski's car past the White House, into the Executive Office Building garage across the street, the intensity of the light pinpointed the boy's location: Al Sitorski Junior was in that den of degradation and moral decay, that cesspool of radicalism: Lafayette Park.

In the park, Lester pounded his drum. The radio was playing "I Got a Feeling," the Beatles' latest; and now John Lennon sang, "Everybody had a hard year, everybody had a good time . . ." and Lester, above it all, was preaching.

"Have mercy on him, Lord," Lester yelled, in between beats of the drum, "whoever it is of you who governs those parts. The Buddha, I s'pose. He's a jolly old bastard usually, you know, but he's being tested something nasty. Christ God's trying to convert the Buddha, see, teach him that you got to fight back. But Buddha knows the war's not about people, see, not about Commies or any earthly bull. It's just principles, who's got it right in the great debate. I got my money on the East."

Al Junior was sitting in the lotus position, palms raised, just a couple of feet in front of Lester.

"Dig it," Lester said. "Dig the sounds of the drum."

He put a long finger to his lips, slowly lifted his arm, then beat down again on the drum.

"Check it out: every bang on the peace drum's another body. Maybe it'll seep into Tricky Dick's soul, if he has one. Maybe, one day . . . We do what we can, you know? With what we got."

Lester beat the drum again.

"Something smells," Lester said. "Like napalm almost. Gasoline or something." He sniffed around him, then looked down at Al Junior. "You spill some gas on yourself, brother?"

Junior didn't say anything.

Lester beat the drum.

"We all got to change our way of thinking," Lester said. "See all these people here? They're trying to as best they can. Look: three years ago we circle the Pentagon, arms linked, minds and spirits rising out and over us and mixed together in a cloud, and we focus our minds on levitating the whole evil thing, spirits and all, and if the police and Uncle Sam hadn't fucked with our karma, we could have lifted that thing up in the air and hurled it like a Frisbee into the sea. Or maybe we were just convincing ourselves we could. But it doesn't matter, see? 'Cause revolution is all about theater. Mirror games, show strength you don't have, so it builds on itself and 'fore you know it you really do have the numbers. And then you got the manpower to dynamite the whole nasty Pentagon building off its hinges, and build a temple in its place, for the new faith, dig? So you really have levitated the thing. What's real? What's theater?"

Lester beat the drum again, caught his breath.

Then Junior opened his eyes, turned to him and asked: "Got a light?"

7 5

TO THE WHITE HOUSE

DRIVING BY THE PARK, Alex Sitorski had no idea his son was there. But he heard the beat of the drum. Sitorski had heard it every trip he had made to the White House for as long as American boys had been dying in Vietnam. Which, Sitorski didn't realize until this very instant—walking out of his car, then out of the EOB garage, onto Pennsylvania Avenue—was exactly the point. The drumbeat was a death roll.

He didn't know where Junior had gone, and the feeling came over him that he would never see him again. He had been given a test, an opportunity to meet his boy, explain things. Action was demanded, something bold and decisive. He had failed.

The image he had been carrying in his head, of Elena and Junior and him all back together again—he couldn't bring it back. He would have his work, from here on out, and that would be all.

He listened to the banging drum, then walked to the side gate of the White House, showed his badge, and was permitted to enter.

ROOM SERVICE

"I GOTTA READ A LITTLE FIRST," Elvis said. He was lying in bed in the hotel, leaning up against the headboard. "For inspiration. Hand me that book, Tommy."

Elvis was pointing to *The Impersonal Life*, which was sprawled open on the coffee table an arm's length away from him.

A couple of bellhops were rolling in room service carts.

Tommy pointed them toward Elvis.

"Wait a minute," Elvis said as the bellhops walked toward the door, "hand me a couple of burgers 'fore you go. I want 'em piled high with mayo, onions, and slaw."

The boys looked, puzzled, at Tommy—the carts were just inches away from Elvis—but Tommy nodded, and they rushed to Elvis's side to prepare his meal.

"And fries, too. Soaked in gravy."

"Yes sir."

Elvis stared at Tommy.

"The book?"

There were reasons, damn good ones, why he'd left working for Elvis. He walked across the room and handed Elvis the book.

"You see," Elvis said, burger in one hand, looking down at *The Impersonal Life* in the other, "there's involution and then there's evolution. What does that bastard Finlator know?!"

"I don't know, Elvis," Tommy said, waving the bellhops to leave. "I don't know."

77

PEORIA AND BEYOND

ONCE SITORSKI WALKED INTO the Oval Office, he felt that he was surrounded. There was Nixon, Haldeman, Ehrlichman, and Popkins, all around him, staring, waiting for an answer to the question the President had asked him the instant he had walked into the office.

"Come on, Colonel," Haldeman said. "The President asked you a question."

"It's not like he asked you the meaning of life," Ehrlichman said.

The President nodded, holding his chin in his hand.

Sitorski now noticed that the President had picked up a thick, squat glass, and was gulping whiskey.

Popkins repeated the question President Nixon had asked Sitorski a moment before.

"Colonel, how will it play in Peoria?"

Sitorski looked up at the President. He recalled the transition days in '68, when a new Polack joke would leap to Nixon's mind each time they were reintroduced. In Richard Nixon's America of niggers and kikes, of Polacks and faggots and hippie-queers, *what name would Nixon call my son?*

"I don't know what *it* is," Sitorski said. "Sir."

Nixon was staring at him, caressing his chin. Haldeman was glaring.

"You know," Popkins said.

"We know you know," Ehrlichman said. "Did you do it because of your boy, Colonel?"

Junior? Sitorski turned around to look for helpful faces. There, in the back, was Max Sharpe. They were friends. Not close, but friends, still.

"Max," Sitorski said, "what are they talking about? In all honesty, I haven't a clue."

Sharpe shook his head, disapprovingly it seemed, then turned away.

"We know you know," Ehrlichman said, "but I'll play along. My Lai. Orange County and the rest. The P.R. campaign you leaked to the press."

Sitorski now recalled that he had been asked this same question two days ago, and he had assumed that all the President wanted to know was how the public might react to the court-martial proceedings against Lieutenant Calley, nothing more.

"My Lai?" Sitorski said, and the heads around him all nodded: Ehrlichman, Haldeman, Popkins, and Sharpe. "A P.R. campaign?"

"That's right," Ehrlichman said. "How will it play?"

"In Peoria," Haldeman added.

Alex Sitorski paused, watched the heads stare at him, heard indecipherable presidential mutterings in the background. Then he spoke.

"It depends," Sitorski began.

"ON???!!!" Haldeman shouted.

Sitorski again looked at Haldeman, then at Ehrlichman, then Nixon. It was as if each one of them was asking "Depends on what?" and their voices were echoing throughout the room, then reverberated down the East Wing and the West Wing simultaneously, and downstairs to the basement conference rooms where low-level technocrats were debating the nitty-gritty of "national security" . . . and somewhere bodies were being counted, dead young American boys and Vietnamese boys and Vietnamese girls and old men . . . and lists were being prepared, and this was information which it was then Alex Sitorski's job to memorize, to report . . . *we all have jobs to do* . . . the information would be packed into brick walls in his skull . . . the bodies of the dead stacked high in walls over which no one could see, never see . . . then transmitted out into the press rooms of the *Post*, the *Star*, the *Times*, CBS . . . then filtered throughout the country itself . . . yes . . . to Peoria and beyond.

Sitorski turned to Haldeman, who was still glaring at him, more impatient than ever.

What does it depend on, the question had been. On what will the American public's perception of the My Lai incident depend?

"On whether they know the truth or not," Alex Sitorski said. "And understand it."

TO BEN

WHEN ELVIS AND TOMMY got down to the hotel lobby, Tubby was at the check-in desk, having just arrived.

"E," Tubby said, "what the hell you been doin'? We were worried crazy. The Colonel, and 'Cilla, and—"

"Y'all been paid, haven't you?" Elvis said.

Which shut Tubby up.

Now the three of them were in the back seat, Channa behind the wheel. No one said anything for a few minutes, until the limo turned up 14th Street, into a bad section of town.

"The White House isn't this way," Tommy said, leaning over toward the driver, "is it?"

"We got something to do first," Elvis said. "A friend I gotta pay back." He was reading *The Tibetan Book of the Dead* as they drove.

"But Elvis," Tubby said, "Tommy here says the President expects you at noon. We'll be late!" There went Tubby's grand visions: when Colonel Parker and Bo wrote the history of Elvis, missing a visit with Nixon would all be the fault of one Tubby Grove.

"Shhhh," Elvis said, laying his hand on top of Tubby's head.

The limo cruised slowly up 14th Street. The streets were largely empty, only a few stragglers, hoboes, and hustlers—Negroes all. Many of the shops were burnt-out shells, still charred from the riots in '68, after news came from Memphis that Martin Luther King Jr. had been killed. Whole lots were empty, save for a few scattered weeds and charred concrete, but amid the waste was a series of identical brick apartment buildings, a small complex that looked like a prison.

"That must be it," Channa said, pulling the limo along the curb. "The dough-nut man said he was on the seventh floor. Apartment A."

A number of colored men flocked to the windows of the limo, peeking in.

Channa opened Elvis's door.

"Tubby, you stay here," Elvis said as he stepped out. "Tommy, come along."

7 9

BREAKDOWN

HALDEMAN WANTED TO KNOW what the hell Alex Sitorski thought he was doing. Wanted to know if Sitorski was under the impression that this was some sort of philosophy class in which he was engaged. Some sort of Socratic shit.

"'The truth'?" Haldeman had stood up and was walking toward Sitorski. His temples were beginning to throb. "'Truth,' you smug motherfucker? What the hell do you think you mean by that? What the hell do you think you know, that the President, the American people, that the greatest motherfucking people on earth—that Billy Graham!—the Good Lord himself doesn't have a motherfucking idea?!"

Haldeman shook his head, his chest heaving with deep, loud breaths. Sitorski thought he was going to take a swing at him, right there in the Oval Office, in front of the President, everybody.

"Truth," Haldeman repeated.

Suddenly Sitorski felt limp-legged, a little dizzy.

Ehrlichman walked over, patted Haldeman on the back to calm him down, then turned to Sitorski.

"That all you have to say, Colonel?" Ehrlichman said.

Sitorski looked at the President. Nixon was sitting behind his desk now, pen in hand. It seemed, to Alex Sitorski, that the President's mind was elsewhere; either he had actually lost interest in the conversation, or that was the impression he wanted to give: of disinterest, being otherwise engaged. *Let Haldeman rage,* was the message; *let my men carry the battle to this rebel, Sitorski. Let my soldiers fight on. I will turn my attentions to the domestic front; shift to a winning theme: urban renewal, inflation, revising the tax code; good old crime, law and order.* And Vietnam wasn't the only foreign hot spot around: *Solidify our allies elsewhere in Asia, other fronts in the Cold War. To Moscow!* The '72 campaign was just around the corner.

Sitorski thought that this was what Vietnam does, this was Johnson at the end, this would have been Kennedy, had he lived. Vietnam sucked you into the jungle, good intentions or vile . . . it sucked you in, and from there—whether you believed that we were good turned evil, or evil to begin with—you returned evil, all morality vanished. What happened there, he wondered: did you become evil, or did you just see your true evil self? Who was transforming whom? . . . whichever (and you could never know), there you were stuck, there you remained, and—admit it: You *were* evil; Vietnam was no sorcerer, America no chameleon; we have one true face and Vietnam was a mirror . . . and America, with each occasional glimpse at its true exposed self, took a step back, a step away from the mirror, from the truth; toward retreat and deceit, because self-delusion was easy . . . yes, Vietnam was a swamp from which you never emerged. The best hope, the only way out, was to disengage. *But what if you couldn't disengage? What if we had become Vietnam?*

Sitorski felt his legs shaky. The heads—Haldeman, Ehrlichman, Popkins, Sharpe—went crooked.

The President glanced up from his desk.

Nobody's gonna die in my office, are they, John?

"We know about you, Alex," Popkins said, waving a memo in his hand. "We found out all about you. The girl. Your boy."

"Who did you leak Peoria to?" Sharpe said. "If you tell us, we can deal with it."

"Nothing's fatal," somebody else said.

Sitorski walked over to the couch, sat down. He wondered where Junior was.

"What 'truth'?" Haldeman said again, quieter this time. "What fucking truth?"

"I don't really . . ." the President muttered, waving with his hands, mumbling, "John . . . ?" *Let's wrap this up. Take the poor guy away for God's sakes.*

Then Sitorski saw, in an instant, everyone who had left him, all standing around him in the room: Junior, Elena. And all the dead he'd committed to memory, brick by brick by brick. Images from the last days rushed at him like a flood: a young black girl, eyes woozy and hopeless. Junior, at My Lai. Everyone in the ditch. He saw it all from his boy's eyes.

Sitorski looked at Nixon, locked in on his eyes for an instant. Thought: *This is a man who could trudge through the swamp, Vietnam, look in the mirror, dis-engage and stroll on to the next battle. This is who survives it all, this is who carries on. This is who wins in the end.* The mirror held no secrets for Richard Nixon.

He stood up, his legs giving way. Tried to focus on the questions being fired at him.

"Who knows about Peoria?" Ehrlichman was saying.

"What fucking truth?" Haldeman kept repeating.

"Did you do it for your boy?" someone else muttered.

Sitorski tried to slow things down, tried to respond, but nothing came out.

He stared at the face of Richard Nixon.

The questions kept coming, faster and less decipherable, and then it seemed there were no words. Only noise.

"Fuck it, John," he finally heard the President say. Nixon had looked at him, then turned away in disgust. "The bastard's crying."

8 0

TO GO OUT IS NOT GOOD NOW

THE ELEVATOR DIDN'T WORK so Tommy and Elvis had walked all the way up the narrow stairway in the center of the building. It seemed to Elvis as they made their way that there were colored faces staring at him everywhere, in the keyholes, open cracks in the doorways, holes in the walls, and the old fears came back to him. Things were scary quiet. Elvis didn't hear anything until they reached the seventh floor when, panting, leaning over and catching their breath on the small linoleum landing, he heard the crying.

Elvis motioned to Tommy to check it out. He knocked on the door—it was marked "A"—but a girl just said to go away. Elvis walked over and tried the knob. The door opened.

The girl was sobbing, kneeling on the floor, her back to the door. Smooth skin, dark brown, her hair pulled back tight against her skull. It looked as if she was petting something, and Elvis could see someone lying down on the floor on the other side of her.

"We're looking for Ben Rollins," Elvis said.

"You the police?" the girl said.

Elvis nodded, pulled out a badge and showed it to her quickly.

"The FBI did it," she said. "Ben didn't do anything, he didn't, he couldn't—" And then she broke down again in sobs.

Elvis stepped inside. He could see that it was the one-armed kid lying on the floor, his head, partly wrapped in a blood-soaked towel, in the girl's lap.

"I'm sorry," Elvis said. He had a silk scarf in his pocket, and he gave it to her. "He was a good man. Helped me out once."

Elvis stood over the body. Ben Rollins's lifeless eyes pointed straight up at the exposed lightbulb overhead, open and unblinking.

"Please, ma'am." Elvis patted the girl on the shoulder, gently moved her away. "We've gotta check out the body."

The girl kept hold of Ben's head, but moved back to let Elvis near him.

"Tommy, c'mere. Take off his shirt."

"What the hell—" Tommy stopped himself in mid-shout; he had watched Elvis play coroner on late-night visits to morgues back in Memphis, but still it disturbed him, this fascination with the dead. And he had never seen a corpse this . . . fresh.

"Now!"

The coroners at Memphis had taught Elvis basic techniques, and had allowed him to conduct enough autopsies himself that he had developed a set routine for examining a corpse. Now, once Tommy finished unbuttoning the shirt, he fell into it. First, he knelt down and scanned the length of the body for general impressions. Well muscled, particularly the thighs, pectorals, and biceps: an athlete, most likely. Then he looked more closely, for scars, significant marks. He lifted Ben's arm, rotated it to check the inside of the forearm. No track marks: the boy was clean, never injected at least. Following the same lead, Elvis checked his hands, then in between the toes. Clean: no punctures. He leaned over and prodded the kid's nostrils up, peeked inside: no prolonged snorting either, cocaine or otherwise. The other arm was just a stub, the skin sewn up just past the shoulder. Elvis checked the armpit. Again, nothing. Next, he rubbed his hands lightly over the torso, feeling for incisions, wounds. There were a few bullet wounds, healed over, on both sides of the stomach and chest; and, turning the body over, he could see more scars on the back. But nothing recent.

Then he nudged Angie aside and gripped Ben's temples on either side and lifted the head, shook it lightly up and down, careful to keep the blood from him. It felt light; the kid had lost tissue, maybe his whole brain. The explanation was obvious enough: on the back of the skull was a gaping hole, blood still sticky around it, though the girl must have wiped a lot off. Two bullets, maybe three, hitting the same target, shattering the skull. An expert marksman, or the dumbest luck. Can never tell.

"This is an important time," Elvis said, as he laid the head down and turned to Angie. "The spirit hasn't left him yet. We must send it off, before it embarks on the Great Journey."

"I don't—" She shook her head.

"We're giving his spirit directions. You don't want him to end up in Avichi, I can tell you that right now. 'Lost opportunities, futile regrets'? Hell no."

Then he pulled out *The Tibetan Book of the Dead.*

"Oh nobly born Ben," Elvis read aloud, "although you liketh it not, nevertheless being pursued from behind by karmic tormenting furies, one feeleth compelled involuntarily to go on. And with the furies in the front, and life-cutters as a vanguard leading one, and darkness and karmic tornadoes, and noises and snow and rain and terrifying hail storms and whirlwinds of icy blasts occurring, there will arise the thought of fleeing them." Then Elvis put the book down on the floor, grabbed Ben's feet in his hands, and lifted them. "Thereupon," he recited, "by going to seek refuge because of fear, one beholdeth the visions of great mansions, lotus blossoms and such which close upon entering them. And one escapeth by hiding inside and fearing to come out therefrom, and thinking, 'To go out is not good now.'" Elvis paused, nodded his head. Then he laid the feet down.

"Pick up the head," he said to Tommy.

"What?"

"Pick it up."

When Tommy jerked his hands away, Elvis glared him down.

"Tommy!"

Tommy cradled the skull in his hands, looked down at the face, then slowly lifted it.

Elvis turned to Angie. "What were his dreams?"

She didn't say anything.

"When he was young. What did he want to be?"

Elvis nodded to her. *All friends here.*

"Different things," she said finally, wiping away her tears. "I mean, at first he wanted to be a football player. Back in high school Ben was the quarterback. But when he came back from the war, that wasn't going to happen. He didn't—we didn't talk much about dreams after that. But—I don't know." She looked down at Ben, into his eyes. "I think he could have been a preacher. Like Martin Luther King."

Then Elvis placed a hand over Ben Rollins's face, covered his mouth, nose, and eyes.

"We do not know what form you will take in the next stage, Ben," he said, "even I can't tell you that. But we know it is a world of justice and peace, that good deeds will be rewarded. For a brief time, there will be no sadness, no trouble, but you will be delivered, from this creature that we are. Close your eyes, Ben. Close your eyes, and when you open them you will be another."

Elvis kept his hand on Ben's face another minute. Then he lifted it, and Tommy laid the head back down. Ben's eyes were closed.

They were silent for a while, looking down at the body. Angelina had stopped crying. Elvis took her hand in his and grabbed Tommy's with his other hand and Tommy did the same so the three of them formed a circle, all kneeling over the body. The sun pierced through the seemingly impenetrable window and a shadow appeared over the body of Ben Rollins, a penumbra, and they all saw it lift up from the body and up through the ceiling, which had vanished, allowing it to rise, unencumbered, to the clouds. For a brief moment their thoughts converged. There were perfect lives, good futures . . . and here their thoughts parted, though overlapped at points, for there in the clouds Angelina and Ben were back in high school, and there was never a war and never would be; and Ben Rollins was alive and so was Martin Luther King and so, Tommy thought, were the Kennedy boys, and America was a vast communal scene and there was sharing and love, and the girls, all the beautiful girls thought he was sexy as Elvis and, Elvis thought, he was young and there were dreams still he hadn't lived and time had stopped long ago and then moved forward in front of him, just out of his grasp — something to reach for — they were all young and things were so simple.

And then they heard the harsh shriek of the police sirens approaching and all of a sudden they opened their eyes, let go of each other's hands. There was Ben Rollins, still beneath them.

Elvis stood up.

"Here," he said, handing Tommy his checkbook. "Give her five thousand." Elvis walked to the door, glanced down at the corpse. "He'll need it."

8 1

WENDY'S BLESSING

BACK IN MEMPHIS, Wendy had tossed a bucket of water on the Colonel and Bo to revive them, Arnell's right-left combination having knocked them each out cold. Then, with Arnell and Sharon's help, he threw them out of the Chili and BBQ Tavern into the street.

The commotion had interrupted the wedding ceremony, and frazzled the bride and groom, so Arnell and Sharon now went to their respective bathrooms to clean up. Arnell (his old anger flared up in the fight) felt he needed it.

Which was all fine with Wendy. The fight with the Colonel and Bo had inspired him to scrawl a few key insights for his all-encompassing History. The two intruders being guardians of Elvis, the scene had, like most everything else in his life, taken on mythic import.

Study how history is made, Wendy wrote, *how religions are created and oper-ate—who takes them over, and why. Compare how the Church distorted Jesus' basically Marxist/Radical message to its opposite meaning with Colonel Parker's Hollywoodizing/Vegasizing of Elvis. Who prospers from this inversion of truth? What interests are served?*

Then Arnell and Sharon emerged from their respective bathrooms, careful this time not to collide with each other. As they closed their doors, they stopped to gaze at each other, eyes transfixed. Arnell walked over and took Sharon's hands in his, kissed her fingers.

It wasn't that she forgot that she'd been married before, or that Hank had been killed in the war: the memory had vanished from her mind. And it wasn't that the war was over, or that Arnell was no longer responsible for his brother Rich's death: neither had ever happened. History had been erased like a blackboard.

They walked up to the bar. Wendy stood back up on the chair before them.

"We must be careful how we choose our heroes," Wendy said. "Elvis gave us freedom, gave us fun. May the two of you, together, live such a life. Love, freedom, and fun. Whatever happens, may you never lose that."

Wendy stepped down from his chair, laid a hand on each of their shoulders, and smiled down upon them.

8 2

BIRTH OF THE PLUMBERS

"I APOLOGIZE, MR. PRESIDENT," John Ehrlichman said. "I didn't expect an outburst like that."

"No one's to blame," Nixon said. "There's this craziness, this madness that's—" He waved his hand in circles before him.

"In the air," Haldeman said.

Nixon nodded.

"A viciousness," Max Sharpe said.

"Exactly," Nixon said.

Ross Turnbull knocked on the open door, then stepped inside. "I've got a man keeping an eye on the colonel," he said. "You're sure we shouldn't pick him up?"

Nixon looked at Haldeman, who looked at Ehrlichman, who glanced at Sharpe.

Sharpe shook his head.

Then Ehrlichman turned to Turnbull.

"No, that's fine. Just stay with him. Maybe we can learn something."

Turnbull saluted the President and left, closing the door behind him.

"Max did quite a job with the colonel," Ehrlichman said, turning to the President. He took an envelope from his inside pocket and held it in the air. "Got good men working on it. Thorough, efficient."

Nixon's hands were on his hips as he looked Sharpe up and down.

"And he was even friends with Sitorski—weren't you, Max?" Ehrlichman said. "But that didn't stop him. He had a job to do, and went about his business."

"You're going places, young man," Nixon said.

"Thank you very much, Mr. President," Sharpe said. "I was just doing my job."

"Perseverance is quite a virtue in this business."

"Yes, well, actually," Sharpe saw, out of the corner of his eye, Ehrlichman waving him to be quiet, "I have this plan—"

"Right," Ehrlichman said, "there is something we wanted to talk to you about, Max. We've been looking toward '72, and we all agree that the problem of these leaks has to be dealt with. It's not just Sitorski; an ad hoc approach just won't do—"

"Better plumbing," the President said. "What we need is better plumbing."

"Right," Ehrlichman said. "We need a unit, a standing division ready to deal with these and other, well, sundry items that might crop up, and someone, of course, has to lead it. It would take some initiative, some independence, creativity."

"And balls," the President said.

"Of course, Mr. President," Ehrlichman said. "Max, we think you're the man."

"I don't know what to—" Sharpe offered his hand to the President. "I'm honored, Mr. President."

Then the buzzer on the President's desk sounded.

Nixon pressed it down.

"Yes, Rose Mary."

"I'm sorry to interrupt, Mr. President, but Mr. Sharpe's office insists that there's an emergency."

"What is it?"

"They say that Elvis Presley is there to see him."

AT SHARPE'S

ELVIS, TOMMY, AND TUBBY were across the street, in Sharpe's office. His secretary couldn't stop them.

"I ain't bein' dicked over like they did me at the FBI," Elvis said.

"Who do they think they are," Tubby said, "not lettin' us right in the White House."

"You know they got security," Tommy said.

"I guess." Then Elvis glanced at Tubby. "A sight better than you and Bo, I'd bet, too."

Tommy walked over to Sharpe's desk, picked up a piece of letterhead and read it.

"'Maximillian Sharpe, Jr., Staff Assistant to the Assistant to the President for Domestic Affairs.'"

"You'd think a fancy title like that'd get you a better office," Tubby said.

Fancy title for a good Nazi, Tommy thought.

"There's a war going on," Elvis said. "These boys have got more important things to worry about."

"Right," Tommy said, picking up a folder from the desk and leafing through it. "Like tailing their own generals."

"'Tailing generals,'" Elvis said. "What the hell's that all about?"

"Look." Tommy handed the report to him. "'Investigative Report.'"

Elvis glanced at it, then tossed it back on the desk.

"Those boys have their reasons, I'm sure," Elvis said. "And anyway, it's just a colonel."

•　•　•

Elvis felt a drag coming, a slight wave of tiredness, so he dug in his pockets. There was one pill left—a red, thank God, that he'd picked up at the hotel—and he popped it in his mouth, let it slide down his throat. Then he held the Magnum in his hand, pointed it at a picture on the wall, squinted his eye to aim.

"You ain't plannin' to use that," Tubby said. "Are you, E?"

Elvis turned around, didn't say anything.

8 4

SACRIFICING JUNIOR

W HEN C OLONEL A LEX S ITORSKI stumbled out of the White House, a crowd had formed across the street at Lafayette Park. Tour buses were parked down Pennsylvania Avenue, and the sidewalk was lined with people, not the sort Sitorski imagined lived in the park: there was a crowd of ladies, middle-aged and older, in flowered dresses, each violently waving a miniature American flag. For the first time since he could remember, that infernal drum was not beating, so he could hear the ladies' screams clearly, as if they were speaking directly to him.

"Freedom to Calley!"

"Fight Like Rusty!"

"Cut Your Hair/Cleanse Your Soul!"

"My Lai? My Lord!"

Sitorski didn't understand the last cheer but he got the general gist. Peoria. It was as if the event were planned for his benefit. He wouldn't put it past Nixon and his men to have arranged these past few days with such precision.

The commotion was beyond the ladies, in the depths of the park. He felt compelled to see it, examine it.

He walked across the street.

In the park a crowd had formed around Al Sitorski Junior. Only Lester was near; the others kept their distance, forming a circle. Junior got up and poured gasoline in a trail that began an inch from where he had been sitting, then tailed away in a circular path that swirled closer and closer around him toward the center.

Then he returned to his spot, sat on the ground, cross-legged, palms raised, holding a butane lighter in one hand. Everything was slow, methodical.

"You know what you're doing?" Lester said. "I seen those Buddhist monks do that trick, and I'll tell you," he shook his head, "it's an awful sight."

The crowd of onlookers circled around Junior and Lester, the usual protesters, hippies, mystics.

"Let the man do his thing," one said.

"Stop him!" said another. "Killing is killing!"

Junior didn't see who said it. Only voices.

"Look." Lester stood his drum up on the ground and stretched out his hand. "Maybe you should hand me that lighter. Let's just talk about this first."

"You think I'm crazy?" Junior said. "The President of the United States thinks if we don't destroy an entire people on the other side of the world, then every country from there to here will fall like dominoes to the Russians. On Christmas we deliver bombs. Napalm. Spread it on their skin, like gasoline jelly."

Lester stepped closer toward the lighter, but Junior snapped his hand shut and pulled it to his chest.

"Please," Junior said. "This is all I have to give."

Lester looked into his eyes—determined, nothing wild about him. *Serious questions here: freedom, a life's final message.* The certainty Lester felt in his heart, how to live, treat each other; it wasn't there.

8 5

ELVIS AND FANS

"Mr. Presley, it's an honor." It was what Max Sharpe had prepared himself to say, though he was not prepared for the sight. Elvis was bigger than he had imagined: over six feet, easy; and broad, fat, though his costume disguised it somewhat. And his face, though partly covered by large green sunglasses (he still wore them inside), was chalky white, and puffy around the cheeks. Long black hair hung over the back of his collar. Now Elvis scratched behind his neck, and Sharpe could see that his neck was covered with red splotches, particularly heavy toward the back. His girth was harnessed by a thick jeweled belt, and there was what looked like a metal handle protruding from it.

"So," Sharpe went on after Elvis didn't say anything, "you're a fan of President Nixon?"

"He's a great man," Elvis said. "I think I can help him."

"And you gentlemen . . ." Sharpe pointed to Elvis's bodyguards. Almost as big as Elvis, both of them. Bigger maybe.

"These are a couple of my boys. Tommy Shelton and Tubby Grove."

They shook hands with Sharpe. Then Elvis and Sharpe left Tubby and Tommy at the office, and walked down the hall.

"We've got to cross over to the White House," Sharpe said. "There's a tunnel in the basement."

"Let's walk outside," Elvis said. "Catch some air."

So they stepped outside onto the sidewalk, began to walk down Pennsylvania Avenue.

"Elvis," Sharpe said, "I've got some ideas about how you could help the President. And he could help you."

Elvis wasn't listening. He was looking around, across the street, at the White House, the traffic on Pennsylvania Avenue. Lafayette Park.

"The way I see it," Sharpe went on, "well—let me just come right out with it. 'Get High on Life!' Not drugs, not demonstrations, not antiwar or anti-South or anti-anything, but life! And you, Elvis, you'd be front and center, leading the campaign. President Nixon, Vice President Agnew, and you, Elvis, on television, with satellites and everything. The President asks you, 'Elvis, what do you get high on?' And you say, 'Life, Mr. President'—or Mr. Nixon, or—hell, you can call him Dick. Have Pat out there, maybe the kids too. You've got a girl, don't you? Priscilla, and the . . . Elvis?"

"Hey, Elvis!"

A kid, seven, eight years old, walking toward them with his mother, had run up and now was pointing his finger at Elvis's belt, almost jabbing him in the crotch. A fluffy cone of cotton candy was in the boy's other hand.

"Hey, Mom! It's Elvis! Cool!"

Elvis stopped.

"We're running late," Sharpe said, grabbing Elvis by the arm, but Elvis knelt down on the sidewalk, to the kid's height.

"That's right, son," Elvis said. "What's your name, little fella?"

"John."

Elvis grabbed a handful of the kid's cotton candy, stuffed it into his mouth before the boy pulled it away.

The mother scurried over, took the boy's hand. Brown hair swooped up in a high, swirling hive, bright blue eyeshadow offsetting the smooth tan skin of her face, just the way Elvis liked it. Sort of reminded him of Priscilla, just after they were married, anyway, when she cared how she looked around him.

"I'm sorry," she said, and Elvis thought for a minute that she really was Priscilla, and he wanted to ask her what exactly she was sorry for, but then decided he didn't want to know. "Oh, you really *are* Elvis!"

She offered her hand, and Elvis took it, raised it toward his lips.

"I used to be so crazy about you," she said, giggling nervously.

Elvis dropped the hand.

"We're really late," Sharpe repeated, and this time Elvis stood up.

"Bless you both," Elvis said, and he walked away.

Across the street, in the park, Alex Sitorski had just breached the first line of pro-war protesters who, according to their banner, called themselves the Daughters of Orange County. Excuse-mes got him nowhere; now he was engaged in hand-to-hand combat, elbowing the fat squat ladies who surrounded him, beehive hairdos prodding him under each armpit, a wooden stake that held a placard in his gut ("America! Calley Loves It / Hippies: Leave It!"). He could see over their heads—the tall American among the slight Vietnamese—saw the backs of a circle of protesters who the ladies were jeering.

"What's going on?" Sitorski said to no one in particular.

A young girl, maybe a daughter of one of the ladies, was next to him, screaming, "Go Back Where You Came From!"

He could hear a police siren behind him.

Everyone was screaming so loud that Lester could hardly hear what Junior was saying, though he was just in front of him. All he could hear was something about sacrifice and sin.

The ladies were behind him now, preferring to jeer at a distance, as if proximity to the protesters would contaminate them. Sitorski could see them in front of him, still yards away. Swirling around him was a cacophony of sounds, music from transistor radios, and sung by guitar players: "Has anybody here, seen my old friend Martin?" "Where have all the young men gone? / Long time ago," "How many deaths will it take, till we know / That too many people have died?"—all under a thick pungent cloud of smoke and incense. Questions, Sitorski thought, without answers.

He walked closer to the circle. Heard someone say—or thought he heard— "Sitorski."

"What's *your* name?" Junior said.

"Lester."

Junior was holding the lighter in his hand.

Everyone was waiting for someone to do something.

"Well, Lester," Junior said, "if someone asks, tell them I don't blame anyone. I blame everyone."

And Junior fell silent.

As he neared the circle Alex Sitorski wondered who knew him, who had spotted him here. Thought he recognized a bum with a mop-top Afro standing in front of him, a face that seemed familiar from sometime during the weekend. Who cared enough to watch him, especially now, after that scene in the White House? They had tested him, and he had lost control. He'd face a discharge of some sort, though he wasn't certain for what. But if the White House wanted to get you, they could.

He was close now, the circle of protesters just in front of him, and he could smell gasoline, the hint of a flame. He felt compelled to discover what was going on there. That had been his career, the gathering of data, the compilation of casualties, numbers nameless and faceless.

There were carolers he heard now, wasn't sure from where, old Christmas songs that didn't fit the scene. But it was Christmas, after all; would be soon.

You have opportunities, brief moments for action, to say, do what you feel. He had had his moment, had others before: Junior growing up, encouraging him to enter the war, and before that, the path he had chosen for himself . . . and he had let it all pass.

Junior remained silent for a minute before he lit the gas, breathing deeply, eyes closed. As the flames fed each other and grew, the heat would be intense, the fire melting the skin down to the bone, but he believed that if he meditated enough, if his thoughts were pure, he would not feel the heat.

Eyes closed, senses shut off, mind emptied, he would leave this earth before the fire ever touched him. The smoke would fill his lungs like helium and then he would float upward, upward. There were clouds above the ditch at My Lai, clouds of gunpowder, fire (yes, to answer the lawyer's question, he could see the tears in the soldier's eyes as he fired, because no one wants to kill another human being) . . . and the clouds were the spirits of the bodies, their souls transported upward when they died. How many souls are up there? he wondered. Lost dreams. The tragic end of things. They look down upon us, all of them, all-knowing, all-seeing, never forgetting. What do they think of us, what have they learned? Teach us? They remind us, torment us. We cannot escape them, those clouds. They are our better selves. Purity. The hope, eternal, we have for ourselves. The hope that will not die.

Alex Sitorski had just reached the back row of the circle of onlookers when the fire erupted. Even at the outer edge of the protesters he could feel the heat slap his face as the flames leapt toward the sky. Then there was chaos; those closest to the fire turned around and ran back, starting a stampede away from the heat. People fell, stomped on those in front of them, grabbed anyone they could for balance, toppling them over. There were screams and cries and muttering asides ("Can't believe he lit it," "Seemed like he didn't feel anything," "Oh, that much pain you gotta feel") and over it all the whoosh of the fire erupting again and the sizzle of the flames.

Sitorski tried to stand firm, clutched his arms around himself and let the herd pass him, elbowing ones who got close, eyes clenched shut. He had seen chaos before. Had seen worse.

They passed, the protesters and the counterprotesters and the onlookers, and when they did Alex Sitorski saw the bum with the huge, odd-looking Afro he had seen earlier, and a young Negro man next to the fire. The bum with the Afro was just watching, while the Negro tossed water at the flames from the inside of a conga drum. There was no point to any of it though: the fire just raged all the more and the body—Sitorski could see the faint shadow of a body in the midst of the flames—wasn't moving. Whoever was in there was dead. *So this is how it all ends.* No, there wasn't a point to any of it but there Alex Sitorski stood, watching the fire.

He knew only that there was a tragedy there in front of him, a catastrophe that he did not fully understand and was powerless to do anything about.

As Elvis and Sharpe neared the gate of the White House, an ambulance raced down Pennsylvania Avenue and screeched to a halt at the park just across the street from them. There was what looked like a small fire toward the back of the park, and Elvis watched the smoke rise up to the clouds.

8 6

TUBBY REPORTS BACK

TUBBY WAS LEANING BACK in Max Sharpe's desk chair, holding the telephone to his ear. As soon as Elvis and Sharpe left, he had dialed up Graceland.

"Colonel, I didn't know you were there," Tubby said.

"You called me, didn't you?" the Colonel barked.

Tubby jerked the phone an inch from his ear to muffle the sound. It was the Colonel, all right.

"Yes sir."

"And I picked up, didn't I?"

"Yes sir. Yes sir."

"Ah, hell. Bo, how'm I gonna explain this shiner to the press? I can see the headlines now: 'Elvis Decks Colonel! Out-a-Control King!' Get me more of that ice, boy!"

"Colonel," Tubby said, "you want me to get you some ice?"

"Lord, I was talking to Bo! You remember Bo, don't you? Man who sits on his fat ass collecting paychecks from the very man he's paid to protect, then he loses him?"

"Sure, I do, Colonel. I just thought you said—"

"Well, Bo and me almost lost our jawbones looking for you."

"Sorry to hear that, Colonel, but I—"

"We'll live, which is more than I can say for some." Tubby could hear Bo muttering in the background. "Now where the hell are you? And not that I don't miss *your* ugly craw, Tubby, but where in God's name is Elvis?"

"That's what I'm callin' about, Colonel. See, I found him. The thing is—I was tracking him down—Elvis, I mean—and I figured it tied back to that Sharon

309

girl, with the airlines. She wouldn't talk in the hospital, so I figured I had to get her someplace more out of the way, put her feet to the fire, so to—"

"Girl you kidnapped from the hospital?"

"Right, well, I mean—"

"Get to the point, boy! I got the godawful press to talk to! I got Vegas on the other line. I got—"

"Well—what I'm saying is, Colonel, I finally found out where Elvis—"

"And you got him?"

"Uh huh."

The Colonel paused a second. "Alive?"

"'Course, Colonel."

"Well then, *where* you got him?!"

"You won't believe this, Colonel. Washington, D.C."

"Why wouldn't I believe . . . ? Ah hell. Send me a postcard, willya? LET ME TALK TO ELVIS!"

"I can't do that one, Colonel. 'Cause *that's* what you're really not gonna believe. He's in the White House. Meetin' with the President."

8 7

ELVIS AND NIXON

RICHARD NIXON WAS STANDING behind his desk, gazing through the French doors that faced out the back of the Oval Office. A moment earlier the screech of sirens had drawn his attention outside. Ambulances, fire engines, police: a wondrous cacophony, full of leitmotifs supplied by the raging chorus that was Lafayette Park, the usual tears, screams, tribal drumbeats. Chaos, random violence. Subversion. *Detritus*, human debris . . . garbage . . . *trash*. Yes, that was the word he was searching for, *trash*. He could hear Spiro letting it slip at a casual press run-in, perhaps later this afternoon, snarled under his breath with a simmering fed-up scowl that contorted his face for emphasis. That was the story for tonight's news, the latest tale of burning trash.

He closed his eyes for a moment, breathed in deep. Oh, it was a beautiful symbiotic conflagration, the madness out there . . . and he, Richard Nixon, was the puppeteer, the conductor orchestrating the symphony, the tune the primal rhythm of life itself (the sirens screeched outside again: an ambulance departing) . . . this was *Dante's Inferno*, and one could only hear it—No, *Experience* It—from *this* vantage point, on top of the world, the Desk, the Office, the House for which heroes fought to sleep for but one night, where only kings did live. . . .

"Mr. President."

It was a lackey, a particularly ambitious one (though his name had not embedded itself in the presidential consciousness), stirring him out of his reverie. Nixon began to do battle with his cheek muscles to prepare a happy face for the imminent task ahead, and just as the pall of a smile fell over his face, the euphoria, the magic of the moment began to fade, and was lost.

. . .

Elvis was in the entryway, before him a woman's outstretched arm entreating him to enter the Oval Office. Sharpe had led him through the halls so fast that he was winded, his legs unsteady *(when had he last eaten?)*, so run-down from the past days *(where had his reds gone?)*, he had only caught glimpses of the paintings of past presidents that lined the walls, portraits strategically arranged to carry you through the saga of American history, from Washington to Jefferson to Lincoln to Kennedy, leading you to the crescendo: this room, this President.

He passed through the door into the office and staggered into a coffee table, knocked a chair down as he leaned on its back for support that wasn't there for him.

The crash jarred Nixon. He turned to see the lackey picking up a toppled chair, and there beside him was Elvis. The President sized him up for a moment. Pat had not graced him with a son, no one to follow in his path, carry the Nixon mantle. Only the girls. He sometimes wondered what a son would be like in this age, these crazy times. The peacenik protesters he spoke with that night at the Lincoln Memorial, they weren't all bad. They listened. Some may even have understood, a little anyway. *You did not have to throw your child in the water, Dad,* that was the message. You could talk things out, maybe. It wasn't all war between the generations. A part of Richard Nixon cried that late night, communing with the young folks, telling them his old football stories. Elvis was older, but still a young man. Somebody's son.

"It's an honor, Mr. President. I just wanted to—"

Elvis was talking, the President could see his lips moving, but he wasn't focusing on the words. There was a pile of metal badges on the coffee table in front of them, Nixon wasn't sure why. Police badges, they looked like, a small child's collection of prize toys.

"These badges can only get me so far," Elvis now said. "There are doors they can't open, things they can't do."

Nixon looked at him, puzzled. Tried to focus. This was work.

"I've got enemies out there, Mr. President, people after me."

"That," the President finally said, "I can appreciate."

Elvis had not had time to think since Sharpe had shepherded him through the halls of the White House, so now he took a minute to just look, breathe in the aura of the President, let it wash over him, cleanse him. There were things Richard Nixon knew, it was so goddamned obvious: the man *knew* what it was like to come back from the dead, to rise again and rule; *knew* America at its core, its spirit; *understood. You give a Master tributes, and you are rewarded with favors.* Messages here. Solutions and resolutions. He was so tired, dizzy, light-headed, but he could pull himself together for this. He had to. A thing or two he had to say, and do.

"I've been blessed with something special," Elvis said. He had rehearsed the words in his head, and now they came back to him. "Next week or so they're going to award me as one of the top ten outstanding young men in America. And I hear one of your own, Ron Ziegler, is too. You see, I know what you're doing."

Nixon looked nervously at Elvis, fear revealing itself across his face for an instant, then he snapped an accusatory glare back at the lackey, Max Sharpe.

Then Elvis said, "It's possible you all could be building the kingdom of heaven right here." Nixon smiled, breathed easy. "It's not too far-fetched from reality."

"Well," the President said, "we're trying. But you know, not everyone sees it that way."

Elvis took off his sunglasses and leaned toward the President. Nixon looked at him: Elvis's eyes seemed red and blurred.

"When I was young, Mr. President, those kids were crazy about me. Lennon wasn't nothing. And there wasn't the drugs, and the black-white thing, and all this craziness. The kids, and me—back in the fifties—"

The two fell silent for a moment, looked into each other's eyes. Then Nixon stood up.

"I want you to understand," Elvis said, his voice cracking as he looked up at the President. He tried to visualize the words he had scrawled in his head over the past days. "They idolized me. I was the hero in the comic book. I saw movies and I was the hero of the movie. Every dream that I ever dreamed has come true a hundred times. But that's not how it is anymore. Mr. President, things have gotten godawful crazy, all out of control and I don't even want to tell you about Priscilla and Graceland like a prison and the phone calls in the night. But they're leading them all against us. This war, it's everywhere. But you can stop them. We can get them out of the way, so they won't bother us and things'll be like they used to. I can be your deputy, Mr. President."

Elvis stood up and stepped toward the President.

"I want you to know how much I support you," Elvis said. "I want you to know how much I want to help."

The President stepped back, smoothed down the lapels of his jacket.

This wasn't the way Elvis had seen things playing out; no response from the President, no acceptance. He wasn't sure what the next step was. He'd played out his lines, the ones he remembered anyway.

Elvis shut his eyes, and when they opened the room was bathed in dark red light blowing in through the shaded French doors, and he stood alone with Richard Nixon.

"You know why you came here?" Still dizzy, unsteady, but Elvis was certain the President had said it.

Elvis didn't say anything. He was sweating from the hot red light that surrounded him and all he knew was that he was now there to listen.

The red light became black, the ceiling vanished into a dark moonless night and the President waved his hand and walked and Elvis followed. They were leaving the office but there was no office anymore, they were walking but there did not appear to be a floor, or walls, only black space. They seemed to walk a long way through the dark, no one speaking, no sounds or light. Elvis wondered whether they were traveling through physical space, how their bodies were transporting themselves. Maybe they were just closing their eyes. Elvis looked up and in the sky was a flashing neon marquee that read, AVICHI.

"There." Nixon pointed and Elvis followed his outstretched finger, down the hallway he had walked to get to the Oval Office. The presidential portraits, the paint on all of them was stripping away, melting, dripping down over the gilded frames, down the walls to the floor, as if the President's elongated finger emitted some sort of acid that eradicated the distinguished mythic profiles, exposing them for what they were—historical illusions, frauds that disguised the truth, behind History lay Reality, a dark, ugly visage . . . the veneer of the portraits vanished . . . Washington, Adams, Jefferson . . . Lincoln . . . both Roosevelts . . . revealed themselves, their true selves, murky, cobwebbed, all with the crooked, ski-jump nose, arching brows, the sinister smiling face . . . by turns dark and brooding . . . of Richard Nixon.

"Lost opportunities, futile regrets," the President said.

"And where do I fit in?" Elvis asked.

"You said it yourself. You were the hero. The hero of the young conquers the old. But you stayed in a goddamned comic book."

There was a feeling Elvis remembered having fifteen years before, and now the images came back to him, flashing before him: Cardinal Spellman calling him a demon, Steve Allen dressing him in tails and a top hat and having him sing to a dog before the nation, cackling at him. Nixon was Vice President back then, chasing Reds with Joe McCarthy, and a placid Ike was on the golf course, and Elvis was shaking and the girls were screaming, swooning. Didn't they all feel the rumble under the manicured lawns of America? If Elvis caught on, if the madness took hold, Ike's golf cart would topple, the young would inherit the land, and all hell would break loose. The powers that be were scared shitless of him. Elvis had dreams, visions, he wasn't sure what they were now but, yes, he *had* been the hero, that was the dream. He had real powers then, didn't he? Could have used them, led the young folks *(but where?)* . . . but then there was the army . . . and then he just coasted, rode that wave of Technicolor movies. It was the easy thing to do. Then he lost track. What dreams? What visions? Then Vegas. And now here he was.

The rage he felt the other morning back at Graceland, with Vern and Priscilla coming after him, he thought now it had begun to simmer inside him even back then, fifteen years ago, just after he'd skyrocketed to stardom and the rush upward peaked suddenly and the sense hit him that he'd bottomed out already, that the plateau was inevitable, just a long boring coast ahead, downhill. Maybe it was the sense of reality setting in, *wasn't no hero, no real powers.* The illusion revealed as illusion. *Hero in a comic book?* The President was right, of course he was right. Real history was ruled with ballots and bullets. But Elvis? Just a show. All a helluva misunderstanding.

"You win in the end." Elvis wasn't sure if he said it out loud.

President Nixon smiled. "I always win in the end." The President's voice echoed through the historical corridors that had so mesmerized Elvis. "I always will."

Was the President laughing at him? Elvis wasn't sure. What he could do was reach under his jacket. There was the godawful beautiful Colt. The grip felt good in his hand, cold and snug. He slipped the gun from his waistband, held it at his side.

Then the room went black, silent but for the sound of a breeze wisping away. Then total silence and a dim light that first illuminated the President's eyes, then the rest of his face, and as the light grew back to daylight everyone was visible again: the photographer folding away his tripod, Max Sharpe walking toward the President, who whispered something to him.

Elvis looked at the President. Nixon was fidgeting, looking at Sharpe, clasping his hands behind his back, then holding his hips, uncomfortable with each position. Elvis rotated his eyes about the room, taking in the scene. The curtains were open now and he could see outside, guards on the grass. Thought he heard sirens and faint screams, and above it all a smattering of low black smoke rising up to meet the high blue in the sky. The reds were crashing now and an image flashed of the young vet on the airplane. There was fear in his eyes, that and loss. Or were they Elvis's own eyes? He shook his head to keep his mind on track.

Looked back at the President.

Then at the pistol in his hand. *Had he loaded it before he left home?* Wasn't sure. Was Richard Nixon a Master or a Rival? A Demon maybe, maybe they all were, the Colonel, Lennon, all the bastards who'd made him grow old, sapped his strength and will. He *was* the hero, had been anyway, when it all began. Could be again. But before he could finish his story he'd forgotten where he was going. You needed bold strokes, great actions.

His finger found the trigger easy. The gun felt snug in his hand.

From his outpost at the back of the room where the President had relegated him, Max Sharpe spotted the gun. Just inches from the President. Gulped. Saw his future in an instant: career dashed, HOLE destined for the landfills of history. Imprisoned as an accessory even—having noticed that goddamned bulge in his pants, but still escorted in this . . . assassin.

The President was oblivious, turned away from Elvis, picking up something from his desk.

Had to warn him, save him.

"There's a—" Sharpe screamed as he tried to leap and run at the same instant, but his legs, attempting to race in all directions, only propelled him into a coffee table, then facedown into the heart of the presidential seal in the rug's center.

Elvis would find in himself the strength to pull the trigger, to fire the gun. The bullet would strike the President in the temple, creating a third eye— *Knowledge? The final insights into the karmic furies?*—and though the thin fixed smile on Nixon's face would remain, frozen, as frozen as those piercing eyes, the President would fall, topple like some towering Egyptian statue, and the stone would crumble as it hit the floor. There would be no police, no Secret Service: No, all would recognize that Elvis was now the king, again, the rightful King, and as the blood poured out of Richard Nixon's skull Elvis would stroll over his dying body, out the French doors to a conquering hero's acclaim: the people, His vast fandom, would be there outside, waiting for him to emerge, to reemerge, the girls would scream and claw like that picture back at Graceland, the applause thundering from the heavens themselves. A magical scene.

He steered the gun steady in his hands, focused his vision on his target, on the present moment. There was the President, hard and cold, a man who would never let anything stop him, not law, not man, not even success, not even his own goals, his own dreams. There were nervous tics in his manner, the bobbing head, the hands grasping each other in front of the waist, then behind the back, but these were only surface insecurities. Beneath it all was a hard, undefeatable shell.

"We'd like you to have," Nixon said as he turned toward Elvis, then handed him something, "this."

Awwww shit. There was a gun, no question. Nixon saw it at Elvis's side. *The ungrateful motherfucker. Wasn't this just more trash?* No son here. There were no good sons, not anymore. His father was right, *Throw the boy in the water, watch him sink, that'll learn him.* He and Agnew were right, Wallace was right. This was war, no time for pleasant chats about football at three in the morning. LeMay was right: Take evolution into your own hands, bomb the bastards back to the Stone Age. Calley was right: Any child could hold a time bomb so every child was a time bomb so . . . throw them all in the ditch, in the water, in the pit. *That'll learn 'em.*

Where the fuck was that lackey?

The President cleared his mind of rage for a moment, focused it on the task at hand, summoned up Richard Nixon's Lessons for Life, those applicable to the crisis of the moment:

1) Look fear in the eye.
2) Embrace madness: swallow it whole.
3) "While those around you lose their heads," etcetera, etcetera.

And one more, the only lesson his mother had ever taught him:

4) Trust in God. For some reason, He loves Richard Nixon.

Max Sharpe had righted himself and now scurried toward the President, buzzed the intercom on the President's desk, muttered a torrent of barked commands, and the other end buzzed back and the voice that followed the buzz was metallic, loud and inhuman. The buzz triggered more buzzes, up and down the hallway, more orders.

The President tried to smile, tried to emit a calm, comforting aura. The hand that held the gun wasn't moving. That was good. He held his hand out.

Elvis looked down. The President had handed him a clear plastic box. He wasn't sure what he expected to be in it, what he wanted, what he hoped for. Things put back in order. A *magic pass.*

Inside was a small brass disc, the size of a dime.

Elvis stared at the box. Saw his face reflected in the plastic cover. Then he looked at Richard Nixon, into his eyes. The President seemed even more ill at ease than before, smiling nervously, and now Elvis saw—the thought flashed in his head: *enlightenment*—that it was all an act. No connection here; no help. Tried to keep his mind on track but couldn't; the reds had greased up his skull so his thoughts and dreams skidded recklessly into each other. His face still reflected in the plastic, and brief flashes of the weekend rushed back at him, his brain a fiery wreck of images. Finlator puffing away at his pipe, laughing at him. Vernon and Priscilla scowling, and somewhere a dark shadow of the Colonel. *You construct a kingdom, lives around you, and then they turn you out.* Angry Negroes at the doughnut shop, *you ain't no genius, you a thief, boy,* the young vet on the plane, the colored boy laid out and bleeding in the arms of the crying girl and that was war too. Channa's inscrutable smile: *hidden wisdoms.* There were James Bond spies and the open-mouthed worshipful girl at the airport who still believed in him. *Pursued by karmic tormenting furies.* The smoke again, the clouds. The photo that had set him off, back at Graceland: young and pure, once, and . . . oh, this was Avichi all right: *a long drawn-out dream of bitter memories, a vivid consciousness of failure without volition; a dream of lost opportunities and futile regrets, of ambitions thwarted and hopes denied, of neglected duties, abused powers and impotent hate; a dream ending ultimately in the oblivion of utter annihilation.* . . . Back in Memphis, he knew, Bo and the Colonel would be preparing for his return, Colonel gonna tighten things up this time around, *your time's too precious, boy, to waste on this crazy bullshit—remember those phone calls in the night?*—gotta clamp down on the money too, and on those late night rides . . . this is what happens, this is what you earn . . . *to go out is not good now* . . . things gotta be different, the Colonel would insist on it, Elvis knew. . . . And there were things he did not know, but sensed: within a year Priscilla would abandon him—for a friend, no less—take Lisa Marie from him. Things—everything—would go downhill: the drugs more frequent, the loneliness more intense . . . all things sliding, inexorably, to the end. . . . Nixon and Hoover would try to deport John Lennon but the judges would screw it up . . . no matter . . . three years after Elvis would die Lennon would be gunned down outside his home . . . Richard Nixon would outlive them all. . . .

"It's a presidential pin."

In this world, you help yourself.

"Mr. President," Elvis said; his eyes were wet and he thought that if he forced his anger up front he wouldn't cry, "what I really need is one of those badges. Real powers. From Mr. Hoover himself."

"That's a good man," the President said, his eyes fixed on the gun. "Talk about building the kingdom of heaven."

Nixon smiled, a fixed vapid smile, tired but firm, a steely-eyed, chin-nodding smile, determined, gazing straight ahead. The clap of galloping wingtips was approaching down the hall.

"It's almost Christmas, Mr. President." Elvis's voice was cracking and he could feel the tears now streaming down his cheeks. Elvis raised the gun—his gold-plated World War II Colt: a beautiful weapon. His hands were shaking, sweaty, but he was able to grip the cold metal hard. "Take this."

PART FIVE

Monday Afternoon

BACK TO MEMPHIS

ELVIS IN THE CLOUDS

ELVIS WAS FLYING. He thought he recognized the cloud directly ahead of him: the form of it looked familiar.

Tubby was in the aisle seat, asleep already, feet up so Elvis couldn't get out if he tried. Not that he had the energy to. The old feeling came over him: *trapped again.*

Lean back and accept it.

In his hand he was holding the FBI/Bureau of Dangerous Drugs badge Nixon had given him just before he left the White House. Elvis had delivered unto the President his Colt, meek as General Lee at Appomattox, and in return received this, the prize of his collection now: a Federal Narcotics Agent-at-Large. It was real, he imagined. One flash and they had let him on the plane, guns and all. So maybe the trip was worthwhile.

Right.

Vague images flashed through his head, of *agents provocateurs,* setup jobs, cults forming around his youthful image. . . . He was the answer to the fall of America or America was not falling, he was falling, or he mattered still, a hero again, a prophet, or he was a joke, his delusions of sacramental sweat-soaked scarves funny. He was black or he was white. A genius, a thief. The young idol, the old king. Richard Nixon and he were Masters or there were no Masters, we're on our own. He was impotent and over with. He was dead.

Which was which . . . ?

And below, a world was spinning fast . . . in Washington, Max Sharpe walked back to his office, that infernal, incessant drum no longer pounding . . . satisfied, but still so much to do . . . he would enlist a band of dedicated souls to stop the President's leaks . . . call his good friend, Gordon Liddy. . . .

Up 14th Street, at Ray's Saloon the television news was explaining that the tentacles of the crime problem had reached into the White House itself, as shown by the story of Benjamin Rollins . . . after tossing his medal in a drug-crazed frenzy, he pulled a gun on FBI officers who came to arrest him for possession, chaos ensued . . . Ronnie Bonnard had just gotten off the phone with John Finlator: the Director had been told how the aforementioned operational complexities had been resolved . . . by termination . . . and Palmer Wilson, listening sadly to the television, raised his glass to the Lord of Dumb Luck . . . and Angie stared blankly at the check Tommy Shelton had given her, unaware that Bo would stop it once Tommy gave him the news . . . and as Alex Sitorski collapsed onto his seat the news went on to tell of the young man who had set himself ablaze in Lafayette Park. . . .

And back in Memphis the Colonel had the press on one line and Vegas on the other . . . and at the Chili and BBQ Tavern, Wendy was behind the bar, reading the last pages of his manuscript into the telephone: "The Sixties are dead," he said, "the Kennedys, Kings—and Elvis as we loved him—gone, Nixon and his cohorts have prevailed" . . . and when Maurice, who was on the other end of the line, asked why "Blue Moon"—Elvis's '54 recording—was blaring, Wendy explained that Sharon and Arnell were dancing, cheeks snug against each other's, to which Maurice responded: "Don't give me any ideas. . . ."

At National Airport, Tommy Shelton had called Bo to tell him Elvis was coming back . . . his chest, tight since he left the White House, was suffocating him now . . . he needed some air . . . staggered outside . . . then pulled out the presidential pin Elvis had given him and held it in his palm—the bald eagle, that vanishing, beautiful bird, crowded out by the American flag in one corner, the face of Richard Nixon in the other—and Tommy clenched the pin tight in his fist so that the sharp point would break skin, and he could coat the medal in blood. . . .

Back at the White House, the President had gathered his troops. On the couch Chapin recited next week's itinerary to Haldeman, the Vice President and Buchanan plotted strategic responses to the latest incendiary protests, Cronkite reported that atheists were protesting the National Christmas Tree, Brinkley narrated fresh footage from the war, Rose Mary rushed in with a whispered message for Ehrlichman, typewriters clacked loudly from the hall . . . and Nixon, standing behind his desk, looking out at the park, listened to his orchestra tuning up as he grasped his elbow with one hand, his chin with the other, and nodded to the rhythmic clatter.

"All these years I never let him out of my sight," he muttered to himself, then let go of the elbow, grabbed a highball from the desk and gulped. "You must keep track of them, no excuses, none. I remember speaking to McCarthy—the rats had chased him from the temple by then—near the end, poor fuck—and he told me, 'Dick, squash the roaches before they grow. Better still: disgrace 'em. Swing 'em from the gallows.'" The President fell silent for a moment, running through the memory in his head. Then he raised his glass high. "To our new special agent," he announced, and as the others turned to him, at attention, Richard Milhous Nixon, son of Hannah, son of Frank, child of Yorba Linda, of North Carolina, of New York City, the length and breadth of California, of Key Biscayne, of Washington, D.C.—*a politician must have so many homes*—he was of America—he was, he *is*, America—Richard Nixon, laughed. . . .

Elvis was still watching the clouds floating by, too fast to make any sense of. If he cared to, he would have thought hard now, tried to decipher what was real and what was not, what had happened and what he had only imagined over the past days.

Out the window now he saw . . . a face straight ahead of him, just beyond the nose of the airplane. Thought it was the colored kid with one arm, but that wasn't it.

Remain there, Elvis whispered, gazing out the window. *I need more time.*

Closed his eyes. Tried to unpack things, unwind.

You turn inward, he thought, *grow scared. Lash out.*

Hold on to what you have.

They would meet him at the airport, Priscilla and Vernon and Bo and the Colonel, his image disappearing from sight as they surrounded him, then back to Graceland. Christmas was four days away and there they would be happy, for a while.

He thought of his last scene there. The picture in the living room, the one that had transfixed him: young and on the road, his face thin and free, bright and hopeful.

That was it: that was the cloud at the nose of the plane. It was his face, his young self. And in that image was captured time and spirit.

I command you to stay in front of us, just beyond the nose of the plane. He said this silently to the cloud; he prayed it. *Stay with me. Travel with us.*

Then he opened his eyes and leaned forward to look out the window, searching the sky.

AFTERWORD

This book is a novel, a product of the imagination; it is not intended to be read as history. However, as many events, characters, and some dialogue are based in fact, some clarifications are in order.

The basic events of Elvis's weekend—as described in the book—are true: he left Graceland in a huff on December 19, 1970; at the airport he was thrown off, then reinvited onto a plane, with his weapons; flew to Washington alone; visited a doughnut shop, ran into trouble and flashed his gun; checked into the Washington Hotel. From there he called a friend and flew to L.A. Then they flew back to D.C. together. In Washington, on Monday, December 21, Elvis met with John Finlator (who rebuffed his request for a BDD badge), and then with President Nixon, who gave one to him, making him a special narcotics agent. Then he went home. The letter Elvis wrote to Nixon has not been changed in any substantial way.

The memos are, for the most part, taken verbatim from actual memos of Nixon White House staffers, though I have changed and added some material. One staffer did mention the concept of Elvis participating in a "High on Life" anti-drug program, though I have expanded on that idea. While the "Nixon Under the Stars" chapter is fictional, Nixon exhibited similar behavior earlier in 1970, when at four in the morning he went out with his chauffeur and attempted to commune with antiwar protesters at the Lincoln Memorial. The rest of the words and deeds of Ehrlichman, Chapin, Haldeman, Buchanan, and (with a few exceptions) Nixon are fictional.

The Peoria campaign is a fictional creation. However, the Nixon administration commonly created artificial public shows of support by writing letters, petitions, etc., falsely ascribed to citizens; in fact, Pat Buchanan and others wrote such letters regarding Vietnam and My Lai, though not at the time or of the type I describe. Although Nixon's first public response to My Lai was one of disapproval, in private his outrage was directed at the "rotten Jews" (Nixon's words) in the press who made such an issue of the "incident" (the U.S. Army's words). A good deal of the public did come around to support Calley, and Nixon did as well. When, in March 1971, Calley was convicted and sentenced to a lifetime of hard labor, Nixon ordered him removed from jail and placed under house arrest in an apartment. In August of that year, the Commanding General reduced the sentence to twenty years. In 1973 the Secretary of the Army cut that sentence in half. When Calley was paroled in November 1974, Nixon had resigned. The My Lai massacre was at least as grotesque and awful as I have described. The testimony the lawyer reads to Junior is from the transcript of Calley's trial.

Many of Billy Graham's comments on My Lai are actual quotes. While there is no recording of Elvis's meetings with Finlator and Nixon (the White House bugging system had not yet been installed), portions of them are reconstructed from memos memorializing those events.

Though John Ehrlichman, H. R. Haldeman, Dwight Chapin, John Finlator, Colonel Parker, Priscilla Presley, and Vernon Presley are real people, their characteristics and proclivities, as described here, are fictional. However, there are germs of truth behind some of their characterizations. John Finlator did work at the FBI's Bureau of Dangerous Drugs when he met Elvis. Colonel Parker was known to tell tales of his carnival scams, including the story of spreading manure at the tent exit.

The strands of thought in Elvis's mind, and his actions, all have bases in fact, though, again, my depiction is not intended to be historically accurate. Elvis was probably on pills during the meeting, as the famous picture with Nixon suggests. He was obsessed with the theosophical and religious writings of Madame Blavatsky and the other mystics referred to; he visited morgues and funeral parlors to examine cadavers; reportedly thought he was "a Master"; thought he could stop clouds, etc. The "Am I? Am I?" story was a favorite of his. Portions of his sermon on the beach are taken from religious discourses he reportedly gave to his Memphis entourage. Elvis was known to quote portions of his spiritual books from memory.

The other characters are fictional. Some are composites of people who worked in the White House or Graceland, but they are not intended to resemble or portray any real individuals, living or dead. All other events are wholly fictional.

SUGGESTED PLAYLIST

SUGGESTED PLAYLIST

PART FIVE: MONDAY AFTERNOON: BACK TO MEMPHIS

Jonathan Lowy graduated from Harvard College and the University of Virginia School of Law. *Elvis and Nixon* is his first novel. He lives in Maryland with his wife, Dawn, and two children, Alessandra and Zachary.